THE SPIDER ON THE CEILING

An Anna Newsom Mystery

Michael J. Grasso

D1523245

Cover design by: Amanda Truax
Library of Congress Control Number: TXu 2-135-879
Printed in the United States of America

The pendulum of the mind alternates between sense and non-sense, not between right and wrong.

CARL JUNG

CONTENTS

THE SPIDER ON THE CEILING

one

The quaint delivery van pulls to a stop at the curb. Unlike utility vehicles that strive for anonymity, this one is designed to attract attention; a nostalgic tip of the hat to an earlier age before television, the internet, and the threat of nuclear annihilation.

It's done up in a pleasing shade of ochre, with cherry red trim and wheels, and a hand-painted sign in a swirling script that announces the arrival of O'Rourke's Organic Dairy in robin's egg blue. It's precisely the effect David O'Rourke sought to achieve when he inherited the farm from his late grandfather.

An affable fifty-four-year old, David jumps from the van and makes his way to the rear doors which split at the middle. He swings them open, retrieves a wire basket with three bottles of whole milk and a carton containing two dozen brown eggs.

Then, as he's done every Friday morning for the last four years, he makes his way up the neatly trimmed sidewalk to the main entrance of the brick parsonage; an imposing, four-story Victorian trimmed out in forest green.

He sets the wire basket with the milk bottles on the worn planks of the front porch and is about to do the same with the carton of eggs when Margret Strawsby, the housekeeper, spots him from the kitchen in the rear of the house.

"David! Let me help you!" she says, yelling down the length of the hallway to the open front door. Standing in her third-floor bedroom window, Elizabeth Barrett stares down at the street through fall-colored branches. The voices filtering up through the floorboards tells her that David has made his way into the house and probably as far as the kitchen.

Elizabeth is fifteen and has been the ward of her uncle, Benjamin Wetherford, pastor of the Clevedon Church of the Divinity, since her parents died nearly four years ago. Thomas and Virginia Barrett, both missionaries, were killed in India in 2016 when the boat on which they were passengers capsized and sank in the Hirakud reservoir.

"Margret! No fish market this mornin'?" David says, setting the bottles on the top shelf of the refrigerator.

"Heavens no. There was a big smash up on the M4, so we said our prayers, turned 'round and come right home."

"Well, it's a fine surprise, seeing you here," David says. "And if you'd be fancyin' lamb this week, we're 'avin a special."

"What's this I hear about lamb?" Benjamin asks, as he rounds the corner into the kitchen.

"Good mornin', Pastor," David says.

"*Organic lamb* to be specific," Margret adds, transferring the eggs from the delivery carton, "for a pound of it we could eat hamburgers for a week!"

"I needn't remind you, Margret, that hamburger is not lamb. None of which has passed me lips since Easter," Benjamin quips.

"Mindin' the budget, that's me job," Margret replies.

"Things are well, David?" Benjamin says.

"We're busy, thank the Lord. By the way, how's Elizabeth?"

Benjamin and Margret exchange glances, silently debating who should answer.

"Why do you ask?" Margret says.

"Devon, me youngest, was asking after 'er, at's all," David says, but his comment is followed by an awkward pause in the conversation.

"Say something wrong, did I?"

"No, not at all, David. Not at all," Benjamin says, but that wasn't the truth. Remote and pensive after the tragic loss of her parents, Elizabeth had been growing…

"…Increasingly distant and self-absorbed," according to

Benjamin. "Alarmingly so."

"There's something going on with that child," Margret had shared with her best friend just the previous week.

"Angry, she is. On account of her parents untimely passin', no doubt," her friend had offered.

Turning from the window, Elizabeth walks to her vanity and reaches for her hairbrush. Staring vacantly into the mirror, she runs the brush through her long, raven-colored hair, once, then twice, then sets the brush back down in its place. Next to the brush is an exact miniature of David O'Rourke's van. He had given it to her a year ago this past summer when she was fourteen and she hated him even more because of it; not only for what he had been doing to her, but then the added insult of seeing her as a child in need of a toy.

Elizabeth's bedroom had, at one time, been reserved as a retreat for Adelaide, Benjamin's late wife. Adelaide loved to knit, and she loved the circular turret which looked out across the Bristol Channel and on clear days afforded a view all the way to Cardiff.

"Sometimes she'd tuck herself away from breakfast to afternoon tea," Benjamin would brag.

After Adelaide's death, he was determined to preserve it as a shrine to her memory, and so it was when Elizabeth came to live; not a stick had been changed; matching wallpaper and drapes, baskets of colored yarn; finished and unfinished needlepoint randomly placed around the room were left just as they had been.

There was also Adelaide's smattering of English antiques and collectibles. Elizabeth could have had either of the bedrooms on the lower floor, but she, like Adelaide, preferred looking out at the sails and shipping vessels on the channel and told Benjamin that she didn't at all mind the way the room presented itself.

Elizabeth turns from the mirror and walks toward the basket at the foot of her bed. Kneeling next to it, she surveys the colorful balls of yarn and the cluster of stainless-steel knitting needles bound by a pink ribbon.

One in particular stands out. The eye of the needle is raised about two inches above the others, as though it had purposefully and with forethought singled itself out for the deed. Elizabeth studies it and then slides it out of the cluster, all twelve inches of it, and inserts it into the lining of the fall jacket that stops at her waist.

Stepping into the hallway, Elizabeth pauses to make sure that no one is near. Most Victorian mansions of the nineteenth century had two entrances; the formal, elaborate front door, and then a second, utilitarian entrance off the kitchen reserved for the servants.

This one, however, had a third, lesser-used entrance in the middle of the house. It was on the east side which was opposite the large windows that faced south and west, and a stairway connected the upper floors to the basement.

Elizabeth steps onto the middle stairway and silently makes her way down the three flights of stairs. Getting to the bottom floor, she stops.

When satisfied that she's hearing all three voices, she slips out the door and down the side lawn. As she reaches the van, she shoots a look in each direction, then jumps through the open rear doors.

She hadn't planned on what to do if there had been nowhere to hide, but luckily there's a green tarp crumpled up in the corner behind the passenger seat. She slides in next to a few large boxes, unravels the tarp and covers herself.

"So, Pastor, will you be 'avin the fall outin' again this year?" David asks as Benjamin leads him to the front door.

"If Margret says we can manage."

"Well, the O'Rourkes will do their part, you can bet on that. The whole of Clevedon is lookin' forward to it," David says, and with that he was out the front door for the last time.

The tarp is old and damp and close, filling Elizabeth's nose with the putrid smell of mildew and silage, and it's making it nearly impossible for her to breath. She pushes the tarp away and takes a few more gulps of air, and then from the porch she hears two voices saying good-bye followed by the front door moaning shut.

She tracks David's footsteps as he moves down the sidewalk, crosses the narrow strip of grass and steps off the curb to the asphalt at the rear of the van. Suddenly, she's terrified that he'll notice that the tarp has been moved, but he doesn't and slams the doors after setting the wire bottle carrier into its cradle.

The parsonage was usually David's last stop as it was the closest to the farm and today was no different. He cranks up the van and pulls a U-turn, heading toward Bellevue Road.

Elizabeth knows the route well enough to recognize every turn and on which street they're traveling, but the lack of oxygen under the tarp and the carbon monoxide seeping into the cargo area is adding weight to her eyelids and she's drifting off.

Stay awake! Stay awake! Stay awake! she keeps telling herself. She's dreamt of doing this a thousand times and now the day had come. After four years of torment she would soon be free of him.

Turn left onto Bellevue... at the roundabout take the third exit onto Elton Road, yes, that's right... then to Old Church Road....and then to Strode Road. I...I... can't keep my eyes open... can't keep my eyes...open...

Just as sleep is about to claim her for good, David O'Rourke opens his window to whistle at his three Australian Shepards, and the rush of cool air and the jarring bounce off the main road jolts her awake.

Elizabeth reaches into the lining of her jacket and feels for the cool smoothness of the stainless-steel shaft. She's seen the farm a thousand times, each detail burned into her memory, and now, in her mind's eye, she sees it again.

The road leading to the modest house; the white, rail fences and the large maple full of fall; the clothesline in the side yard right of the house, and the single stack of hay in the field beyond.

David's wife, May, has just pulled a load of laundry from the line and on hearing the van approaching, perhaps a hundred yards off, picks up the basket and begins walking toward him, waving and smiling.

She had been debating about what to fix for dinner, but it being Friday night, David may be wanting to have his meal in town. Williams, one of the many dairy hands on O'Rourke's farm, stops to light his pipe, then continues crossing a field from the left. He picks up a stick and flings it toward the dogs that are now close enough to tear at Elizabeth through the open windows had she been sitting at one.

IT'S TIME! she tells herself, and using her free hand, she yanks the tarp from her face. It's time because she can see the large maple in the front yard sliding through the rear windows of the van, and the pounding in her ears has turned into a rushing roar, and one way or another in the next split second the universe is going to change, and there must be an end to him, so it has to be *NOW!!!*

In a flash, Elizabeth lurches to her knees. The sudden movement causes David's eyes to dart from May at the clothesline to his rearview mirror.

Allowing him no quarter, she grabs the stainless-steel knitting needle in both hands as tightly as she can and plunges it through the back of David's neck.

Just as suddenly, the entire panorama crystallizes in front of her as she remembers each moment his hand or his mouth or that abominable thing between his legs were in places they shouldn't have been.

She sees David clutching at his throat with a raspy, gurgling growl and the streak of red pulsating through his fingers; the Australian Shepherds with bared teeth, snarling and barking, whipping drooled saliva through the air; and the stickiness of David's blood smelling like hot tin in her nostrils; and a woman with a laundry basket; smiling and waving and then frozen; her smile turning to terror; and her laundry basket falling to the ground.

From May's point of view, she thinks David is grinning, happy to be home, but then to her horror realizes that he's grimacing.

She drops the basket and begins racing toward him. The van, careening wildly, throws Elizabeth from side to side, shattering milk bottles and flinging wire baskets against the interior walls until it crashes headlong into a fence post, sending Elizabeth flying into the back of the front passenger seat.

Dazed and disoriented, she scrambles out the passenger side door, gets to her feet, and spins back toward the van to revel in the glory of her handiwork, only to be tackled by Williams the farm hand and slammed to the ground.

All this at the exact moment May reaches the front of the van, shrieking at the sight of her husband through the blood-splattered windshield; splayed out against the back of the seat, his eyes wide and fixed on a point in the sky somewhere over the barn, and his hands clenching the steel knitting needle protruding from the front of his neck.

two

The slight shift in engine pitch was enough to wake her. Landings had never been Anna's favorite part of flying, and over the years she had trained herself not to miss them - better awake in case of a crash landing, she told herself. She didn't like missing a proper meal either, which was just one more reason to wake early.

Anna pulls the airline blanket up to her chin and raises her shade. Sliding into view below are the Monach Islands. A group of low-lying, sandy outcroppings that nearly all of Scotland has long forgotten. The morning is clear and a low sun rakes across the grouchy, granite fingers that splay out from the coastline into the frigid, green waters of the North Atlantic.

It brings to mind a story Anna once heard during her second year of women's studies at Georgia Southern. It was about a certain Lord Grange who had his wife kidnapped and abandoned on the Monachs in 1732.

We've taken the northern route today, she tells herself.

"Good morning, Dr. Newsom. Will you be joining us for breakfast this morning?"

Anna turns from the window and glances up at the young, pretty, and very English flight attendant that had served drinks and dinner on the climb out from JFK the night before.

"Good morning, Sarah. Yes. And coffee with milk, please."

"Of course. And your choice, miss. Bangers and scrambled or porridge."

Anna thinks for a moment, then the flight attendant adds,

"I just pinched a morsel of banger, you can't go wrong."

"Then bangers it is!" Anna says.

Before walking away, the flight attendant spots the open

book on Anna's tray table, cover side up.

"If you don't mind me saying, miss, you've created quite a stir in me grand-mum's book club."

Anna smiles.

"She says your theories are astonishing."

"Well, thank you. Just means I'm doing my job, I guess."

The flight attendant glances back at the cover and is about to add something when Anna preempts her.

"You know, I have some extra copies with me. Who should I make it out to?"

"Oh! If it's no problem, miss."

"None at all."

"Uh, me grand-mum, then. Isabel Quivers."

Anna takes the pen that had been laying near the book and writes the name on a paper napkin.

"Isabel Quivers. What a wonderful name. I'll have it for you after we land."

"Lovely," she says, and as she begins to walk away, Anna stops her, whispering in a conspiratorial tone.

"Sarah! What's happening in row five?"

The flight attendant raises her head and sneaks a peak toward the rear of the first-class cabin. The young couple that had been sharing one another's tongue from Long Island to Greenland have fallen asleep and are now wrapped, one around the other.

"It appears they're taking a breather, miss."

Anna shuts the door and sits down on the small toilet, trying not to think about how far above the earth she is. Opposite her is a stainless-steel sink and a small mirror and she studies her reflection.

"The Spider on the Ceiling" is her first book, published just six years after going into practice as a forensic psychologist. It's been on the New York Times Bestsellers List for more than a month, and it has thrust her into the limelight, a place that she's not entirely comfortable with.

The trip to London is being paid for by the BBC, which means she'll have to earn it; a television interview later this morning, a book signing tomorrow, and a speech on Monday stands between her and the return trip home to Macon, Georgia.

Anna pulls paper from the roll, flushes, and stands. From her toiletries bag she takes out a lipstick and a hairbrush. She can admit to herself that she's pretty - in that simple, Southern, willowy kind of way. When she was eight, one of the boys in her neighborhood nicknamed her Sparrow, but that was when she was eight and no boy has called her that since she was eleven.

She's okay with the shape of her mouth and has no real issue with her nose and someone once described her eyes as the color of Spanish moss, which pleased her. But her hair is another story. Naturally, it's a strawberry blonde and flat as a pancake. She keeps it medium length and on occasion resorts to color or perms or curling irons to give it some encouragement. This morning she only has time for a brush and some spray.

Anna reaches for the plastic onyx lipstick capsule with brass-colored trim and removes the top half, exposing the pinkish, waxy bullet inside, and she studies it for several seconds. When Anna was a teenager, her therapist had warned her that lipstick might be a trigger, and she had been right. For years she had sworn off lipstick. But now, with her fifteen seconds of fame and the public attention that's come with it, her friends have kindly shared that "a little bit of glam" wouldn't hurt one bit.

So that is why on this 11th day of September 2020, Dr. Anna Newsom stands in the restroom of a passenger jet, twenty-four thousand feet above Scotland, applying the waxy substance to her quite satisfactory lips. And in spite of all the years, the memory comes flooding back.

three

It's 1999 and Anna is thirteen. It's late August, and although she and her cousin, Chloe, have had a great summer, Anna is beginning to feel her annual, peculiar foreboding at the approach of fall. She has, on occasion, attempted to describe the feeling to her mother to see if she shared it also, but to no avail. Never having been very comfortable hanging out in what she described as *'the feelings department,'* Vivian was more at ease in the housewares department, with tangibles like spoons and knives.

Anna's and Chloe's families had spent nearly two weeks together on a houseboat in Branson, Missouri. Vivian and her sister, Trudy, rarely had the opportunity to spend this much time together, and the husbands, Frank and Tim, pretty much agreed on all the important things such as hunting and politics and the proper temperature of beer.

The houseboat was large enough to accommodate everyone comfortably - all five Andersons - and the four Newsoms - Vivian, Anna's father, Frank, and Anna's older brother, Jason; who, along with Chloe's two brothers, Chris and Jack, contented themselves with scoping out potential, bikini clad quarry from the top deck of the houseboat. Anna and Chloe had their own room with a small double bed on the opposite end of the boat from the boys who shared a room with bunks.

One day at the end of the second week, the adults organized a trip into town.

"Okay, show of hands," Frank, Anna's father barked, "who's going to shore?"

The older boys were quick to respond, jumping at the chance to test their skills with the native girls on dry land, and

Anna and Chloe shot each other a look sensing that this may be their opportunity.

The older boys were quick to respond, jumping at the chance to test their skills with the native girls on dry land, and Anna and Chloe shot each other a look sensing that this may be their opportunity.

"No unsupervised swimming. Remember?"

"Okay, no swimming. We'll stay and watch a movie."

Needless to say, watching a movie was the last thing they had on their minds. It was agreed at the beginning of the trip that if the opportunity arose and they were left alone, the girls would slip into their new swim suits, pilfer a few cigarettes from one of Trudy's ubiquitous packs, and position themselves with Budweisers on the top deck of the houseboat to see what kind of attention they could attract.

They wait for the distinctive, putt-putt of the dinghy's engine. As it bobs around the houseboat and comes into view, the girl's give half-hearted waves, pretending to be more interested in deciding which film to choose.

"Girls? Remember what we said!" Vivian yells out, but as soon as Chris, Chloe's eighteen-year-old brother swings the dinghy in the direction of the pier, Chloe jumps up.

"Okay, let's go!

"I want to take a shower first," Anna says, "I'll see you upstairs."

"Alright, but hurry!"

Waiting for warm water in the bathroom below decks, Anna undresses in front of a small mirror on the back side of the bathroom door. Turning one way then the other, she begins making her daily assessment of progression into womanhood.

To what degree her breasts had manifested since the beginning of summer was a matter of debate, but her pubic hair was definitely different now - not nearly as soft as it had been at the end of May, and to her horror, it was getting thicker. Like the hair on her head, she thought, and was dismayed when she considered that boys may not like that sort of thing. She promised herself to ask Chloe.

Leaning back under the shower, she rinses out the shampoo, then reaches for a soap container sitting on the ledge in front of the small, open window. She squeezes the silky liquid into her palm, then spreads it along each calf and up to her thighs, widening her stance. She pauses for a moment and then slides her right hand up toward her crotch, to the spot that she has often heard about and just recently discovered.

She lets her fingers linger there for a moment, pressing inward, then begins moving her hand in alternating clockwise and counter-clockwise circles, concentrating, trying to decide which was more effective. With her heart quickening, she glances out the open window toward the distant shore and catches sight of the tiny dinghy docking at the pier, bobbing in the waves stirred up by a distant storm.

"HURRY UP!" Chloe yells from the top deck.

On shore, everyone but Chris has clamored out of the dinghy.

"What are ya doing? Tie it off and let's go eat," his father says.

"I, um, just remembered, I forgot my wallet."

"That was dumb. Make it quick, everyone's hungry."

"I will, don't sweat it."

Chris kicks the dinghy into reverse, pulls away from the dock, spins it in the direction of the houseboat and hits the throttle. Over the noise of the engine he hears the low rumble of thunder and, glancing westward, he spots the growing thunderhead.

Anna has finished drying off and has put on her pink bikini bottoms, but not her top. Standing at the mirror she reaches for her Michael Jackson toiletries bag, pulls out a thick tooth comb and begins to run it though her hair. She got the bag from someone, she can't remember who now, on her ninth birthday. Maybe it's time for another, she thinks to herself.

As Chris gets closer to the houseboat, he spots a figure on

the upper deck.

"Shit."

He grabs the pair of binoculars the boys had been using all week and sees that it's Chloe, not Anna, then does a quick scan of the rest of the boat. He drops the binoculars, then swings the dinghy left, making sure that he stays out of Chloe's line of sight.

Killing the engine so as not to be heard, he grabs an oar from the bottom of the dinghy and begins to paddle his way around to the rear end of the houseboat.

The water is rougher now, making the approach more difficult. Chris reaches the ladder and the rear platform that sits just above the water line, and pulls the dinghy in, firmly securing it with rope.

In the bathroom, Anna reaches back into her toiletries bag and pulls out her plastic pink lipstick tube, removes the top and rotates the mechanism at the bottom. She leans into the mirror and begins applying it the way her mother showed her two years prior, upper lip first.

Suddenly, she notices something moving in the corner of the mirror but before she can react, he's at her back, his arm around the front of her neck.

"Ahhh, what are you…?" Anna says, struggling to speak.

"Shut up! Make one sound and I'll tell everyone it was your idea," he threatens. YOU HEAR ME!!!"

"Stop, DON'T! You're hurting me…!"

"ANNA! WHAT'S TAKING SO LONG?" Chloe yells from the top deck.

"Answer her, dammit!" Chris says, under his breath.

Anna barely manages to eek out a response.

"Uh, hey, sorry, be up in a minute!"

In a split second, Chris shifts his arm to the back of Anna's neck and slams her body up against the wall, pressing her face hard against the cool mirror where her warm, panicked breath condenses.

"You want this as much as I do and you know it," he says, in her ear as he drops his pants.

From that point on, it was though Anna had stepped out of her body. Years later, in college, she would learn that what she was about to experience was TID. Trauma Induced Dissociation.

With her face and left arm pinned against the glass, she raised the lipstick with her right and slowly, methodically, began applying it first to her upper lip and then to her lower lip.

How long the ordeal lasted, she's never been able to say. Through hypnosis, however, she was able to recall, in minute detail, each pass of the pink, waxy bullet; filling in the lines and outlining the shape of her lips. It was her escape from the reality of the pain and humiliation being inflicted upon her, and it would become the foundation of her career.

four

From her window, Anna watches as England rises up to meet her Airbus 350. The landing is exceptionally smooth, prompting most of the passengers in economy to break into warm, appreciative applause. Those in first-class, however, restrain themselves, choosing instead to display the cool nonchalance of the seasoned traveler.

Anna takes note of the different reactions in the two cabins, a social and psychological phenomenon to be sure, and promises herself to give it more thought when she has the time.

She retrieves her Tumi backpack from under the front seat and pulls her small carry-on from the overhead. Sarah, the flight attendant, is positioned at the exit door with another flight attendant, a male. They're sprinkling 'so longs' and 'goodbyes' over the departing passengers, most of whom offer thanks in return. As she reaches them, she hands the signed copy of her book to Sarah, who beams with appreciation.

"Miss Newsom. You've made me grand-mum's day, I assure you."

"Just promise you'll give me a ring or send an email telling me how she liked it," Anna says, as the male flight attendant taking a peek over Sarah's shoulder, takes note of the title.

"The Spider on the Ceiling? Sounds Scary. Not one of those Stephen King horrors is it?"

Anna smiles and is about to respond when Sarah jumps in.

"Don't mind him. Tell the BBC 'ello for us."

Anna exits the plane, wheeling her carry-on up the long jetway and then out into one of the many long corridors at Heathrow that feeds the international security and customs hall.

This morning, like most, it's jammed with thousands of travelers from all over the world. After retrieving her single suitcase from a woman who mistakenly thought it was her own, Anna gets into an unimaginably long line leading to the customs desks. She reaches into her Tumi backpac, pulls out her phone and hits speed dial. After a moment she hears fumbling on the other end of the line.

"Ethan?"

In Anna's house, her long-term boyfriend, Ethan Barnes, is in bed and groggy, and he squints at his phone.

"Hey, geez, what time is it? I tracked your flight until you flew over that place in Iceland that sounds like something's stuck in your throat, then fell asleep."

"And you say it's true love. How did the job interview go?"

"Um, not so good. I had an episode, and by the time the meds kicked in, I had missed it."

Anna goes silent.

"Anna? You there?"

"I'm here. Did you call them?"

"What for?"

"To reschedule, Ethan. That's what for. You've been looking forward to getting into that company," Anna says.

"I don't know. Didn't think it would do any good."

Anna hesitates, not really wanting the answer to her next question.

"You've remembered to feed Louis, haven't you?"

"Of course."

"Sorry, Ethan, I've gotta get my luggage."

"Yeah, sure," he says.

"You okay?"

"Listen, Anna, we need to talk."

"When I get home, I promise."

five

Devon O'Rourke, seventeen, the youngest of David's two sons, has just opened the taps of the hot water boiler and is beginning to spray down the milking parlor when he's suddenly aware of the faint, discordant shrieks of police and ambulance sirens somewhere in the distance.

Fire and violent crimes are fairly uncommon in the rural country-side, but accidents occur frequently, and when he hears sirens, Devon has learned to plot a mental map of their trajectory and likely destination.

He turns the nozzle of the hose to maximum and begins spraying at the far end of the parlor, so when he's finished, he's closest to the house and his mother's proper English breakfast; bacon, sausages, eggs, potatoes, and a variety of toasts.

This morning is different, however. Instead of turning away and fading in the distance, the sirens are growing closer and louder, then so close that the alarm bells start going off in Devon's head.

Without turning off the flow of hot water, Devon drops the hose and tears out of the milking barn. He makes a hard, right-hand turn and then another, which brings him into full view of the horror playing out two hundred yards away.

Sprinting as hard and as fast as he can through the muddy field, Devon spots the line of police cars and rescue vehicles screaming up the main road toward the entrance of the farm, and he can just make out his mother, on her knees, in front of the O'Rourke delivery van which is pitched over at an odd angle against the fence.

Behind and to the right, he sees Williams struggling with something or someone in his arms. The vehicles tear up the gravel road leading to the farmhouse and one by one skid to a grinding halt.

Chief Inspector Hayden jumps out of the first patrol car and rushes toward Williams, who has Elizabeth in a choke hold. Hayden motions for two officers to approach and subdue her.

"What's happened here!?" Hayden says, yelling over the last of the sirens.

"See for yourself!" Williams says, nodding toward the front of the delivery van as the two officers free him of Elizabeth.

Hayden moves quickly around to the front and sees May on her knees, moaning and in shock, and as he follows her gaze up to the windshield of the truck, he spots David splayed out against the seat.

"Good, Lord," he says, under his breath.

At that moment, Devon, his lungs scorched from the long sprint, arrives winded and barely able to speak.

"Mother? Wha...wha...what's happened?"

"Who are you!?" Hayden says.

"Her son!"

Williams runs around the van and latches onto Devon's arm.

"Dev, come with me son..." Williams says, as he tries to draw Devon's attention away from the van.

"NO!" Devon says, ripping his arm away, "what's, what's... going on here? Where's my fath...?"

In the middle of his sentence, Devon spots David through the bloodied windshield.

Suddenly, everything about him slows. He pulls away from Williams and putting on his bravest self, approaches the driver's side window to get a full view of the atrocity.

"Who...did...this?" he mumbles under his breath.

Now it's Hayden who approaches him.

"Son, come with me."

"NO!" Devon yells, and as quickly as he went silent, he's now wild with rage. Glancing up toward the gravel road, he spots Elizabeth Barrett being placed into one of the police vehicles and tears off in her direction.

"ELIZABETH!" Devon screams.

"STOP HIM!" Hayden says, yelling to the other officers in the group, two of which are able to catch Devon and restrain him just as he's reaching the window of the car in which Elizabeth has been placed.

"Elizabeth! Why?" is all Devon can manage to say, and in return, all Elizabeth can offer is a vacant stare through the bullet proof glass of the patrol car.

six

Margret has her arms elbow deep in a bowl of bread dough and the persistence of the person at the buzzer has caused her to resurrect words she hasn't used since her team lost the lawn bowling tournament to Tickenham.

She trudges down the long hallway and finishes wiping her hands just as she reaches the front door.

"Ma'am, sorry to be a bother. Would Pastor Wetherford be available?" says the older of two policemen.

"Come now, another fundraiser officer? Your boys were 'round no more than a fortnight ago!"

Margret turns back into the house and as the officers follow, she continues her admonition.

"We're on a shoestring these days, what with the return to sin and all, but I'm sure the pastor can pinch a quid or two for the good of the community," she says.

"Sorry, ma'am, but I'm afraid this, uh, isn't about money."

The officer's tone makes Margret stop and turn back in his direction, and she now sees that two additional patrol cars plus several more uniformed officers are assembling on the street in front of the parsonage.

"Oh my. I see," she says.

Margret and the two officers are standing in the front parlor when Benjamin enters the room.

"Good morning, gentlemen. Margret said it's something serious. Wasn't my last sermon, was it?" Benjamin says, expecting a light-hearted response, but it never arrives, and the more senior of the two officers clears his throat.

"Pastor. We met at the parsonage picnic last year. I'm Sergeant Poole."

"Of course. Nice seeing you again, Poole."

"And this is Officer Murray. I think it best you both take a seat."

"What? What's happening?" Margret says.

The two officers remain standing as officer Poole continues speaking.

"It's about your niece."

"Lizbeth? Why, she's been in her room all morning, shall I go fetch her?"

"That, regrettably, isn't the case, ma'am."

Perplexed, Margret turns to Benjamin who continues the questioning.

"Then where is she? Is she alright?"

"I'm afraid she's fine."

"*Afraid* she's fine? I don't understand," Benjamin says.

Officer Poole swallows and continues.

"Two hours ago, your niece was arrested."

"Arrested! Good heavens!" Margret cries, turning to Benjamin who immediately attempts an explanation.

"Pinched a new pair of undies, did she? Is that what it is, officer? The girl is always complaining about having too few, isn't that right, Margret? Juveniles today, puerile behavior and utter contempt for private property. As her guardian, you have my word that... "

"I'm sorry, Pastor. It's, uh, nothing as simple as that, I'm afraid."

Poole looks to his fellow officer for support. Delivering bad news has never been his forte.

"Then out with it, Officer. What's happened? What's she done?"

Officer Poole takes a deep breath, clears his throat and continues in a more formal tone.

"I regret to inform you that Elizabeth Barrett has been arrested... for the, uh, murder...."

"MURDER?" Margret gasps, holding her hand to her mouth.

"of…David O'Rourke."

"AHHHHH," is all Margret can manage and, as she begins to swoon, she rushes out of the room.

As for Benjamin, had he been run over by a team of horses the effect would have been no more devastating.

"Wha, wha, wha…what are you saying, man, you can't be serious?"

"Afraid, I am. I'm sorry, sir. Chief Inspector Hayden will be here momentarily. He'll be wanting to take a statement, if you're up to it, and then the forensics men will commence an examination of the girl's things."

"I, uh, don't', don't know what to…"

The shock has left Benjamin dumbstruck. He reaches into his pocket for a handkerchief, then he wipes his brow and holds it over his mouth in horror.

Weak-kneed and trembling, Benjamin makes his way across the large expanse of lawn that separates the parsonage from the church. After Margret rushed from the parlor, she flew upstairs and may be dead on the floor for all he knows.

What started as a pleasant fall day with full sails on the channel and swirling whimbrels in a deep blue sky has morphed into a churlish prelude to winter. The smell of rain is on a bitter wind blowing from the northwest and dark clouds roil low over the Welsh coastline. Chief Inspector Hayden will be here at any time and Benjamin needs a moment to collect himself before he's overtaken by the nauseating knot in his stomach.

Rather than using the heavy front doors reserved for Sunday services, Benjamin chooses the side entrance, rounds the sixteenth century Welsh altar, and takes the worn stone staircase to the basement.

He enters his office, dark and dank, and moves to a wooden shelf on the far wall. On it stands a bronze crucifix flanked by two candle holders. He reaches for the crucifix, turns it over and carefully extracts a small key from a notch carved into its base. He sets the crucifix back on the shelf, then settles into his chair behind the desk.

Using the key, he unlocks the lower drawer and pulls out a bottle of Irish whiskey and a glass tumbler. His hands are shaking so badly most of the whiskey spills onto the desktop, but he manages to get enough into the glass to make a difference in the way he feels and downs it in two large gulps. He wipes his mouth, settles himself, then delivers the bottle back to the drawer.

Stepping out of the stairway from the basement, Benjamin is startled to hear the voice of his organ player yelling down to him from the choir loft.

"Mornin', pastor!"

"Blevins! Didn't expect you here on a Friday," Benjamin says, calling back up to him.

"Too cold to do much else. 'Twas such a fine day 'and now it's lookin' like the devil."

"It'll blow over, Blevins. Never fear, it always does."

Blevins, as he chooses to be called, is Celwin Blevins, a plump, sixty-eight-year-old, born in Wales and as dedicated as the day is long.

Benjamin takes a seat in one of the front pews and begins to calm as the whiskey takes its full effect.

"Blevins?" Benjamin says, calling over his shoulder.

"Yes, pastor."

"Play Hyfrydol for me."

"Now, sir, what would made you think of that one?" Blevins says, and he begins searching the pile of sheet music on a table next to the organ,

"I don't know, just the day I guess."

Finding the sheet music at the bottom of his stack, Blevins sets it onto the organ and begins to play.

"Me father used to play this on his dulcimer," he says, shouting over the sound.

The lilting melody of the old Welsh hymn, carried by the rich warm tones of the eighteenth-century Brindle pipe organ, begins to fill the church and gifts Benjamin with a moment to reflect on whatever and how much responsibility he might have for the morning's catastrophe.

As he prays, the nauseating knot in his stomach starts to loosen, his chest settles, and he begins to get his legs back. Then, under the sound of the organ, Benjamin hears the discordant moan of the heavy front doors and opens his eyes just in time to catch a diffused beam of grayish, wintry light falling onto the seventeenth century painting on the rear wall of the altar.

s e v e n

To her surprise, the customs line moves quickly, and like an on-ramp without traffic controls, Anna gets caught up in a tangle of luggage carts and passengers, most of whom have been trapped in airports or on airplanes for the better part of a day.

Suddenly, everyone and everything is being funneled toward the exits and oxygen is becoming a scarce commodity. It reminds Anna of a friend from college who based her doctorate on the behavior of large numbers of people in public places and why panicked crowds stampede, even though it's the worst possible thing they could do.

Fortunately, as those in the front begin to spill out into the main greeting area, the knot of bodies and carts around her begins to fray and loosen, scattering in all directions.

Breathing freely again, Anna crosses the last boundary between airport limbo and freedom when she spots an elderly man in a blue suit holding a neatly printed, handwritten sign with her name on it.

"Ah, it must be Dr. Newsom," the Englishman says, calling out as Anna approaches.

"Yes, good morning."

"Call me Henry. I'll be your driver while you're in London. Allow me," he says, smiling and reaching for her luggage cart.

"Thank you, Henry."

Once inside the cab, Anna sits back with a sigh of relief. Having made it across the North Atlantic and through customs, she takes a moment to get her bearings and assess her well-being.

All systems are go, she tells herself. *Let's just get through the next few days.*

"Excuse me, miss, if ya don't mind me askin'..."

Anna shifts her gaze from the window.

"Sorry, what's that?"

"First time 'ere, in our part 'o the world?"

"Yes. It is," Anna says, hoping that this isn't the beginning of a long interrogation. Henry looks into the rear-view mirror and centers her reflection.

"I told me wife over tea this mornin' that I was driving a Miss Anna Newsom today. She's always wantin' to know who me clients are; so she can pop off at bridge, I imagine."

"I'm sure," Anna says, politely.

"She tells me you're a writer. I 'ave always admired those who can put pen to paper."

"Actually, I'm not a writer, per se. I'm a forensic psychologist."

"Oh my. Psychologist is it? Don't tell the Mrs. or she'll be wantin' you to give me own noggin' a once over!"

"No, I'm a *forensic* psychologist. Unless you've attacked or killed someone, you're safe."

"Then clean as a whistle, I am."

Anna smiles, Henry is kind of growing on her.

"How long have you been driving?"

"Before retirin'? Long haul lories it was. For the BBC? Coming on ten years now. They pay well enough, and I've gotten a stack of squiggles as long as me forearm out of it, too."

"Squiggles? she asks.

"Squiggles. You know, auties."

"Sorry?"

"Don't mind me, miss, autographs!" he answers.

"Oh, of course!"

"Last week had Sir Paul McCartney right where you're sitting. Nice as the day is long, too. A gentleman. The bigger the star, the nicer they are, is what I've learned, and Sir Paul did not disappoint. No, by George, he did not."

"I can't imagine he would." Anna offers, smiling.

She turns back to the window, Henry's monologue playing against the rush of morning commuters and for a moment Anna has the feeling that she's in a movie. *It must be the jet lag, she thinks to herself.*

eight

Benjamin turns over his shoulder and sees the silhouette of Chief Inspector Hayden making his way down the length of the church. Outside the large wooden doors, Benjamin can make out the shapes of several uniformed police officers.

"Pastor Wetherford?" Hayden says, his voice echoing through the church over the sound of the organ.

"I am," Benjamin says, struggling to stand.

"We've come to have a look around. Can you lead me to the girl's room, please?"

"Yes, of course. How's Margret? Have you seen her?" Benjamin says.

"Resting."

From the choir loft, Blevins sees what's taking place and stops playing.

"Something amiss, pastor?"

"We'll speak later, Blevins. Keep playing, please. Just keep playing."

As Benjamin exits the church, he sees that a phalanx of police and patrol cars have descended upon the neighborhood, along with television cameras and news reporters. The Chief Inspector, along with four officers, lead him to the front entrance of the parsonage, and Benjamin wonders why they couldn't have taken him around to the rear, out of view of the gathering crowd.

"How many entrances in the house?" Hayden asks.

"Three. The front that we're going through now, one on the east side of the house and then of course, the servant and delivery door off the kitchen," Benjamin says, the wobble in his knees returning.

As they reach the top landing Benjamin stops to catch his

breath.

"It's, uh, it's the turret room, next door on the right," he says, as Hayden continues down the hallway.

When he gets to the doorway Hayden stops and slowly scans the room, taking note of the view of Bristol Channel outside the windows. Early in his career, a Chief Inspector Wiley, a mentor and a veteran of hundreds of investigations taught him his secret to approaching a case.

"Peel it away like an onion, me boy," Wiley used to say. *"First things first. And eventually you'll get to the heart of it."*

In the case of the murder of David O'Rourke, however, Hayden is fairly certain that there are only two layers to this onion. Love and Hate.

"When we're finished here, I'm going to need a statement," Hayden says, stepping back into the hallway.

"In the meantime, may I sit, Chief Inspector?"

"Yes, of course," Hayden says.

Benjamin takes a seat on an antique bench off to one side of the landing near the room and tries to catch his breath. A man in street clothes carrying a small briefcase steps in beside Hayden.

"Go on in," Hayden tells him.

"Who is he?" Benjamin asks.

"We're going to be dustin' the room for prints," Hayden says, "and then we'll be taking photographs."

Benjamin struggles to his feet.

"My God, man, this was my wife's dearest room, her sewing room, and I've preserved it just the way it was when she was alive, and I would prefer it not be disrupted. On top of that, what bloody good are fingerprints when Elizabeth wasn't the one murdered?"

As he's about to respond, Hayden's cell phone rings and he steps off to the side to answer it.

"Hayden."

"Rieger here. No chance in Hades the widow can make a statement today. Possibly not for the next week."

"Chief Inspector!" the fingerprint man yells from inside the room.

Hayden hangs up from the call, walks to the bedroom and steps inside. With gloved hands and large tweezers, the man grasps the miniature model of the O'Rourke delivery van that had been sitting on Elizabeth's vanity and raises it to give Hayden a closer look.

nine

Henry pulls up to the hotel and a bellman approaches the cab.

"Morning, miss, welcome to the Shangri-La Hotel," he says, as he opens Anna's door. Henry turns in his seat to face her.

"They've given you three hours to rest and freshen up a bit. Not that you need it, mind you."

"You're too kind, Henry," Anna replies, through a yawn.

"Not at all, miss. I'll be back at 10:30 sharp."

The Shangri-La Hotel occupies several floors in the center of the tallest and most modern building in Great Britain. Cynically dubbed, "The Shard" by outraged citizenry, its 95 stories slice through the London skyline, looking for all intents like a gargantuan shard of glass that has lodged itself in the front yard after a wayward baseball has shattered the living room window.

The design, by Italian architect Renzo Piano, has led some of the more acerbic critics to claim that *'the eyesore is proof positive World War Two never actually ended.'*

If she had had a choice, Anna would have much preferred the cozy tradition of a Brown's Hotel on Albemarle Street where Rudyard Kipling wrote his first book; Alexander Graham Bell placed the first telephone call, and where one can have a warm, home-made scone and afternoon tea at street level if so desired.

All of this compared to The Shard, whose management wasted no time in claiming the record for the most selfies taken in London since the skyscraper's opening, due mainly to the *'Irresistible views from its 72nd floor observation deck.'*

Anna's room is on the fortieth floor of the building. The motif is modern Oriental, combining sharp angles with softer, Pan Asian iconography; all set against floor-to-ceiling windows, plush, oversized bath towels and heated marble floors in the bathrooms.

For a moment she wonders how an unassuming Southern girl from Macon, Georgia, ended up with a forty-story view of one of the great cities of Europe, the Thames beckoning at her feet; but then decides that in second guessing the experience, she may be cheating herself out of a reward she has apparently earned.

Anna unpacks her suitcase and undresses, pulling one of two plush robes from out of the closet. She walks to the bath with the heated marble floor and approaches a wedged shaped tub that appears to be teetering on the edge of some urban precipice, then turns the gold-plated handle engraved with the shape of a lotus flower and begins to fill the tub.

Even though she's some four-hundred feet above St. Thomas Street, Anna still feels uncomfortable being naked, right there in front of God and London, and it doesn't help when a police helicopter suddenly appears from out of nowhere, passing within a hundred yards of her room.

As the beating of the chopper blades fade around the opposite corner of the building, the phone on the marble wall rings with an odd, beep-beep that sounds nothing like an American ring; one that tells her that she is indeed in a foreign country.

"Miss Newsom?"

"Yes, this is she."

"Hold please."

Anna reaches for her robe and holds it to her as a second voice comes on the line.

"Anna? Cynthia here!"

On the call is Cynthia Smythe, the producer for the BBC show that Anna is scheduled to record later this morning.

"Cynthia, good morning."

"Welcome to London! How was the flight? Was Henry on time? He's a love, isn't he?"

Cynthia is an obvious A-type personality and, with her rapid-fire style, Anna surmises that Cynthia neither wants nor expects an answer.

"Um, good, fine,"

"Brilliant!" Cynthia fires back. "Get some rest, enjoy the view, and we'll see you at the studio around eleven.

Cynthia's voice departs as quickly as it arrived. Anna lets the robe slip onto the marble floor, reaches for the room service menu laying on a bench nearby, and steps gingerly into the soothing, warm water, wondering if the helicopters ever get any closer.

Henry was at the hotel at 10:30 sharp, just as he promised.

"'Ello, miss! he says, cheerfully, as Anna gets into the cab. "Nab a few winks, did we?"

"I tried, Henry, but the phone kept ringing," Anna replies.

In reality, the phone had rung twice. The first was hotel management asking if everything was okay, and the second was the London office of Anna's publisher, also asking if everything was okay.

Everything was fine, Anna had assured them, and went back to her pillow, but could only manage a hypnogogic montage with strange voices hallucinated in the low hissing of the air conditioner.

Travel to the BBC studios took every second of the estimate Henry had given her. A visiting dignitary's motorcade had forced the re-routing of most of central London, tangling traffic and threatening a late arrival, but Henry's incredible mastery of the ancient maze of streets and alleys had them to the iconic circular structure of BBC Television right on time.

"It's me hippocampus," Henry says, offering it as the explanation for his grasp of what Londoners call, The Knowledge - the mental map of London's 35,000 thoroughfares.

"Bigger than most, it is," he adds proudly. "One day, two young blokes and a lassie from Queen Mary U take a ride in me cab. Next thing I know, they're asking if, for a hundred pounds, they can take a photo of me brain. So, I talk to the Mrs. and she says, 'for a hundred pounds, they can have the whole thing.'"

"She has quite the sense of humor," Anna says.

"So, yes, I says, and before you know, it I'm layin' flat on me back in a tube and then right after, them telling me I got an 'atypical hippocampus'."

Henry was right. Anna had read about the brain's newly discovered plasticity and how the learning or forgetting of certain skills can actually increase or decrease neuronal connections in the areas of the brain specific to those skills. Although not considered germane in Anna's area of expertise, the importance of brain plasticity was gaining traction across many fields, and Anna made a mental note to give it further study.

After several minutes of waiting at the front desk, Cynthia Smythe bursts through a heavily fortified door leading to the rest of the complex and thrusts out her hand. As Anna has surmised, Cynthia is about fifteen years Anna's senior.

"Anna, it's so nice to finally meet you," Cynthia offers.

"And you as well."

"We'll get you all checked in, sorry for the tight security, and then to make-up if, you like. Not necessary, though."

"I don't know, what do most women do?" Anna asks as they walk through the security door.

"Don't be daffy, love. They take the free makeover."

Contrary to what Anna might have imagined or wished for, a television studio is not a warm and inviting place. In fact, they're cold, damn cold, and intimidating, and Studio A in the BBC Television Complex was no different.

"Electronics are happier in lower temperatures," Cynthia Smythe explains.

The set for The Evolving Mind, the show that Anna is

scheduled to appear on, occupies one corner of a studio measuring some 100 feet square. In fact, it's so cavernous that one can't see into its corners, as the bright lighting for the set diminishes dramatically at approximately the distance of the television cameras, of which there are three.

The set itself is simple. Two high-backed upholstered armchairs sit on a blue, carpeted riser. Between the chairs is a small table with a carafe of water, two glasses, and a copy of Anna's book.

Hanging just behind the chairs is a large illustration of a human skull with an exposed brain, areas of which are highlighted, reminding Anna of those old illustrations nineteenth century Phrenologists would use. It also makes Anna wonder if the BBC has all but concluded that the mind resides exclusively within the head, a concept that cutting edge science and Anna herself are not entirely comfortable with.

"This is where you'll be sitting," Cynthia says, pointing to a chair on the left side of the set. "Mr. Edwards sits here to your left or, as we in the industry say, camera right."

"Of course," Anna says, citing Cynthia's Type A personality as fertile ground for study.

Edwards is John Edwards, the English host of The Evolving Mind. Anna has heard from her literary agent that he's an experienced, even-handed journalist and has a psychology degree to boot, but a review of him that Anna read during the flight over put it somewhat differently, describing him as…

> *A pompous narcissistic; swaddled in the gentleman's trappings of Saville Row and drenched in Penhaligon's; a dinosaur from the last century, desperately struggling to stave off extinction.*

"You're wondering why interviewers normally sit on the right," Cynthia says, anticipating a question she's gotten a hundred times. "It's simple, really. It's because it makes them appear powerful. In Western culture, we read from left to right, count from left to right, and most people, when they think of the week or the year ahead, produce mental images which are also laid out left to right. The interviewer sits at the right, because no matter how famous the guest may be, sitting to the left makes him or her seem subservient."

Anna hesitates, savoring the moment.

"Um, actually, I knew that. I was going to ask where the nearest restroom is."

"Oh. The loo. Of course," Cynthia answers, a little flummoxed. "Through the door behind the set."

Anna steps up to the mirror in the restroom to get a closer look at what damage the young make-up girl might have inflicted. She grabs a brush from her purse and tries to make some sense out of her hair, then grabs some tissue out of a holder on the counter next to the sink and begins to dab some of the color from her eyelids and cheeks. Finally, she reduces the amount of color on her lips. Then, thinking that she's removed a little too much, she reaches for her tube of lipstick, stares at it for a moment, then applies a touch more and tosses the onyx tube back into her purse.

When she returns, the set is a beehive of activity. There are camera operators and sound people and an assortment of assistants flitting about doing things that seem awfully important.

"Anna?" a male voice calls out from behind.

Anna turns to see the show's director approaching from the other side of the set.

"Looks as though you've drawn the short-straw this morning," the man says, in a likable, self-deprecating way.

"I'm Mitchell Walker, your director today, welcome to the BBC."

"Good morning," Anna replies, reaching for his hand and not agreeing in the least with the short-straw analogy.

Mitchell Walker is thirty-four and about the best-looking

Englishman she's seen since landing. Something behind his eyes, however, tells Anna that he already knows that. He's of moderate height with thick, curly black hair and a mouth that turns up at both corners when he smiles.

"Cynthia has given you the run down I assume?" Mitchell adds.

"Yes, she..." Anna begins to say, when a man in his late sixties enters the studio.

"Ah, here's Edwards, now," Mitchell says, taking a couple of steps in Edwards's direction.

"John Edwards, meet Dr. Anna Newsom."

"Good morning. I see you've met the 'Dictator of the Day,'" Edwards quips, referring to Mitchell as he extends his hand.

"I have," Anna says, reaching for his. "Good morning."

Anna pauses a moment to take Edwards in. He's tall, with thick salt and pepper hair combed to one side and back. His eyes are steely grey, and this morning they're bloodshot. He seems altogether too tan for living in England year-round, and Anna knows that the 'Dictator of the Day' statement, although meant to be humorous, is really John Edward's way of saying that, while directors are dispensable, he's the permanent fixture around here and, contrary to what her agent told her, he's got 'asshole' written all over him.

"Mitch, take a look at the way she's studying me," Edwards says.

Mitchell glances at Anna and breaks into a wry smile.

"She is, isn't she?" he says.

"I trust your analysis is on the house, young lady," Edward's quips.

Anna smiles politely and has the distinct impression that she smells alcohol.

"Not everything is about you, John," Cynthia says, as she joins the group. "Good morning, everyone, let's get this party started."

And with that everyone fans out to their various stations.

Anna has taken her seat and watches as Edwards pulls a

small bottle of Visine from his jacket pocket.

"Damn studio air, as dry as the bloody Kalahari."

"Stand-by!" a floor assistant shouts and with that the interview begins. Edwards and Anna are plunged into darkness, silhouetted against the lighted rear wall of the set.

The assistant holds one hand in front of the main camera and with fingers splayed starts the countdown, retracting one finger for each number.

"Five, four, three, two, one," he says.

After which the introductory theme song begins. In the control room, Mitchell watches the clock as the theme song enters its last few moments.

"Ready lights… lights up," he says into the microphone on his headset.

Instantly, the set is bathed in intensely bright light.

The second sunrise of the day, Anna thinks to herself, the first being earlier this morning over Scotland, which now seems ages ago.

"Ready to cue Edwards. Cue Edwards," Mitchell continues.

On the set, the floor assistant standing next to the main camera points at Edwards, who takes his cue.

"Ladies and gentlemen," he begins, "welcome to another installment of The Evolving Mind. Tonight's guest, Dr. Anna Newsom, is the author of the best-selling book, The Spider on the Ceiling."

Anna is now suddenly aware that a red light has been illuminated on the camera pointed directly at her and takes a deep breath.

"Dr. Newsom, welcome to The Evolving Mind."

She swallows, then manages a response.

"Thank you for having me."

"You seem so young to have a best-seller on the New York Times list," Edwards begins, striking a blow even before Anna's eyes have adjusted to the lights.

"The youngest, Jake Marcionette, was twelve. I'm old enough to be his mother," Anna quips in reply. "In any case, it's not so much what I've written as the discoveries we've made."

"Very well, then. You start your book with a quote."

"Yes."

Edwards reaches for the book and with great affect, pulls his reading glasses from his jacket pocket.

> "'If the mind isn't occupied by one thing, it may be occupied by something one wishes to be less occupied by.' Quite poetic."

"It's a quote I borrowed from a professor in graduate school."

"You majored in Women's Studies, I understand, and…"

"Minored, in Women's Studies. My major was Forensic Psychology."

"I stand corrected."

"The quote changed my life. And it informed everything that I did after."

"Please explain."

"The Spider on the Ceiling contains five case histories of women who were serially raped by a single perpetrator and who were accused of murdering or attempting to murder said perpetrator."

"And how did you come to select these particular women?" he asks.

"They were patients of mine."

"Patients?"

"It's important to remember that these were cases where NO physical evidence of abuse was available. It was my job, working with law enforcement, to determine if and to what degree each of these victims was telling the truth, as that would lead to a conviction or a judgment of justifiable homicide."

"And what relevance does the quote have?"

"It's simple really. Try thinking of nothing."

"When I try thinking of nothing, I'm thinking that I'm trying to think of nothing," Edwards answers.

"Which is most of the time," Mitchell quips, as he and Cynthia watch the progress of the interview from the control room.

"Correct," Anna says. "People who practice transcendental meditation do it, but not without years of training. Now imagine that you're a woman being raped."

"Do I have to?" Edwards offers sarcastically.

"He's such a bloody bugger," Cynthia says, under her breath.

In spite of how offensive Edwards is, Anna continues.

"Your mind is consumed by the unthinkable offense that's being committed against you. The only defense mechanism the victim has in these cases is to either think of nothing, which is impossible. Or something else entirely."

"Then the corollary is also true," Edwards adds.

"Correct. If the mind is occupied by something it wants to be less occupied by, then it must find the something to replace it with. What I discovered was that in every case of serial rape or molestation we studied, the victim had consciously or unconsciously latched on to an object in their physical environment that would divert his or her attention and help facilitate a conscious escape from the horror of the moment. I've named it the Psychic Lightning Rod, or PLR for short.

"With all due respect, Dr. Newsom, this is hardly a new concept. The notion of a psychic retreat was formulated by Steiner decades ago. All you've done is rename it."

"Hardly. We're into entirely different territory now," Mr. Edwards.

"Explain."

"In each of the five cases I present in my book, the victim identified a PLR in her environment. In one particular case, however, not only did she identify a PLR, but over time, the object manifested physical changes."

"What exactly are you saying?" Edwards asks, leaning back into his chair. "That these victims were somehow able to perform paranormal feats like psychokinesis?

"Unconsciously, yes. We call them Causal Tele-trans-mutations or CTT's. And yes, that's what my research has shown."

"I've read the case histories," Cynthia says, to Mitchell. "bloody amazing."

Edwards pauses for effect.

"Well, from where I'm sitting, young lady, it seems you're using voodoo science to set murderers free."

Suddenly, Anna has become keenly aware of the flashing red light on the television camera in her peripheral vision. That, plus the lack of sleep and too many cups of coffee are all having an effect on her ability to think and respond.

"Dr. Newsom? You haven't responded to my statement."

"You, um, wouldn't think so if you...if you were one of these women," Anna says, as she reaches for a glass and pours herself some water from the carafe.

"Of which you are one, as revealed in your book."

Anna stops for a moment, struggling to regain some mental clarity.

"I, um... based my master's thesis on my particular experience. In the book I use it as a way of establishing the foundation upon which I base my psychological evaluations."

"You say in your book that you were raped by your cousin when you were thirteen."

"Yes."

"Were you serially raped?"

"No."

"But you say you used the same technique for creating the Psychic Lightning Rod, as you call it."

"Yes, to escape the reality of the moment. I just wasn't consciously aware of what I was doing when I was doing it. Many women aren't. It wasn't until therapy afterwards that I was able to retrieve the memory."

"And your particular PLR?"

"A tube of lipstick."

"Did your lipstick 'tele-transmutate' over time?" Edwards says, sarcastically.

"As I said, no time-frame existed, as it was a single episode."

"Nevertheless, if someone were to have given you a psychological evaluation based on your theory, you too, would have been declared the innocent victim; theoretically justified, then, in committing the capital crime of the murder of your cousin."

"Theoretically, yes."

Edwards stops for a moment, readying for the final assault.

"I hope the audience will forgive me, but I've got to say this sounds like bloody tommyrot."

In the studio control room Mitchell Walker turns and whispers to Cynthia Smythe.

"Christ, he must have been on real bender last night.

"A doozy, I'd say," replies Cynthia.

Edwards now senses he has the advantage.

"Can you tell me, and the audience watching at home, how it came to be that your cousin was acquitted and found innocent of the crime of rape? Statutory rape in this case."

Anna is quick to respond.

"He lied."

"And you told the truth, I presume?"

"Of course."

"So, we're back to, 'he said, she said.'"

"Oh, fuck. We just lost half of our female viewers," Cynthia says, turning to Mitchell, "tell the floor manager we're going to a break."

Mitchell flips a switch on the control panel and barks into the microphone on his headset.

"Sam, we're going to a break. No. Now."

"I was not the one on trial," Anna says sharply, her jaw tightening. "The difference here, Mr. Edwards…"

"John, please," he says, patronizing her, but Anna ignores

him.

"....is that in my case, the theory of the Psychic Lightning Rod was years away from being formulated." Anna pauses and then adds, "I was thirteen."

Satisfied that he's been able to get under her skin, Edwards rewards himself with a small smirk.

"You can see how dangerous this is, can't you, Dr. Newsom?" Then, spotting the floor manager signaling him out of the corner of his eye, Edwards lets the question hang in the air and turns to camera one.

"After the break, we'll be taking a closer look at the first case in Dr. Newsom's book, *The Spider on the Ceiling*".

"Wanker," Mitchell exclaims under his breath, as Cynthia stands and bolts for the door.

ten

Anna was furious at herself. First, for letting Edwards get the better of her, and second, for allowing herself to be talked into doing the interview at all.

Her literary agent, Evelyn Hardwick, is of the opinion that any publicity at all is beneficial, but Anna's father had warned her about the press, especially those who consider themselves intellectual superiors, which, of course, most do. But Edwards was another beast entirely, and Anna had him pegged from the start.

With nothing else scheduled for the rest of the day, Anna was looking forward to a trip to Harrod's, but the balance of the interview had been no easier and had left her exhausted; so now she was thinking of saving it for another day.

"Thanks, Henry. I won't be needing you this afternoon," Anna tells him.

"You do look all in, miss. Why not sneak a few winks and ring me up when you're ready to venture out."

"No, Henry, I'm sure. Thank you."

Henry's face drops and he turns away.

"Whatever you say, miss. But now I'll be havin' to take me wife and her girlfriends to the shopping mall in Hammersmith."

Anna makes her way through the lobby of the Shangri-La and takes the elevator to the fortieth floor. In her room she draws a bath and chooses some music on her phone. Although she can listen to most anything, she prefers the nostalgia of Southern bluegrass ballads with their honey-like blend of Scottish and Celtic chords. It must be genetic, she thinks, as both of her great-great grandfathers fought in the Civil War.

She climbs out of her clothes right in front of the floor-to-ceiling glass windows, then steps into the warm water. A copy of *The Spider on the Ceiling* is laying on the small oriental table next to the tub and she reaches for it, opens it to the first case study, but immediately closes it, having had enough of the subject for one day.

Her twin theories of the Psychic Lightning Rod and the Causal Tele-Transmutations that sometimes follow do sound outlandish, she understands that, *but the science is there,* she tells herself. Anna leans back in the tub and closes her eyes to a song from the group Elephant Revival.

> *There's a ring around the moon*
> *There's a ring around the moon*
> *There's a ring around the moon*
> *Neath the Halo of the moon*
> *Blew down on her sail*
> *Seasons changing*
> *I can smell it in the air*

Suddenly, she's aware of the distant thumping of an approaching helicopter and tries to guess from which direction it's approaching. The glass skin of The Shard, however, tends to amplify the pulsating sound, making it difficult to determine direction and distance.

Anna is experiencing the full onslaught of jet lag now and is trying to resist the temptation to sleep. She knows how important it is to adapt to the local Circadian rhythm, but somewhere a small voice tells her that shutting her eyes for a few moments couldn't hurt. As the beating blades of the helicopter die away, the song returns…

> *I can see it in their paintings*
> *And I can hear it in the wind,*
> *hear it rise and descend*
> *Through the many-colored trees,*
> *Forms a many-colored breeze*

Made of many-colored leaves,
departing ever so gracefully…

…and Anna sinks into that twilight state, intensified by jet lag, where the conscious mind melts into the surreal, other worldly landscape of the sublimal…

It's early summer and she and Ethan are hiking in the Shenandoah Valley. It's been two weeks since they met on a blind date and both are experiencing the sharpening of senses stoked by elevated hormones.

They've been following a trail through a dense forest of yellow poplars, but now the single trail is splitting into two, with each trail ascending hills on either side of the stream.

"Which one?" Ethan asks, deferring to Anna.

"You choose," she answers.

Ethan turns to the left and they begin the rise. Leaving the stream below, six-foot-tall Osmunda regalia ferns give way to Dryopteris Goldiana and eventually to Woodsia Ilvensis, which clings to the cliffs in the higher elevations and where chestnut and red oak line the ridges. Having made the summit, they hike along the ridge line, eventually coming to a saddle in the hill which opens to a view of the valley between the two ridges 3500 feet below.

Ethan stops them in the middle of a patch of purple and yellow wildflowers as a Blue-winged warbler takes note of their arrival. The sun in a summer sky shimmers across the landscape.

"That's strange," Anna says. "I can still hear the stream."
Ethan turns to her, steps in close, and gives her a gentle kiss, first on the forehead, then each cheek, and then her lips.

"It's funny, I can't hear anything, I can't see anything, I can't feel anything, but you," he says, gently pulling her down onto the bed of wildflowers. As bees whiz away to other blossoms, Anna lays back and Ethan follows her down.

Gently pressing himself against her, she can feel him harden on her leg and he kisses her again, but Anna turns away, distracted.

"Ethan, listen. The stream. It's louder."

"What?"

Ethan turns his head toward the valley below.

"What in the hell is that?"

Then suddenly, without warning, the low rumble breaks into an unimaginable roar as a wall of water nearly two thirds the height of the ridge crashes upward out of the valley. Smashing through maples and birch as it climbs, gigantic waves and swirling vortices rush in to the fill the voids in the cliffs just below where Anna and Ethan are laying.

"RUN!" Ethan shouts jumping to his feet, his voice barely audible above the roar. "RUN! RUN! FOR GOD'S SAKE!"

Without thinking, Anna tears off in the direction opposite the thundering, rising tide and yells for Ethan over her shoulder.

"ETHAN!!! ETHAN!!!", she cries out in desperation. Reaching the taller side of the saddle in the ridge, Anna begins to scramble up the pile of loose gravel and decomposed granite. She claws at the broken rock, bloodying her hands, and digs in with her hiking boots, straining to get some purchase against the rising tide behind her. Then, with no strength left in reserve, Anna reaches the crest, and turns back just in time to see a massive secondary wave as it slams against the far ridge. It ricochets 40, 50, 60 feet in height across the massive body of turbulent, roiling water and then crashes up and over the near ridge just below her, engulfing the patch of wildflowers where she and Ethan were laying just moments ago.

Then all at once, it's dead silent; and now she feels the water rise up around her body, up to her breasts and neck, and she's trying to hold her breath because she can feel its fingers playing at the corners of her mouth and she doesn't dare scream but she can no longer not breathe, and with a jolt and shudder she gasps, awake, in her tub in the Shangri-La Hotel, rising bath water lapping at her chin.

For a second Anna has no idea where she is. Then she remembers the morning and the interview and the helicopters and the warnings her mother had given her about unprotected sex and falling asleep in the bathtub.

eleven

Although the forecast was for rain, Anna decides she needs to get out and get some air and, who knows, there may be a sale at Harrod's. She grabs one of the umbrellas that the Shangri-La holds in reserve for hotel guests, then opens her phone to her maps app.

"Harrod's," Anna says into the phone.

A female voice responds to her command.

"Harrod's. One hour and twenty-three minutes. 3.8 miles. This is your best route."

A hotel bellman who happens to be passing overhears.

"That's quite a trudge, miss, especially at this hour on a Friday. Pedways will be jammed. Call you a cab?"

"No, thank you," Anna answers, then decides she may be better saving Harrod's for another day when she'll have Henry at her beck and call. It's already nearly three and, with the days getting shorter, Anna decides the bellman is right, better to roam closer to the hotel this afternoon.

*After the book signing tomorrow, s*he tells herself. From the map on her phone she plots a route that will take her across the Thames and around the Tower of London; then the Tower Bridge to travel back across the Thames; through Potter's Field Park and the London Bridge railway station which connects to The Shard.

It's a mild September day, but the sun's proximity to the horizon and the slight chill coming off the Thames sparks in Anna that peculiar sense of foreboding; and although she can't recall the first time she experienced it, she also can't recall a time when she hasn't.

Then she remembers what Cynthia Smythe had said about Westerners, producing mental images which are laid out left to right when thinking of the week or the year ahead.

For Anna, the opposite is true. She imagines the days of the week moving from her upper right down to her lower left, and months moving in the same direction, descending into some dark, indiscernible smudge as they approach winter.

While rain seems possible, the broken clouds are moving quickly, and random patches of yellow sunlight skip across the grey landscape. Crossing the Tower Bridge, she notices some sort of Naval ship at anchor on the opposite bank in the direction of the Shangri-La. She can see human figures crossing a footbridge from the shore and concludes it must be a museum of some kind.

When she arrives, Anna is greeted by a sign that reads, 'The HMS Belfast', accompanied by a concise history of the light cruiser's *long and admirable service to the country*', which to Anna meant that it probably killed a lot of people.

"She's open every day from 10 to 5, miss," says the elderly male docent at the ticket kiosk.

Anna considers boarding, but then changes her mind in favor of a coffee and decides to make her way into the newly renovated London Bridge Railway Station, which she read is more like an underground shopping mall.

This afternoon it's thronged with passengers, some arriving and looking forward to a weekend on the town, but mostly populated with weary, urban warriors, scrambling to make their connection home. Weaving her way upstream, Anna reaches a cafe situated next to a news kiosk and grabs a seat that is just being vacated. A middle-aged waitress appears and scoops up the change left behind by the previous occupant.

"What'll be, miss?"

"Coffee, please. With milk."

Anna leans her Shangri-La umbrella up against her chair and glances around her. Spotting a news kiosk, she turns to the middle-age man sitting next to her.

"Um, excuse me?"

"What's 'at, miss?" he replies, turning from his paper.

"Can you hold my seat for a minute?"

The man gives Anna a quick once-over and flashes a sliver of a grin.

"Longer, if you like," he quips.

Anna's smile vanishes.

"Really. Was that necessary?" she says, incredulous.

"Just joking, I was. Go ahead, I'll watch your things."

Anna stands and as she's walking away, wonders how men like him still exist in 2020.

On one side of the newsstand are racks of periodicals and newspapers. On the other side are shelves with hardcover novels and paperbacks. She spots a stack of her books on a table that's partially hidden by a display of carry-on rollers. She picks up a copy and turns it over to look at the back cover.

Her agent explained that the book's description may be slightly modified depending upon the country or territory in which the book is being sold. Seeing that it's different from the U.S. edition she decides to buy a copy, but before bringing it to the counter, she stops to scan the local tabloids. Most carry headlines about national and international politics, of which Anna has no interest. But one catches her eye. THE EVENING TATTLER is carrying a story with a headline that reads:

'TEEN GIRL ARRESTED FOR MURDER
Victim David O'Rourke Was Respected Clevedon Resident.'

She pays for her book and the tabloid and when she returns to her table, her coffee has already arrived.

"Ah, there you are," says the man seated next to her.

"Your coffee's going cold and I was about to leave for my train."

"Thank you," Anna replies.

She sits and places the newspaper and book on the table, takes a sip of coffee, and begins to read the back cover. As the man collects his things, he glances down and notices her photograph.

"Well, blimey! It's you, is it?"

"Yes, it is."

"Here I am, sitting next to an author and all I can manage is a bloody joke. And a bloody poor one at that. My apologies, miss."

"Accepted, thank you. Can you tell me? Where is Clevedon?"

"Due west. By train, three hours or so," he says, then the man tips his hat and disappears into the crowd.

Anna takes another sip of coffee, quickly scans the rear of her book, and then turns her attention to the story in the paper. The Evening Tattler is published in Bristol, a city of some 724,000 souls in Southwest England, which sits astride the Frome and Avon Rivers. Clevedon, where the murder took place, is a seaside suburb about thirteen miles west.

The paper states that the murder occurred in the early hours of this morning, and Anna is about to read further when her cell phone rings.

"Hello?"

"I hear that you made quite a splash at the BBC."

On the other end is Anna's agent, Evelyn Hardwick; a literary firebrand and a consummate New Yorker.

"John Edwards is an ass," Anna reports.

"Doesn't matter. According to Cynthia Smythe you held your ground, and that's all that counts. I just got off the phone with her. She told me that they feel the subject matter is so compelling they want to run it as five episodes over five nights instead of a single show. You should be very proud of yourself. How's London treating you?"

"It's ignoring me, basically."

"Not for long, sweetheart. Say hello to Tom Hiddleston for me," and with that, Evelyn was on to another client.

Anna glances at the time on her phone and sees that it's nearing six. It's been an exhausting twenty-four hours; now she's ready for a couple glasses of wine and a relaxing dinner, something typically British, she tells herself.

She slips the newspaper and her book into her Tumi backpack and slings it across her back. She picks up her change, leaving a couple of coins for the waitress, and then heads toward the station exit.

"Eve'nin', miss, much obliged," the waitress says approaching the table.

"You're welcome," Anna replies, over her shoulder.

The forecast was spot on and it's raining when she steps outside. The sky has darkened and it's much colder than it was an hour ago. Anna opens her Shangri-La umbrella and makes a right turn up St. Thomas Street, and then remembers she could have taken the underground walkway.

Too late now, she tells herself.

About half the distance to the hotel, the rain turns into a torrential downpour delivered by heavy winds and dark clouds that bristle with lightning.

Not surprisingly, the umbrella is no match for the storm, so Anna breaks into a sprint and dives through the hotel entrance just as a large lightning bolt strikes a power pole across the street, sending a flash of hot white light skidding across the hotel lobby. It's followed immediately by a sharp crack and a deafening roll of thunder that could easily compete with a summer storm in Georgia.

In all the excitement and confusion, Anna doesn't notice the group in front of her and she crashes headlong and sopping wet into the back of Mitchell Walker, the director from the BBC who is just saying goodbye to a friend.

"What the...? Anna!" Mitchell blurts out, as he turns.

Swinging the Tumi backpack off her shoulder, Anna glances up at the familiar sounding voice.

"Mitchell! I'm so sorry!"

"We could feel the electric discharge from here! Are you okay?"

"I could, too!" she says, slipping out of her jacket. "Look, the fuzz on my arm is standing straight up!" Anna says, then

66

runs her hand through her sopping hair.

"I look like the Bride of Frankenstein, don't I?"

"Hardly," Mitchell offers.

"Then as bad as a Monday mop, I'm sure."

"Best looking Monday mop I've ever run into. Or that's run into me, I should say," Mitchell says, as he flashes the up-turned smile Anna had noticed this very morning at the BBC.

My God, she thinks to herself, *It's still the same day.*

"Is this your hotel?", he asks.

Anna shakes her head, feeling a little chill.

"They used to put guests up at Brown's. No longer smart enough, I suppose," he says.

"The way of the world now, isn't it?" Anna replies. "Well, good night."

As Anna begins to move off in the direction of the elevators, Mitchell calls out to her.

"Anna! Um, listen, I was here having a drink with friends and they had to dash, so I was battin' 'round the idea of grabbing a bite," Mitchell says.

"Well, I'm going to sit in the tub, have a couple glasses of wine, and then try the English restaurant here," Anna replies, and, as she begins to turn away, Mitchell calls out again.

"Then why not this? You get out of those damp clothes and have a nice, warm tubby while I pay another visit to me friend, Mr. Jack Daniels. Ting's is gourmet British, if there can be such a thing, and I've heard good things. Plus, we won't need to leave the hotel."

"That's very nice, but no, thank you. I've got work and phone calls and…"

"Look, nothing serious, I promise. Just a friendly bite between two professionals. You need to eat and why eat alone?"

"No, thank you, but no."

Anna is just about to leave when a passing bellman spots her tattered umbrella.

"Allow me, miss," he says, reaching for it, "looks like this soldier has 'ad its day, I'm afraid."

Anna watches the bellman walk away and hesitates a moment, reconsidering Mitchell's offer.

"You know, why not. Say, 30 minutes?"

"Tings, thirty-fifth floor! See you there!" Mitchell replies.

Mitchell takes another sip of wine and continues his story.

"Then, when I was twelve, I started making pretend TV cameras out of cardboard boxes and would coerce everyone in my family to sit for an hour at a time and pretend they were news readers," Mitchell says, sipping his wine.

Anna slices off another piece of her entree and pops it into her mouth.

"Then Edwards was right."

"How so?"

"You are a dictator!" Anna says, with a smile, reaching for her wine glass.

"I stand convicted!"

There it is again, Anna thinks to herself. The way his mouth turns up at the corners when he's pleased with himself and how it always seems to be accompanied by a glint in his eyes.

Anna and Mitchell are seated at a table for two next to the floor-to-ceiling windows, the exact view of the city that Anna has from her bathtub five floors above. Mitchell notices Anna's glass.

"Where are my manners?"

He reaches for the bottle of New Zealand Sauvignon Blanc that's been chilling in an ice bucket next to their table. Two feet away, occasional bursts of rain mottles their view of the city and transforms the lights of London into dancing splotches of color. The center of the storm, however, has moved off to the East providing Anna with sporadic flashes of electric blue on the distant horizon.

Psychic Lightning Rods, she thinks to herself.

Anna swallows, sets down her knife and fork, and wipes her mouth with her napkin.

"I must say, this is the best Surrey Dairy Cow with anchovy ketchup I've ever had."

"You're being sarcastic. You don't like it? It's totally British, just what you wanted!"

"I do. It's just, um, let me say, different."

"Well, I've heard you Southerners manage all kinds of odd edibles."

"I stand convicted!" Anna says in a quid pro quo, making them both laugh out loud. She takes another sip of wine and begins a story.

"One weekend when my parents were away, my brother and I went Crawfish hunting."

"I've seen those, like big beetles, right?"

"No, no. More like tiny lobsters. Anyway, we went down to the river about a mile from our house and stood in knee deep water for three hours or so, scooping them out of the thick mud and tossing them into an old pillowcase.

"Poor buggers."

"We must have collected a hundred or so. We took them home and boiled them and tried to make our own kids' version of a gumbo, but we couldn't get it right, so we'd rinse them out of the sauce and try it again."

"No way!" Mitchell says, reaching for his wine.

"Those crawdads must have been drenched five or six times in everything from barbecue sauce to Campbell's tomato soup before we gave up on the whole enterprise and made grilled cheese sandwiches."

"To the crawdads!" Mitchell says, raising his glass.

Anna follows suit and raises her glass as well.

"To the Surrey dairy cows!" Anna says, and they both laugh again.

Settling for a moment, Mitchell grows a bit more serious and runs his hand through his thick, curly black hair.

"Listen, I'd, uh, like to apologize for Edwards this morning."

"No need."

"Yes, there is."

"No, there isn't! I can take care of myself, okay?"

"Okay."

Mitchell hesitates, allowing himself a moment to take in Anna's delicate features; her reddish, blonde hair just touching her shoulders, the grayish green eyes the shade of moss and the lips that form a small heart at the philtrum just beneath her slightly upturned nose.

*She's quite adorable, h*e thinks to himself, clearing his throat.

"Anyway, Cynthia has promised the BBC one show for each of the five cases, and I guess I'm slated for the job."

"Fantastic, good for you."

"Since it's also the title of the book, they'll probably lead off with The Spider on the Ceiling, unless, of course, you have a problem with that."

"No, not at all."

Their waiter appears from out of nowhere and empties the bottle of Sauvignon Blanc into each of their glasses.

"Another?" the waiter asks, raising the bottle.

Mitchell looks at Anna.

"No way. I've got to be up early."

"A compromise. Two glasses," Mitchell says, looking back across the table.

"No, really. Thanks."

Mitchell turns to the waiter.

"I guess it's a no, then. I'll take the check."

"Very well," the waiter says and walks away.

"How did you come to all this, anyway? Your work, I mean."

"I was in college, minoring in Women's Studies and felt that I wanted to do something to become an advocate of women's rights. I knew I didn't want to be a lawyer..."

"Good decision," Mitchell says, interrupting, "world certainly doesn't need one more of those buggers," he adds, jokingly.

Anna savors the moment before responding.

"My father's a lawyer."

"Put my foot in it, didn't I. Sorry."

"Anyway, I had no idea really of which way to turn, and then one day I was standing in line at the grocery store and there was one of those tabloids that always feature weird stories. On the cover was a story about a woman in the 1950s who had murdered her husband claiming that he was sexually and physically abusing her. It was accompanied by old black and white photos and I couldn't resist, so I bought it and took it home, but it sat on my coffee table until the next weekend when I had some time to give it a read."

"So, what happened?"

"What always happened back then. Nobody believed her and she went to the electric chair."

"So, what's so weird about it?" Mitchell asks.

"The husband kept a diary, and had it hidden behind a wall in their house."

"No!"

"Yep. He kept copious notes of when and how he abused her, what he used, and what he planned to do in the future."

"And if that had been known at the time of her trial, she would have been acquitted, right?"

"Probably not."

"You've lost me."

"Any attorney worth his salt could have made a jury believe that the husband was living in a fantasy world and that the diary was nothing more than his way of living out that fantasy. Remember, she's still alive and in one piece at this point."

"Now, I'm really lost."

"It's simple. A forensic psychologist could have, through analysis and hypnotherapy, brought tens if not hundreds of minute details of the abuse to the surface of her conscious mind. From that point her defense attorney could have tied those details directly to corresponding entries in the husband's diary; essentially transforming her husband's fantas-

71

tical musings into irrefutable evidence that she had acted out of self-defense, which, of course, is totally legal."

"But what if the husband never created a diary?"

"That's when it gets really interesting," Anna says, sipping the remaining drops of Sauvignon Blanc.

"Your check, sir."

Mitchell takes a look at the bill, pulls a money clip from his pocket and drops several bills onto the table.

"When do you head back to the States?"

"Tuesday. Book signing tomorrow. King's College on Monday morning. Shopping Monday afternoon."

"Then dinner Sunday?"

"No, really, Mitchell, I can't. This was amazing and fun and…" Anna hesitates. "I can't."

Without warning, Anna stands, collects her things and reaches for Mitchell's hand. Dismayed at the sudden end to the evening, Mitchell stands and reaches for hers.

"It was very nice meeting you, Mitchell. Thank you for dinner and good luck with the series."

And with that, she was off, leaving Mitchell standing alone in the middle of the dining room.

twelve

Anna undresses and then slips into her white tank top and men's boxers, the same way she's dressed for bed ever since college, and she's practically asleep by the time her head hits the pillow.

There's an old World War Two movie, one of her father's favorites, called "The Longest Day", and Anna's sure that the day to which the title refers couldn't have been any longer than the one she's just experienced.

The rain has softened, and the gentle patter against the floor-to-ceiling windows provides a welcome palliative, as does the crisp 800-count bed linens and the silk 'Goldilocks' comforter embossed with a lotus pattern; not too heavy and not too light.

As she begins to slip the bonds of consciousness, Anna is bombarded with a flurry of fragmented sounds and images.

Waking Ethan to tell him she was leaving and good luck with the job interview and to not forget to take his medicine or feed the cat; her father's goodbye hug; Macon falling away and disappearing through broken clouds; scrambling to make her connection in Atlanta; Sarah, the flight attendant, Romeo and Juliet in row five; the hundreds of travelers and carts piled with luggage and the frenzied dash to freedom and Henry holding the sign; Cynthia Smythe's outstretched hand; John Edward's cynical sneer; floor-to-ceiling glass windows; and now naked with helicopters thumping outside her window and then falling asleep in the tub and the terrible dream of the massive tidal wave, and all of it fading into a swirling grey mist; and now, from out of nowhere, vaguely aware of Mitchell's upturned grin and the hu-

morous glint in his deep brown eyes; and a thought far off, wondering why she's thinking of him at all.

In his robe, Mitchell switches off the kitchen light and makes his way to the living room. Glancing out the second-story window, he takes note that the rain has eased up a bit.

His flat, in the Kensington area of London, is a lucky find. It's north of the city center and within walking distance to the BBC, and the cafes and nightlife provide welcome relief from the drabness of his last address, which was in Bromley. Bromley was a neighborhood insisted upon by his ex-wife due to its proximity to his in-laws, thereby giving Kensington another tick in the plus column.

Although this building is pre-war, Mitchell's done it up with mid-century American art and antiques, something he couldn't have done with Carolyn, who was deeply committed to flowered wallpaper and chintz drapes.

He takes a sip from his glass of Jack Daniels, grabs Anna's book from a 1950's bird's-eye maple coffee table and stretches out on his vintage Tuxedo mohair sofa.

He glances at the cover, then flips the book around. He takes note of Anna's photo, lingering on it a little longer than he's comfortable with, and then opens the book to the first chapter.

THE SPIDER ON THE CEILING

Rayanna Mae Carter, a white female, 16 years of age, was arrested in November of 2016 by officers of the Savannah Police Department for the murder of her step-father, 43-year-old Kenneth (Kenny) Jules Griffin. After processing, she was transferred to the Georgia Department of Juvenile Justice and brought to the Regional Youth Detention Center to be held until her hearing in a juvenile court. As the investigation into the crime progressed, the prosecutor in the case was developing a the-

ory that the murder was actually born of a plot hatched between the murderer and her 17-year-old boyfriend, Alton Dean Wilcox. Parallel to this effort, a decision was made by Rayanna's defense attorney to proceed with psychoanalysis. I received a phone call late in June requesting that I travel to Savannah and schedule a series of sessions to determine the suspect's mental state and to make a determination as to her ability to stand trial...

thirteen

Looking up from the large eighteenth century desk, now used as a book signing table, Anna can see John Hatchard's portrait staring down at her through the spindles of the creaky staircase leading to the second-floor landing. Before leaving Macon, Anna had paid a visit to Hatchards website. Clicking the history tab, she learned that;

> 'Its customers have been the literary, political, art-
> istic, and social lions of their day and, since its incep-
> tion, a link has been forged between the fine booksellers
> of Hatchards and the royal households of Britain and
> Europe, as demonstrated by the three royal warrants
> it currently holds. Eight generations of customers and
> booksellers have come and gone since the shop first
> opened its doors. Many things have changed, but the es-
> sence of the place remains the same and is unchange-
> able. Hatchards is a unique British Institution.'

The rain has given way to warm sunlight kissed with the hint of a cool, gentle breeze, and because it's also a Saturday, the sidewalks and streets are teeming with fall shoppers. Sales have been brisk; Anna has probably signed two dozen books at this point, but, as for 'social lions' and 'British royalty', she gathers that they've more than likely slept in this morning.

Henry delivered her a few minutes before opening, so she had had a chance to grab a coffee and get acquainted with the neighborhood. When Hatchards opened, promptly at ten, she was warmly greeted by the store manager, Clive Anderson; an Englishman proper to the point of caricature, he dutifully gave her a quick tour before setting her up at the large signing desk, to which Clive gave Anna a formal introduction.

"Smashing, isn't she?"

"It's beautiful," Anna replies, noticing the stack of books waiting for her signature.

"Quite a history in this old girl. 'Maggie', as she's known around Hatchards, has been sitting right where you see her now since 1832."

"Maggie?"

"Short for Mahogany. Solid through and through. Don't be shy, give her a test drive."

Anna slides into the chair behind the desk, scoots up close, and runs her hands across the finish.

"Her first owner was a John Marley, a captain he was, of an enemy ship; the 32-gun fast frigate, the USS Hancock. That is until the Hancock was overwhelmed and captured in a brave and daring maneuver on the high seas by the Royal Navy's HMS Rainbow during the harebrained escapade you Yankees call the War of Independence. It was at that moment that Maggie became the indisputable property of his highness King George the Third."

"Harebrained is a little harsh, don't you think?" Anna asks as she circles behind the desk. "Anyway, how did she, I mean Maggie, come to find herself here at Hatchards?"

"No one knows for sure. For decades rumors abounded about gambling debts and unseemly liaisons in Parliament or some such poppycock; but that, my dear author, is irrelevant. The point is that she's here now and, for this morning at least, steadfastly at your service."

Anna humors herself with a quick, dime-store analysis of Clive Anderson;

He's forthright and loyal to a fault due to his being haunted by a perceived fatal flaw for which he must make amends.

It reminds Anna of a syndrome known as Rejection Sensitive Dysphoria; an extreme emotional condition triggered by the perception, at least, that a person has been rejected, teased, or criticized by important people in their life.

I shamefully admit that, as an infant, I was denied my

mother's breast, Anna chuckles to herself, imagining Clive's stoic disclosure through his facade of implacable superiority.

Anna estimated that the signing of each book, taking into account introductions, questions, and small talk, took roughly two-and-a-half minutes. The signing was scheduled to last from 10:30 to 12:45, but went longer, as several customers were already in line when Clive Anderson closed the queue. By 1:15, Anna was out the door enjoying the bright sunshine. The pubs were teeming now, having taken the burden from the streets and the pedways, and the walk was pleasant.

Just before leaving Hatchards, she Googled Brown's Hotel and discovered that it was around the block about a third of a mile away. It also said that Agatha Christie had been a regular at Brown's and that she had used the hotel as a setting for one of her mysteries, so Anna could think of no better place to read the newspaper story about the murder in Clevedon.

When she arrived, there was a bright yellow, overstuffed chair that was just being vacated by a large man with a small dog. Tucked into the corner of the room and out of the main traffic areas, it appeared, judging from the sagging, sunken cushions, to have served decades of satisfied customers.

Anna slides her Tumi backpack off her shoulder and before she has a chance to sit, is met by a polite but prickly waiter in a short, white jacket.

"Welcome to Brown's Hotel. High tea today, miss?" he asks.

"Oh, um, yes. Please. And I understand you have warm, homemade scones served with butter and jam?

"Everyday," he answers.

"I'll have one of those as well, no, sorry, make it two," Anna says.

"Ahem," the waiter says, clearing his throat as he hands her a menu.

"Not to disappoint you, miss, but this is NOT a hot dog stand," then, just before disappearing around a large fern, he adds, "the prices are to the right. In pounds."

Anna now has the very clear feeling that she's done something terribly inappropriate and as she sinks into the chair, takes a slow look around. The room is full of what her mother would call *'the well-heeled'*, and, by all appearances, *'the well-fed'* also.

On each table are stacks of scones, crocks of butter, honey, jams, and assortments of sandwiches and finger foods. The items are not inexpensive, which is not surprising, and Anna can afford most anything on the menu, but what she really wants is tea and scones. That's all. Until she spots watercress sandwiches, which she's never seen on a menu and has always wanted to try, as she's always liked the way it sounded when people ordered them in old movies.

Anna reaches down and pulls the copy of The Evening Tattler from her Tumi backpack. She rereads the headline and then the bi-line.

'*TEEN GIRL ARRESTED FOR MURDER.*'
'*Victim David O'Rourke Was Respected Clevedon Resident.*'

"Ready to order, miss?"
Anna looks up from the paper.
"Yes, um, scones, please. And watercress sandwiches."
"Very good, miss."
As he moves away, Anna turns back to the paper.

> *'Elizabeth Barrett, 15 years of age, was arrested this morning for the murder of Clevedon resident David O'Rourke, fifty-four. According to the Avon and Somerset Constabulary, the suspect has been the ward of Pastor Benjamin Wetherford of the Chapel of the Divinity in Clevedon for the last four years. Miss Barrett, whose parents were killed in India, has, since that time, been residing inside the parsonage along with the pastor and the housekeeper of 12 years, 72-year-old Margret Strawsby.'*

"Here you are, miss," announces the waiter as he rolls a trolley up to Anna's chair. He carefully places the items, one at a time, on the small oval table to Anna's right.

First the teapot, then the scones, then butter for the scones. Then the jams and finally the watercress sandwiches; twelve of them piled like a pyramid, which, to Anna's dismay, are nothing more than little triangles of crustless white bread separated by a thin green line of vegetable.

"Thought you might find it interesting, miss, being an American and all, that this is exactly the same chair occupied by Napoleon the Third while he was here consulting with his British allies during the Crimean War."

"Really?" *My God, I hope I don't spill something,* Anna says to herself, and then wonders why being an American makes a difference.

"May I pour?" the waiter asks.

"Please," Anna says.

Had she asked him, he would have told her that one-half cup is the proper pouring level for tea, as it allows for the addition of milk and sugar if a customer so desires. The waiter returns the pot to its home under the cozy, and then moves off to more demanding clientele.

Anna grabs her teacup in both hands and takes a sip. She sets it down, takes one of the warm scones and breaks it in two, then spreads a good amount of butter on each half.

'While reluctant to provide too many details, a spokesperson for the police department did say that the murder was the cruelest and most grisly that he's seen in his twenty-five years on the force.'

Pleased to see that it's melting, she takes a bite, then licks the butter from her fingers and keeps reading.

'It appeared that Mr. O'Rourke was killed by a single puncture wound clean through the neck, although the official autopsy reports are not yet available. Since

the accused is being held and will be tried as an adult juvenile, all aspects of the case will be open to the public. The defendant has refused to make any statements to the police. Mr. O'Rourke was the heir to the O'Rourke Dairy farm on Lower Strobe Road and had made regular, weekly deliveries to the parsonage for the last several years. The Pastor, Benjamin Wetherford, and Ms. Strawsby were not available for comment, although friends of Ms. Strawsby told The Evening Tattler that Strawsby had confided that of late, the suspect had appeared to be displaying signs of anxiety and depression. Miss Barrett is being held at the Avon and Somerset Constabulary. Mr. O'Rourke is survived by his wife, May Latham O'Rourke of Bristol, and two sons, Samuel, aged twenty-two and Devon, aged seventeen.'

Anna finishes the last morsel of her last scone and is brushing her hands of crumbs when the waiter reappears. He's about to ask if there is anything else she might like when he notices the banner on Anna's newspaper.

"The Eve'nin' Tattler, miss?"

Anna flips the paper around to read the banner and then turns back to the waiter.

"Yes, it is, why?" Anna says.

"This is Brown's Hotel, miss. It just isn't done."

The distance from Brown's Hotel to the Shangri-La is nearly the same distance as the Shangri-La is to Harrod's, and even though the bellman advised that it was a trudge, Anna decides to walk and give the scones something to do. Harrod's can wait till Monday.

It's mid-afternoon, the weather seems to be agreeing with the forecasts, and Anna calculates that by the time she gets to her room, she'll be ready for some wine and a peaceful dinner alone; maybe a small, quiet place near the hotel.

Thinking that she should call her parents, Anna slips her phone from its pocket. She hasn't spoken to either of them since her arrival, plus she needs to call Ethan, who was going to attempt some repairs around the house; but just as she's about to hit her speed dial, she gets an incoming video call. On her screen pops up a live image of Lyla Patterson, thirty-five, African American, and Anna's office manager.

"Lyla!"

"You were supposed to call when you landed, you've had this girl worried!"

"My bad. It's been crazy here."

"That's what I figured. You okay?"

"It's had its moments. I'll fill you in when I see you." Anna says.

"Okay, guess. Where am I?" Lyla asks.

"Aren't you in Macon?"

"I had the week off, remember. I'm out of town." Lyla replies.

"Gee, Lyla, I don't know, I have no idea."

"C'mon, guess! Name a place, any place!"

"Um, visiting family in Savannah," Anna says.

"Nope."

"New York City?"

"Negative."

"Okay, Nova Scotia."

"You'll never guess!"

"You just asked me to!"

"Want me to tell you?"

"Okay, I give up."

"Heathrow, girl!"

"Heathrow?!!! What?!!!"

"We just landed!!!"

At that moment Lyla's boyfriend, Caleb, pops into view over Lyla's shoulder.

"Hey, Anna. We were going to surprise you at the hotel, but you know this one, can't keep a secret to save her soul."

"Hi, Caleb!" Anna says.

Caleb Williams is thirty-seven, African American, and Lyla's longtime boyfriend.

"Since I had the time, and Caleb had a bunch of miles, we thought, why not pop over the pond, see England and spend some time with you?"

"Wow, that's…" Anna begins to say.

"Don't worry, you've got the night off. Caleb found an amazing Air BnB in Chelsea and we're heading there now.

"Hey, I see our luggage, gotta go. See ya tomorrow, Anna."

"Bye, Caleb."

"There's a public house near our room that he's itching to get to. How about brunch tomorrow?"

"Sounds amazing. Lyla, I'm so glad you're here, really. There's a lot to talk about," Anna adds, somewhat relieved that her evening is still intact.

"You sound a little tired, girl. Get some rest and I'll call you in the morning with a name and address for brunch."

Rather than venture out for the evening, Anna decides to stay in and order room service. She puts on some bluegrass ballads, slips into her Shangri-La robe, and surveys the substantial minibar to see what adventures await. Tucked behind a bottle of Veuve Clicquot sits a split of the same New Zealand Sauvignon Blanc that she shared with Mitchell the previous evening.

She opens the bottle, pours herself a glass, then grabs her laptop and settles onto the sofa facing the floor-to-ceiling windows that frame the panorama of London. She remembers watching a documentary about the bombing of England and tries to imagine what it must have been like;

> …searchlights sweeping the night sky and German bombers silhouetted against the fires, and the RAF flying up to greet the bombers with blood red bursts of tracer fire…

St. Paul's Cathedral is off to her right. Anna quickly Googles it and finds a photo of its great dome, rising triumphant out of the thick, dark swirling smoke that was London burning. She takes a sip of wine and asks herself, Why do foreign places feel so strange and foreboding at dusk?

Shying away from a replay on the Surrey Dairy Cow, Anna opts for a bowl of tomato soup and a turkey sandwich. The room service waiter has the cart at her door just as the last light of day settles in the west, in the direction of Clevedon, and sets her up at the small dining table perched next to the windows.

The soup is good and perfectly comforting, and just as another song is beginning, it's interrupted by a phone call. She gets up and walks across the room to her phone, which she left laying on top of the minibar. On the caller ID she sees that it's Mitchell, then remembers exchanging numbers with him before leaving the studio. She hesitates and then hits the button to send it to voicemail.

I can't let this happen, Anna says to herself.

fourteen

It's been forty-eight hours since the murder of David O'Rourke, and Benjamin is sure that neither he, nor the parsonage, will ever be the same. Margret has been in her room since her dash from the parlor and has only journeyed out for tea and an occasional biscuit.

The police have cordoned off Adelaide's sewing room pending further investigation. Of the reporters, a few of the more rapacious have set off for fresh meat; the ones remaining being satisfied with the random arrival or departure of a police cruiser or the occasional sighting of poor Benjamin through the open drapes of the windows.

For two days the citizens of Clevedon and the surrounding area have been bombarded with leaked details of the murder. The heinous nature of the crime has only served to heighten the mood over what would have been a dull and dreary weekend and has livened both pubs and dinner tables alike.

Now, it's Sunday morning, The Lord's Day; and as Pastor of the Church of the Divinity, it's Benjamin's duty to greet the parishioners, to smile and to shake hands; to sing along with Blevins' organ; and to admonish, cajole, and offer sustenance from the pulpit.

He dresses and shines his shoes, as he has every Sunday morning for twenty-four years; foregoing his usual bowl of porridge, however, as he hasn't been able to keep anything down since Friday morning.

He exits from the kitchen, which is the shortest distance to the church and the one that will provide him the greatest cover from the hoots and howls being hurled from across the street.

Blevins is just finishing a moving rendition of, *'I Come to the Garden Alone'* and Benjamin is sitting in his usual chair on the altar, eyes closed. The church is at capacity today, which confirms what he's always known; that the Bible is no match for The Evening Tattler, and that there's nothing that brings forth one's own piety like than the salacious sins of another.

As the music comes to a close, the congregation is stirred to a rapturous if not discordant denouement. With his eyes closed, Benjamin has learned to tell which voice belongs to which parishioner and can't help but feel that the ones who sing the loudest are the ones most confident of their salvation. And, as he does every Sunday, he scolds himself for his cynicism.

As the old Brindle organ issues forth its final note, the parishioners rustle their hymnals, shuffle their feet, clear their throats; cough, sneeze; moan, sigh, and settle into the cracked and creaking seventeenth-century pews. There will be the one more sneeze from the right front and then the raspy, smoking cough from the left rear, followed by the sodden nose being blown somewhere in the center.

Benjamin slowly opens his eyes and struggles to his feet, waiting to feel his legs. Hopeful that he may actually make it, he wobbles toward the pulpit, then painfully ascends the twelve steps cut from the single block of Jurassic limestone quarried in Cardigan, Wales, sometime in the year 1690.

Reaching the top, he approaches the eighteenth-century Bible and says a silent prayer. After ten seconds, he looks up to the congregation, looks from the left side of the aisle to the right, and realizes that he hasn't the faintest clue of what to say.

The murder was the main event, Benjamin thinks. *I am just the sideshow. But one worth every shilling. They're here to see the spectacle. To rub elbows with evil from the safety of the pew.*

After thirty seconds, they begin to shift in their seats. After a minute, there are whispers and coughing, and the occasional sneeze and clearing of throats. And after a minute more, just at the threshold of his hearing, he begins to pick out phrases like…

"What's wrong with him." "The poor chap." "He's had quite a shock." "Perhaps someone should call a doctor."

He can see them stirring, whispering, sneering, accusing; perhaps, even conspiring.

Benjamin's pulse begins to race and his breathing gets shallow; and, as a respite from the stares, he glances above their heads through the large wooden doors carved from English walnut and sees the full sails on the Bristol Channel and the two grey gulls strutting across the roofline of the parsonage, and leaves falling from the ancient silver maple that was planted long before his great grandfather was a child.

And then, without warning, it appears the maple, no, the entire scene, is swaying back and forth where a moment ago it was still; and then Benjamin hears gasps of "Oh, no's!" and "Oh, my Gods", and then he catches sight of Blevins, up from his organ, mouth agape, arms outstretched as if to catch him; then a billion stars spinning and he at the galactic center, and then the slow turn-up toward the ancient marble statues peering down at him from the nave of the church, followed by the sudden crash of hard stone against the back of his skull.

fifteen

Anna, Lyla, and Caleb are seated at a table in the middle of Khan's restaurant. An endearing Indian waiter in his mid-twenties is nearly done taking their order, his accent and broken English giving him away as a recent arrival.

"So, dear peoples. To start, one Paapri Chaat, one Mango and Avocado Chutney, and one Chilli Paneer. Afterward, special lady number one..." he says, pointing to Anna, "...enjoy Tarka Daal. Second special lady number two, enjoy Murgh Tikka, and gentlemans with big stomach enjoy King Prawns Bhuna and one Kolkata Roll."

Is Aneesh correct?"

Anna, Lyla, and Caleb smile and answer at the same time.

"Correct! Good job! Thanks, Aneesh!"

He smiles with pride, retrieves the menus, and is about to leave the table when Anna stops him.

"Aneesh? I'll take the check, please."

"Yes, good lady."

"Anna, no..."

"You came all this way, it's the least I can do."

Caleb tears off a piece of the flatbread sitting on a plate in the middle of the table, slathers it with butter, and turns to Lyla.

"I'm telling you now, keep your fork outta my Chilli Paneer."

"Okay, there, Mr. Big Stomach."

Lyla takes a sip of her drink and continues.

"Anyway, where were we?"

"The BBC," Anna says, taking a bite of flatbread.

"My God, how was that? Weren't you nervous?"

"A little. No, a lot. John Edwards was supposed to be a

good guy, but, wow, what a jerk."

"Gave you a hard time?"

"First, he had been drinking before the show."

"No, c'mon."

"I heard that Winston Churchill was drunk constantly," Caleb adds.

"And, he's the consummate narcissist. Rude, condescending, and a bully."

"Three of my favorite traits in a man," Lyla says.

"He's a news guy. Aren't they all?" Caleb says taking a sip of his drink.

"Anyway, instead of a single show, they're doing them in installments, one for each of the five case studies. The first one airs tomorrow night."

"Great! We'll be able to see it, then. You still get to come home this week though, right?   "

"I can't leave Ethan alone any longer than that."

The reference to Ethan triggers a glance between Lyla and Caleb, just as Aneesh reappears with a second server.

"And here we go. Paapri Chaat. Mango and Avocado Chutney."

Anna has taken a seat facing the front windows of the restaurant. It was overcast when she went to the gym this morning, but the day has turned vivid. The crisp, clear air has given everything a brilliant edge and as the traffic moves on Harrington Street, multiple windshields send reflected shafts of light skidding through the interior of the restaurant.

As Aneesh places the last appetizer on the table, a cab pulls to the curb and stops at just the right angle to shoot a blinding streak of light through the windows and right into Anna's eyes, forcing her to squint and turn her head.

"And one Chili Paneer."

"Right here, my man," Caleb says.

"Every people, please enjoy," Aneesh says.

Moving away, he crosses Anna's line of sight and breaks the beam of light, allowing Anna a brief instant in which she catches sight of a familiar silhouette entering through the front door.

She blinks, but before her brain can process the image, the cab moves away, pulling the blinding glare along with it and depositing within Anna the opposing sensations of delight and dread.

"Hey, what's wrong?" Lyla says. "Are you feeling okay?"

"I'm fine, why?" Anna replies, reaching for her drink, surprised that her reaction to Mitchell's appearance had been that obvious.

Out of the corner of her eye, Anna watches as he steps up to the bar that borders the right side of the restaurant. Wanting to avoid eye contact, she quickly turns her attention to the table and reaches for the plate of mango and avocado chutney.

"This is amazing," Lyla says, taking her first bite of the Paapri Chaat. "Don't you think?"

"Delicious," Anna says.

"Sweetie," Lyla says, to Caleb. "Can't I have just a teeny, tiny taste of the Chili Paneer?"

"Not a chance," Caleb says, glancing at Anna. "You should have seen what she did to my cannoli the other night."

As Lyla and Caleb engage in their familiar banter, Anna sneaks a peak at the bar at the very moment Mitchell spots her reflection in the mirror. He picks up his drink, turns into the room, and heads in their direction. Even from a distance, she can discern the upturned corners of his smile.

"Anna!" Mitchell says as he approaches the table.

"Mitchell! What a coincidence."

"Not really, this is my neighborhood, remember? I rang you up last night to see if you wanted to join me here. Didn't you get my message?"

"Um, no. That's strange, I didn't. Darn cell phones."

"Well, you're here now, no harm done."

Anna turns to Lyla and Caleb.

"This is Mitchell Walker. He directed the interview on Friday. This is Lyla."

Lyla quickly swallows and reaches for Mitchell's hand, obviously taken with his looks.

"Hi, Mitchell. Nice meeting you."

"Lyla is my right hand at the office," Anna says.

"From the States, then! Pleased to meet you."

"Uh-huh. Had a few days, thought we'd surprise her, and here we are."

"And this is Caleb," Anna adds.

"Hey, Mitchell. Good to meet you, man. You Brits eat like this all the time?"

"Except when there's a war on," Mitchell says jokingly, the glint in his eye and the upturned smile eliciting in Anna the familiar, fleeting palpitation, causing her to quickly look away.

"Anna's been telling us all about the BBC, but she hasn't mentioned a word about you," Lyla says, egging Anna on.

"No need really. Just a cog," Mitchell says, glancing down at Anna, whose coolness has him wondering if he said or did something wrong during dinner on Friday night. There's an uncomfortable pause in the conversation, and Lyla can't quite figure out what's going on, but decides someone needs to take up the slack.

"Why don't you join us. We've got entrees coming and I'm sure there'll be plenty…"

"No!" Anna blurts out, forcing Caleb to look up from his Chili Paneer.

"It's that, um, I'm sure Mitchell's got a million things to do this afternoon. Being a director and all."

Mitchell is also taken aback and, then, from out of the blue, Anna bolts straight up from the table.

"Excuse me," she says, snatching her purse from the back of her chair. "I don't think the chutney agrees with me."

"Back and to the left," Mitchell says, without skipping a beat, and the three of them watch as Anna darts toward the loo at the rear of the restaurant.

"Must be the Paapri Chaat," Caleb quips, then Lyla turns to

Mitchell.

"Don't take it personally, Mitchell."

"No, of course not. Actually, I do have a few things to get done today. The first being to finish this drink. Cheers," Mitchell says, raising his glass. "Hope London treats you well."

Anxious to make a getaway with at least some of his dignity intact, Mitchell turns and begins to walk away when Lyla stops him.

"Mitchell?"

"Come again?" he says, turning back toward the table.

"It's just that she's sort of, sensitive, when it comes to certain things."

"Like men, you mean?"

Mitchell leaves the question hanging in the air and he turns and walks away. Lyla watches him for a moment, then picks up her fork and turns to Caleb.

"I'm having a taste of your precious, damn Chili Paneer, even if it kills you!"

"Okay! Okay! Caleb says, sliding the plate in her direction.

sixteen

Lyla and Caleb want to see the Tower of London and offer to share a cab back to the hotel, but Anna declines, deciding instead to walk the afternoon away. She purchased a new pair of earbuds before the trip and is glad she did, as her music sounds incredible, and they cancel most of the city's unwanted noise, which in London is quite substantial.

Replaying the scene at the restaurant over and over in her head, Anna feels like she could kick herself. But she knows that if she had allowed Mitchell to join them, it would have signaled an open door and only prolonged the inevitable.

By the time she gets to the hotel, the wind has picked up and it's started to drizzle. With only one more day in London, she hasn't even visited the observation deck yet, so she takes the elevator up to the sixty-ninth floor.

It's crowded for a Sunday evening and filled with folks taking pictures and who can't get it through their heads that using a flash for a wide shot at night is like trying to eat soup with a chopstick. Not to mention the annoying reflections of the strobe lights off the glass partition.

Thoroughly peeved, Anna decides to take the stairs to the partially open deck on the seventy-second floor. Exposed to the inclement weather, it has, thankfully, begun to whittle away the crowd.

There is certainly nothing like this in Macon or even Atlanta, she's thinking, looking at the city below, when her phone rings.

It's Ethan wanting to FaceTime, and she considers not taking it, but she really does owe him a call. Anna accepts and, after a beat, Ethan's face appears on her screen.

"Hey, good morning," Anna says.

"Hey."

"I was going to call last night, but I was just, you know, so…" Anna begins to say.

"Too tired. Yeah, I get it. Where are you? You look cold."

"Standing outside the hotel."

"Why aren't you in your room?" Ethan says.

"The bloody windows don't open. I needed some fresh air," she says, and then catches herself, not believing how easily she's picked up the ubiquitous British term.

"Louis wants to say hi."

Ethan maneuvers the phone to give Anna a view of the black and white cat sitting on Ethan's lap.

"Hey, Louis! How 'ya doing, bud?" Anna says, in her small, baby voice.

"I Googled your hotel this morning. Pretty amazing."

"It's just okay."

"Right," Ethan says, shifting the phone back to himself.

"Anyway, I, uh, was checking our credit cards and, uh, looks like you had quite a time today. Something you're not telling me?"

"Dammit, Ethan. Really?"

"Yeah. Two hundred dollars, really!"

"Lyla and Caleb are here, okay?"

"That's a good one."

"Look, I'm exhausted. I've flown across the Atlantic, been cross-examined by a drunken playboy, my hotel is surrounded by helicopters, the traffic is hell, I've had terrible nightmares, and I've got a huge presentation tomorrow and the damn lunch bill is part of the expenses covered on the trip. And yes, Lyla and Caleb flew in yesterday to surprise me."

In frustration, Ethan brings his hand to his face and, for a moment, all Anna can hear is the sound of Louis meowing from Ethan's lap.

"Listen, I know this is hard on you," Anna says.

"Forget it, okay?"

"I'm going back inside. Try to have a good day, okay?"

"Yeah. 'Night."

Anna pushes a button, bringing the blackout shades down on London and the rain. She undresses and then slips into her white tank top and men's boxers; washes her face, brushes her teeth, and then runs a brush through her hair, stopping to look at herself in the mirror.

I'm still kind of okay, she thinks to herself, reminded of the shock of her tenth high school reunion. She takes one last peek at her laptop before shutting it down, then makes her way to the bed and switches off the last remaining light. Anna slides between the crisp linen sheets and pulls the silk comforter up to her chest.

About a year after she and Ethan met, Anna went to the shopping mall in Macon and splurged on a set of sexy lingerie, hoping to surprise him for Valentine's Day. Ethan was already in bed, but when Anna slid in and cuddled up against him, he jumped up and switched on the light.

"What in the hell?" he yelled, pulling back the covers.

"I thought you'd like it!"

Ethan thought about it for a moment and got back into bed, but then started telling Anna the story of the day when he was about fourteen and snuck into his parents' bedroom to sneak a rubber.

Rummaging through his father's nightstand, he accidentally unearthed several photos, professional photos taken in a studio of his mother dressed in some kind of silky lingerie; posing in positions that a son really doesn't want to see or ever think about again, and that is the reason he's always preferred Anna in tee shirt and shorts.

The truth was that Anna didn't particularly like the lingerie either. She had gotten them because she though it would please him, something she hadn't really ever been able to do.

When she and Ethan met, Anna had been clear that sex was difficult for her, that, in essence, she was frigid. It wasn't that she didn't have a desire for intimacy; it was just that the rape had made it impossible for her to abandon fear in favor of trust, and to feel fully safe. Ethan said he didn't care; that he could be patient, that they could work through it, and they even tried going to counseling together.

That was six years ago, and they had basically been living like roommates ever since. Yes, they would sleep together occasionally and occasionally Anna would try to please him in some other way, but it wasn't working; they both knew it, but neither could face the alternative.

The sound of one hand clapping is how Ethan describes it when he's been drinking. For penance, Anna continues torturing herself, looking at Instagram posts of contemporaries with swollen breasts and maternity clothes; driving their kids to soccer, or sewing the newest costume for the latest school play.

Reaching up into her tee shirt, Anna does a cursory examination of her breasts and gently circles each areola. She brings her finger up to her lips, wets it in her mouth, and then slides her hand down, slipping it under the elastic band of her boxer shorts and down toward her crotch. She starts with small, easy circles, and, as her heartbeat quickens, she summons Ethan the way he was the first summer she knew him; strong and kind and gentle and hard; an arrow of truth on a single-minded mission to the fountainhead; as all men are when they're young and strong and earnest; the way he was before he discovered there would be nothing more.

She widens the circle and presses harder, her breathing growing deeper and then, suddenly, at the edges of her consciousness appear swirling, paisley shapes of something curled, or curling, like thick, black smoke, and then the smile with the turned-up corners and the glint in the eye that has never heard the word 'no.'

seventeen

Monday morning dawned rainy and cold. Henry was idling at the curb, and when he spotted Anna exiting the hotel, he shifted into gear and pulled up to the entrance. A bellman with an umbrella helped her into the cab.

"Mornin, miss," he says, as Anna slides into the rear seat. "Rainin' kittens and canaries, just as they said."

"Good morning, Henry."

"Smash-ups all over London. What time is your meetin'?" Henry asks, looking at his watch.

"Ten-thirty. How was your weekend?"

"Me wife had me to and fro, never did get a peak at the pitch. Not a one."

"Peak at the pitch?" Anna says.

"Sorry, miss. Cricket! Essex at Surrey. One for the record books is what the papers are calling it, and where was I? Me wife had me plucking parsnips in Wokingham."

"Well, that's just not fair, Henry."

"How about you, miss, your weekend?

"Nice. I had the book signing on Saturday, and after walked to Brown's for tea. Then friends surprised me from the States."

"Oh, marvelous. This all must be very excitin' for you, miss. Your book and The BBC and all."

Henry's cab pulls to the front of King's College at 9:45, so Anna has a few moments to get her bearings and meet the woman responsible for bringing her here to speak.

The school was founded in 1829, and, at that time, the study of philosophy was restricted to courses within the Departments of Theology and English Literature. In 1906, a separate Department of Philosophy and Psychology was established; and, in 1912, Psychology split to form its own division, The Institute of Psychiatry, Psychology and Neuroscience.

Anna is greeted at the door by an earnest young man in a white shirt, black pants and black tie who was obviously told to be on the lookout and recognizes her the moment she enters.

"Dr. Newsom! You made it! Dastardly weather this morning. I'm Justin by the way," he says, reaching out his hand.

"Good morning, Justin," Anna replies.

"I'll take you to Adrienne, straight away."

She doesn't know why exactly, but Anna was expecting to be met by a building that would speak to her from the sixteenth century; walls and ceilings dinghy from years of cigar and pipe smoke - creaky, wooden floors and low hanging globes that cast a warm glow over stacks of dusty, leatherbound books and decades old, graffiti covered desks. Instead, the Institute looks and feels more like the campus of a Silicon Valley juggernaut; high tech and ultra-modern.

They walk down one long hallway and climb two flights of stairs bordered by tall windows looking out at an atrium of silver maples before rounding a corner and entering the anteroom to Adrienne's office.

"Dr. Anna Newsom. We're so excited to have you all to ourselves today!" is how Adrienne Owens, Director of the Institute, greets Anna as they shake hands.

"Thank you, Professor. It's good to be here."

"Adrienne, please."

"Tea or coffee before I leave?" Justin asks, "and let me take your coat."

"Coffee with milk would be great, thank you."

"Ms. Owens?"

"I've had mine this morning, thank you, Justin."

"We've got a little time, let's sit for a moment," Adrienne says, leading Anna to two high backed chairs flanking a small coffee table inside her office.

"Now, tell me. How was your trip? And how was your interview at the BBC?"

Anna was expecting to be nervous and is relieved by Adrienne's maternal nature and comforting body language. She took note that, as Adrienne asked her questions, she leaned forward and locked onto Anna's eyes as if what Anna was about to say was, at the moment anyway, the most important thing in the world to her.

"The trip was fine. I was able to sleep, and the interview went well enough that they've decided to expand the series. The first is tonight."

"Brilliant. What time? I'll make sure to watch."

"8 pm, I believe."

"One coffee with milk," Justin says, entering the office.

"Thank you," Anna says.

Out of courtesy, Adrienne waits for Anna to take a sip and then continues.

"Congratulations, Anna. You've heard it elsewhere, but I wanted to tell you personally that the work you've done, the theories and the proof that you've put forth, are revolutionary. That's no exaggeration."

"I'm embarrassed."

"Don't be. On a more immediate level, you've given forensic psychologists a potent tool. One that could save the lives of hundreds of women facing criminal prosecution."

"Well, that was my hope."

Adrienne smiles, taking in the young woman sitting across from her.

"I'll save the rest for my introduction."

Chief Inspector Hayden drops a coin into a vending machine and watches as the hot tea dispenses into a paper cup. At the same time, a man wearing a gun and holster exits the room next to the machine.

"She's ready now, Chief Inspector."

"Can you believe it, Randolph?"

"What's that, sir?"

"They call this tea."

"Can't imagine how, sir."

Hayden takes a sip and enters a room no more than twelve-feet square to find Elizabeth Barrett seated at a small table positioned under a two-way mirror. She has her hands folded, and she's staring blankly toward the floor. Hayden takes a seat opposite her.

Another officer moves from one side of the small room to the other and settles to a stop. Hayden looks up and over his shoulder to the camera looking down from the corner of the room. From a small speaker mounted underneath the camera comes a female voice.

"On and recording."

Hayden takes another sip from his paper cup and sets it down on the table.

"Elizabeth?"

No response.

"Elizabeth? My name is Chief Inspector Hayden. Can you tell me your last name?"

No response.

"Elizabeth?"

"I don't have a last name."

"Everyone has a last name. Tell me your last name."

Inside the room behind the two-way mirror, a woman wearing a pair of headphones is monitoring the video picture and the tape recorder. Seated behind her is Dr. Fielding Goddard, a bearded, pipe-smoking, old school psychologist who fancies himself an intellectual. In his mid-sixties, Goddard is also the chief psychologist for the prosecution.

Since there is no doubt that Elizabeth is the killer, the trial balances on mental state and motive, and Goddard is here to continue the process of discovery, to determine Elizabeth's current state of mind, and her possible motives for the grisly murder of David O'Rourke.

The door from the hallway opens and Simon Mercer, early forties, enters and takes a seat on the opposite side of the small room. Simon is the state appointed defense attorney.

"Morning, Goddard," he says.

"Simon. Bloody dreary out there."

"Paying for the weekend, I suppose," Simon replies, turning his attention to the video screen.

"How long have lived with your uncle?" Hayden asks.

No response.

"You live with your uncle. He's a pastor. His name is Benjamin."

No response.

"You live with Benjamin Wetherford."

"I'm waiting for me mum and dad."

"Your mother and father are dead."

Elizabeth is silent for a few seconds.

"You're lying. They're away. In India. On an errand for God."

Elizabeth looks up from the floor and stares blankly into Hayden's eyes, and then shifts her gaze to the officer standing against the wall.

"Who is that man?"

"He works for me. Can we please get back to my question?"

No response.

"What is your last name, Elizabeth?"

No response.

"Elizabeth. Have you ever met, or had you ever heard of a David O'Rourke?"

Elizabeth turns to her left and looks into the two-way mirror.

"What's in there?"

"Where?"

"In that room. Behind the mirror."

"How do you know there's a room there?"

"Are me mum and dad in there?"

"Have you ever met a David O'Rourke?"

No response.

"Did David O'Rourke, each and every Friday, come to the parsonage where you live?"

Elizabeth shifts her gaze from the two-way mirror and back to her right and stares at the officer standing against the wall.

"That man."

"What about him?"

"Does he have a penis?"

Hayden hesitates for a moment and behind the two-way mirror Goddard and Simon exchange glances.

"How do you know about penises, Elizabeth?"

"Do all men have penises?"

"I suppose so. Why?"

"That's my question. Why?"

Simon reaches for his phone as he exits into the hallway.

"Mornin', Eva."

"'Ello, sir. Aren't you due in court this hour?"

"New assignment, Eva. The Barrett girl."

"Oh, my, how did you find her, sir?"

"What you'd expect, the poor thing. Listen, call the lab and schedule a full rape panel for this afternoon."

"Straight away, sir," Eva replies.

As Fielding Goddard exits the room, he overhears Simon's conversation and stops.

"I'll be in the office this afternoon," Simon says, then hangs up and pockets his phone. As he heads to the front door, Goddard follows.

"You're wasting your time, Mercer. And constabulary funds. David O'Rourke was a beloved member of the community and the girl didn't say a wisp about rape. Nothing of the sort. Not a hint of an accusation toward the deceased. I'm not saying she doesn't take a fancy to the male anatomy, mind you. Or didn't have a crush on the man himself."

"That's quite a rush to judgment, Fielding, even for you," Simon says as they reach the exit.

"Nothing of the sort. It's a textbook case, really. Her parents are killed, and the ensuing trauma catalyzes an attachment to a man who could be her father but isn't. With each day that passes, and he doesn't act as her father, the more traumatized she becomes. Like I said, you're wasting your time. I'd stake my career on it."

"I think you just have, Fielding."

Anna is standing on the stage of the largest lecture theatre in the King's College Institute of Psychiatry, Psychology and Neuroscience. The coliseum, semi-circular design holds two hundred and fifty attendees, and this morning it's filled to capacity. Anna has just been introduced by Adrienne Owens and is about to begin her presentation.

"...and I'd like to personally thank Professor Owens for the invitation and the opportunity to come here today," she says.

Anna is joined by a polite round of applause, and, as she scans her audience, she spots Lyla and Caleb entering through the rear doors at the top of the lecture hall. They pause for a moment to join in the applause, and then take a couple of seats in the back row.

"This is so amazing for her," Lyla whispers to Caleb, as Anna continues.

"Well, this morning, the first is also the last. The Spider on the Ceiling was the first, real opportunity I had at solving a case through the application of my concept now known as PLR, the Psychic Lightning Rod. And to date, it's the last case I've solved where my assistant was an arthropod," Anna quips.

The audience appears taken with Anna and rewards her with a sincere round of laughter before permitting her to continue. Caleb leans into Lyla.

"What's an arthropod?"

"Arthropods are animals with their skeletons on the outside."

Caleb thinks for a beat and then responds.

"Like lobsters."

"Shhh."

"And crabs."

"Is food the only thing you think about?

"When I'm not thinking about you, yes."

"This murder took place in Savannah, Georgia, on June 11, 2016. Rayanna Mae Carter, a white female, sixteen years of age, was arrested on June 16th of that year by officers of the Savannah Police Department for the murder of her stepfather, forty-three-year-old Kenneth Jules Griffin, nicknamed Kenny. The prosecutor in the case was developing a theory that the murder was born of a plot hatched between the murderer and her sixteen-year-old boyfriend, Alton Dean Wilcox. The motive being...?"

"Money!" some call out in response.

"Right. But parallel to this effort by the prosecution, Rayanna's defense attorney, Ms. Maya Sonders, was growing firm in the belief that Rayanna killed her stepfather in self-defense; that Rayanna's anxiety, depression, and withdrawal had nothing to do with the murder but, rather, were long term effects manifesting from a much deeper psychic schism; the months of molestation and serial rape that the defendant was alleging. The problem was, of course, how to prove it."

eighteen

"'Ello, miss. Who have we here?" Henry says, as Anna, Lyla and Caleb slide into the rear seat of the cab.

"These are my friends, Lyla and Caleb. Lyla works with me back home."

"Hi, Henry," Lyla says, and Caleb joins in.

"Hey, Henry, what's up? And what's with this weather?" Lyla rolls her eyes.

"Caleb? England. Remember?"

"Any friends of Miss Newsom are friends of mine," Henry says, then he shifts the cab into gear and they merge into the heavy traffic.

"You look pleased, miss. Went well, I trust?"

"They loved her, Henry," Lyla says.

"They didn't throw anything at me, so I'm taking it as a good sign," Anna replies.

"Jolly good, miss. Harrod's to celebrate, then?"

"Harrod's?" Lyla says, turning to Anna.

"Yes, please!"

The rain and the traffic haven't let up a bit since morning, which makes the three-and-a-half-mile trip to Harrod's from King's College that much more tedious; and when Henry finally rounds the corner at Brompton Road, they're met with a scene right out of a Hollywood film.

The entire block is cordoned off, and Harrod's is surrounded by police cruisers with flashing lights and at least a hundred-armed men in SWAT gear positioned at various intervals on the street and the roofs of neighboring buildings.

"Holy shit," Caleb says.

"Henry, what do you think it is?"

"Whatever it is, miss, it's a safe wager you'll not be getting anywhere near the Ladies' Department this afternoon."

Henry rolls down his window and they come to a stop next to a man in full body armor holding an assault rifle.

"What seems to be the trouble, officer?" Henry asks, as if he's addressing a cop on a country road, and he nearly has his head taken off.

"BOMB SCARE. KEEP IT MOVING. THAT WAY. NOW!"

The officer jabs his arm to the right, and Henry quickly swings his cab in that direction.

"Those guys are serious," Caleb says, looking through the rear window.

"Ya think," Lyla adds.

Looking into his rearview mirror, Henry is relieved to see the man with the assault rifle getting smaller.

"You know, blowing up trains stations and airports are one thing, miss. But Harrod's? Now, they're asking for it."

Simon Mercer shakes off his raincoat and hangs it on the rack above the umbrella holder. He wipes the remaining drops from his face and makes a quick swipe over his thinning brown hair.

"Brutal this evening," he says, as he enters the modest kitchen. Karen is watching BBC News on an inexpensive portable they keep on the counter. Simon steps into her and gives her a peck on the cheek.

"Fix yourself a drink. Be awhile before supper," she says.

Karen Mercer is forty-four, blonde, and not beautiful exactly, but pretty, in an easy, comforting way.

"Smell's good, whatever it is."

"Your mother's lamb stew. If you've had it once, you've had it a thousand times."

Simon moves to a cupboard in the small kitchen and retrieves a bottle of scotch, raising it to see how much is left.

"Would you like one?"

"I'll have wine with dinner."

Simon pulls a tumbler from the shelf, closes the cupboard

door, and then dispenses a few ice cubes from the ice maker. He pours a couple of finger's worth over the ice, swirls it around in the glass, and slowly sips.

"God bless the Scots," he says.

As he settles against the kitchen counter with his drink, his eyes come to rest on the news footage from the day's bomb scare.

"Madness about Harrod's, isn't it?"

"Should anything surprise us anymore?" Karen says. "I can't stop thinking about poor David O'Rourke. And that girl. My God, how terrible."

Simon quiets and looks down at his drink.

"What's wrong, Si? You look all in."

Karen can read Simon like a book, and the look on his face this evening says volumes.

"Oh, no! Simon, don't tell me..."

"Found out first thing this morning."

For a moment, Karen doesn't say a word. She and Simon had met the O'Rourkes on more than one occasion, the last being at a fundraiser for the UK College of Agriculture.

Karen turns away, picks up a dishtowel, and begins wiping her hands.

"You've managed murders before. And you've been desperate for something important."

"I saw the girl today. I'm afraid she's mad."

"Wouldn't she have to be? And won't it make your job that much easier. Getting her declared and all?" Karen says, lifting the pot from the stove.

"I think there's something else going on here," Simon says, as he tops off his drink.

"Something like, what? I mean, what do you think her motive could have been? A young girl driven to madness by unrequited love?" Karen says.

"That's just it. Not unrequited at all."

"What does that mean?" she says, taking off her apron. "Good Lord, Simon, you don't think he was having sex with that girl?"

"No."

"Well, thank God for..."

Simon looks down at his drink and swirls the ice into the liquid.

"I think he may have been raping her."

Karen looks up sharply.

"David O'Rourke? How is that even possible, Simon?"

Simon takes another sip and heads to the dining room table.

"Remember the Jack Nicholson movie, Chinatown?" Simon says, as they sit down.

"Kind of."

"Remember what John Huston said when Nicholson asks him about his daughter?"

"Not really."

"I do. He said, *'most people never have to face the fact that at the right time and the right place, they're capable of anything.'*"

"Helluva view from here," Caleb says, standing at the windows in Anna's room, sipping a beer. "What you can see of it."

The rain hasn't let up, and the intermittent squalls temporarily obscure the view of the city.

"It must cost a bundle to insure this place; hear how close that chopper was?"

"Okay, I want this bathtub," Lyla adds.

"Pretty cool, right?" Anna says. "Kinda going to hate to leave."

Lyla pours herself another glass of wine and turns to Anna.

"I don't blame you. What time's your flight tomorrow?"

"Late afternoon."

"How about you?" Anna says.

"Flying home Friday. I'll be back in the office fresh as a daisy on Monday."

"Hey, it's about to start," Caleb says, reaching for the remote and turns up the volume.

"Although today's bomb scare was a false alarm, it was also a wakeup call to the very real threat that we all face every day. For BBC News, I'm Jake Ritter. John Edwards is up next with The Evolving Mind."

Anna's heart jumps at the sound of the announcer's introduction.

"You have to wonder if that whole bomb threat was real," Caleb says, as he grabs a handful of pretzels from a bowl on Anna's dining table.

"What's that supposed to mean?" Lyla says. "Why would someone fake something like that?"

"We had a client once who made a claim after their factory was hit by a small electrical fire."

"So?"

"Two months later it was completely destroyed. By another, much larger fire."

"So, you're saying Harrod's is going to get blown up?"

"I'm saying they may be setting the stage for a huge insurance payout!"

"Right. As if there aren't a million terrorists who wouldn't love to see it blown sky high."

"No, because Amazon's killing everybody, and it's a way out," Caleb says. "Hey, are we going to order some dinner?"

"Shhh! After, okay?" Lyla says.

The three turn their attention to the flat screen TV mounted over the wet bar as the theme music for The Evolving Mind signals the start of the show. As she and Caleb take a seat on the sofa, Lyla sneaks a peak at Anna.

She's nervous. I can see it, Lyla thinks to herself.

At first there are two silhouettes, and then the lights come up and the music ends.

"Ladies and gentlemen. Welcome to another installment of The Evolving Mind. Tonight's guest, Dr. Anna Newsom, is the author of the bestselling book, The Spider on the Ceiling."

"You look great!" Lyla says.

"God, look at my hair."

"That's a good color on you," Caleb offers.

"Dr. Newsom, welcome to The Evolving Mind."

"Thanks for having me."

"You seem so young to have a best seller on the New York Times list."

"You're right, he is an asshole," Lyla says.

"Told ya," Anna replies, taking a sip of her wine.

"The youngest, Jake Marcionette, was twelve. I'm old enough to be his mother."

"Ha! Score one for my girl," Lyla says.

"In any case, it's not so much what I've written as the discoveries we've made."

"Very well, then. You start your book with a quote."

"Yes."

"'If the mind isn't occupied by one thing, it may be occupied by something one wishes to be less occupied by.' Quite poetic."

"It's a quote I borrowed from a professor in graduate school."

"Sweetkins, as long as you're up, can you open another bottle of SB?" Lyla says, raising her empty glass in the air.

"Coming right up," Caleb says.

Anna's phone dings on Mitchell's incoming text message and she picks it up to read...

'Hey, just want to let you know that I'm watching.
I assume you are, too. Where are you?'

Lyla glances at Anna and can tell by Anna's expression who it's from.

"Now, who could that be?" Lyla says, playfully.

Anna considers answering him, glances up to Lyla and then back to her phone.

"No one."

"If you don't answer him, I will. That boy is gorgeous."

"Hey!" Caleb says, as he opens the wine. "You better be talking about me!"

"The Spider on the Ceiling contains five case histories of women who were serially raped or molested by a single perpetrator, and who were accused of murdering or attempting to murder said perpetrator."

"And how did you come to select these particular women?"

"They were patients of mine."

"Patients?"

"It was my job, working with local law enforcement, to determine if and to what degree each of these victims was telling the truth, as that could lead either to a conviction or a judgment of justifiable homicide."

"You go, girl. You sound great."

"You think? I don't know, it's strange seeing and hearing myself. Darn, I gotta pee," Anna says, running off to the bathroom.

Suddenly, a high, shrieking sound, accompanied by flashing white lights blares from the fire alarm on the wall next to the door.

"Ahhh! What the..." Lyla says, covering her ears.

"It's the damn fire alarm!" Caleb yells, just as Anna runs back into the room.

"What's going on!!!?"

"Fire. We gotta get outta here!" he says, turning to Anna.

"Fire? Shit!" Anna says.

She scrambles for her computer and a jacket, and then follows Lyla and Caleb as they grab their coats and head out the door.

"We've gotta walk down!" Caleb says.

"How high are we?" Lyla asks.

"Forty floors."

"You've got to be kidding me."

As they descend, other guests pour in from the floors below, making it not only more difficult to move, but now the air is getting thick with carbon dioxide, and the fact that Anna has to pee is only making matters worse.

Not soon enough, Anna, Lyla, and Caleb burst out of the stairwell and into the lobby, which is now overrun with hotel guests in various stages of dress and undress. The bellman who took Anna's battered umbrella on Friday night recognizes her and stops.

"'Ello, miss. You alright?"

"The loo, please?"

"Of course. Around the reception desk to the right!"

Anna has just begun heading away when the bellman calls her back.

"Your computer, miss. Don't want that in the rain. It'll be at the front desk."

"Thank you," Anna says, as she hands him the laptop and bounds toward the restroom.

Suddenly, there's a voice from a loudspeaker:

'Everyone, please stay calm and proceed to the exit doors. Stay calm, walk, don't run, and proceed to the way out.'

Anna looks over her shoulder at Lyla and Caleb.

"Go! Don't worry. We'll wait outside," Caleb yells.

Fortunately, the rain has let up, making it somewhat easier for Lyla and Caleb to navigate their way through the police cars and fire trucks.

"Hey, we're just across the street," Lyla says, on her cellphone.

"Coming out now. Okay, I see you."

"There she is," Caleb says, as he spots Anna squirming her way through the throng milling outside the front doors.

"Anybody say how long this might last?" Lyla asks, as Anna steps up onto the sidewalk.

"Apparently, there was a fire in the restaurant."

"Great, there goes room service," Caleb says, and Lyla shoots him a look of incredulity.

"Really?"

"Listen, Caleb's hungry; there's no way we're getting back in anytime soon, and there's a pub around the block. Follow me." Anna says.

"Now we're talking," Caleb says, flashing a grin in Lyla's direction.

Anna had passed The Horniman Pub when she was out for her walk on Friday afternoon. It looked like an inviting atmosphere, and she made a note to give it a try if she had the time.

"That was the best yet," Simon says, reaching for his napkin. "There's something different tonight."

Karen smiles pleased to see his spirits somewhat lifted.

"A bit more sherry, maybe. There was more in the bottle than called for, but not enough to save, so I used it up."

Karen stands and begins collecting the plates.

"There you go, that's it," Simon says, as Karen walks the dirty dishes toward the kitchen.

"I bought a pie today."

"Brilliant," Simon says, as he drains the last of his scotch. Karen sets the dirty dishes in the sink, then pulls the pie from the refrigerator. She sets it on the counter next to the portable television that is now playing Anna's BBC interview.

The sound is low but clearly audible, and Karen is drawn by what Anna is saying.

"I had participated in several previous cases of self-defense where the female accused of murder was found guilty and the rapist, the real perpetrator, had been exonerated. By the time I received her call, I had been obsessed with the problem of how,

absent an eyewitness account or physical evidence of abuse, a defense attorney could move a case beyond the uncertainty of 'he said, she said', and into the realm of empirical science."

"Simon! Come here, quick."

It's been a long day and he's exhausted, but he also knows that Karen is not one to overuse the alarm bell, so Simon pushes himself back from the table and heads to the kitchen.

"Sounds serious. Pie's gone missing, has it?"

"Look at this," Karen says.

Simon turns to the television, then raises the volume.

"... contains five case histories of women who were serially raped or molested by a single perpetrator and who were accused of murdering or attempting to murder said perpetrator."

"And how did you come to select these particular women?"

"They were patients of mine."

"Who is this woman?" Simon asks.

"I've no idea. An American, obviously. I'm sure they'll say at the end of the interview."

"After the break, we'll be taking a closer look at the first case in Dr. Anna Newsom's book, The Spider on the Ceiling."

The crowd at the bar was six-deep when Anna, Lyla, and Caleb arrived at The Horniman Pub, and not a few were refugees from the fire at The Shard. The three made their way upstairs and nestled into a small table off to the side. Not that it was any less busy.

It took seven minutes to get their first round of gin and tonics, and now they've been waiting over ten for their fourth. Anna was right about the atmosphere, though. The Horniman is typically British, with warm tones and cozy seating; from their table Anna can see the HMS Belfast anchored in the Thames, not more than a hundred yards away.

"Our waiter's been kidnapped, I'm sure of it," Caleb says, timing the absence on his watch. "Ten minutes and thirty seconds... right... now."

"That guy's been watching you since we got here," Lyla says, looking over Anna's shoulder.

"No, he hasn't."

"Uh, wanna bet?"

Anna takes a gulp from her last gin and tonic and then turns around, pretending to look for their waiter.

"Whaddya think?" Lyla says. "Thirty-four?"

"Shoot, I don't know," Anna replies. "I have to look again."

The man is standing alone and leaning against one of the wooden columns. He noticed Anna the moment she arrived, and he's been contemplating a move for the last half hour. He saw her look the first time, and now he sees her look again.

"Not a day over thirty-five. I'm bloody positive," Anna says with a distinct slur.

"Hey, missy, you sure you need another?" Lyla says.

"Bloody positive," Anna slurs in reply.

"She's had a tough few days, let her relax a little," Caleb says.

"Whatever, you say, Dr. Oz. but you're not the one flying tomorrow."

Anna's cell phone rings and she pulls it up off her lap, squints at the screen, and glances at Lyla.

"It's Ethan."

"Aren't you going to take it?"

Anna debates whether to answer, and then decides that the pub is too noisy, and Ethan will want to know where she is and what she's doing, and she just doesn't have the energy to explain.

"Looks like someone's going to the post office," Anna says, with yet another slur, and pushes a button to end the call.

"Come again?" Caleb says.

"Going to the post office. Voicemail. Haven't you heard that before?" Lyla says, but before Caleb can respond, Lyla's phone dings. She looks at it, then turns it in Anna's direction for her to see. It's a text from Ethan;

'Hey, Lyla. Where are you guys? Are you with Anna? I just tried calling but she didn't answer.'

"He's checking up on you," Lyla says, and she too sends it to voicemail.

"I gotta pee," Anna says.

"Uh-oh," Lyla says, sipping on her straw. "Too late."

The man has left his post at the column and has made his way to Anna's table.

"Eve'nin'."

"Hey, how 'ya doin?" Caleb says.

"Couldn't help but notice the definite lack of waiterin' going on 'ere, so I told me friend who owns the place. Drinks'll be round soon, I guarantee it."

"Wow, thank you. I'm Lyla. And this is our friend, Anna."

Anna is taking a sip and doesn't say a word, but waves in the man's direction.

"Anna, is it? Correct me if I'm wrong, Anna, but didn't I see you on the Belfie this Friday past?"

Anna swallows, hiccups, and then says,

"What in the hell is the Belfie?"

"Yeah, what's the…uh, what's it called? Caleb adds.

"She's right out there," the man says, pointing out the window. "The HMS Belfast. I work on her."

"Ah. Belfast. Belfie. That's cool, man. Whaddya do?"

"I dress up like a World War Two sailor and flirt with the ladies."

"Wow. What does something like that pay?" Caleb quips.

"Finally," Lyla says, turning toward the approaching waiter.

"Sorry for the wait. Dogs dinner here tonight. Two blokes never showed," the waiter says.

"On me," the man says, plucking cash from his pocket.

"No, really, we couldn't…." Anna starts to say, but it's too late. Before anyone can react, the bill is paid and the obligation to ask him to sit is hanging in the air.

"Thanks, man. What's your name?" Caleb asks.

"Liam."

"Hey, Liam, I'm Caleb and this is Lyla and, well, you know who this is.

Anna glances up to Caleb, and then turns to Liam.

"Come sit next to me, Liam," Anna says, patting the seat of the chair next to her.

Simon and Karen have decided to settle in and watch the rest of Anna's interview in the living room. Karen is sitting in a high-backed chair sipping from a coffee cup and Simon is laying on the sofa.

"This is fascinating, Simon."

"Let's see how she makes her case."

"Before my discovery, it was believed that when a person is experiencing shock or trauma, it is common for them to, what we call, "dissociate." To, in effect, separate themselves from their identity, consciousness, or self-awareness. Dissociation, however, presents a problem in mounting a self-defense case, because the significant memories and details of the crime may be lost."

I discovered that concurrent to dissociation, is physic transference or what I have termed PLR or the Psychic Lightning Rod. In these cases, the victim not only dissociates from the trauma, but, at the same time, latches onto an object in their trauma environment. In essence, the PLR is the anchor to the real world that allows the mind to proceed with dissociation. In this case, the PLR was an Anahita Punctulata. Commonly known as the Southeastern Wandering Spider."

Her workday not yet over, Adrienne Owens is sitting behind her desk, taking care of paperwork as Anna's interview plays on a flat screen TV above a credenza on a side wall.

"Anything else for today, Ms. Owens?" her assistant, Justin, asks from the open door.

"No, Justin, thank you. Safe travels home." Adrienne says, then turns her attention back to the interview.

"...*During our sessions, I was able to learn that the spider hunted during the day, coincidently at the time most of the rapes took place. Due to the fight-or-flight hormones pouring into her system, Rayanna was able to 'zoom in', as it were, and single out the smallest details of the spider and its movements.*

She could recall exactly how it looked, from where it had appeared, how it hunted, what it hunted, and where it had stashed its prey. I knew then, if we could link the details in her memory to physical evidence in the environment, it would prove her claim of serial rapes, as there could be no other reasonable explanation..."

Watching in his flat, Mitchell pours himself another drink and sits back down in front of his television, paying particular attention to how Anna is coming across on camera.

"...*The suspect, her defense attorney, and me, along with two assistants, one to keep a journal and the second to video the process, went on a field trip to the scene of the murder.*

Although highly stressed, Rayanna was able to enter the shed. She took us to the sofa where the rapes had taken place and then had us look up at the corner in the rafters where the spider would appear. The next question was the most critical. I asked if she was sure of where the spider had stashed its prey. Rayanna closed her eyes and went deep inside herself and, after a rather long interval, she answered.

'*The light fixture. I wasn't sure, but now, seeing it again, I am.' We all looked up. On the ceiling was a glass globe, the inverted kind that's open to the ceiling. One of the assistants grabbed a ladder and set it within arms-reach of the fixture.*

My heart was pounding as I climbed, and when I reached the top, I took a deep breath and looked down inside. And there they were, every one of the insects that Rayanna had identified as prey were either wrapped in webbing or partially eaten and cast aside..."

"*And where, may I ask, is your eight-legged suspect at this* point?" Edwards says.

"The spider itself was nowhere in sight. Could we mount a defense without it? We believed so. But how much stronger would our case be if we had him. So, we set up the video camera and pointed it directly at the corner of the room from where Rayanna said it would appear. And you know what happened...?"

At this part of the interview, Simon sits up and perches himself on the edge of the sofa.

"There's more pie, if you like," Karen says.

"It'll keep. Thanks."

"...Nothing. For at least thirty minutes. It was now one o'clock and we were starving, so one of the assistants ran out for cokes and sandwiches. Then Rayanna reminded us that the rapes usually happened around three. So, we ate the sandwiches and waited two more hours. Then three o'clock came and went. Then three thirty, and then three forty-five. More than disappointed, we began packing up; and, just as the assistant was about to shut down the video camera, our Anahita Punctulata appeared from a small crevice between one of the rafter beams and the wall. Just where Rayanna had said he would.

'He's an hour late but he made it, Maya Sonders said.'

And then we realized, he was an hour late because of OUR schedule, Daylight Saving Time. In November, when the murder had taken place, he would have been right on time."

In her office, Adrienne tosses down her pen, leans back in her chair and smiles...

"Brilliant."

At the bar in The Royal Thames Yacht Club, John Edwards has just polished off his third Manhattan and turns from the television to the bartender.

"Like I said. Tommyrot. Complete and utter tommyrot."

"Bloody amazing," Simon says, turning to Karen. "If she can prove my theory about Elizabeth Barrett being serially raped, we may be able to keep her out of prison."

"It may even save her life, Simon."

"I'll find this girl first thing tomorrow."

In his flat, Mitchell picks up his phone and taps out a text message to Anna.

'Knocked it out of park as you Yanks say!"

Lyla and Caleb make their way through the crowd and spill out onto the sidewalk in front of The Horniman.

"Whew!" Lyla says, taking a deep breath. "Where's Anna?"

"Weren't they right behind us?"

Lyla and Caleb spin around toward the front door and spot Anna and Liam stumbling out behind them.

"Steady there, girl." he says, to Anna then turns to Lyla and Caleb, "we had to go back for her phone."

"I'm, okay, really," Anna says, wobbling on her shoes.

"C'mon, let's get some air." Liam says, as he leads her toward the stone wall that separates the Thames from the walkway, but Lyla steps in and reaches for Anna's arm.

"Liam, nice meeting you, but it's late and we really have to get her back to the hotel," Lyla says. "C'mon, sweetie, let's get you home."

"I'm fine, let me go!" Anna snaps.

"Caleb? Little help, please," Lyla says.

"Hey, you! Let's go. Time to get tucked in," Caleb says, and this time Anna allows herself to be pulled away from Liam.

The three of them begin walking toward the arcade that leads to the pub from the hotel when Liam yells out to them.

"Hey! How 'bout a nightcap! On me?"

Lyla and Caleb turn and are about to say *'thank you, no'* when Anna breaks free of Caleb's arm and rushes back toward Liam.

"Shit! Caleb?" Lyla says, and they watch as Anna runs up to Liam hooks her arm around his neck and dives tongue first into his mouth.

"Holy crap. What was in those drinks?" Caleb says.

Several seconds later, Anna pulls herself away and looks dreamily into his eyes.

"So long, sailor," she slurs, and then, nearly falling off her shoes, she joins Lyla and Caleb and the three of them head off in the direction of the hotel.

nineteen

Simon bounds through the front door of the outer office, coffee cup in one hand and a donut in the other.

"Morning, Mr. Mercer," his secretary, Eva, says from her desk, "you look up-and-at-'em today and as dry as a dog biscuit, if I may."

"Rain's finally let up, thank goodness. Eva, do me a favor and get a Cynthia Smythe on the line for me. She's at BBC television. A producer."

"Straight away, sir."

Simon enters his office, puts the donut in his mouth, sets the coffee on his desk, and takes off his hat and raincoat. The room is on the small side with furniture that pokes through several layers of varnish.

He bites the donut, does a quick brush of his hands to remove the crumbs, and then sits and reaches for the pile of neatly stacked folders to his left. Eva has labeled each of them in preparation for the O'Rourke case, and they have yet to be filled.

Simon shuffles through them and pulls the one labeled *'Claim of Serial Rape',* just as Eva appears in his doorway.

"Ms. Smythe on two for you."

Simon swivels to his right and picks up the handset.

"Hello, Ms. Smythe."

"Good morning, Mr. Mercer. It's not often that I get a call from the public defender's office.

"And it's not often that I speak to a television producer."

"No, I suppose you're right. How can I help you?"

"I was watching one of your shows last night, and I think the young American woman, the psychologist, can be some help to us."

"Dr. Anna Newsom?"

"Yes, that's her. I'd like to be able to sit down and have a chat with her, if that's possible."

"Sorry, it's not."

"Oh?"

"She's leaving the country today. Headed home."

"Damn. What time is she leaving?"

"4:00 p.m. From Heathrow. I can give you her phone number, if you'd like."

"Brilliant."

Simon reaches for a pen and a piece of paper.

"Ready."

Somewhere off in the distance, Anna can hear the muffled sound of a ringing cell phone. Her tongue is like carpet and her head feels like a concrete weight. She hasn't been this hungover since college.

Wha…what is that ringing…wait, no, now it's stopped. Where am I? What day is it? Now it's ringing again. When it stops, I'll go back to sleep. Please, just let me sleep.

But it doesn't.

"Damn…"

Anna flings the pillow off of her head and barely manages to sit up.

"Oh. My. God," she whimpers.

When she went to bed, she had forgotten to close the blinds, and now the morning sun is white hot and blaring into her room. Anna rests her elbow on her knees and cradles her head in her hands, and the evening slowly starts coming back to her. The BBC interview. The Fire. The Horniman. The Gin and Tonics. And Liam.

Oh, God. Liam.

Her phone starts ringing a third time, but it's nowhere in sight. She gets on her hands and knees and starts rummaging through the sheets, extracting it just in time to see a number she doesn't recognize.

"Dammit."

She tosses the phone on the table next to her and let's herself fall back against the pillows.

Simon is sitting in his office, and this is the third time he's tried calling. He double checks the time, does a quick calculation in his head, then jumps to his feet, grabs his coat and hat, and as he runs past Eva, she calls out to him.

"Where to, sir?"

"Any reason why I shouldn't make Heathrow in two hours?"

"Other than a smash-up, you should be fine."

"Emergency calls only, Eva."

"Right that, Mr. Mercer," she replies, but Simon is already out the door.

Anna jerks awake at the sound of the doorbell, blinks several times at the ceiling, and then reaches for her phone and brings it closer.

*They must have hung up, s*he tells herself, and is about to set it back down when the doorbell sounds again. She hesitates for a moment, and then, through her brain fog realizes that it's someone ringing her doorbell.

I don't remember ordering room service.

As she swings her legs over the edge of the bed, the doorbell rings several more times and with far more determination.

"Miss? Are you in there, miss?" a voice yells from the hallway.

"I'm coming!" *Really, I am. Just stop that infernal buzzing!*

Anna gets to her feet, steadies herself and reaches for her robe, but then realizes that she's still dressed from the night before.

Oh, my God. What did I do.

She wavers for a moment, wobbles to the door, and peers through the peephole at a bellman standing in the hallway.

"Hello, I'm here, I'm fine. What's wrong?" Anna says, through the door.

"It's one o'clock, miss, and a Mr. Henry has been waitin' downstairs for the last hour. He was gettin' concerned, so he asked me to come up."

The bellman's words send a shockwave through her entire body.

OH, GOD! HENRY! THE AIRPORT!

"Tell, tell him I'll be down as soon as possible!!! Anna yells.

"Very good, miss."

Anna spins on her heels, turns one way, then the other, then rushes for her suitcase, flings it onto the bed, and makes a beeline for the closet.

Simon retrieves his blue Ford Fiesta from the car park and swings it onto Barton Hill Road. Getting out of Bristol shouldn't be too difficult, and the northbound M32 is fairly lenient this time of day. It's the M4 that he's worried about.

It starts just outside Llangennech in Wales, skirts Cardiff, goes up the coast, crosses the Bristol Channel at Caldicot, and then continues all the way to London. It can be brutal if everyone decides to head east at the same time, but it doesn't look like that's the case today.

Anna has packed and gotten out of her room in record time. As she bounds out the front doors of the hotel, she stops dead in her tracks.

"My computer!"

She runs back and through the lobby to the front desk.

"My computer, please. Anna Newsom. Room 4012."

"Right away, miss."

"Please, hurry."

"I'll do my best, mum."

The young woman leaves the desk and exits behind a door to a storage room.

"Please hurry. Please!" Anna says, calling after her.

"Sorry the for rap on the door, miss." Henry says, as Anna jumps into the rear seat, "but I can't say that I was just a little worried."

"Henry, I am so sorry, are we going to make it?" Anna says, trying to catch her breath.

The hangover, not having had breakfast, and the stress of missing her flight is wreaking havoc on Anna's head and stomach.

"Barring an act of The Almighty, we should be fine. But I'll put me foot in it, just to be safe."

Henry pulls the cab out of the hotel driveway, heads right on St. Thomas Street and, in an uncustomary burst of acceleration, whips the cab onto the A3 toward the airport.

"Please don't get a ticket on my account!" Anna says.

"Don't you worry, miss, me wife tells me I got eyes in the back o' me head."

Simon merges onto the M4 ten minutes later than he had expected to. *Time enough,* he tells himself, and his GPS is saying that it's clear sailing until Chieveley. He flips on his radio, punches a button for his classical music station, and then sets the cruise control for ten kilometers above the limit.

"Blast!" Henry says.

"Oh, no. What's happening?"

"Doesn't look good, miss, highway work!"

Anna reaches for her phone and dials Lyla, and after four rings is about to hang up when Lyla answers.

"I was just going to call you," Lyla says, "not thirty seconds ago, I was telling Caleb that she's probably through customs and having a drink in the lounge."

"God, please, don't talk about drinks."

"Sorry. Not doing so well myself today."

"Lyla, I overslept."

"What!?"

"Thank God, Henry sent the bellman up to wake me. We're still in the cab…"

"Oh, no!"

"Do me a favor, go online and see if there's a later flight. It's gotta be British Airways though."

"Will do. I'll call you back."

Simon passed through Chieveley with no problems, so whatever it was must have been cleared by the time he arrived. That was an hour ago, and now he's just twenty minutes from the airport and is thinking about how to approach Anna Newsom when he meets her, and then notices some kind of confusion on the opposite side of the highway about a half mile ahead.

At first, he can't tell what the problem is, but cars seem to be splayed every which way, and now the traffic on his side is slowing down to a crawl.

"Damn," he says, looking at his watch again.

Inching closer, he can make out a lorry turned over on its side and indistinct, fuzzy white shapes scattering willy-nilly in every direction; but then, wait, it seems as though the white shapes have, what? Legs!

Within a minute or so, Simon finds himself in the midst of a thousand or more chickens that have swarmed onto the highway, evidently sprung from their cages when the lorry tipped over.

Traffic on both sides is at a crawl, and, had a video news crew been present, they would have captured scenes of laughing, cheering kids and angry adults, and police cruisers with flashing lights and scores of officers fanning their batons in a futile attempt to corral the escapees. Not to mention the occasional reprobate seeking to exploit the tragedy with a free supper.

As the waylaid lorry slides past to his right, Simon is able to catch sight of the sign on the side of the truck, which reads,

'McAdoo's Famous Free-range Chickens.'

Life imitating art, I suppose. Or is it the other way 'round? Never quite sure how that works, he's thinking to himself, as his Ford Fiesta breaks free of the chaos.

Anna and Henry are at a dead stop now, just east of Brentford and with only thirteen miles to go.

"We're not going to make it," Anna says.

"Steady as she goes, miss. Henry has never let a client down yet," he says, as Anna answers the incoming call from Lyla.

"Hi. You won't believe it," Anna says.

"You're not there yet?"

"Nope."

"I checked. Everything is booked until tomorrow evening. Same flight."

"Darn it. Okay, go ahead, let's take that…"

"Already done."

"You're amazing. I'll let you know what happens. Thanks."

Anna slips her phone back into her backpack as Henry's cab slides up to a police officer who's been monitoring the safety of the road crew.

"Good afternoon, officer."

Uh-oh, here we go again, Anna says to herself.

"Is it, now?" the officer says.

"'T'ain't rainin', me boy," Henry reminds him.

"I guess you're right."

"And I got Miss Anna Newsom right in the back seat here."

"Well, good for you."

"A famous psychologist, she is, maybe you saw her on the telly last eve'nin'?" Henry says.

"The telly, was it?"

His interest piqued, the officer leans away from his vehicle and strolls to Henry's cab, then leans down and peeks through the rear window.

"A psychologist, you say?"

"Home to the States she's goin'."

"'Ello, miss."

"Hi, officer," Anna says, giving him a little wave.

The officer studies Anna's face for a moment, and then lights up.

"Blimey! Of course! Me wife was watchin' this very same young lady last night! While I was tying me flies!"

"Gonna miss her flight, poor girl," Henry says, with dramatic effect.

The officer thinks for a second, and then heads toward his cruiser.

"Not on my watch, she's not. Follow me."

To Anna's amazement, the officer makes a beeline for his cruiser, jumps in, and turns on every flashing light he has. He guides Henry out of the traffic and onto the shoulder of the roadway, then quickly gets them up to a respectable speed, leaving the traffic jam in the dust.

Henry smiles and looks into his rearview mirror.

"What did I tell 'ya, miss!"

With tires squealing, Simon makes the final turn up to the top level of the car park. Each floor below has been chockablock, but, as he rounds the corner from the ramp, he spots an empty space dead ahead.

He dives into it, shuts off the engine, leaps out, and charges across the length of the top level to the escalators. At ground level, he darts across the main road in front of the terminals, weaves his way through the crowd of travelers dragging carry-ons, and bolts through the doors.

He pulls to a stop to make way for an Indian family with three luggage carts, then makes his to the British Airways information counter.

"Cheers," he says, nearly out of breath. "Can you tell me which counter for flight 293?"

An older woman who looks like she's seen it all points to

her left.

"Window four," she says, but Simon has already taken off in that direction.

"Hello," Simon says, gasping for air as he gets to the window.

The prickly, young man behind the counter is looking down at his cellphone and doesn't respond.

"Sorry, but I..."

"Yes, what can I do for you?" the young man says, finally looking up.

"I'd...I'd... like to know if a certain passenger has checked in or not?"

"You're joking, right? What do you think this is, 1975?"

"Right. What I was thinking," Simon says, finally getting some of his breath back.

"Sir, if there's nothing else, it's, uh, time for my break."

"Right, well..." Simon says.

With Simon still standing at the counter, the young man grabs his bottle of Evian water and begins to leave his position.

"Hello! Sir! Don't leave, please!" Anna yells.

At the sound of her voice, Simon spins around and spots Anna rushing up to the window and he steps aside.

"Cutting it kind of close, aren't we?" the young man says.

Anna hands him her ticket and heaves her suitcase up onto the scale.

"Um, excuse me, Miss..." Simon begins to say.

"Sorry, I don't have any spare change," Anna says, nearly as out of breath as Simon is.

"No, I'm not..."

"Just the one?" the young man at the counter asks her.

"Yes."

"Listen, I've tried calling you, but..." Simon says.

"Really, please. I'm going to miss my plane."

Simon decides he needs to dispense with formalities and cut to the chase.

"Dr. Anna Newsom, my name is Simon Mercer. I'm a public defender in Bristol, and I've just driven two hours and I need your help."

"I'm sorry?"

"A public defender. There's a young woman accused of murder and I believe she's the victim of serial rape."

"Look, I'm about to get on a ...."

"Let me ring you up, at least."

The young man behind the counter hands Anna her ticket and takes a sip from his Evian bottle.

"Chop chop, miss," he says, as Anna slings her Tumi backpack over her shoulder.

"Really, I've got to..." Anna says, and as she peels away from the counter and rushes toward the security area, Simon follows.

"I saw you last night!" he says.

"Mr...?"

"Mercer."

"Mr. Mercer, I need to get home, and I really can't miss this flight."

"For God's sake, a girl's life is at stake," Simon says.

Anna thinks for a second, and then remembers the murder in the paper.

"Did you say Bristol?"

"Yes."

"Your client wouldn't be in Clevedon, would she?"

"Yes, as a matter of fact she is."

"Is this the O'Rourke case?"

Simon, ragged, out of breath and somewhat relieved, shakes his head.

"Yes! Yes! Yes!"

Anna turns on her heels and yells to him over her shoulder.

"Call me at 11:00 tomorrow morning."

"But where will you..."

"Atlanta time!"

"You'll answer your phone? You promise?" Simon says, yelling after her.

"Yes! I promise!"

twenty

Even though she slept most of the way, Anna was still exhausted when she landed in Atlanta. At Heathrow she had to run to make her flight, and they were closing the doors as she arrived at the gate. There were headwinds which added thirty minutes to the flight, and the luggage took longer than usual to come off the plane, so, by the time she got to the curb it had been ten hours and twenty minutes since she had left London.

She had asked Ethan to be there and waiting at 7:15 and he's just pulling up at 8:20, and now she's faced with the ninety-minute drive to Macon.

Ethan pulls Anna's white Subaru Forester up to the curb and waits as Anna opens the rear door, tosses in her suitcase and her backpack, then slams it shut.

"Hey," Ethan says, as Anna slides into the passenger seat.

"Hey. Glad I wasn't here on time."

"There was traffic."

"There's always traffic."

Anna glances over at him and decides to let up a little, so she leans in and gives him a peck on the cheek.

"That's better," he says.

On the way home Ethan listened to Johnny Cash, and Anna tried to sleep but couldn't with all the distractions. At one point she rolled from the window and watched him. Ethan is two years Anna's senior, but people take him for much older.

He looks like he's lost weight again.

Ethan has thin, sandy colored hair and sharp features, and there are times when she can clearly picture him in the butternut-colored uniform of the Army of Virginia.

Tonight he's wearing a flannel shirt over a black tee shirt and faded jeans with sneakers, and the totality of his wardrobe is just a variation on the same theme.

Anna can't help but think of him as he used to be, and although she tries not to draw a comparison between Ethan and Mitchell, or even Liam, for that matter, it's hard not to. Generalized Anxiety Disorder with Agoraphobia is how he's been diagnosed, but Anna feels the current methodologies are too simplistic to provide an accurate picture of what's actually occurring.

It was already late afternoon in London and, although she never completely adapted to the time zone, she was getting hungry. They stopped for a burger and fries and were able to make small talk, and, by the time they got home, she was ready for bed.

Ethan helped bring in the luggage, so he must have gotten the message when she slammed the car door at the airport, but when they got inside the house, she couldn't believe her eyes.

She had only been gone four days, but it could have been a month. The living room was strewn with magazines, candy wrappers, and Chinese food containers; and if that weren't enough the dishes from her Thursday night going away supper were still in the sink.

"My God, Ethan, look at this place."

"I was going to take care of it, but it got late."

"You promised you'd do the dishes. That was five nights ago!" Anna is so shocked by the condition of the house, she hadn't noticed that Louis wasn't around.

"Where's Louis?"

"Didn't I tell you?"

"Tell me? Tell me what?"

"Easy. I took him to the vet 'cause he got himself into a little scrape down the street and they said they wanted to keep him overnight."

"A little scrape. And when were you going to tell me?"

"I said, I thought I told you."

"Oh, God, Ethan. Please."

Anna grabs her suitcase and stomps down the hallway, yelling to him over her shoulder.

"By the way, when did you start smoking again?"

"You mean the pack on the coffee table?"

"Yeah."

"I just felt like having one, and you can't buy just one, so I bought the pack."

"That's why there's only half a pack left?"

After Anna graduated with her master's degree, her father helped her get a place of her own out of town, in Bolingbroke, a rural area northwest of Macon. The house was small, but it was on five acres, and to Anna it was heaven. She kept it just the way she liked, shabby chic, and had goats and sheep and chickens.

She found Louis in a neighbor's barn and decided that he belonged in the menagerie. Ethan moved in a year later, and a year after that his business fell apart. From that point on, he was no longer interested in doing anything around her little farm, so Anna decided it would be best to move closer into town. They found a place on Spring Street, which seemed perfect at the time since it was within walking distance of the small office Anna had sub-let from a psychiatrist.

Anna swings her suitcase up onto the bed and opens it to the same mess that she closed it on nearly twelve hours earlier. There wasn't time to properly pack, so she literally just jammed it all in without folding. As she slips out of her blouse and leggings, her phone dings on an incoming message.

'Hey. Early production meeting here at The Shard. Not the same without you. Hope you had a brilliant trip home. BTW, you looked and sounded great in the interview. Mitch.'

As she's reading, Ethan knocks on the door.

"Why are you doing this?"

"Doing what?"

"Acting this way. Like I'm the enemy or something."

Anna takes a second look at the text then tosses her phone on the bed.

"I'm just, so, tired, of living this way, Ethan."

"Yeah, well, we both are."

Anna slips into her white tank top and boxers and heads for the bathroom. She brushes her teeth and runs a quick brush through her hair, then walks down the hallway and finds Ethan sitting in front of the television.

"Okay, so what do we do?"

Ethan ignores her and then grabs the remote and begins scanning through the channels.

"You're not working. You don't contribute. You don't care about yourself and you don't care about me." Anna says.

"I'm here, aren't I? And don't talk to me about caring! You told me we'd try, that we'd go see someone, but we never really did. How long do you expect me to go on this way? I can barely touch you without getting my knuckles rapped, for chrissake!"

"That's why the mess! And not telling me about Louis, Isn't it?"

"What?"

"It's passive aggressive behavior and you do it just to get back at me."

"Please, spare me your two-bit analysis."

"My two-bit analyses are paying for this place, okay?"

"And there it is, ladies and gentlemen. Ethan's a bum. Go ahead, say it! That's what you're thinking!"

"No, Ethan, that's not what...."

"Sure, it is."

"Ever since the thing with Butch you've treated me like a... a fucking science experiment, your goddam personal lab rat!

'Let's take Ethan to a shrink cause his best friend stole his business! Let's take some pictures to see what's happened to his

brain! Let's get him on anti-depressants! "

"That's not fair, Ethan…"

"*'Then, let's spend all day, every day, at work and see how long Ethan can go without sex. And maybe, just maybe, if we go on this way long enough his dick will shrink and fall off and I'll never have to worry about it again!'*"

"And what have you done, Ethan!?" Wallowed in self-pity. You used to be so bright, so alive, now look at you. Get over yourself. Other people go through tough times and come out the other side, but not the great Ethan Barnes!"

As always, Anna and Ethan have reached the point of no return, and neither seems prepared to take the next step.

"Listen, I really didn't want to get into all of this…"

"Of course, you didn't."

Anna hesitates, afraid as to how he'll react at the news.

"They've asked me to go back to London."

"Really? What now? Another interview or have they given you your own show? *Dr. Anna Newsom, God's Gift to Psychology!!!*"

"I told them I wouldn't go if you didn't want me to."

"Oh, no! Don't put this on me!"

Anna hesitates, then continues, softer now.

"Why couldn't you have just told me about Louis?"

"Jesus. That again?"

"You know how important he is to me, why wouldn't you tell me something like that?"

"Listen, I'm sorry."

Ethan stands, moves toward her, and extends his arms to offer an embrace.

"No. Don't touch me," Anna says, pulling away.

Ethan hesitates, then seems to come to some decision. He snatches the package of cigarettes from off the coffee table and heads toward the front door.

"Why should tonight be any different," he says, slamming the door behind him.

twenty-one

When Anna makes it out to the kitchen the next morning, she's surprised to see that that Ethan has picked up the living room and done the dishes. He's also packed her a sack lunch. Although she usually comes home to eat, he's probably thinking she won't have time with all the work she has to catch up on.

Strange, I didn't hear him come in last night, Anna thinks to herself as she heads down the hall to the bedroom. *No need to wake him.*

After she's dressed and about ready to leave, she remembers the small souvenir she had bought for him on the HMS Belfast. It was a surprisingly accurate scale model of the ship, and, being a World War Two enthusiast, she thought he would like it. She places the ship where she knows he'll spot it, right next to the television remote on the coffee table. Reaching the front door, she spots a handwritten note.

'Picking up Louis around noon, see you tonight.'

Very thoughtful. Anna thinks. *Maybe things are changing after all.*

As Anna steps out onto the front porch, her neighbor across the street, Jaylynn Morrisson, is just getting home from a jog, and the two wave to one another the way women do when they're not really friends.

Jaylynn and her husband, Ron, are divorced with two kids in grammar school. Word has it that the divorce was Ron's idea, although Anna can't understand why a man would want to leave a brunette as cute as Jaylynn.

Ron visits on the weekends or takes the kids to his house, and, even though they're the same age as Anna and Ethan, the two couples have never socialized; except maybe for the occasional Fourth of July picnic, which always includes the whole neighborhood.

Leaving the car with Ethan, Anna walks from their small house on Spring St. to the much larger, converted three story Georgian on Arlington that houses six other psychologists. Anna had loved the handsome mansion as a child, and, when she went into practice, was excited to learn it had been converted to offices.

The only space available had been two rooms in the rear on the second floor; not ideal, but not bad, either. There was a separate stairway leading down to the rear parking lot, which she liked, and, as she was about to venture out on her own, the thought of being with other psychologists was reassuring.

This morning she takes the front entrance and retrieves the mail from her box in the foyer.

"Good morning, Judy," Anna says, as she passes the secretary of one of the other doctors.

"Anna! How was your trip? How was London?"

"The trip was good. London was amazing. Ever been?"

"Have not, but it's on my bucket list!"

Judy is nearly twenty years Anna's senior and as Southern as they get. Warm and kind and always thinking of others first.

She's been married only once, to a first responder from Atlanta who was called up to New York the day after 9-11. He worked on the debris pile for two months and died from a mysterious lung ailment two years later.

Anna takes the stairway up to the second floor, makes a right and heads down the hall to the last door on the left. She unlocks it, drops the mail on Lyla's desk, and then heads into her office. She has two windows, one behind her desk and another on the adjoining wall that faces the parking lot. Each has blinds and, when she has a patient, she always leaves the one over her desk open, as it affords a view of the American chestnut said to be over a hundred years old.

It'll be a good conversation starter, Anna thought to herself when she first saw it.

She wakes her desktop computer, takes off her fall jacket and hangs it on a coat rack next to the door. Then she sits down at her desk, scoots her chair under her keyboard, and starts a Google search.

She types, **Clevedon, UK. Murder.** Almost immediately, up pop several links. One is the original story she saw when she purchased The Evening Tattler at the train station.

But, since then, it appears that many more papers and media outlets have picked up on the story, giving it the potential of becoming one of Britain's highest profile cases. And in one column, where the voice of the reporter is decidedly female, there are bizarre hints that Elizabeth Barrett could become a feminist folk hero.

As an example, someone in the meme world has created a feminist logo around Elizabeth; it shows a young, idealized woman, obviously computer generated; her hair is actually different colored yarns, and it's blowing in the breeze.

She's wearing a white Che Guevara style beret and is holding across her chest two very long and highly polished steel knitting needles which glint in the sun. The most disturbing thing, though, is on the white beret. In the style of a parking sign, there is a red, block lettered M (for men, apparently) within a red circle bifurcated by a red line.

Anna is mesmerized by the imagery and the speed at which the stories and images have promulgated.

"How about some coffee?"

Anna nearly jumps out of her chair when Judy pops her head in the door.

"Oh! Love one, thank you."

As Anna turns back to the stories her cell phone rings.

"This is Anna."

"Anna! Simon Mercer!"

"Simon!"

"Sounds like you made your plane, thank goodness. Hope I didn't wake you."

"With seconds to spare, and I'm up and at work."

"Listen, awfully sorry about calling before eleven, but there was a last-minute change in court schedule..."

"No, I'm glad you did. Just reading the papers and watching some of the news reports. Your case seems to be getting a life of its own."

"That's what I'm afraid of. At the center of all this is a young woman, and I'm troubled that, between the busybodies and the scandalmongers, she's going to be tried and convicted before we can get her through the front door of the courthouse."

"Have you had a chance to see the girl?" Anna says, as Judy enters with the cup of coffee.

"Yes, I sat in on the police interrogation on Monday. The girl is mentally unstable, probably mad, and the prosecution isn't going to bend an inch if we get a negative result on the rape test. They're going to say it was a crime of passion, that she had been infatuated with an older, married man, and they'll seek the maximum, which in Elizabeth's case could be the whole of her life in prison."

"She's being tried as an adult then."

"The way it's done if they're older than ten years of age."

"So, what do you think happened here?" Anna asks, sipping from her cup.

"For most of the interrogation she was remote, unengaged, elusive. Displayed, what is it? A flat aspect?"

"Yes. I'm making notes, if that's okay."

"Of course."

"Asked several times where she lived, she always answered, '*with me mum and dad*,' but as we know her parents were killed, tragically. Then, something happened. Rather odd, really. Elizabeth shifted her gaze and stared at the police officer standing against the wall. '*Does that man have a penis?*' she asked. Hayden, the Chief Inspector, hesitated, then replied, '*how do you know about penises, Elizabeth?*'"

"Was this her first reference to male anatomy?" Anna says.

"Yes, and then Elizabeth asked if all men have penises.

Hayden waited awhile and then answered, *'yes, why?'* and would you like to know how Elizabeth answered? She said, *'That's my question. Why?"*

"As in, why do all men have penises?" Anna asks.

"Correct."

Anna takes another sip from her cup, taking in what Simon has just told her.

"That statement combined with her psychological state leads me to believe the girl was raped; but, of course, I'm not a psychologist."

"Well, the problem, of course, is that if the rape test comes back negative, how are you..." Anna begins to say,

"How am I going to prove it?" Simon says, finishing her thought.

"Right."

"That is precisely why I need you on this case."

"Oh, Simon, I can't really. I've got a heavy caseload here, and responsibilities at home. Thank you, though, but it's just not possible."

"Anna. You've seen the papers. Can you imagine what's going to happen to this girl?

"I understand, I really do..."

"One paper has dubbed her the *'Lizzy Borden of Bristol Channel,'* and a lunatic called and asked if Elizabeth would endorse a brand of knitting needles he was having manufactured in China."

For a few seconds, Anna doesn't respond.

"Anna? Are you there?"

"I'm here."

"Sorry, thought I lost you. As I said, I saw your first interview on the BBC. It was brilliant. I really think you'll be able to help this girl. Not to mention a middle-aged public defender."

Anna really, really doesn't want to go back to England, but this case never would have come her way if she hadn't been asked to England in the first place, so maybe it's all part of God's plan.

But what about Ethan? And Louis? And the house? And the small, fall garden she had planted the week before she left. Who's going to take care of them?

"Listen, Simon."

"All 'ears I am."

"Why don't we just wait until the rape results are in?"

"I can't, Anna. Even if it comes back positive."

Simon was right. Even if the rape test were to come back positive, it would only be confirmation of a *single* rape, not serial rape, and the murder was obviously premeditated. Making a case for self-defense would be nearly impossible.

Anna thinks about it from all angles, but deep down she knows it's something she should do.

"Okay. But I've got to speak to my boyfriend. How long will I be gone?"

"Five, maybe six weeks at the most."

"That's an awfully long time, Simon. I can't promise. But if it somehow works out, I'd like my assistant there with me."

"Your wish is my command. Welcome aboard, Anna!"

"Not until I talk to my boyfriend."

"As you wish," Simon says, not a little relieved that the door is still open.

The morning has flown by, and now it's nearly noon and she's famished.

No wonder, it's dinnertime in London, Anna says to herself; and then her thoughts wander to *The Shangri-La, and the Thames and the warm scones with melting butter at Brown's Hotel and the dinner with Mitchell. Mitchell with the upturned smile and the glint in his eye.*

But she won't let her thoughts go any further. She grabs Ethan's sack lunch from the drawer in her desk and peeks inside the bag.

A turkey sandwich. A few pieces of cheese. An apple. And two Hershey's kisses. How sweet. Strange that he would make me lunch today. A peace offering, perhaps.

Anna pulls the apple from the bag, thinking that she'll have it on her walk home, and then plans to eat the rest on the front porch while she waits for Louis. Afterward, Ethan can drive her back to work for her afternoon client.

She exits the office, retrieves her Bluetooth earbuds and selects her bluegrass station on Pandora. It's a beautiful fall day, and the walk will do her good. Anna's been meaning to get back into her workout routine, but it's next to impossible with a work schedule that's so unpredictable.

At least you don't need to lose weight, Lyla tells her.

The maples, white ash, and yellow birches are at peak color, and the weather is unseasonably mild. Even so, she still senses that peculiar feeling of foreboding hovering just over the horizon. It's irrational, she tells herself, to have that feeling, but, in the last few years, she's learned just how little we know or understand of the human mind.

The distance from home to work is a little over half a mile and about a twelve-to-fifteen-minute walk, depending on how anxious one is to get from one place to the other, and today she's excited to see Louis.

She heads down Arlington Place, then turns left onto Forsyth Street. A half mile later, she makes the right onto Spring Street and spots her house in the middle of the block, a single-story brick bungalow on the right. As she gets closer, she's disappointed to see her car still sitting in the driveway.

Ethan should have left for the vet by now. Maybe he's home already!

She finishes the apple and tosses the core into the garbage can waiting at the curb. The Wednesday before she left for London, there was a notice in the mailbox that gave them a head's up about the neighborhood tree trimming to be done today. The men hadn't arrived by the time she left for work, but now they're here, in full force.

The woodchipper is whining and grinding, being fed from a huge pile of branches in the yard next to Jaylynn's house; two men are roped into the trees cutting more, and two others are waiting down below to retrieve the dropped branches. The woodchipper plus two additional trucks have magnetic signs that read... *'Out On A Limb Tree Service'*.

Anna walks up the driveway from the sidewalk, her headphones providing little relief from the irritating, high-pitched noise of the chipper. As she passes her Forester, she happens to glance in the front seat and stops dead in her tracks. Not only is Louis' travel bag sitting in the passenger seat, but Louis himself is in it!

She rounds the car, flings open the door and grabs the bag from the seat.

"Louis, honey, how's my boy? Are you okay?"

He meows and except for the small bandages on his leg and over his eye, he seems fine. She rips the headphones out of her ears and bounds up the porch, tosses her lunch sack onto a chair, and bursts through the front door.

"Ethan? Ethan!! Where are you?"

She sets Louis' bag on the couch, and then opens the zippered flap. Louis meows a couple of times, and then jumps to the floor and scrambles to his food bowl. Anna follows him into the kitchen.

"Ethan!!!"

With no response, Anna heads to the bedroom expecting to find Ethan there.

"Ethan! What were you thinking....?"

But to her surprise the room is empty. Growing angrier by the second, Anna stomps to the window facing the backyard and pulls back the blinds.

Maybe, she thinks, *Ethan is tending the garden*; but he isn't there, either and now her wrath is turning to worry.

As irresponsible as he can be at times, doing something like leaving Louis in the car isn't like him. She pulls her phone from her purse and hits speed dial.

Anna's heart is beating faster now, and her mind is racing. *Did he have an episode? Is he in the hospital?*

She heads back into the living room to find that, thankfully, the woodchipper has taken a break. She pulls her phone from her purse and hits speed dial. Ethan's phone rings once, twice, four times, and goes to voicemail.

"Oh, God," she says, then she hangs up and hits speed dial again. This time, on the fourth ring, he picks up.

"Hey."

"My God, are you okay?" Anna says, with a sigh of relief.

"Why, what's up?"

While the sound of his voice has relieved her worry, there's something else which is hitting her antenna full force.

She decides to take another tack.

"I, uh, just wanted to thank you for the lunch."

"You're welcome."

He sounds distracted, Anna is thinking. *And nervous.*

"I was sitting here in the office wondering if you had picked up Louis yet."

"Um, yeah, of course. He's, um, he's eating right now, too."

"He's okay, then?" Anna says, now positive that something isn't quite right.

Suddenly, the woodchipper fires up, and the two men on the ground begin chucking in more fallen branches.

The high-pitched whining and grinding is unbearable, so Anna reaches over the sofa and closes the two windows which look out onto the street.

"Yeah, he's fine."

With the windows closed, Anna hears something very strange. She can hear still hear the sound of the woodchipper, but now it's coming through Ethan's phone.

"Wow, what's that noise?" she says.

"Uh, um, some guys are doing something with the trees. Remember the thing we got in the mailbox?"

Anna takes another look at the chipper parked next to Jaylynn's house, and then it hits her like a fist in the stomach.

ETHAN IS IN JAYLYNN'S HOUSE!

Immediately, Anna's heart starts racing again, faster now, and her breath is growing shallow, and a nauseating knot is starting to form in her stomach.

"Hey, you know..." Anna pauses, trying to catch her breath.

"I really can't wait to see Louis and my afternoon appointment canceled so I'm going to run home. Bye."

"Wait!!! I can bring him to you, if you..."

But, before Ethan can finish, Anna hangs up and bolts out the front door. She grabs her lunch bag off the chair, marches out to the street, smashes it between her hands, and throws it into the garbage.

Then she stomps back to the porch and parks herself on a chair. And stares. And waits. Not more than two minutes has gone by since she hung up when Jaylynn's front door swings open.

The woodchipper is still grinding away as Ethan zips the last inch of his zipper; then looking in the direction that Anna would be arriving from and not seeing her, Ethan makes a dash across the street.

As he jumps the curb, he glances up to see Anna glaring at him from the chair and stops cold. She waits a few beats, stands, then steps slowly off the porch and walks toward him.

Ethan yells over the whine and grind of the chipper.

"I was just there to do her a favor and had to take a piss, okay?"

Anna approaches and passes him without saying a word.

"Hey, what are you doing?" he yells.

Anna heads toward the curb, steps off, and begins to make her way across the street toward Jaylynn's house.

"You're crazy, you know that?" Ethan yells, as Anna stops in the middle of the street.

"That's better. C'mon, let's go see Louis."

When she turns back, it gives Ethan the impression that he's been given a reprieve, but it's only temporary. Instead, Anna walks to the garbage can, retrieves the mashed-up lunch sack, and again proceeds to cross the street.

"Shit! Anna!"

When she gets to the front door of Jaylynn's house, Anna stops, raises her hand to knock, but realizes that Jaylynn won't be able to hear over the sound of the woodchipper, so she just swings the door open and steps inside. She slips through the living room and heads down the hallway.

The floor plan differs little from Anna's as they were all designed and built in basically the same way in the 1930's; the master is always in the rear at the end of the hall, either on the left or on the right.

Anna comes to the first door on the right, and, when she swings it open, sees it's empty save for a couple of hand-me-down armchairs and an old saltwater fish tank that hasn't since a fish for years.

"Ethan? That you, babe?" she hears Jaylynn say.

Anna turns and takes three steps toward the door on the left which is partially open. She pushes on it and swings it wider. There, on her Walmart sheets in the middle of her Walmart bedroom is Jaylynn Morrison, slim, trim, and buck naked.

She's laying on her stomach, and her long black hair flows down her back. With a Coke bottle and a cigarette in one hand, she's checking emails on her cell phone with the other.

Anna takes note that Jaylynn's cigarettes are the same brand as Ethan's.

"Grab me another coke, would ya, darlin'?" Jaylynn says, thinking that Anna is Ethan.

Four-or-five-seconds pass and, when she doesn't get a reply, Jaylynn rolls over to see Anna framed in the doorway.

She pauses, looks Anna up and down, and without skipping a beat, says;

"And while you're at it, get one for yourself."

When she was crossing the street, Anna had entertained thoughts of heaving the sack lunch in Jaylynn's face but now it seems a childish and totally inadequate response to Jaylynn's pithy rejoinder, so all Anna can do is turn around and stomp out of the house.

Across the street, Ethan is sitting in the chair on the porch, his head in his hands.

"Don't say a word. I'm going into the house. I'm going to pack. I'm taking the car and Louis and going to my parents'. Louis will be there until I get back to town.

By Monday, I want you out of the house. Whether you have a job or not. I'll have my father come by. If you're still here, he'll call the police."

The tree trimmers and the woodchipper are done, and the day has taken on the tones of a late fall afternoon. Anna has finished packing and is taking one last look around to see if there's anything she might have forgotten, when she spots the scale model of the HMS Belfast.

I'll be damned if I'm leaving this, she thinks to herself. She scoops it up, tosses it into her backpack, and grabs Louis' bag from off the dining room table.

Jaylynn has been sitting on the front porch of her house, sipping a Coke and smoking cigarettes while watching the drama unfold across the street.

Exiting the house, Anna slams the screen door, throws the last of her things into the Forester, then deposits Louis in the front passenger seat before going around and sliding in behind the wheel.

As she peels out of the driveway and heads down Spring, Ethan comes out of the house and saunters across the road.

"Who put the bee in her bonnet?" Jaylynn says, as Ethan steps up onto her porch.

"Bound to happen sooner or later, I guess."

"You guys were together a long time."

"Yeah, we were."

"She wasn't very good for you, Ethan."

"Guess, not."

"What's that saying? Physician heal thyself?"

"She wasn't always so bad."

149

"Whaddya gonna do now?"

"I dunno. I'll figure it out."

Jaylynn shakes another cigarette from her pack and lights it from the butt of the one she's been smoking, then drains the bottle.

"Well, in the meantime, can you do me a favor darlin' and grab me another Coke?"

Tearing down Spring Street, Anna took one more look in the rearview mirror and saw Ethan crossing the road to Jaylynn's house. Suddenly, she begins pounding on the steering wheel.

"Dammit! How dare he!" Anna cries.

She reaches into her purse, fishes around for a used tissue and begins to wipe her eyes and her nose.

"It's just not fair, Louis!!!"

And just as if he knew what was going on, Louis lifts his head and meows in Anna's direction.

Anna makes a right onto Mulberry Street, then a left onto Second until she gets to Emery Highway. Her parents live in a suburb near the Bowden Golf Course. Vivian and Frank belonged to the club for years; but, when her father traded in his golf clubs for a fishing pole, Vivian decided to find something else to do as well, although they still have an occasional dinner with friends in the golf course dining room.

Dear God, what have I been thinking? she says to herself as she grabs her phone.

"Siri, call Simon Mercer," she says, still sniffling.

"Simon Mercer. Calling now."

Anna can hear the change in ambient noise as the call shifts from one satellite to another and notes that even the rings sound different. She's surprised that Simon picks up so quickly.

"Anna!"

"Hi, Simon, hope it isn't too late to call."

"You've spoken already? Now did he take it?"

"Let's just say I'm yours for as long as I'm needed."

"Understanding chap! Good for you!"

Anna hears Simon pull the phone from his ear and yell over his shoulder to his wife.

"Karen! Anna Newsom's on board!"

"Fantastic! When does she arrive?" Karen says, as Simon returns to the phone.

"How soon can you make it?"

"I can leave Saturday. That'll give me two days here to wrap things up."

"Brilliant. I'll have Eva, my secretary, make the arrangements and email the particulars. You'll be staying near Bristol this go 'round. Oh, and Anna, what's your preference, would you like to have a look around the girl's bedroom prior to your first interview with her?"

"No, the interview first please. And don't forget I'll have my assistant, Lyla, with me. She's already in England, so no flight is needed."

"Oh, right, thanks for the reminder. I'll pick you up Saturday morning for the drive out.

"Perfect. See you then. Oh, Simon, I almost forget, my email is, Anna Newsom 007 @ gmail.com."

"007 is it? Brilliant!"

t w e n t y - t w o

Lyla and Caleb have just stepped into one of the thirty-two oval shaped capsules on London's massive Ferris wheel, the London Eye, when Lyla's phone rings. She reaches into her coat pocket, pulls out her phone, and answers.

"Hey, they said no phones, remember?" Caleb says, so Lyla whispers.

"Hi, listen, I can't talk right now."

"I'll make it quick. It's over with Ethan…"

"WHAT!???"

"Shhhh," Caleb says.

"I'm going to stay with my parents for a couple of days. Your flight home was on Friday, right?"

"Yeah."

"Well, cancel it."

"What!???"

Several passengers in Lyla's vicinity turn in her direction and stare.

"Sorry," Lyla says, in response to them. "Emergency."

"Listen, I'm coming back Saturday. We've got a case. A big one, I think. Google, Clevedon murder. C-L-E-V-E-D-O-N."

"Got it."

"I'll call you later, and I'll send you my itinerary as soon as it arrives. Bye." Anna says, and hangs up.

"Hallelujah!" Lyla says, as she puts her phone away.

"There's a sale at Dillard's?" Caleb quips, looking out at the rising panorama.

"Very funny. No! Anna and Ethan are history."

"Wow. Who's next? Harry and Meghan? What's that boy going to do now?"

"I don't know about Ethan, but you're going home alone."

"What!???" Caleb says, drawing further stares. "Shhhh. I'll explain later."

twenty-three

"Elizabeth. There's water in the pitcher. If you'd prefer something other, please ask."

Dr. Fielding Goddard sits across a small table from Elizabeth Barrett. The room is similar to the one that Chief Inspector Hayden used during his first interview of Elizabeth. It has the same two-way mirror and recording devices, but today the guard is standing outside the door in the hallway rather than inside the room.

Behind the two-way mirror today is the Prosecutor for the Crown, Ms. Diana Lynch. In her early fifties, Lynch is an attractive, yet hard-nosed barrister who cut her teeth in the Eastern districts of Cambridgeshire, Essex and Norfolk, and who has achieved something of star status within the Crown Prosecution Service with an eighty-eight percent conviction rate. Next to Diana is her assistant, Daniel Morrison, mid-thirties and no less a zealot.

"Do you remember me from yesterday, Elizabeth? My name is Dr. Goddard. I'm here to help you."

Elizabeth doesn't respond or even acknowledge Goddard's presence and displays the same flat affect as she has during her previous interviews.

"Can you raise the volume please?" Diana says, to the male technician at the controls.

"Are you hungry, Elizabeth? Are they feeding you well?"

Elizabeth ignores the question.

"That's a very nice outfit you're wearing this morning."

The mention of Elizabeth's wardrobe creates a minuscule flicker in her eye. Noticing the response, Goddard continues.

"Did you choose the outfit especially for our meeting today?"

No response.

"Do you know why you're here, Elizabeth?" Goddard says, and out of the blue, Elizabeth answers.

"I'm waiting for me mum and me dad."

"That's what you told Chief Inspector Hayden."

"I'm still waiting."

"Your parents are dead, Elizabeth."

"You're lying. They're away. In India. On an errand for God."

Goddard lets the last statement lay for a few moments, then continues.

"Who told you that?"

Elizabeth doesn't answer.

"Do you know who David O'Rourke is?"

Elizabeth is silent for a moment, and it appears to Goddard that the name has registered, but she doesn't answer and turns her head away.

"I'd like a Coca Cola, please."

In the control room, Diana and Daniel hear Elizabeth's request.

"I'll get it," Daniel says.

Goddard slows down his questioning. It's imperative that he earns Elizabeth's full trust and cooperation before proceeding to the next level of inquiry. Just as he's about to begin again, the guard comes into the room with the can of Coke and sets it down in front of her.

"Elizabeth, can you describe your bedroom for me?"

Elizabeth picks up the can in both hands and studies it for a moment before taking a sip.

"Where is the man who brought the Coke?"

"Outside," Goddard says, "he's here to protect you."

"You're lying. He's here to protect you."

"From what, Elizabeth? Are you going to hurt me? I'm here to help you."

Elizabeth looks toward the door and then back to Goddard.

"Do you have a penis?"

"That's rather personal, don't you think?"

"But you're asking me all sorts of personal questions."

"Yes, I am. That's my job."

In the control room, Diana Lynch turns to Daniel.

"Do me a favor and Google Elizabeth Ann Barrett."

Daniel opens his laptop and types in Elizabeth's name. Within seconds there are several thousand hits.

twenty-four

Anna pulls into the driveway of the modest, single-story house in the Macon suburb known as Cross Keys. The homes here are made mostly of brick and stone, which, when built, were meant to convey an aura of substance and stability that...

'Nowadays seem to be in short supply,' as Anna's father is fond of saying. And unlike the newer homes with stingy lots that offer barely enough space for a clothesline, Anna grew up on half an acre where neighborhood kids and dogs could roam at will; not to mention the occasional raccoon and possum and skunk.

I can't remember the last time I spent the night here, Anna thinks to herself as she's getting out of the car. *It must have been after graduation and before Ethan.*

"C'mon, Louis," Anna says, as she grabs his bag and her backpack and heads inside the house.

"Anybody home?"

Anna sets Louis' bag on the kitchen table, then swings her backpack off her shoulder and onto a chair. Not hearing a response, she goes back out to the car for her suitcase and carry-on.

"Anna? That you?" her father says, as he comes into the kitchen from the stairs leading to the basement.

"Hi, Dad," Anna says, as she comes back through the door.

"Hey, Sparky. We didn't expect to see you until this weekend. Your mom's at the store. What's with the luggage? Wait a second, weren't you supposed to get in last night?"

"I did. But I need to spend a of couple nights here, if that's okay."

"Don't be silly, why wouldn't it be?"

"Well, Mom isn't exactly the queen of spontaneity," Anna says, stepping into him for a hug.

"She's really trying, Anna. Last Wednesday, she threw caution to the wind, and at the last minute we had mac and cheese instead of spaghetti and meatballs."

"Wow, life in the fast lane," Anna says, and they share a laugh, but sensing something isn't quite right, Frank glances out at the driveway through the kitchen window.

"He's not here," Anna says, and moves to the kitchen table and unzips Louis' bag.

"What's going on?"

"I, uh, really can't talk about it right now."

"Is he okay?"

"Really, Dad. Not now."

Louis manages a couple of meows as he clamors out of his bag and jumps down to the kitchen floor. Frank pauses a moment, knowing his daughter well enough to not pursue the topic any further.

"Well, make yourself comfortable, I'll be downstairs. We can't wait to hear all about your trip!" he says, turning back down the steps.

Anna grabs her suitcase and carry-on and wheels them down the hardwood floor hallway. The walls, that particular beige that was so popular in the 90's, are still lined with old family photos, but not nearly as many as before the incident on the houseboat.

Anna's room is the second on the right. It's just the way she left it, and not because she asked; it's just that Vivian hasn't gotten around to doing what she said she was going to do which was to make it an art studio. Anna sets her luggage to one side and takes a look around.

The twin bed is on the right wall under the Gwen Stefani poster that she got from her grandparents when she turned seven, and her desk is under the window that looks out to the side yard where they used to play badminton. Beyond the yard and across the street is where Joey Kern used to live before his parents threw in the towel and uprooted the family for California.

Anna sinks onto the bed and flops back onto one of her Michael Jackson pillows, staring up at the deep blue ceiling with glow-in-the-dark stars that she painted one day when her parents were playing golf.

Why is coming home so strange? Anna asks herself. *Is it because everything looks the same and smells the same, in spite of the passage of time? Or is home like a measuring stick or, better yet, a control in a science experiment against which we compare our wins and losses; to what degree we've advanced and succeeded, or, in some cases, how far we've been blown off course.*

As her eyes start to water, and not wanting to lose control, Anna forces herself to think of things other than Ethan; like London and The Shangri-La, and the horrific murder in Clevedon...

Unlike young men, young women rarely murder without motive, she thinks. ***This case will be difficult. Maybe even dangerous. Hello, it's your intuition knocking.***

Anna closes her eyes, and then, from far off, she thinks she hears Vivian's voice, but perhaps is only imagining it.

'Where is she Frank? How does she seem? Should we let her sleep? Look, she left everything in the middle of the kitchen... Should we have mac and cheese or spaghetti and meatballs? It is Wednesday isn't it, Frank...?'

Or is she calling Anna to hurry up and finish packing because we have to leave for Chloe's and the summer of her thirteenth year that will end in such pain and humiliation on the houseboat.

She can't forget the expressions on her parents' faces when she finally told them what had happened. And then Chloe changing her story and siding with her brother; and then *'he said, she said'* and the trial and the two families never to speak again, not even her mother and her Aunt Trudy.

And then the trip to J.C. Penney's to pick out the new

bedspread and the new sheets and the matching drapes for her room, because they were supposed to help her forget; or was it really Vivian trying to scrub away the vile thing that had happened, and the nagging doubts that perhaps Chris was telling the truth; but new, fresh dresses would take care of that, wouldn't it?

Her favorite doll. The one sitting on the shelf above her small TV; the one she thought she had lost the winter when she was eight, but found when the snow melted, laying in the sandbox right where she had left it two months before the record-breaking storm; she knew Anna had been telling the truth.

Anna lets her mind wander to animals she read about in biology class, the ones that shed their skins as they grow. Like snakes and hermit crabs. Humans are like that, but we shed things and each other, and she can't help but feel the overwhelming guilt that she has shed Ethan and left him to curl up and dry in the sun.

But then, it hits her like a freight train; that maybe she's the one that's been shed. That Ethan and Jaylynn might go on and have a family of their own, and now Anna is swamped by an overwhelming dread that at some point she will be old and empty and falling back to earth like a spent rocket that never quite made it into orbit.

"You think we should wake her?" Frank asks.

"No. Let her sleep," Vivian says. "The mac and cheese will keep."

twenty-five

"Mr. Wetherford?"

"Yes, what is it?" Benjamin says, turning from his television to the nurse standing in the doorway of his hospital room.

"Chief Inspector Hayden to see you."

Benjamin hesitates for a moment and then responds.

"Yes, show him in."

The nurse nods toward her right and steps away as Hayden appears in the doorway.

"Good morning, Pastor."

"Chief Inspector."

Benjamin is sitting up in bed, and a massive bandage covers the top of his head and wraps around his chin. He reaches for the remote and turns down the volume as Hayden enters the room, taking off his hat.

"Was wonderin' how you were comin' along. Heard it was quite a fall, and judging by that bandage, I'd say they were right."

"Well, considerin' this thick Welsh skull, I think it was the stone floor got the worst of it," Benjamin says, then he motions to the visitor's chair at the end of the bed.

"Please."

Hayden takes him up on the offer and pulls the chair a little closer to the bed before sitting.

"So, tell me. How did all this come about?"

"I climbed the steps of the pulpit and was about to begin me sermon when, when...the whole world started spinnin'."

"Never happened before?"

"Never. But I'd be lying if I said it had nothing to do with the murder of David O'Rourke."

"I imagine that the shock has been…"

"You can't imagine, Chief Inspector. The girl is like me own daughter."

"But she's not, is she?"

"I'm sorry?" Benjamin replies.

"Nothing. Forget I said it."

For a moment there's an uncomfortable pause, and then Hayden stands and moves toward the door.

"Well, just stopped by for a quick hello. Good to see you on the mend."

Hayden is starting to walk out when he turns back toward Benjamin.

"Pastor, if you'll allow me another minute or so."

"I'm a little tired, Inspector."

"I'll be quick. I understand that you and the housekeeper go to the fish market each Friday morning."

"In Caldicot. For Margret, nothing else will do."

"What time do you normally leave the parsonage?"

"4:00 a.m. or so, but no later than 4:10."

"And how long do you stay, on average?"

"Depends. On rare occasions Margret will spot the fish she wants straight away, and have it held while she walks into town for some window shopping. Most days, however, she'll mosey about comparin' the whiting to the cod or the bass to the pollack looking for the best and the cheapest."

"Either way, you leave to return to the parsonage at what time?"

"Never later than 7:00 a.m."

"Were you usually back by the time David O'Rourke arrived?"

"Actually, no. We were back early that morning because of the smash-up on the M4."

"So, on most Friday's when David arrived, there was no one home."

"No one. Well, except for Elizabeth, that is."

"Only Elizabeth?"

"Yes. No one else."

"One more thing, Pastor Wetherford. Am I correct in assumin' you and Margret are together for the entire time? At the fish market, that is?"

Benjamin hesitates, not understanding the purpose of the question, and clears his throat before he speaks.

"Not always. Sometimes I'll take a walk along the breakwater. Other times I may drive into Somerton or Christchurch, or any number of the other quaint towns on the other side."

"Don't you think it odd, though?"

"Odd? How do you mean?"

"Here she is shopping for the parsonage and you just up and leave."

"Not odd at all, Chief Inspector. My God man, have you ever spent two hours watching a woman shop for fish?"

"I suppose I haven't." Hayden says, allowing himself a chuckle, then he puts on his hat and heads toward the door.

"Good day, Pastor."

"Good day, Chief Inspector."

twenty-six

"I could have mac and cheese every night," Frank says, as he ladles another spoonful from the bowl in the middle of the table.

"We'd save money, that's for sure," Vivian replies, but, on noticing the size of Frank's portion, she changes her mind.

"Lordy, that reminds me. That client of yours. With the ice cream. What was her name?" Vivian says, as she takes a healthy sip of her wine.

"Right. Um. Stevenson. Ella Stevenson," Frank says.

"That's her! Your father was hired by the Stevensons when Ella found a metal screw in a bowl of ice cream," Vivian says.

"What does that have to do with mac and cheese?" Anna says, studying the cheesy noodles on her fork before taking a bite.

"Nothing, except that when your father settled the case, Ella had her choice of money or ice cream and she settled for a year's supply of Tin Roof Sundae. That was the kind she was eating when she found the screw; and, knowing her, she was a large woman, you see, we guessed she had it every night until the settlement ran out."

"Isn't Tin Roof Sundae Ethan's favorite?" Frank says, not thinking, and then realizing what he's said, turns to Anna.

"Sorry."

"It's okay, Dad."

"So, how long did you say you'd be gone?" Vivian says, changing the subject.

"Five weeks or so. Why?"

"Because we're your parents and we'd like to know, that's why," Vivian says, the three glasses of wine now having their intended effect.

"That's a long time, Sparky."

"I know it is, Dad."

"What about your work here? Aren't you afraid of burning bridges?" Vivian says. "Pour me another would you, Frank."

"My clients will be here when I get back."

"Don't be so sure. You know how people are when one of their own goes off to greener pastures," Vivian says.

"No, mom, I don't. How are they?"

"Well, I'll never forget what Bette Midler said about success…," Vivian begins to say when Frank interrupts her.

"You mean the singer Bette Midler, or the pain in the ass at the post office Bette Midler?" he quips, and he turns and smiles at Anna.

"You know darn well who I mean," Vivian says, not pleased with being the butt of his joke.

"Go on, Mom."

"She said, and I quote,

'The worst part of success is trying to find someone who is happy for you'… unquote. People don't like to see other people make good. I don't know why. It's human nature I suppose. Didn't they teach you that in psychology school?"

"Not in those words exactly," Anna says, sipping from her wine glass.

Vivian pushes her chair back, gets up from the table, and begins to collect the dishes.

"Believe me, I'll never forget how people talked when we moved to Macon from Box Springs."

Anna rolls her eyes at Frank as Vivian walks the dishes to the sink.

"That true, Dad?"

"Frank, you know it is. When we'd go back for a visit, I couldn't step into the Kut 'n Kurl without the whole place going quiet," Vivian says, as she turns on the faucet.

"Well, if that's the case the damage has already been done. Not many people can brag that their daughter is on the New York Times Best Sellers List and flying to London to be on TV."

He smiles at Anna and then glances up to Vivian, expecting her to chime in, but instead sees that her shoulders are shaking.

Here we go again, Anna says to herself.

"Vivian, if Anna says it'll be fine, then I'm sure it will be."

Reaching for a tissue in the pocket of her house dress, Vivian attempts a response.

"It's not that."

"Then what?" Anna says.

Vivian takes a few seconds to answer.

"How long were you with Ethan?"

"I knew it," Anna says, pushing herself away from the table.

"I'll tell you..."

"Not now, Vivian. She's told us what happened," Frank says, but Vivian ignores him and plows on.

"We thought that one of these days you'd want to...to do what your brother's done. Look how happy he and Linda are!"

"I tried, Mom. I really did."

"It's not your fault, Anna," Frank says.

"Nobody's perfect. Ethan may have had his faults, but he was sweet, and he loved you," Vivian says.

"Damn it, Mom, I told you why! It's okay that he was sleeping with our next door neighbor? Is that what you're saying? That you'd be okay with Dad and Ms. Bullet Boobs across the street getting it on every night? Would you?"

Anna stands, throws her napkin down on the table, and begins pacing the floor.

"Easy, Sparky," Frank says.

"No, that's not what I'm saying, and you know it, but you've got work here, you said so. Isn't one murder like any other for God's sake. Why traipse all the way to London?"

"Because this girl needs me, that's why!"

"A murderer. And Ethan doesn't?"

"Mom, I just told you! I found him cheating with the woman across the street!"

Vivian, the tears having turned to anger, rips the apron from around her waist and tosses it on the counter.

"And why not! He was probably lonely, Anna! Who could blame him?"

The room quiets and for several moments all you can hear is the sound of the water running in the sink and the occasional meow from Louis.

"Okay, you're crossing the line here, Mom. You don't understand."

Vivian softens and leans back against the counter, her hand to her mouth.

"I just pray that it isn't something I've done. That keeps you from, well, committing. If I did something, anything, you'd say so, right? Shouldn't she, Frank? If I did something?"

Anna hesitates, and then decides she can't hold back any longer.

"Anna, don't," Frank says.

"Goddam it, Mom, it isn't always about you, but it always has to be doesn't it?"

There's a full moon and, as Anna crosses the length of the back yard, she can make out the line of birch trees along the rear of the property silhouetted against the sky.

When she gets to the largest, she stops and takes out her cell phone. She switches on her flashlight and points it at the tree. About five feet from the bottom and hanging from a nail is a homemade plaque. Anna was eight and Jason was ten when they made it. Jason cut the wood from an old piece of lumber tossed behind the garage and Anna painted the epitaph, but, even though the wood has weathered and the words have faded, she can still see what it says:

'Here lies Baxter. The best dog God ever made. November 11, 2001.'

Anna switches off the light, and then takes a flash photo of the plaque. At that moment, she senses Frank coming up behind her, and she bursts into tears.

"Oh, God, Dad."

About to tear up himself, all Frank can manage is to put his arms around his daughter and say...

"We are so damned proud of you, Anna. Don't you ever forget that."

twenty-seven

"Simon Mercer's office," Eva says, answering the phone.

"I'd like to speak to Mr. Mercer, please."

"May I tell him who's calling?"

"Cynthia Smythe."

"Good morning, Ms. Smythe! I'll put you right through."

Eva puts Cynthia on hold and hits the intercom button into Simon's office.

"It's Ms. Smythe again! From the BBC! On line one! Wait till me mum hears! A television producer on me own phone!"

"Thank you, Eva," Simon says, as he hits the flashing button on his phone.

"Mornin', Ms. Smythe."

"I was calling to see if you were ever able to connect with Anna Newsom?"

Simon can't help but notice Cynthia Smythe's lack of a *'hello', 'how are you',* or even a *'good day',* and how her manners seem inversely proportional to her sense of self-worth.

"Good of you to ask. A fairly herculean feat, but I managed to catch her at Heathrow, in the nick of time, I might add and, thanks to you, she'll be returning to London this week."

"Returning to London? This week? What in heavens for?"

"The murder in Clevedon. Have you seen it?" Simon asks.

"Something about knitting needles and a teenage girl and unrequited love?" Cynthia replies, "it's all over the birdcage liners."

"That's the one."

"Not my cup of tea, I'm afraid."

"Well, for better or worse, it's mine, and Dr. Newson has agreed to work the case for us."

Simon takes no little pleasure in being able to one-up

Cynthia Smythe, who, for the moment, is uncharacteristically at a loss for words.

"You don't say."

"She's coming in late Friday, and Saturday morning we're heading out to Bristol Channel."

Not to be outdone, this news has started the wheels turning in Cynthia's head.

"How long will she be involved, do you suppose?"

"Could be a month or more, really. We're putting her up at The Sandringham, in Weston."

"The Sandringham?"

"It's not the Shangri-La, I'm afraid, but it's the best we could do."

"Right. Of course. Listen, Simon, I've got to run, but do you mind if I call you in a day or so?"

"Not at all."

"Thank you, Simon."

"Good day, Cynthia."

"Why not this. We take the opening statement of the installment and split it in half, making the first portion a part of a teaser?" the young editor says, turning to Mitchell, who is sitting next to him.

They've been working on the subsequent shows in Anna's series and are now on the one that is titled, 'The Crack in the Chimney.'

"I think you'll need more than that," Mitchell says. "Play it again."

Mitchell and the editor, Brian, are sitting in one of several editing suites at BBC Television. Brian is young, about twenty-four, and will be interning for the next six months. Cynthia has assigned him to Mitchell in the hopes that Mitchell's experience and expertise will rub off on the lad.

The rooms are small and well insulated for sound and dimly lit, making the editing screen the center of attention. As Brian hits the 'play' button, Anna's face appears on the screen.

"No doubt about it," Brian says.

"About what?" Mitchell replies.

"She's pretty hot."

Mitchell studies Anna in the monitor and can't help but agree.

"Never mind that. Listen to what she's saying."

> *"The Crack in the Chimney is the final case study in my non-fictional book, The Spider on the Ceiling. I save this one for last because it goes beyond PLR and enters the realm of the paranormal. The specific name I've given to the phenomenon in this case is Causal Tele-transmutation."*

"See there. You need something to explain what Causal Tele-transmutation is," Mitchell says, just as the door to the edit bay swings open, providing a gap for Cynthia Smythe's head and a beam of light that penetrates the room.

"Working on a teaser," Mitchell says.

"I need you to take a break."

"Now? About to wrap it up, Cynthia."

"Sorry, can't wait. Brian can finish.

"What!? Who me!?" Brian says, looking up from the editing console. "Wow, thanks, Ms. Smythe!"

"I'll be in conference room three." Cynthia says as she disappears into the hallway.

Mitchell knows better than to push back when Cynthia is on a tear, so he puts his notes to one side and slides back from the editing console.

"She's all yours, ole man."

Mitchell rounds the corner into the room to find Cynthia, two producers, and four assistants sitting around the large oval conference table. He goes to a credenza, pours himself a cup of coffee and takes a seat across from Cynthia, who begins the meeting.

"I know this is short notice and you've all got other assignments, so I'll make it as brief as possible."

Mitchell takes a sip from his cup and settles into the chair.

"I'm assuming everyone here has heard of the murder in Clevedon. If not, please say so."

The news of the killing has been hard to dodge, so, to varying degrees, everyone at the table has some idea of what occurred. Cynthia looks around the table and, satisfied with everyone's familiarity with the case, continues.

"I just found out that the public defender assigned to the suspect in this case has hired Dr. Anna Newsom to assist him."

Mitchell has just taken another sip of coffee and nearly chokes on the news.

"Something wrong, Mr. Walker?" Cynthia says.

Mitchell swallows, coughs a couple of times, and taps his chest with his fist before setting his cup down on the table.

"Down the wrong alley. Sorry."

Cynthia turns from Mitchell and continues addressing the table.

"If you don't know who Dr. Newsom is, she's the forensic psychologist we've been featuring this month on The Evolving Mind."

"The one from the States?" one of the assistants asks.

"Yes. Anna has become fairly well known for her ability to determine whether women who've murdered, claiming serial rape as the motive, are telling the truth or not."

"This a rape case, then?" a producer asks.

"No one is sure yet," Cynthia says.

"Anna will be arriving tomorrow and will probably be on the case for a few weeks. I've brought you all in to consider the feasibility of producing a real time documentary around the murder and the analysis of the suspect, which Anna will be conducting."

The table goes quiet as each person tries to understand what Cynthia Smythe is asking of them.

"Quite exciting, Cynthia," says, Hal Boyd, one of the senior producers. "Never seen it done, before."

"It hasn't been done before."

After thinking about it for a few moments, Mitchell responds.

"If I may, Cynthia, what exactly do you mean by real time?"

"What you'll find in reading her book, is that each of the cases are resolved in very different and very startling ways. Rather than read about it or discuss it after the fact, I want our audience to see it play out exactly as it happens. And I need your advice as to how to accomplish it."

"Where is Anna's analysis going to take place?" one of the female assistants asks.

"I imagine it may take place in several locations." Cynthia says.

"But it's more than that," Mitchell says. "Each case is solved by combining interviews with the patient with evidence found at the scene of the rapes, which is generally the same location where the murder has taken place."

"Well, I'd start by planting cameras in all locations pertinent to the case," an assistant offers.

"Somewhat of the cart before the horse, isn't it?" says another assistant. "What about legal clearances? Will the suspect even allow us to videotape her? And what about Dr. Newsom, will she have any of it?"

"Good questions," Cynthia says. "First, I believe that we can get permission from the public defender on the basis that we are providing a video record of the entire procedure for legal purposes, which they could and should do themselves, but at great cost. We're offering it, gratis. Written into our agreement, however, will be that once the case is resolved, we will have permission to use the raw material from which to cut the documentary."

"I still think you may have problems with getting Dr. Newsom to cooperate. She may see it as an intrusion and a distraction from her duties," says an older male assistant.

"That is exactly why I'm assigning Mitchell Walker to the project," Cynthia says.

Mitchell had been checking messages on his phone and looks up sharply at the mention of his name.

"No, Cynthia, please. I've got enough to do with…"

"Sorry. Anna likes you, Mitchell. She trusts you. God knows, we can't count on Edwards to make her feel at home here."

"But…"

"Enough. You'll direct and Hal will produce."

Hal Boyd is several years Mitchell's senior and has been producing shows and documentaries for the BBC for nearly two decades. His even-tempered, avuncular nature complements Mitchell's intense creativity, and, as a team, they have shared several successes together.

"Cynthia, you don't understand…" Mitchell says, pleading.

"Forget it, Mitchell, it won't work. I want a production plan on my desk Monday morning. Good day, all."

As Cynthia and the rest of the team stand and leave the room, Hal walks over to Mitchell's side of the table.

"Cynthia filled me in an hour ago. Just think, 'ole boy, Walker and Boyd together again, just like Warwick." he says.

"Bloody bollocks, this," Mitchell says, angrier now.

"Buck up, mate. It's a hell of an idea she has, and we may even walk away with another Bafta. Plus, Dr. Anna Newsom seems a bit of the bee's knees, if you ask me."

Mitchell stands, grabs his coffee cup and heads for the door.

"That, my dear producer, is precisely the problem."

twenty-eight

The kettle is rising to a whistle as Margret enters the kitchen. She shuts off the burner, places a crocheted potholder around the handle, and carefully pours the boiling water into the blue and white Staffordshire pot.

After setting the kettle back on the stove, she covers the teapot in a pink and green crocheted cozy. She can't help but notice how translucent the skin on her hands has become, and how it stretches like parchment over her blue veins and swollen joints.

She sets the teapot on a tray next to a small plate, which holds two biscuits. The potholder and the tea cozy are a matching set that Benjamin's wife made sometime before Margret arrived at the parsonage. She had only been there a year when Adelaide passed on, but, while she was alive, the two defied conventional wisdom about women occupying the same household and actually got on well together.

Shortly after hearing the news of the murder, Margret's friend Agatha came around with two dozen Shrewsbury biscuits. Although Margret's appetite hadn't returned, she shared with Agatha that the biscuits...

'...have, nonetheless, been a comforting reminder of happier times.'

Carrying the tray slowly up the stairs to her room, Margret hears the strains of Blevins organ echoing across the large expanse of lawn that separates the church from the parsonage.

It's just dusk as she reaches the second-floor landing.

He certainly seems in a mood tonight. Margret thinks to herself.

Bach's Toccata and Fugue in D Minor is one of the pieces that Blevins rarely indulges himself in and, when he does, it's only at the end of rehearsal for the coming week's services. But tonight, it appears that he is beginning with it.

Poor Blevins. He so loves the Church. And Benjamin.

Margret makes her way into her room and sets the tray on a table under the window. The tragedy has taken its toll on everyone, and, with Benjamin still on the mend, it seems likely, barring a visit from a neighboring pastor, that Blevins will have to, for a time at least, fill Benjamin's shoes.

In the choir loft, Blevins is lost, absorbed in the music, when he hears a voice echoing up from below.

"Blevins?"

Startled, Blevins looks up sharply and abruptly stops in the middle of the concerto.

"Who's there?" he says, staring down into the darkened church.

"Are you Celwin Blevins?"

"I say, who are you?"

"I'd like a word, if I may."

"At this hour?" Blevins says.

"It's important."

Blevins stands from his bench, snaps off the small light that illuminates the keyboard, and peers down into the darkness. As his eyes adjust, he can make out the silhouette of a man against the moonlight filtering in from the open door next to the altar. It appears that he's wearing a wide-brimmed hat and some kind of raincoat.

"If it's that important you should be speaking to Pastor Wetherford."

"Stay there. I'll come to you."

The choir loft is illuminated by a single bare bulb in the plaster ceiling that casts an eerie light over the folding chairs and music stands. As the man makes his way up to the loft, Blevins marks his progress by the squeaks and creaks of the centuries-old stairs behind the stained, shiplap partition.

Blevins turns to his bench, raises the lid and retrieves the billy-club given to him by his uncle when he retired from the police force.

"No need for that," the man says, hesitating in the shadows at the top of the landing.

"Tell me why not, then."

The man reaches into the inside pocket of his trench coat causing Blevins to flinch.

"Here," the man says, as he presents Blevins with his business card.

"On the music stand, there," Blevins says, aiming the billy-club at an open stand in the middle of the loft.

The man steps forward into the dim light and places the business card on the stand.

"Now. Over there."

As the man sits down in an open folding chair near the back wall, Blevins can see that he's somewhere in his early forties. He moves to the music stand and picks up the card, reading out loud...

"Hugh Archer. Reporter. The Eve'nin' Tattler."

Blevins looks up.

"I don't like reporters, Mr. Archer. Especially your kind."

"News is news, Mr. Blevins."

"You're keeping me from me supper."

"I'll be quick."

The man hesitates, collects his thoughts and begins.

"There are rumors. Just rumors, mind you, that the girl... is, uh, claiming she was raped."

"Get out."

"Listen, please..."

"This house, this church, has been through enough, Mr. Archer! A fine man, Mr. O'Rourke was! Murdered! And now you say she's crying rape! What calumny!"

"But think, Mr. Blevins. What if it's true?"

Blevins pauses for a moment, then sinks back onto his bench.

"True?" he says, as if he's never heard the word before. "If it's true, then…"

"Then there's much more to the story," Archer says.

Blevins sits stone still as the meaning of the man's words sink in.

"Why me, Mr. Archer?"

"You're here. You see things."

"I've no idea what you're driving at…"

"You may not be pastor here, but you're a man of God. I can see that. And I could hear it before I came in."

"I'm just a man, Mr. Archer," Blevins says.

Archer stands, makes his way toward the dark stairway and turns back to Blevins.

"*Where I found truth, there found I my God, who is truth it-self,*" Archer says.

"Saint Augustine," Blevins replies.

"A man of God, just as I said. All I'm asking is for the truth, Mr. Blevins. Wherever it may lay and to whatever it may lead. You've got my card."

And with that, Hugh Archer, reporter from The Evening Tattler, heads back down the stairs and disappears into the darkness.

twenty-nine

"We're just pulling into the airport now."

"Were you able to get into the house?" Lyla says.

"Yep. Found the key. I got your heavy wool coat, three sweaters, two light jackets, four pair of leggings, and two knit caps, the white one and the black one with the matching scarves."

"You're a dear."

"How did Caleb take the news?"

"About being gone so long or having to go home alone?"

"Both."

"He's okay. He's got a ton of work to keep him busy and the World Series is coming up and he's looking forward to football season. All good. Plus, when I told him the stewardess would probably let him have my entree as well as his, he lit up light a Christmas tree."

"Well, hopefully we'll be home before Thanksgiving!" Anna says, laughing.

"You're joking, right?"

"I hope so."

"By the way, I happened by a newsstand yesterday. The newspapers have this girl tried and sentenced already."

"It's a good thing we're doing this, Lyla. I know this is hard on you two. Thank you."

"Forget it. It's what we do, right?"

"Right. It's what we do."

Anna hangs up and continues the conversation she was having with her father.

"You're sure you want me to go to the house on Monday?"

"Of course, why?"

"You were together a long time Anna. There must have

been a reason."

"I can't get past what he did, Dad."

"You know, your mother can be a real pain in the ass sometimes, but she's not always wrong. You know what they say, *'no matter how thin...'*

"I know. *'No matter how thin the pancake, there's always two sides.'*"

"That's all we're saying. Spend this time weighing things out, and if you feel the same way when you get back, then do what you need to do."

Anna thinks about what he is saying and considers it for a few seconds.

"Sorry, Dad. I've made up my mind."

"Okay, then. Just hope you won't regret it.

Frank swings the car to the curb and he and Anna step out into the chilly fall air.

"Seems busier than usual here this morning," Frank says.

"College."

"Oh, right."

Frank shuts the trunk lid and hoists the two large suitcases up onto the curb. Anna pulls the handle up out of her carry on and swings her Tumi backpack over her shoulder.

"Thanks, Dad. I'll get a baggage guy to help from here."

Anna turns and wraps her arms around him.

"What time do you get in?"

"Super early. Love you."

"Love you, too. You be safe, okay?"

Anna pulls herself away and steps up onto the curb and is about to head off when Frank calls out to her.

"Sparky!"

Anna turns back and gives him a little smile. He had given her the nickname one Fourth of July when she couldn't get enough of the sparklers Frank had bought for her at the parade in Macon. It stuck, and she didn't seem to mind.

"The bases are loaded. You know what to do." he says.

Anna shoots him a look that's more than a smile and then disappears into the passengers heading toward the terminal.

Anna slips her earbuds out of her Tumi backpack before sliding it under the seat in front of her. It's hard to believe it's just over a week since her first flight to London, but it is, and this second flight is going to be longer than the first one from New York.

"Ladies and gentlemen. Welcome aboard British Airways flight 7012 from Atlanta to London's Heathrow airport. This is First Officer McGrath. Our pilot tonight is Rebecca Swift, but don't let that get your hopes up; it's still going to be an eight-hour flight."

The quip from the first officer sends up a round of chuckles that ripples through the plane.

"Our flight plan tonight has us going up the eastern seaboard, which will provide stunning views for our passengers on the left side of the plane. From there we'll skirt past New England, and then on to Newfoundland and Nova Scotia."

Anna had hoped that Sarah, the flight attendant on her first flight to London, would be on this flight, as well, but she's not in the first-class section which, thanks to Simon Mercer, is where Anna is sitting tonight.

Before leaving, Simon's secretary sent Anna flight and hotel Information, as well as newspaper and video links to the O'Rourke murder, which she downloaded and saved to her computer.

"Welcome aboard, ma'am. Would you like something to drink before take-off?"

No one had ever called her *'ma'am'* before, so Anna thought the young male flight attendant was speaking to the greying, middle-aged woman in the seat next to her.

"He's asking you a question," the woman says, politely diverting Anna's attention from the messages on her cell phone.

"Oh! Sorry. Um, yes please. How about a gin and tonic?"

"That was quick," Vivian says, as Frank enters the house

through the garage.

"Three hours and twenty minutes. Not bad."

Frank tosses his keys down on the small entry table and heads to the kitchen.

"How was she?"

"Conflicted. Worried about Ethan and excited about the trip."

"Well, she should be worried," Vivian says, as Frank goes to the Mr. Coffee on the counter next to the refrigerator and pours himself a cup.

"No, she should be excited. She's an incredible young woman, Vivian. Look at what she's accomplished."

"She was really hard on that boy."

"How can you say that? He hasn't pulled his weight for years. They're… what's the term now? Unequally yoked. It may be good for him," Frank says, taking a sip.

"It's hard these days, Frank. You think she's going to find someone decent on one of those sleazy dating sights?"

"So, she doesn't find someone. It's not the end of the world, although it may be coming the way things are going."

"Mr. Doom and Gloom. What are you doing this after-noon?"

"I thought about dusting off my golf clubs and hitting some balls. What are you doing?"

"Anna didn't seem so pleased to see her room, so I thought maybe I'd start on the redecorating."

Frank rinses his cup, sets it in the sink, and is about to walk out the door to the garage when Vivian stops him.

"Frank?"

"Yup?"

"What about Ms. Bullet Boobs?"

"Who?"

"Across the street."

Frank crosses the kitchen, steps up to Vivian and plants a small kiss on the cheek."

"No idea what you're talking about."

"Nice try." Vivian replies.

Anna finishes her spaghetti Bolognese just as the Airbus 350 slides over the eastern tip of Nova Scotia. She decided she would skip the sugary desert and accepted another glass of the Italian Brunello instead. Out her window, the lights of Cape Breton pass underneath the darkened shape of the left wing some thirty feet behind her.

"Ma'am, may I take your tray?"

Not able to hear the flight attendant with her earbuds in, the woman next to her taps her on the arm.

"He'd like to know if you're finished," she says, leaning into Anna.

"Oh, sorry. Yes, please."

Anna hands him the tray and then reaches into the seat pocket in front of her and pulls out her laptop. She sets it on the tray table in front of her and, once it's booted up, she opens the folder containing the latest news about the O'Rourke murder.

Based on the number of articles and photographs, it appears that the murder has moved to center stage in the tabloids. The crime took place just over a week ago, and it has already ballooned to near historic proportions. The headlines range from the macabre to outright fabrications.

LOCAL DAIRYMAN SKEWERED BY TEEN LOVER
CLEVEDON THRUST INTO HEADLINES
PARSONAGE LOVE PERCH PASSION
RAPE REPRISAL BLOODBATH
O'ROURKE DIARY HIDDEN SECRETS
SLAUGHTER ON LOWER STROBE ROAD
KNITTING NEEDLE NIGHTMARE
BRISTOL'S LIZZY BORDEN
NEIGHBOR HEARS SCREAMS OF PASSION

In addition to the headlines, many of the more enterprising papers had photographers positioned around the parsonage, round the clock, so there are photos taken with long lenses showing Benjamin in his bathrobe or Margret in the kitchen making a pot of tea.

Also, there are schematics of the house with large arrows pointing at the *'Room of Rape'* side-by-side with crime scene photos of the *'Delivery Lorry of Death'* taken by the police.

There are enlargements of Benjamin, Margret, and an organist named Blevins that appear to be taken from the files of the Driver and Vehicle Licensing Agency.

There are photos of Elizabeth from the Clevedon Secondary School, which show her in a school production of The Sound of Music; dressed as a stalk of wheat in a Love the Earth Day Parade; and a volunteer during the Keep Our Channel Clean Initiative.

There is no paucity of interviews with neighbors of the parsonage, school chums of Elizabeth, and parishioners of the Clevedon Church of the Divinity. Also featured are interviews with many of O'Rourke's long-time customers.

While no official statements have been made by the police regarding the claim of rape, it appears the media have been able to 'buy the rumor and sell the news', turning David O'Rourke into a sex-starved milkman and Elizabeth Barrett into a lovestruck, teenaged Jezebel.

Anna finishes her glass of wine and takes her small toiletries bag from her backpack and stands.

"Excuse, me. Sorry," Anna says to the middle-aged woman on the aisle and heads for the restroom at the front of the first-class cabin.

Once inside, she washes her face, brushes her teeth, and runs a comb through her hair, pulling it back into a loose ponytail with a hair tie.

She allows herself a few seconds in the mirror, hoping that the events of the last few days haven't taken too much of a toll, and then remembers the look on Ethan's face when she said it was over.

Maybe it was all my fault. Maybe Vivian was right. Take the next few weeks and see how I feel without Ethan and then decide. Or not. He's probably across the street with her right now.

For a fleeting moment, Anna remembers the way Jaylynn looked laying naked on the bed, and then imagines she and Ethan together under the sheets.

She shakes it off, packs up her toiletries, and heads back to her seat in the middle of the cabin.

"Sorry, one more time," Anna says.

"No worries. I was just about to wash up me self. Nothing like a good warm wash up before bedtime, that's what I always say."

"No, I suppose you're right," Anna says, as the woman swings her legs allowing Anna to pass.

"I didn't want to disturb you with those whatchamacall-its in your ears, but I couldn't help but notice what you was readin'. Nosy as the day is long, I am. Especially for a good murder mystery. My husband used to say it was my biggest flaw. It's just a weakness I 'ave."

Anna can't help but like the woman's earnest and honest demeanor and gives her a warm smile.

"I know what you mean. My name is Anna."

"And I'm Sally. Nice to make your acquaintance. Feel sorry for the lass, me self."

"It's hard not to," Anna says.

"What do 'ya think will 'appen to her?"

"I honestly don't know."

"Poor dearie," the woman says, as she stands.

Anna puts the earbuds back into her ears and lowers her seat back to the point where she's comfortable yet can still see outside the window. The flight attendants have turned off the cabin lights making it more conducive to sleep, and Anna can now see a waning moon racing alongside them, appearing and disappearing through the clouds.

We'll have a full moon over the Bristol Channel, Anna says to herself and then lets her thoughts wander to Elizabeth Barrett and the case to come.

The girl is going to be put through hell, regardless of the out-come. If she wasn't raped, she'll be found guilty and probably spend her life in prison. If she was, the jury may find justifiable homicide and she'll become a cult hero. Either way, she'll be fodder for the media grist mill for years to come.

As the wine takes its full effect, Anna begins to doze, and even through her earbuds she can make out the low drone of the two engines and the irregular vibrations sent through the body of the plane as they go in and out of sync; and then, as though it's materializing out of a mist, she remembers the whirring of the fan; large and black and hung in the corner of the courtroom where the rape case against her cousin was heard.

The trial had been set for early spring but was postponed to summer and took place during one of the hottest months on record. After the attack, Anna had been terrified to say any-thing at all, fearing that she would be the one blamed, but she also did a terrible job at hiding it.

Even before leaving Branson, her mother knew, instinct-ively, that something had happened; and she hounded Anna and Chloe to fess up and tell the truth, thinking that some-how the two of them had gotten into some kind of trouble together.

Vivian had tried to enlist her sister, Trudy, in the quest, but that also failed; and one night when Chloe's father, Tim, had finally had enough and yelled at Vivian to *'cut out all this crazy crap'*, a fissure was created that would culminate in the trial and the complete rupture of the two families.

Not long after their return, Frank and Vivian took Anna to see a child psychologist in Macon by the name of Dr. Cal-vin Street. It took Dr. Street two sessions before bringing in a hypnotherapist, and it took three more under hypnosis before they were able to get Anna's complete story.

By that time, months had gone by, and a medical examin-ation would have been useless as a means of proving the veracity of Anna's story. Except for the fact that Anna said Chloe had been an eyewitness, all Frank and Vivian were left with was a case of *'he said, she said'*.

So, without fully considering the consequences, Frank and Vivian, along with their attorney, made the decision to move forward with charges and to call Chloe as a prosecution witness.

thirty

"Anna, over here!" Simon says, calling out toward the group of passengers exiting the terminal. Anna glances through the crowd in the direction of the voice and spots Simon outside his car alongside the curb.

Not exactly Henry's style of service, she thinks, and then reprimands herself for sounding like such a prima donna.

"Here, let me get these, why don't you take a seat in the car," Simon says.

Anna grabs her Tumi backpack from the top of the luggage cart and brings it with her into the front passenger seat of the blue Ford Fiesta. Simon heaves the two large suitcases into his trunk, slams the lid shut, then hops into the driver's seat and starts the car.

"Anna, I can't believe it. You're actually here. Odds were fairly slim on this, I'd say."

"Some things are meant to be. Don't you think?"

"Yes. Yes, I do. 'Bit warmer than when you left, but it's bound to get colder in the next week. How was the flight? Fine, I trust."

"Long, but thankfully, I slept. So, fill me in, what's new?"

"Plenty. Things are moving quickly. Fielding Goddard, the prosecution psychologist, has interviewed Elizabeth twice already. You received all the newspaper clippings and media stories?"

"Yes, Eva sent them. You were right. One way or the other, they've nearly tried and convicted this girl. By the way, Simon, I've changed my mind."

"Not about the case, I hope."

"No, sorry. I mean about Elizabeth. I think I'd rather see her room first. Where she lived."

"Perfect, I'll arrange that on Monday. You must be hungry, how about a bite of breakfast?"

"Coffee sounds amazing."

"Should I stop now?"

"No, let's get into town. I can wait."

"Forgot to mention, Lyla stayed on the Shangri-La last night. I'll ring her up when we're on the M4, and then we'll all head out to the channel together."

"Brilliant."

"Ha, now you're catching on!" Simon says, regarding Anna's use of the popular British term.

"Really, If I caught Caleb with another woman..." Lyla says, as she and Anna make their way out of the lobby of the Shangri-La. "...it would be Lorena Bobbitt time. You know, 'snip-snip.'"

"My mother was practically defending Ethan," Anna says.

Anna and Lyla cross the driveway toward Simon who is leaning up against his car reading a tabloid he's just purchased at the hotel's newsstand.

"Simon Mercer meet Lyla Patterson."

Hearing Anna's voice, Simon looks up from the paper.

"Nice meeting you, Simon," Lyla says, extending her hand.

"My pleasure, Lyla. Good to have you onboard."

"Hope I can be of some help."

"Anna insisted on having you here, so I'm sure there's no doubt that you will."

A bellman swings Lyla's suitcase onto the rear seat of Simon's Ford Fiesta as Lyla gets in the opposite side. Anna has just grabbed a cup of coffee in the lobby and takes her place in the front passenger seat.

"Doing the trick?" Simon says.

"A life saver."

Simon starts the car and they head out of the driveway, making a right onto St. Thomas Street, which will lead them to the M4.

"Today is Saturday, so the traffic should be somewhat agreeable. I'd say three hours and a half. Four max."

"And we're headed west?"

"That's right, Lyla. You and Anna will be staying in a village near Clevedon called Weston-Super-Mare, don't ask me how they came up with the name, but it's a delightful town.

The Sandringham, your hotel, overlooks the Bristol Channel, and there's plenty nearby to keep two young ladies occupied. Bars, restaurants and shopping. That sort of thing."

"Sounds amazing. Simon, tell me again, how you found Anna?" Lyla asks.

"The BBC. My wife, Karen, and I saw the first installment Monday past. Remarkable, really. I got in touch with the producer, who put me in touch with Anna."

"Poor Simon. I was so hungover I missed all of his calls, so he drove all the way from Bristol to Heathrow to track me down."

"Like a madman I might add."

"Oh, God, that's right. The morning after the infamous night at the Horniman."

"The Horniman was it!? And you survived!? There are three pubs right there in that area of the Thames. Locals call it 'the Bermuda Triangle' because many don't make it out alive!"

Anna, Lyla, and Simon all have a good chuckle at the reference and then Simon's phone rings.

"Well, look at this. Speak of the devil."

Before answering, Simon turns to Anna.

"Cynthia Smythe."

Anna turns over her shoulder to Lyla,

"It's the producer from the BBC. The one I told you about."

"Miss Tight Ass."

"That's the one."

Simon lifts his phone and answers.

"Cynthia! You'll never guess who I have with me."

"That's right. Just picked her up."

"Uh, huh. Working on a Saturday."

"No, no, I haven't said a word."

"Haven't had a chance."

"I don't know. Hold for a moment, won't you?"

Simon mutes his phone and turns to Anna, clearing his throat.

"So, ahem, I'm not quite sure that this is the time or place, but Cynthia has made a proposal. I wanted to tell you about it when we were alone and quiet, but, well, you know Cynthia. She wants to do it herself. Now."

Anna looks to Lyla and then to Simon.

"Okay, let's hear it," Anna says, with no little apprehension and Simon unmutes his phone and puts Cynthia on speaker.

"Cynthia?"

"Yes."

"We're all here, now," Simon says.

"Hi, Cynthia."

"Anna, so nice to hear your voice, again. How was the flight home?"

"Fine. Thank you."

"And kudos to Simon for bringing you in on the Clevedon case."

"Well, thank you for the introduction."

"So, Anna. I think you know me by now. Not one to banter about the barbecue, as they say."

Anna turns to Lyla who rolls her eyes.

"We want to do a show around the O'Rourke murder. Your involvement, specifically. In real time, as it happens."

"I'm sorry, what did you say?" Anna says, not quite sure if she understood.

"We've told Simon that we want to record everything that happens, beginning to end. And that it will only be made into a show with the permission of yourself and Elizabeth Barrett."

"What exactly do you mean by everything?" Anna says.

"Well, let's say, short of brushing your teeth. In fact, had we been able to get this arranged sooner, Mitchell would have had a couple of cameras in Simon's car already."

"Mitchell?"

"He'll be co-producing and directing."

"Oh, no. Cynthia, listen, I really appreciate you thinking of me, but, really, this flies in the face of...."

"Simon, are you there?"

"Hi, Cynthia, I'm listening."

"Help me here."

Simon hesitates a moment, and then turns to Anna.

"In Britain, it's not against the law or against doctor-client privilege to tape-record events. Actually, it's now encouraged, as it provides a much more accurate account of what actually transpires.

A documentary, based on the work you do, Anna, could go a long way to saving other women in Elizabeth's predicament. Cynthia has made us an offer we really shouldn't refuse. For Elizabeth's sake."

"Well said, Simon. I'm meeting with my producers first thing Monday. Please send me your schedule, so we can co-ordinate locations. Bye for now."

And with that, she's gone.

Simon hangs up and waits for Anna's response, but it doesn't come.

"No comment? I thought you'd be pleased," Simon says.

"Sorry. I'm a little tired and this is, uh, a lot to take in."

"Completely understood. Why don't you lay back and sneak a few winks? Lyla and I can keep ourselves occupied, right, Lyla?" Simon says, glancing into his rearview mirror at Lyla who is busy looking at her phone.

"Oh. Right. Says here that *Weston-Super-Mare is actually nicknamed, Super-Mud,* about a mile of it right outside our window when the tide is out. *Perfect for metal detecting and digging for clams!*"

"Wonderful," Anna says, under her breath.

thirty-one

The knot of reporters outside the North Somerset Hospital set upon Benjamin like a school of piranhas on a drowning rhino, and the two young ambulance attendants, whose duty it is to get him safely home, are at wit's end to even get him to the lorry.

"How many times was she raped, Pastor?"
"Who's sayin' she was raped?" Benjamin says.
"Did you ever see David O'Rourke in her bedroom?"
"Of course, not!"
"What time did you leave on Friday mornings?"
"It's none of your business."
"Who else was let into the house?"
"Pastor, it happened on your watch and right under your nose, how did you not know?"
"Did Elizabeth invite him up?"
"What does Elizabeth wear to bed?"
"Do you and the housekeeper sleep in the same room?

Fortunately, hospital security guards are called to intervene and, together with the attendants, they're able to extract Benjamin from the crowd and get him up and into the waiting vehicle.

"My God, 'ave these poor souls nothing better to do?" Benjamin says, exasperated and out of breath, once the lorry doors have been closed.

"'Fraid not, Pastor," says the younger of the two attendants.

"That's why they're reporters, sir," adds the other.

The ride from the hospital to the parsonage should only take a few minutes, but the driver has been instructed to take a less direct route should an enterprising reporter consider hijacking the vehicle and Benjamin for an exclusive.

"Don't you worry, sir. We'll get you there in one piece, I assure you."

"From your lips to God's ears, son," Benjamin replies.

As the ambulance rounds the corner to the parsonage, the attendants discover that they're now going to face an even bigger gauntlet.

"Bloody, bastards."

"What do we do?"

Just at that moment, three police cars with sirens blaring and lights flashing, round the corner from the opposite direction and pull up to a stop in front of the parsonage.

"Nothing to fear, but fear itself, gentlemen. It appears that, once again, the cavalry has arrived in the nick of time," Benjamin says.

When he's safely inside the parsonage, the ambulance attendants and the police officers drive away, leaving the media encampment looking like a kicked over ant hill.

"Pastor, Benjamin," Margret says, with a tremble in her voice as she greets him at the door.

"What's happened to us, Margret?"

"Dark night of the soul it 'tis."

"Bless you, Margret. Tea, if you don't mind."

"Where would you like it, Pastor?"

"Anywhere we can't be seen, please."

thirty-two

"Knock, knock," Lyla says, as she pokes her head into the open door of Anna's hotel room.

"Hey," Anna says.

Lyla steps into the room to find Anna sitting in one of two chairs facing the windows.

"You're supposed to say, 'who's there?' Pretty cool place, don't you think?"

"I suppose."

"Sorry? There's a shopping mall right behind us, bars and restaurants all up and down the street and, look, the Bristol Channel right out your window. C'mon! Let's take a walk, I'd like to find a pair of binoculars."

"Don't bother."

Lyla shifts her gaze from the window and the view of the channel to Anna's open suitcase laying on the bed.

"What's going on, you haven't unpacked."

"I think we should we leave."

"Something wrong with the hotel?"

"No, the hotel is fine. It's great actually."

Lyla takes a seat in the chair opposite Anna.

"I think we should go home," Anna says.

"You're kidding, right?"

"No. I'm not."

"It's funny, you were the picture of enthusiasm when you picked me up at the hotel this morning. What changed?" Lyla asks, knowing the answer.

Anna stands and walks to one of two windows overlooking the waterfront.

"I don't know, it's...."

"Anna. You know exactly. It's Mitchell, isn't it?"

"Mitchell?" Anna says, with a dismissive laugh. "Absolutely not!"

"Of course, it is! There's no logical reason not to memorialize this case with video recordings."

"No. I just don't like the idea of anyone, I don't care who or what it is, interfering with the discovery process."

"That's a disingenuous argument, and you know it. Elizabeth won't even know the cameras are there."

"But I'll know they're there!"

"And so? Like it's the first time you've been on camera, for God's sake? In the end the video may never be used, but it also may save Elizabeth Barrett's life. How can you deny her that?"

"I'm not denying her anything, they can go on without me; and I really don't think it's your place to...."

"Not my place? After six years, you're telling me what I can or can't say? I thought you valued my opinion, isn't that what you pay me for?"

"Yes. In business."

"But not in your personal life. That's what you're saying. Just be honest with yourself. There is something going on with you and Mitchell, and you're freaked out over losing control."

"There is absolutely nothing going on between us! You were there at lunch. We hardly spoke."

"'Cause you put in him deep freeze. Admit it! You're willing to shortchange Elizabeth Barrett because you can't face your feelings or the possibility, God forbid, that Anna Newsom may fall in love and actually have to entrust herself to another human being."

Lyla reaches the door and then turns back for one final reply.

"I'm going for a walk. Send me a text when you're ready to leave," she says and then exits the room, leaving Anna frozen at the window.

Anna waits until Lyla appears and watches as she crosses the street to the Grand Pier which extends a couple of hundred yards over the channel.

She turns from the window and lays down on the bed. She hits shuffle on her bluegrass playlist and closes her eyes; and, as chance would have it, the first song up is Never Happy Till I'm Full of Sorrow by Blue Moon Rising, a group from Tennessee.

Got a couple of friends that I really don't know
And they really don't know me either,
A guy to cheer me up when I'm feelin' low
He don't know it but I'm gonna leave him
Hound dog layin' in the kudzu vine,
Lord, he acts like he's glad to see me
But he'd rather run rabbit than to hear me whine
'Bout self inflicted pain and misery
Well, I've got everything that I'll ever need
And most of all I've ever wanted,
But the more I have the more it seems
I walk away feelin' haunted...

By the time the song hits the bridge, Anna has drifted into twilight; and like her first trip nine days earlier, she's besieged by a hypnogogic montage of fleeting images and hallucinated sounds. The last thing she remembers before sinking beneath the surface is a sign she spotted on the cafe two doors down from the hotel when they arrived. It read... *'Toasted Tea Cakes. Eat in. Take Out.'*

When Anna wakens, her room is dark save for the lights on Parade Street. She can make out the faint sound of laughter coming from a television in the next room, and footsteps, female she guesses, from the floor above.

She swings her legs over the edge of the bed and pulls out her earbuds. She hadn't intended to sleep, and could kick herself, because now she'll be up for hours and out of sync with the entire English world when morning comes.

Peering through her window blinds, Anna discovers that a thick fog snuck in while she was asleep and has turned the lights on the Grand Pier into diaphanous globes suspended above the black water of the channel.

She pauses to entertain herself with the thought that, if this were a film noir, she'd be reaching for a cigarette and a highball right about now, both of which are sounding pretty good.

She glances at her phone, it's 10:30, then sees that Lyla sent her a message two hours earlier asking if she was packed yet. She decides she could use a decent meal and wanders into the bathroom, splashes some water on her face, runs a brush through her hair, and throws on a raincoat and scarf.

Leaving, Anna nearly steps on a copy of The Evening Tattler that has been slipped under the door. She picks it up and reads the headline…

'BRISTOL LIZZY HEADED FOR BRONZEFIELD?
Could Spend Life in Notorious Woman's Prison'

'Bristol Lizzy' is an obvious reference to Elizabeth Barrett and the result of some enterprising journalist having crafted a rather obvious conflation of Elizabeth and Lizzy Borden, the American woman accused of murdering her father and step-mother with an axe.

Anna studies it for a beat, then folds the paper, slips it into the pocket of her raincoat, and heads out the door. She makes her way through the modest lobby, and, stepping out onto Parade Street, turns her collar up against the wind.

Rather than reaching for her phone, Anna stops a young man and woman who look as though they might know a thing or two about the local pubs.

"Nick's Bar. Three blocks straight up. Can't miss it. Cheers!"

"Cheers," Anna says.

Nick's is no more than a minute from The Sandringham and from the sidewalk it appears warm and welcoming. Anna enters and is greeted by a young girl in her twenties.

"Eve'nin'. Table?"

"No, thanks. Do they serve food at the bar?"

"Anywhere you like."

Anna moves into the room, removes the paper from her pocket, then hangs up her coat, and takes a seat at the bar. In the back of the restaurant, a lone man with a guitar covers songs from the 1970's.

"Ello, miss' what'll it be?" says the bartender, a man in his forties.

"Guinness and a menu, please."

"Sure thing, specials on the wall," he says with a nod.

Anna glances at the chalkboard and then opens The Evening Tattler. First, it's obvious that the article is based entirely on conjecture as to the outcome of Elizabeth's case. Secondly, it becomes clear rather quickly that the whole point of the article is to present the more sordid and sensational side of Bronzefield Prison. That being said, it doesn't negate or ameliorate what Elizabeth will face if convicted and sent there.

"'Ere's your draft, miss. Eyin' some dinner, are we?"

"How about the, um, fish and chips."

"Comin' right up," he says, and Anna continues reading.

Bronzefield, also known as HMP Bronzefield for 'Her Majesty's Prison', is a Category A prison in existence solely for female offenders. Category A offenders, which is how Elizabeth would be classified, are:

'...those whose escape would be highly dangerous to the public or national security. Offenses that may result in consideration for Category A or Restricted Status include:

Murder, Manslaughter, Wounding with Intent, Rape, Kidnapping, Indecent Assault, Robbery or Conspiracy to Rob; firearm offenses, importing or suppling Class A controlled drugs; possessing or suppling explosives; and offenses connected with terrorism and Offenses under the Official Secrets Act.'

"Fish and chips," the bartender announces as he sets the plate and condiment bottles in front of Anna. "Ketchup and vinegar here if you like, tartar sauce is on the plate. Another Guinness?"

"Please."

Anna pops a couple of chips into her mouth and continues reading. As she makes her way through the article, it becomes absolutely apparent that, if Elizabeth is convicted and not placed into solitary confinement or 'segregation' as it's known in the UK, she'll be exposed to the vilest and most violent women the country has produced.

Skipping ahead in the article, Anna reads down the list of past and current inmates. The first is a woman who was convicted in what came to be known as the Peterborough ditch murders.

'In March 2013, three male victims were found stabbed to death and dumped in ditches outside Peterborough.'

Another case was the attempted murder of a British MP by a female Islamic extremist, who was also jailed at Bronzefield.

Yet another, involved a woman who conspired with her husband and his friend to kill her own children.

'The Allenton House Fire occurred on May 11, 2012, in a semi-detached home in Derbyshire, England. Five of the children died at the scene, while the oldest died later in hospital. The woman is serving a life sentence.'

The last on the list in the article is a woman who was given a life sentence for murdering three men and stabbing two others.

Anna has finished her fish and is polishing off the last few chips when the bartender brings her one last beer.

"Anything else, miss?"

Mesmerized by the case studies in the article, Anna is brought back to the present by the voice of the bartender.

"Oh, um, no, thank you. Just the check."

The bartender reaches into his apron, retrieves his order pad, rips off the top sheet, and sets Anna's bill on the bar.

"Sorry, but I couldn't help notice what you've been readin'. Into women's prisons, are ya?"

"Not particularly."

"Sorry, never mind, then."

"But why did you ask?"

"It's just that, well, the female cousin of a friend of mine was sent up to Bronzefield."

"Oh, no. You're kidding?"

"Funny way you Americans have, saying, 'you're kidding', even though a person isn't."

"Sorry, it's kind of stupid, isn't it?" Anna replies.

"Not from you it ain't, miss. Anyway, sweet young thing she was. Went head over heels for a fast talkin' hood and got thirty years, she did, as an accessory to a string of jewelry robberies."

"Sounds like an awful lot of time for that kind of crime."

"It would have been, had she made it. Point is she didn't. Not even close. One morning they found her with her throat opened, ear to ear."

"How awful," Anna says.

"The friend told me she had declined an invite to be another inmate's, well…paramour. You get me drift."

It's nearly midnight by the time Anna heads back to the hotel. A light drizzle has started falling and the streets are empty. The yellowish beams from the streetlamps reflect off the wet asphalt and, for the first time, Anna notices the bellow of a foghorn somewhere in the bay.

The distance to the hotel is only three blocks, and to say she was glad to get back to her room would be an understatement. She makes quick work of changing into her tank top and boxers and slides underneath the covers.

The flight to London, the drive to Weston, and the argument with Lyla has left her drained and exhausted, and the article of The Evening Tattler isn't going to make it any easier to get to sleep.

And then it hits her. It was Lyla who left the paper under the door.

thirty-three

Anna is standing in the lobby of The Sandringham when her phone rings.

"Good morning, Simon."

"Anna. How was your rest?"

"Better than I expected."

"It's that good salt air. Works wonders. Listen, Anna, I spent all last night thinking about it. I know you're not keen on the whole BBC thing and...."

"No, Simon. I'm okay with it. Really, I am."

"You mean you want to go on? Recordings and all? We don't have to, you know. Wasn't part of the deal." Simon says.

Anna turns from the window in time to see Lyla getting out of the lift.

"I know it wasn't. Let's just say that I spent all last night thinking about it."

As Lyla approaches, Anna offers her an exploratory smile.

"And, well, I was wrong."

On hearing those words, Lyla returns the smile.

"Bloody good. Listen, why don't you head out to breakfast while I get in touch with Cynthia. I'll ring you up with the schedule as soon as I know something."

"Will do. Thanks, Simon."

Anna hangs up, puts her phone in her pocket, and turns to Lyla.

"How about a toasted tea cake?"

"Sure. Whatever that is."

Anna and Lyla exit the hotel and make a left up Parade Street. The little cafe where Anna saw the sign is open. They walk in and scan the menu board on the wall behind the counter.

A young, pimply faced teenage boy wearing an apron and a paper hat finishes with a customer and then turns to the girls, speaking with the thickest English accent Anna has heard since arriving.

"What would you ladies be 'avin'?"

"Um, one coffee, one tea and oh, can you tell us, what's a toasted tea cake?" Anna says.

The question seems innocent enough, but the teenage boy looks at Anna as if she had just dropped to Earth from a spaceship.

"What, is a toasted tea cake?" he says, drawing out the line for maximum effect.

"Yes. What is a toasted tea cake?" Anna says, repeating the question.

"Well, miss, let me put it this way. It's a tea cake... what's been toasted."

In an instant Anna and Lyla freeze because they can't believe what they've just heard. Then, it's all Anna can do to keep from guffawing out loud especially when she hears Lyla next to her choking down a laugh.

As the two girls exit the cafe with drinks in hand they explode into laughter and try their best at mimicking the young lad.

"Well, miss. It's a tea cake..." Anna starts, and then together they both finish the line.

"What's been toasted!!!"

Laughing hysterically, the two cross the road and walk toward the Grand Pier and both are not a little relieved that they're back on an even keel and on the same page for what's ahead of them.

"Mitchell, how was your weekend?" Cynthia says, as she sits down at the conference table.

"What weekend?" Mitchell says.

"Where's Hal?"

"Right here, Cynthia, Hal says, as he enters the room.

"Morning, all."

Seated around the conference table are the same assistants that were present at the Friday meeting when Cynthia announced her idea.

"I spoke with the public defender, Simon Mercer, on Saturday. Quite fortuitously, he had just picked up Anna Newsom from the airport, so she was on the call as well."

At the sound of Anna's name, Hal throws Mitchell a sideways glance.

"And I just got off the phone with him again and, just to confirm, they're all on board."

"Great." Mitchell says, to himself, under his breath.

"So, here's what we've got," Hal says, jumping right into their plans for the show. "We propose three levels of coverage. The first is to place miniature cameras within each venue. No one will even know they're there."

"Which venues, specifically?" Cynthia asks, looking at Mitchell.

"Elizabeth Barrett's bedroom. The location where Anna's interviews will take place. Simon Mercer's car. Any BBC-provided vehicle that may be used as transport. The public areas of the parsonage and the church," Mitchell says.

"The second level of coverage will be on-camera interviews with all the main players. Simon Mercer. Chief Inspector Hayden. Dr. Anna Newsom. Dr. Fielding Goddard. And the prosecutor, Diana Lynch." Hal says.

"Can we add John Edwards to the list?"

"Edwards? Why?" Mitchell says.

"Because he's our resident psychologist, Mitchell. He may be a boorish pain in the ass, but he's the only one we've got, that's why." Cynthia says.

"The third level of coverage will be a live camera crew," Hal adds.

"Is that necessary?" Cynthia says, as Mitchell jumps in.

"I think it is. A live crew will give us the flexibility to take advantage of opportunities fixed camera positions can't."

"Let's not forget the release forms, please," Cynthia's young, female assistant says.

"When can all this be ready?"

"Once you get the green light to go into the locations, we can place the cameras in a day and a half. If you get it today, we'll be ready to go by Wednesday afternoon."

"I'll make sure we get it today. Thanks, everyone."

Hal is the first one to stand as the meeting breaks up. He collects his things and heads out into the hallway.

"Mitch, I'm going to see the whiz kids about securing the hardware."

"Roger, that," Mitchell answers.

Waiting for everyone else to clear the room, Cynthia calls out to Mitchell just as he's about to make it to the door.

"Mitchell?"

On hearing his name, Mitchell reluctantly stops, and then swings around to face her.

"Yes, Cynthia."

"This isn't like you."

"I've no idea what you mean."

"You know exactly. Normally, you'd be all cock-a-hoop over a chance like this."

"C'mon, Cynthia, can't you see? I've got cock-a-hoop written all over me." Mitchell says, sarcastically, then turns and heads out into the hallway.

thirty-four

Tuesday dawned dismal and cold, as a storm that had been forecast to hit farther north shifted south overnight and then stalled over the Bristol Channel.

From their rooms, Anna and Lyla can see the churning white caps and several different species of seabirds being tossed by the strong winds. They each slept fitfully, as the wind and the torrential rain battered and rattled their windows for the better part of the night.

"Good morning," Anna says, answering her phone.

"Is it? I'm exhausted," Lyla says.

"Me, too. And freezing."

"I think it's warmer in the lobby. Wanna meet for coffee?" Lyla says.

"Give me five minutes."

Margret and Benjamin are just finishing their morning tea when Margret hears the sound of commotion on the street in front of the parsonage. The heavy wind and rain has driven many of the reporters into their vehicles, and they're caught unawares by the arrival of the BBC production van and equipment vehicles which now jockey for the prime positions on the street.

"They're here," Margret says, to Benjamin as she stands and takes her cup to the sink. "The whole affair is tragic enough without bringing in television people."

"This is for Elizabeth's good, Margret. Not ours. I thought we agreed."

"We discussed it. We never agreed."

Margret takes off her apron and exits the kitchen toward the front of the house. She opens the door just as Mitchell is about to press the buzzer.

"Oh, good morning," Mitchell says, "you must be Margret."

"I am."

"I'm Mitchell Walker from the BBC."

"I noticed."

"May I, uh..."

"Of course. Come in. Terrible weather to be drivin' all the way from London."

"Yes, ma'am. it is."

Mitchell steps out of the cold wind and into the foyer, and Margret closes the door behind him.

"So, I believe you spoke to Hal, our producer."

"Pastor did."

"We're not shooting or recording today. The plan is to come in, set up our cameras, and be ready for Dr. Newsom when she comes tomorrow afternoon."

"As I understand it, Pastor Benjamin has given you the run of the house."

"Yes, ma'am. And the church."

"This was his idea. Not mine. Try not to break anything."

The placement of the cameras in and around the parsonage goes fairly quickly, so by mid-afternoon Mitchell, Hal, and the technical crew are moving into the church.

"I'd like two cameras in the choir loft. And one overlooking the church proper."

"Roger, that," Mitchell's assistant director says.

"I'm heading outside for a second."

As Mitchell exits, he meets Blevins who has just gotten out of his car and is making his way across the gravel parking lot.

"Young man!" Blevins says, calling out to Mitchell who stops and turns.

"What's happening here?"

"Sorry?"

"All these men. And these trucks."

Mitchell extends his hand and Blevins reaches with his.

"No one told you?"

"Told me what?"

"We're from the BBC. We're producing a documentary about the murder."

"You must be bloody joking." Blevins says. "See here now, did you request permission for such a thing?"

"Got it from the pastor, himself. Excuse me."

Mitchell gives Blevins a nod, and then heads out to the production van, where he passes Hal coming in the opposite direction.

"Watch out for that one," Mitchell says, pointing back towards Blevins who is just approaching the side door of the church.

"Who is he?" Hal says.

"Haven't the slightest. Had no idea we were coming, and he's not happy about it."

"I'll toss him a quid or two, that should help," Hal says, and as Blevins disappears through the door, he turns back to Mitchell.

"So, looks as though we've got seven cameras left. After the church, that is."

"Okay. We'll need four for wherever the interviews are taking place. By the way, do we know where yet? Mitchell asks.

"A room at The Sandringham."

"Then two for Mercer's vehicle and one for Henry's cab. That accounts for all of them."

Devon O'Rourke stomps into the house, heads for the kitchen, and finds his mother sitting at a small table in the middle of the room.

"Number 28 is sick again."

"Make sure your father knows," May says, staring into her cup of tea.

Devon throws her a look of concern, then goes to the large cookie jar, extracts a few English pounds, and then shoves the bills into his jacket pocket.

"Please, Mum, get some rest," he says, kissing her on top of the head.

He darts out the front door, hops into one of the farm trucks, and cranks the engine. He throws it into gear and heads down the gravel driveway to the main road where he's met by a phalanx of reporters that descend upon him, shouting questions.

"Did you fancy Elizabeth?"

"Why was a model of the farm truck in her bedroom?"

"Did you know your father was raping young Elizabeth?"

"How did you not know?"

"Where is your mother?"

"Does rape run in the family?"

"Have you and your brother sought psychological counseling?"

Determined to run the gauntlet, Devon keeps his foot on the accelerator and races forward, forcing the reporters to scatter.

"BLOODY, LAZY SODS! THE LOT 'O 'YA!" he yells out, and speeds past the last of them.

"Everything Simon's secretary sent is in the folder on my desktop," Anna says.

Lyla takes a seat at the small desk in Anna's room and opens her computer.

"Password the same?"

"BAXTER 2001. Be careful."

"What's that?" Lyla says, looking up.

"Crime scene photos."

As Lyla opens the files related to the O'Rourke murder, Anna pulls her camera bag from her suitcase.

"Have you looked at them?"

"Right after I received them."

"And?"

"I'd like to hear what you think."

"That bad, huh?"

"I just wanted to make sure you were prepared."

Anna takes her 35mm digital camera from its bag and begins prepping for their first visit to Elizabeth's bedroom. She has two lenses, one wide angle and a telephoto with a macro function that allows her to take extreme close-ups.

As is their usual procedure, Anna will survey what she sees, taking photographs and offering commentary, as Lyla takes notes and makes additional observations. She uncaps each and wipes both ends of the lenses with a microfiber cloth and watches as Lyla opens the folder labeled O'Rourke and then the sub-folder labeled CSP's for Crime Scene Photos.

When the photos begin opening, Lyla raises her hand to her chin and then from her chin to her mouth.

"My God," she murmurs under her breath.

"That's exactly what I said."

"That poor man."

Lyla scans through the photos, pausing on each. Anna sets the camera down on the desk and peers at the photos over Lyla's shoulder.

"Let's go through them, step by step."

"Photo number 001. Wide posterior," Lyla says.

"This is looking forward from the cargo area. Look at the amount of blood splatter on the windshield," Lyla says, with Anna looking on over her shoulder.

"She obviously punctured an artery," Anna says, as Lyla goes to the next photo.

"Photo number 002. Close posterior. Here we can see that the needle was thrust nearly to the large eye at the end. The next one should be from the right."

Lyla clicks to the next photo revealing a close-up taken through the driver's side window.

"Obvious startle reflex," Lyla says.

"There, notice something?"

Lyla leans into the screen to take a closer look.

"First of all, the exit puncture wound is oblong, not the

pure, rounded shape of the shaft."

"Right, now zoom in," Anna says.

Lyla taps on the keypad to enlarge the image.

"And pan over to the tip of the needle," Anna says.

Lyla scrolls to the right, bringing the tip of the needle into view.

"You see what I see?" Anna says.

"The tip is bent."

"Right. Just about two inches behind the point of the needle, the shaft is bent at approximately eighteen degrees."

"How?" Lyla says, turning to Anna.

"The needle must have hit one of the cervical vertebrae. Judging from the photo, I'd say the third for fourth. Considering Elizabeth's size and age, that should have stopped the penetration then and there."

"But it didn't," Lyla says.

"That tells us one of two things. Either the delivery van came to a sudden stop and inertia propelled Elizabeth and therefore the needle deeper, or...."

"Or?"

"When faced with the task at hand, her adrenals released a tsunami of epinephrine giving her a momentary burst of superhuman strength."

"Meaning that the needle was thrust in two distinctive maneuvers," Lyla says.

"That's right. The initial thrust and then the secondary plunge that required far more force to tear through the cervical structures."

"The prosecution is going to say that she was a young girl infatuated with an older man, you know that." Lyla says.

"But, we know, there's only one thing that can produce this kind of rage. Persistent, pernicious abuse. We just have to prove it."

Blevins enters through the side door of the church, and, as he begins his slow climb up the stairs to the choir loft, he meets a young, energetic woman coming down the stairs in the opposite direction.

"Mind the cables up top, please."

"Yes, of course," Blevins says, as the girl passes him.

As he reaches the loft, two technicians are completing the process of mounting two small cameras in the rafters.

"That's it for these two. You check the Wi-Fi signal?"

"Strong. No issues."

"Word to the wise, miss," Blevins says to the young woman at the top of a ladder. "Wouldn't be putting me hand up in that dark corner."

"Sorry?" she says, glancing down at him.

"Spiders. False Widows, to be exact. They make their home, there in the rafters. One bite and you're finished."

The young man and young woman pause and look at one another.

"Thanks for the warning," the young man says to Blevins, then they quietly pack up the rest of their gear and head down the stairs, disappearing behind the shiplap partition.

Blevins sets down his music books and lifts the gooseneck lamp off the organ. Taped to the bottom of the lamp is the business card given to him by The Evening Tattler reporter, Hugh Archer. He peels away the card and sets the lamp back down on the organ.

"Mr. Archer?"

"Yes. Who is this?"

"Blevins. Cedric Blevins. Do you remember me?"

"Yes, of course. What can I do for you, Mr. Blevins?"

"I think it's more a matter of what I can do for you."

"Is that right? Where are you calling from?"

"A phone in the basement of the church. I thought you may find it interestin' that the BBC is here."

"Didn't quite get that. What about the BBC?"

"They're here. Swarmin' the place."

"The BBC? There? You're sure?"

"As sure as the sun shines, Mr. Archer, doing a show on the

murder is what they told me.

"I say, Blevins, looks like Auntie has something up her sleeve."

"Looks that way, Mr. Archer. Thought you should know."

After he hangs up, Blevins starts to tape the business card back under the lamp, then thinks better of it. He reaches for his wallet and slides the card underneath his driver's license.

"Hard takin' me eyes off this one," the bartender says, staring up at the television behind the bar.

"Well, when you bloody manage…"

"What's that you say?" the bartender says, glancing back at Devon.

"I said, when you bloody manage, I'll have another," Devon says, draining the last of his pint.

"Maybe you've had enough already, mate."

"And maybe you should shut that bloody thing off."

One of several men sitting at the bar, Devon is in a place called the Little Harp Inn, a public house overlooking the Bristol Channel. It's not his usual stop, and he dropped in hoping for a bit of anonymity.

Just after he arrived, the patrons in the bar had moved on to topics other than his father's murder, but now, to his chagrin, a news report on the television has rekindled the conversation.

"Poor chap, deliverin' milk one minute and the next he's skewered like a Shopshire hare," says a drunken man sitting two stools down.

The bartender slides Devon's newly-filled glass in front of him then looks back up to the television.

"There's talk he was 'avin 'is way with the lil' missy. Rouses the mind, a sweet young thing like she."

"Serves 'im, right, I say. I 'ave a daughter of me own that age," a second man says.

Devon grinds his teeth and holds his tongue, takes a pull from his pint, and glances up to the television to see Simon

Mercer being interviewed by a local television reporter.

"My name is Simon Mercer. I'm the public defender."

"So, you'll be acting as advocate for Miss Barrett?"

"That's correct, Ms. Wilcox."

"I say! Bristol Lizzy's bloody barrister!" a man yells.

"Turn it up!" yells another.

The bartender shoots the man a look, and then reaches for the remote behind the bar. The interview is being conducted by a young, attractive reporter named Nan Wilcox.

"Wouldn't mind a go at the strawberry creams on that one," another says.

"I understand it's still rumor at this point, but are you indeed considering a defense based on justifiable homicide?"

On hearing the question, Devon looks up sharply.

"We've made no final decision, Ms. Wilcox, but we are in the midst of gathering evidence that may support the allegation that Mr. O'Rourke had been, for a number of years, serially raping the defendant."

At this news, the men at the bar erupt with all manner of lascivious jokes and comments.

"See there! Exactly what I just said! He was diddlin' the young thing!"

"I guess the goats n' Guernsies t'weren't enough for him!!!"

For the men at the bar, the news story promises an endless source of entertainment, but, for Devon, it's as though his entire world has imploded.

He grabs a pencil setting next to a cup of dice, scribbles Simon's name on a napkin, and stuffs it into the breast pocket of his flannel shirt. He drains his beer, tosses a couple of coins onto the bar and stomps out.

"Delicious," Lyla says, as she pops another piece into her mouth.

Simon and Karen have invited Anna and Lyla for dinner,

and the four are sitting in the modest dining room at the front of the house.

"Beef Wellington. One of my favorites," Simon says.

"We thought you ladies might enjoy something typically British."

"It's perfect, Karen." Anna says, sipping from her glass of wine.

"Caleb would love this. Is it difficult to make?" Lyla asks.

"Would she admit it if it was?" Simon says, taking a healthy bite from his fork.

Karen turns from Simon, and then to Lyla to answer her question.

"Not at all. Tenderloin, pate', mushrooms and onions wrapped in puff pastry. Then a quick trip to the oven."

"One would think that simplicity in the kitchen would earn a greater frequency at the table," Simon says, shooting a small smile in Karen's direction.

"But then it wouldn't be as special, Simon," Anna says.

"Well said, but I respectfully disagree," Simon adds, lifting his glass of scotch. "Cheers, everyone."

Anna, Lyla, and Karen follow suit and lift their glasses, as well.

"Truth be told," Karen says, "Simon would be happy with most anything, as long as it wasn't fish."

"Ghastly creatures!" Simon replies, as he slices another piece of meat. Karen shakes her head, and then turns to Anna.

"So, Anna, what you were saying about depersonalization... fascinating."

"Well, there was a famous German psychoanalyst..."

"Weren't they all?" Simon quips.

"This one really was. His name was Paul Schlider. In 1928, that long ago, he wrote, let me see if I remember this...

'to the depersonalized individual the world appears strange, peculiar, foreign and dream-like. Objects appear strangely diminished in size, sometime flat. The emo-

tions likewise undergo marked alteration. Patients complain that they are capable of experiencing neither pain nor pleasure. They have become strangers to themselves.'
"

"Very impressive, Anna," Karen says, and Lyla joins in.

"That's my girl."

"Not really. I better remember it, I used it often enough in my master's thesis," Anna says with a chuckle.

"To carry it a step further, then, what your theory says is that, even though a victim is experiencing depersonalization, they...." Simon begins to say, and Anna finishes the thought.

"...they may have an unconscious desire to connect to something in the real world and do so through, what I call, the Psychic Lightning Rod, or PLR."

"And to find that in the patient requires analysis..." Karen says.

"Cognitive therapy, yes," Anna adds.

"And hypnosis?" Simon says.

"If necessary. By the way, no word on the DNA test?

"Too soon. Not for another week, at least. However, the results of the medical examination arrived today."

"And...?"

"Negative."

"Negative? That means that the most recent attack must have occurred more than a week prior to the murder?" Karen says.

"Not necessarily," Anna says, "there are a number of reasons why a rape might not be detected. Timeline is certainly one, but all too we often think of rape as something that always involves force and always involves penetration."

"Lyla, something wrong with your supper?" Simon says, bringing Lyla, who's been in deep thought, back around to the conversation.

"Oh, no, it's wonderful. But, your comment about fish reminded me of something I read in one of the witness statements your secretary sent over."

"Which one?" he says.

"The housekeeper's. I remember her saying that they couldn't go to the fish market because of a traffic accident and turned around and went home. They were there when David O'Rourke arrived with his delivery."

Simon wipes his mouth and reaches for his glass.

"Go on."

"She said, that was unusual because, normally, they were at the fish market when he arrived and they rarely saw one another," Lyla says.

"Meaning?" Simon asks.

"If the rapes occurred on Fridays, when Elizabeth was alone in the house, the pastor and the housekeeper's unexpected arrival home may have prevented a rape on that day."

"Not sure I understand," Simon adds, then Anna continues with Lyla's train of thought.

"What Lyla is saying is that the rape tests may come back negative because there is nothing there to find."

Devon stomps into the men's room of the Little Harp Inn and steps up to a urinal, fuming. He unzips and glances up, seeing his reflection in the small, cracked and stained mirror on the wall just in front of him. He grinds his jaw and clenches his fist, then punches it once, twice, then again, the third time cutting two fingers on a shard of glass.

"Dammit! Fuck!"

He zips up with his good hand, rinses the blood under the tap, and then wraps a paper towel around the wound. Bounding out of the restroom and toward the front door, he spots a pay phone hanging on the wall above a shelf with several dog-eared phonebooks.

He pulls the napkin with Simon's name out of his pocket, flips open one of the phonebooks, and scans the pages until he finds the listing for Simon Mercer. He rips the page out of the book, and stomps out into the night.

Heading out to the parking lot, he pulls a pack of cigarettes from his jacket pocket, shakes one up, and pulls it out with his lips. He retrieves his Zippo lighter and, just as he's about to jump into his truck, he spots a row of bricks laid out around a small patch of grass just in front of his tire.

He pries one of the bricks out of the dirt and gravel, and tosses it onto the bed of his truck. He gets in, cranks the engine, and peels out onto the main highway.

Keeping one eye on the road and clenching the cigarette in his teeth, he opens the GPS app on his cellphone and reads aloud from the torn sheet of phone book.

"Twenty-one eleven, West Park, Bristol," the female voice says in response to Devon's input.

"In 0.7 kilometers turn left onto Old Church Road."

"You're not going to believe what Karen made for dessert."

"Let us at least help with the dishes," Lyla offers.

Anna wipes her mouth and scoots her chair away from the table.

"I'm sorry, where's your powder room?"

"How thoughtless of me. Around that corner and to the right."

Anna excuses herself and heads to the restroom, as Karen and Lyla begin clearing the dishes.

"Simon, I wish we'd thought of it before dinner, why don't we have a fire with dessert?"

"Brilliant. Just as soon as I fetch another scotch."

Devon's tires squeal as he takes the slight left turn onto Cleve Hill.

"In 0.6 kilometers turn right onto Badminton Road," the female voice says, barely audible over the music blaring from Devon's radio.

Fog has rolled in making it hard to see, so Devon slows and takes a moment to get his bearings. He rolls down his window, shakes another cigarette from the pack, and lights it. He makes the right onto Badminton Road and enters the roundabout but then misses the second exit.

"Fuck."

He takes a long drag on his cigarette, circles the roundabout one more time and makes the exit.

"In 0.5 kilometers turn left onto West Park Road."

Simon has just finished pouring another scotch and makes his way back into the living room.

"Simon?"

"Yes, dear?"

Several years of marriage has taught Simon that he can pretty much guess at what Karen is going to ask based on her tone of voice.

"Sinatra or Matt Monroe?" he says, preempting her.

"You're a doll. Either one. But build the fire first, okay?"

"200 , arrive at the destination. On the left."

Devon slows his truck, and shuts off his music. He peers out through the driver's side window and sees Simon's street number materialize out of the fog. He slows to a stop, snuffs his cigarette in the ashtray, and lets the engine idle.

He steps out of the truck and, making sure that no one is around, reaches for the brick, rushes to within twelve or fourteen feet of the glass window, and heaves it as hard as he can; then flies back to the truck, dives in, and squeals down West Park Road in the direction of North Street.

Had the event been recorded in slow motion, one would have seen the reddish, average-size brick shattering the glass and wooden mullions of the large picture window into hundreds of high-velocity projectiles.

Simon took the brunt of the attack, as it should have been, he said, since he was obviously the intended target. He was hit by several pieces of wood and glass, one larger shard having grazed his cheek, causing a bleeding wound. Thankfully, it was no worse.

The brick itself came to rest on the floor just in front of the fireplace hearth.

When they recounted it for the police, Anna remembers just having left the bathroom and being able to see the living room from the hallway.

Lyla recalls pulling the dessert plates from the kitchen counter and just beginning to turn toward the dining room.

Karen had her back to the front of the house, as she was leaning down into the open refrigerator.

And Simon had just turned from the fireplace to the stereo where he was about to put on a record album.

Within minutes, several emergency vehicles converged on the street and now a crowd has gathered.

"Any idea who could have been behind this, Mr. Mercer?"

"Could've been most anyone, I should think. Ouch!" Simon says, as the ambulance attendant applies ointment to the cut on his cheek.

"Come now, sure you can't do better than that?" the officer, who is taking the report says.

"Not tonight, I can't."

"Well, sleep on it then. Chief Inspector Hayden will want to see you tomorrow."

As the police officer moves away from him, Simon spots another officer exiting the house with a large, plastic bag containing the brick.

"You're good to go, Mr. Mercer. Someone was looking down on you tonight," the ambulance attendant says, as he begins packing his medical bag.

"I imagine you're right."

The first officer then reappears from out of the house and heads back to Simon.

"The two Americans are in my car. I'll take them back to

the hotel."

"Very good. Thank you," Simon says.

Anna and Lyla are both still shaken when the police cruiser drops them off in front of The Sandringham.

"I don't think I can sleep," Anna says.

"Me either. I need a drink." Lyla replies.

"Let's go to my room."

"I was in a car accident once," Lyla says, as Anna hands her a glass of wine. "But it was nothing like this."

"There's the difference. That was an accident. This was an intentional attempt to inflict damage. There's a psychological element at work here."

"And why Simon? He's a public defender, for God's sake, not a prosecutor."

As the girls sip their wine, the answer comes to each of them at nearly the same moment.

"Are you thinking what I'm thinking?" Lyla says.

"He's defending Elizabeth but, in doing so, he's prosecuting David O'Rourke."

"Right. And so are we."

The two girls go silent and then Anna's phone dings with an incoming text message.

'I know it's late, but it didn't feel right not reaching out and saying good luck with everything. M'

Lyla looks up just in time to catch Anna's reaction.

"God, I nearly forgot about tomorrow," Anna says.

"We better get some sleep."

"Listen, why don't we both sleep in this room tonight?"

"Good idea. I don't feel like being alone, either. I'll go get my things."

Lyla finishes the last of her glass, and then exits the room as Anna re-reads Mitchell's message. She debates sending a reply and then decides she should.

'Thank you. See you tomorrow. A.'

thirty-five

Anna and Lyla both sleep fitfully, neither of them able to shake the events of the previous evening.

Lyla gets up early and goes to her room to prepare for the day; and, when Anna wakes about an hour later, she decides to take a walk along the shoreline.

The tide was at its highest two hours earlier, but there are still fishermen on the Grand Pier, as well as die-hard clammers and screeching sea gulls chasing the ebbing tide.

Noting that the opposite shore is still cloaked in rain-clouds, Anna decides to wear her black leggings and flat tall boots, a pullover sweater, a vest and a scarf. She grabs a cup of coffee and the proverbial toasted tea cake and heads back to the hotel.

Back in her room and dressed, she takes a closer look at herself in the mirror and decides to add a little more color to her lips. She reaches for her tube of lipstick and hesitates, noting how odd it is that this small, nearly inconsequential object is, in some way, responsible for her being here today.

She also takes note that her peculiar foreboding at the approach of fall has given way to even greater apprehension of the coming investigation, and she fears that being in a strange country, even though English speaking, will make her job more difficult, and Elizabeth's future more precarious.

Anna applies the color, replaces the cap, and tosses it into her purse, then grabs her Tumi backpack and her camera bag and heads out the door.

"Good morning, Miss Newsom," the man at the front desk says.

"Good morning, Williams, has Miss Patterson come down yet?"

"Outside, ma'am."

As Anna steps out of the hotel, she's greeted by a familiar voice.

"Now there's a sight for sore eyes!" Henry says, looking up from his newspaper.

"Henry! What are you doing here?"

"Been enlisted in the cause, I 'ave. Mr. Mercer probably forgot to mention it with all the goings on last night. Heard the news, I did. A terrible thing it is."

"Yes, it is. Have you seen Lyla?"

"Miss Lyla is procuring a morning beverage. Something for you, miss?"

"No, thank you, Henry, I've had mine."

"Here she is now," Henry says, as Lyla steps out of the small cafe next door.

"Morning," Lyla says, coffee cup in hand.

"Well, we're off then!" he says.

The girls slide into the rear seat of the car, and Henry jumps in and cranks the engine.

"Headed to the parsonage, right miss?"

"Yes, thank you," Anna says, as Henry continues.

"Excitin' this. Never been on a murder inquiry. By the way, miss, the BBC has seen fit to place a camera in me car. Right there."

"Oh, geez, you're kidding me," Lyla says, as she attempts to make a little more sense of her hair.

"Henry, you're not driving back and forth from London everyday, are you?" Anna says.

"Oh, no, miss. The BBC has put me up at a small house right up the road."

"I hope your wife is okay with all this." Anna says.

"As fate would have it, me wife is gone on holiday with her bird watchin' friends. In search of the elusive Scottish Kittiwakes, they are. As well as the lesser known public houses, if you get me drift."

Just as Henry turns back to the wheel, it starts to pour and he hits the windshield wipers.

"Goin' to be rainin' kittens 'n canaries today. Guaranteed."

Anna is answering an email on her cell phone when Henry rounds the corner on Old Church Road.

"Oh, my God!" Lyla blurts out.

"What? What's wrong?" Anna says, glancing up to Lyla.

"Look!"

Anna follows Lyla's gaze through Henry's rain-splattered windshield and spots the grayish, looming hulks of the church and the parsonage. Although they're what she expected based on photograph in the papers, in person they are far more imposing.

The church is a gray and gloomy Gothic structure made up of large stone blocks supporting a single spire. The parsonage is a four-story Victorian constructed of red brick, which Lyla later describes to Caleb as being, 'totally suitable for an Alfred Hitchcock film'.

As they get closer, however, Anna realizes that the look of the place is not what Lyla was reacting to. What neither could have expected was the size of the media circus playing out on the street in front of them.

"Something tells me we're not in Kansas anymore," Lyla says.

"Certainly not," Henry says.

"I was afraid of something like this," Anna says.

At first glance it's apparent that the BBC has taken control over the entire area, including the street in front of the parsonage. There is a large production van and several support vehicles and young, twenty-something production types scurry about with umbrellas and an elevated sense of purpose.

Cordoned off behind a barricade of large sawhorses across the street, the rest of the media, at least fifty strong, are encamped in a makeshift conglomeration of pop up tents, cameras, and lighting gear.

Not yet out of the car, the women are immediately bombarded with abrasive, rapid-fire questions, and bright flashes from the strobe lights on the cameras.

"Are you with the prosecution or the defense?"
"Are you a relative?"
"How many times was she raped?"
"Where is Simon Mercer?"
"What about last night's attack?"
"Is Elizabeth going to spend life in prison?"
"Are you the Americans?
"What are you girls doing later?"

"Careful, ladies! A pack of wild hyenas, those reporters!" Henry says, jumping out into the pouring rain.

"Lyla, you go with Henry! There's an umbrella back here."

"Gotcha!"

Anna grabs the umbrella laying under the rear window, reaches for her backpack and camera case, and dives out into the downpour.

So much for my hair, she thinks to herself.

Inside the production van, Mitchell is sitting at the control panel doing camera and sound checks when he hears the ruckus coming from the media circus on the street outside.

"Bloody morons," Mitchell says, jumping up.

He grabs his umbrella and exits the van just as Anna, struggling to get her umbrella open, is getting to the curb.

"Mitchell! This darn thing is stuck!"

"Here!" he says, popping open his umbrella. "Quick, get under."

Anna ducks under Mitchell's umbrella and wipes the rain from her face.

"Wow. Crazy here this morning," she says.

"Those tossers 'cross the way aren't makin' it any easier," Mitchell says, glancing down at her.

"Anyway, good mornin'! Seems like we're always meeting in a rainstorm," he says, as they slosh their way up the puddled sidewalk.

At the front porch, Mitchell stops and lets Anna get herself up the steps to the front door.

"So, uh, if there's anything I can do today…" he says.

"We should be fine. Thanks."

Mitchell gives Anna a quick thumbs up and turns and gets about halfway down the sidewalk when he stops and looks back.

"Oh! Just remembered…." he says, calling out over the rain.

Just having reached the top of the steps, Anna stops and turns.

"What's that?" she yells.

"Heard we're having Surrey Dairy Cow for lunch!"

For a moment Anna thinks he's serious, but, in the next second, Mitchell's face breaks into a larger version of the familiar up turned smile, and Anna can't deny the small flutter somewhere inside her.

"Just joking. Cheers."

Anna sets her umbrella next to the door, stomps the rain from her boots, and enters. Inside, she's greeted by a young, female production assistant clipping a walkie-talkie to her belt and wearing a headset.

"Anna? My name is Claire. I'll be your assistant today."

"Good morning, Claire."

"I'll take your bags upstairs. Coffee, tea?"

"A coffee would be lovely. Milk please."

"Coming right up. Oh, Lyla's in the loo. Down the hall to the right."

"Thanks, Claire."

Anna takes off her vest and scarf, hangs them on a coat rack in the foyer, and pauses a moment to catch her breath.

The interior of the parsonage is pretty much what she expected, only more so. A sunny day might make it tolerable; but, on a dark, rainy morning, the dingy, yellow light from the ceiling fixtures makes the place drearier and more forlorn than it already is.

Anna heads down the long hallway and stops at the arched entrance to the large parlor on the left. The furniture, lamps, and area rugs are an eclectic mélange stitched together by multiple parsons and their wives over tens, if not hundreds, of years.

Rococo, Victorian, and traditional sofas and chairs, tired and threadbare, find themselves side-by-side within lathe-and -plaster walls adorned with chintz wallpaper, and faded draperies and patterns that vary, depending upon the room.

On a spring or summer day, the open windows would catch the fresh air off the Bristol Channel. Today, however, with everything shut tight as a drum, the smell in the grand old house is overtaken by the life that's passed through it.

How many thousands of meals, how many cigars and cigarettes and spilt brandies, Anna thinks to herself. *Or the hundreds of accidental pees and poops from loved and long forgotten pets.*

The whole effect is one of faded glory harkening back to a time when The Church was the social and cultural center of the community, and sin was something to be shunned, rather than enshrined.

"Dr. Newson!" Hal says, as he enters the parlor with her coffee cup.

Anna spins on her heels.

"Good morning! I'm Hal Boyd, co-producer of this extravaganza! I believe this belongs to you."

"Yes, thank you."

Anna takes the cup from Hal then reaches out to shake his hand.

"Pleased to meet you, Hal."

"Sorry 'bout the bloody mess outside. Nothin' to be done about it, I'm afraid."

"Just as long as it doesn't affect what we're doing in here," Anna says.

"We'll do our best to see that it doesn't. I know you're anxious to get started. Simon should be here momentarily."

The words are no sooner out of his mouth when there's a rise in the tumult outside.

"That must be him now. Cheers."

Hal heads down the hallway and disappears through the front door, and Anna sips her coffee and continues in the opposite direction, down the long hallway toward the kitchen, making mental notes of the rooms along the way.

The main staircase is about ten feet inside the front door on the right. The parlor is just after, on the left, and the second, narrower staircase with an exit to the side yard is in the middle of the house, and it too is on the right.

"Hey," Lyla says, under her breath as Anna reaches the kitchen. "This place is pretty creepy, dont you think?"

"Have you seen the parson or the housekeeper yet?" Anna says.

"Heard they're not going to be here today," Lyla says, taking a bite of biscuit.

"Darn, was hoping to get at least a glimpse of them."

"Hi, Ladies."

Claire enters the kitchen holding two sets of small microphones and transmitters.

"We need to get you wired."

"Wired?" Anna asks.

"It's the only way we're assured of good audio. Clip the small microphones to a blouse or sweater, and then clip the transmitter to the outside of your clothes somewhere."

Claire hands each of them their units and is about to walk away when she stops and takes her voice to a whisper.

"Oh, and it's always a good idea to turn them off when you're headed to the loo. Switch is on the side of the transmitter. Cheers."

"Thanks for the tip," Lyla says, mimicking the whisper as Claire exits the kitchen.

"At least she warned us," Anna says.

Hal enters the production van just as Mitchell turns towards, James, the technician seated next to him.

"Okay, let's do a sound check."

"Roger, that," James says.

The girls, however, don't realize that their microphones have already been switched on and are being heard in the van.

"So, um, have you seen Mitchell this morning?" Lyla asks.

Mitchell and James exchange glances.

"Uh, yeah. When I got out of the car."

"How was it?"

> *(Anna doesn't answer)*

"I said... how was it?" Lyla teases.

Hal and James both stifle a laugh.

"How was what? There's nothing there. Exactly what I've said. There's nothing there." Anna says.

"Low blow 'ole boy," Hal quips.

"Bugger off. Both of 'ya," Mitchell says, and turn those bloody things off.

From the kitchen, Anna hears the front door open and the sound of Simon's voice.

"I hope he's okay, today."

"Yeah, me too," Lyla adds.

Simon hangs his coat and hat on the rack and is approached by yet another production assistant, this one a male.

"Simon Mercer?"

"Possibly. Haven't had my coffee yet."

"That way to the kitchen. Coffee, biscuits, and the like."

"Brilliant," he says, and as he heads down the hallway, he rubs his hands together to get some warmth flowing.

"Simon! We're in the kitchen," Anna says, calling out to him.

"Cheers everyone."

"Good morning, Simon." Lyla says.

"Got your coffee, good," Simon says, as he heads to the large urn surrounded by bagels and biscuits set up on the kitchen table.

"Sorry about this morning. About Henry, I mean. Meant to tell you last night that Cynthia had offered his services, but it totally escaped me what with the police and all."

"It's not a problem. Really. How are you feeling? And how's Karen? My God, what a night," Anna says.

"I'd be lying if I said we weren't a bit shaken. Took Karen forever to get to sleep, and I was up most of the night with this damn cut on my face."

"Didn't they give you pain medication?

"Let's just say that it worked. Eventually. After some encouragement from a Scottish friend of mine."

Simon surveys the assortment of breakfast items and chooses a rather plain looking biscuit.

"Not much of an appetite this morning," he says, taking a small bite.

"Do the police have any idea who it could have been?" Lyla says.

"Not yet. Frankly, it's unusual for a public defender to find himself at the receiving end of this kind of thing. Usually, it's the prosecutor."

Anna and Lyla give each other a glance, recalling last night's discussion about David O'Rourke; and, after a few sips of coffee and a couple bites of biscuit, Simon is beginning to look more like himself.

"Well then," he says.

"I'm going to head upstairs and get ready," Lyla says, and Simon turns to Anna for a bit of a pep talk.

"Today's the day, isn't it?"

"Yes, it is. Thank you, Simon. For having us here."

"Nonsense. I'll be the one thanking you. No, Elizabeth will be the one thanking you. I'm sure of it. Let's get started, shall we?"

"Yes, let's."

Mental notes are as important as written or spoken ones, and her experience in writing the book has taught her not to underestimate their usefulness. Before beginning the climb to the third floor, Anna makes a quick assessment of the dimensions of the staircase.

From the first to the second floor, it is approximately eight feet wide and has a slight sweep to the left, the purpose being to create a sense of elegance and grace.

As she ascends, she can't help but notice the uneven steps and the creaking underfoot. The wallpaper is different here. Whereas the parlor was a floral pattern in yellows and pinks and lavenders, the paper here is striped in alternating mint green and maroon.

At the second-floor landing, she turns left and left again to reach the straight and narrower staircase to the third floor. As she reaches the third-floor landing, she notes a window seat under two large drafty windows, and ten feet farther on the right is the entrance to Elizabeth's room.

Down the hallway, beyond Elizabeth's room, stand two more production assistants and two police officers, who are speaking with Simon.

"Here's your camera," Lyla says, "there's still police tape on the door."

Anna takes it and swings the strap over her head.

"That's a good sign."

"Here she is now," Simon says, to one of the officers.

"Good morning, Miss Newsom," the officer says, and then proceeds to remove the seal and the police tape from the doorway.

Anna steps forward and Lyla, pad and pen in hand, follows just behind.

In the production van, Mitchell studies the four television monitors that display the four camera positions within Elizabeth's bedroom. From the two cameras in the far corners he sees Anna step into the room.

"There she is. Begin recording." Mitchell says.

One of the first things she shared after Lyla came to work for her was that she was a firm believer in working from large to small...and generally left to right.

'We take in the broad stokes first and work downward in ever smaller scales of detail.'

"Bed on the left. Closet on the far wall. Vanity on the short wall to the right that leads to the circular windows of the turret. Matching wallpaper and drapes. An assortment of needlepoint scattered throughout the room," she says, then raises her camera to her eye and begins taking photos.

click, click, click...

"The bed is a standard queen with wrought iron head and footboards..."

click, click, click...

"And a heavy knitted bedspread in a herringbone pattern of alternating pink and white."

Anna moves to the foot of the bed and kneels.

"At the foot of the bed is an open wicker basket containing several balls of various colors of yarn and a cluster of stainless-steel knitting needles bound by a pink ribbon."

click, click, click...

Anna stands and moves from the bed to the vanity and Lyla follows.

In the hallway, Simon approaches one of the two production assistants and whispers.

"I'll be in the production van. Let me know if there's anything she needs."

"Of course, Mr. Mercer."

"On the vanity, which appears to be late art nouveau, are three knitted doilies that match the bedspread. A large one in the center and two smaller ones of the sides."

click, click, click...

"On the center doily is a hand mirror and brush and comb set made of ochre-colored Bakelite..."

click, click, click...

"And... oh, wow." Anna says, "Lyla, look at this."

Lyla steps forward as Anna shifts her lens to macro for extreme close ups.

"A toy truck," Lyla says.

Anna brings the camera back to her eye and zooms in as tightly as she can.

"On the side it reads, 'O'Rourkes Organic Dairy'."

click, click, click.

"Good grief. He was giving her toys?" Lyla says.

Simon manages to deflect the rain and the shouts from the reporters, and dives into the BBC production van.

Hal, who is standing just behind Mitchell, turns to the door.

"You must be Simon. I'm Hal Boyd."

"Are we public defenders that obvious?" he quips, wiping rain from his face and stomping his shoes.

"The bandage," Hal says, pointing to his own cheek. "Heard about last night. Nasty business."

"Line of duty, I suppose."

"This is Mitchell, co-producer and director."

"Sorry. Not my usual entrance," Simon says, as Mitchell turns over his shoulder.

"No worries. Pleasure, Simon."

Hal slides one of the chairs up closer to the console.

"You can watch and hear what's going on up there on the monitors."

As Simon takes a seat, Anna continues her description of Elizabeth's bedroom.

"From the windows of the turret there is a view of the street below..." Anna says, pointing the camera through the window.

click, click, click...

She then raises the camera to capture the view of the channel, which today is roiling with heavy waves and white-caps.

"And a view of the Bristol Channel."

click, click, click.

Anna pauses for a moment, lowers her camera, takes another look around the room, and moves back toward the vanity.

"Above the vanity are two shelves containing what appear to be an assortment of collectibles."

click, click, click…

"Lyla, would you please see if one of the production people can find a step stool?"

In the production van, Mitchell hears the request and keys his microphone.

"Claire or Thompson."

"Go for Claire."

"Two step-ups for Anna, please."

"Roger that."

Before Anna can count to five, Claire enters the room with two wooden boxes and sets them down next to her.

"You guys are quick!"

"It's what we do," Claire says, with a smile, as she disappears out into the hallway.

Anna steps up onto the boxes and begins to survey the shelves.

"The uppermost shelf contains several stuffed dolls, antiques, with porcelain heads, and several are likenesses of old Hollywood movie stars."

"Laurel and Hardy,"

click, click,

"Charlie Chaplin…"

click, click,

"Shirley Temple…"

click, click,

"actually…they're kind of frightening…." Anna says.

She lowers her camera and then moves down to the shelf below.

"On the second shelf is an assortment of toy musical instruments, which includes a saxophone…a piano…a guitar…

click, click, click…

"…and a miniature organ with the name, um, Magnus, M-A-G-N-U-S, etched on the front.

click, click, click.

In the van, Simon looks up at the mention of the name Magnus.

"I say. Did she say, Magnus? My old aunt had a Magnus organ. A miniature, just like that one, but the bloody thing actually worked. I played it as a child."

"Whoa…" Anna says, suddenly.

"What was that?" Lyla asks.

"Slight vertigo. Make a note, please," Anna says, instinctively recognizing the feeling as the onset of what she's termed ESS, or Empathic Shared Sensation, even though she can't be sure of who she's sharing the sensation with.

Lyla checks the time on her watch and makes a notation in her notebook.

Anna steps gingerly off of the boxes and moves to the wall just to the right of the bed.

"The room is decorated with matching wallpaper and drapes which, from a distance, appear to have a repeating pattern of some kind of outdoor tableau."

Anna takes a wide shot of the wall and then steps forward, stopping about three feet away.

"On closer examination, we find…."

Suddenly, Anna stops, and a quizzical expression crosses her face.

"Sound check. Is she still speaking?" Mitchell says.

"Appears she's just staring at the wall," Hal adds.

"Sound is fine. Wind has come up, though," James says.

Lyla looks up from her notepad, also wondering why Anna has stopped in the middle of a description.

"Anna? Are you okay?"

"I don't know."

"What's going on?" Simon says.

Anna shifts her camera lens back to telephoto, raises it to her eye, and zooms in all the way, so each of the tiny elements in the farm scene fills her frame.

"...on closer examination the tableau becomes..."

click, click, click...

"She's starting again," Mitchell says.

"...becomes, obvious. It appears to be a scene of, um, a farm. Perhaps a reproduction from an older work of art or an illustration from a book."

"What did she just say?" Simon asks.

"Some kind of farm scene," Hal replies.

"...the same image is repeated from floor to ceiling and wall to wall....Lyla? How many times would you say the image is repeated in this room?"

Lyla takes a moment to size up the dimensions of the room.

"Paper and drapes? About five or six hundred times," Lyla replies, as Anna continues her description.

"A picket fence rests on each side along the bottom and frames the driveway heading toward a single-story farm-house."

click, click, click...

"A large tree....and, um..."

Anna hesitates again.

"....a maple perhaps, sits to the left of the house...."

click, click, click...

"and...and....and...two large dogs run up the driveway chasing a truck of some kind."

"Anna, I think we should take a break," Lyla says.

"I'm, um, I'm feeling a little dizzy..."

click, click, click...

"Why don't you sit for a...."

"Something rather odd about this," Simon says, turning to Hal. "You're sure she's okay?"

"....where did I leave off?"

"Two large dogs run up the...."Lyla, says, reading from her notes.

"....two large dogs run up the driveway chasing a...a...."

"What, Anna?"

"....chasing a... a... delivery van. An old one, from the early nineteen....hundreds....is my guess...."

Suddenly, the sound of the pounding wind and rain is compounded by multiple crashes as the storm shutters outside the room tear loose from their latches and begin slamming against the window frames of the bedroom.

"What the hell is that?" Mitchell yells into his microphone.

Claire picks up Mitchell's transmission on her headset and rushes into Elizabeth's bedroom.

"Bloody shutters, Mitchell! They've come undone!"

"How in the hell did that happen?" Mitchell replies.

"No, idea, sir!"

Struggling with her words, Anna continues.

"In...in... the background, a woman holding a basket... of...of..."

"Mitchell? I'm having a hard time hearing her!" Lyla says, turning to one of the cameras.

"Claire!"

"Yes, Mitchell?"

"Ask Lyla if we should break!"

As if the slamming of the shutters wasn't enough, it seems that the weight of the storm has now moved in over the top of them. Like cannon fire, thunder begins to rock the parsonage as bright flashes of light slice through the room.

"Anna! Maybe we should take a break!" Lyla yells over the noise.

"Claire! Stay with them!" Mitchell snaps into his microphone.

"Roger, that!"

"Really…. I'm okay," Anna murmurs.

"I didn't copy that! What did she say?"

"She wants to continue, Mitchell."

"…a woman holding a basket…of …of…um, flowers, it looks like, waves to the…the…delivery van…"

click, click, click…

"…oh, my…a delivery van…"

With her breathing more difficult and her heart racing, Anna pulls the camera from her eye, glances up toward the wall just above her head, and then gasps.

"Lyla!!!"

"Oh, my God!" Lyla cries out.

Responding to Lyla, Claire, too, looks up in shocked disbelief.

"O-M-G!!!"

"CLAIRE! WHAT'S GOING ON IN THERE?"

"Mitchell, you're not going to believe this. The bloody wallpaper is coming apart!" Claire fires back.

"Where? Which camera?" Mitchell yells into his microphone.

"Um, camera three. You may have to tilt up."

"Tilt up! Tilt up!" Mitchell barks at the technician.

"I'll lose Anna!" James says.

"We've got her on three other cameras! Tilt up, dammit!"

Simon stands and moves closer to the monitors.

"Good lord, man, is she okay?"

Anna struggles to speak, her words now coming in short, rapid bursts.

"…the…the…wall…paper is, um…peeling…and cur, cur, curling along the seam lines."

"Mitchell, I'm going in," Hal says, jumping to his feet.

"Go! But wait outside the room! If she wants to finish, let her finish."

As Hal exits the production van, the wind nearly takes the door off its hinges.

To Anna, it seems her camera has literally tripled in weight. In spite of the effort, she manages to raise it and takes several photos of the peeling wallpaper.

click, click, click...

"Anna, let's take a break!" Lyla yells out.

"...no...not yet..." Anna gasps, her breathing growing shallow and erratic. "In the far distance..."

"....be... behind the woman, are...are...stacks of hay...."

click, click, click...

"and...and...several...cows...Guernsies...and...and...a barn and, a silo."

click, click, click.

"Good Lord, of course!" Simon shouts, jumping to his feet. "It's the O'Rourke place!!"

Mitchell whips his head up toward Simon.

"The what?"

"THE BLOODY DAIRY FARM!"

The words are hardly out of Simon's mouth when his cell phone rings. Looking down at the caller ID, he rushes to answer it.

"Simon here, make it quick! Are you sure? Straight away!"

Simon stuffs the phone in his pocket and bolts for the door of the production van.

"I don't know what the hell is going on here, but they just found Elizabeth Barrett unconscious in her cell!"

"NO! NO! NO!" Anna begins screaming and moaning "...no, no... please, no...."

"Anna!!!" Lyla screams, "Stop!!!"

"CLAIRE! Mitchell shouts into his microphone.

"Go for Claire!"

"We're shutting it down! Get her out of there! NOW!"

"Straight away, sir!"

"...no, no... please, no...stop...please...no...."

The last thing Anna remembers before passing out was

receiving the fleeting image of a man entering the bedroom from the hallway. There was some kind of coarse, cloth bag over his head, and it was fixed with a cord around his neck to prevent it from coming off. Three of the four ragged holes that had been cut for his eyes, nose, and mouth were pools of black, but protruding out of the one for his mouth were two plump lips framing a tongue wet with saliva.

As Margret slams the front door behind her, the questions being hurled from the few reporters that haven't left for the day fade away.

She sets the grocery bag on the side table in the foyer, removes her raincoat and hat, and hangs them on the rack next to the mirror, then picks up the bag and heads down the long hallway to the kitchen.

"Benjamin!" she yells out, in no particular direction, and, by the time she gets to the kitchen, she's received no response.

As she begins emptying the brown paper sack of its contents, she calls out again.

"Benjamin?"

Even though the BBC production crew did its best to leave no trace of their presence that morning, there were still a few telltale reminders.

Two of the power cables were still in place, as per the agreement, and Margret was able to spot an odd assortment of items meaningful only to those employed in the arcane endeavor generously called 'news and entertainment.'

She places the last of her items in the refrigerator and then notices that the teapot had been moved.

He must be upstairs, she tells herself, and heads toward the stairway in the middle of the house.

"Look at what's happened, Margret," Benjamin says, when she finds him in Elizabeth's bedroom.

"My Lord. What in the...?"

"It's as though Satan himself had been here."

Benjamin is sitting on the edge of the bed, teacup in hand,

and pays no attention as Margret circles the room, taking note of the wallpaper which has curled up and away from the walls.

"Do you think the TV people did this?"

"I don't know. Really, I don't. When I met them, everyone seemed pleasant and perfectly professional."

Benjamin lets out a perceptible sigh and struggles to get to his feet.

"What would my dear Adelaide say?" he says, as he leaves the room.

thirty-six

"Right this way, sir."

Dr. Fielding Goddard hands his coat and hat to the attendant and then follows the maitre'd through the main dining room of Le Gavroche, London's premiere French restaurant.

"Mr. Edwards has already been seated," the maître 'd says, as they approach a booth in the far-left corner.

"John, sorry I'm late," Goddard says, as they reach the table.

"My apologies for the short notice," Edwards says, with knife and fork in hand, "there was only one of these beauties left, so I..."

Goddard glances down and sees the large, pinkish arm of an octopus curling toward the ceiling.

"Bras De Pouple," The maître 'd says, as he sets Goddard's menu on the table. "Magnifique."

He waits for Goddard to sit, and then leaves the table.

"No apology necessary, although I've never understood the appeal of dining on something smarter than I am."

"Eat or be eaten. Comes with the territory, I guess."

"If I may. What's it, um, resting on?"

"Puree of fava bean, I think."

"Lovely," Goddard says, sarcastically.

As Edwards slices off a piece and pops it into his mouth, a waiter in a white jacket approaches.

"Good afternoon. My name is Fredric; may I offer the gentleman a cocktail?"

"What are you having, John?"

"Tanqueray martini. One olive," he says, chewing with relish.

"The same, please."

As the waiter leaves the table, Goddard takes a sip from his water glass.

"Speaking of 'eat or be eaten,' how is your show being received?

"I'll put it this way. 'the Evolving Mind' is not a term I'd use to describe much of England these days. Too busy with bloody sports or shopping or going to Boris Johnson rallies to care what their bloody brains are doing."

"Here you are, sir."

"Thank you," Goddard says, as the waiter sets his martini in place.

"Fresh sole amandine, today, if I may, sir?"

"You may," Goddard says with a satisfied smile. He closes his menu, hands it to the waiter and reaches for his martini.

"Tough times, these," Goddard says, taking a healthy sip. "The wild west all over again. Everyone in it for themselves. No personal accountability."

"One has the impression that all this bloody nationalism is simply the same syndrome on steroids," Edwards adds.

"Well put."

As Goddard glances over the menu, Edwards goes back to his octopus and shifts gears.

"So, uh, you mentioned that you've met with the young girl."

"Elizabeth Barrett. Three sessions. Textbook case. Her parents are killed, and the ensuing trauma catalyzes an attachment to a man who could be her father but isn't. With each day that passes, and he doesn't act as her father, the more traumatized she becomes…"

"Sole amandine!" the waiter says, arriving at the table.

"I'm doubling down, Fredric," Edwards says, draining the last of his drink and handing him the glass.

"Very good, another martini, sir."

As the waiter leaves Goddard picks up his knife and fork, and bites into his fish.

"The amplified trauma of further rejection eventually

morphs into GSA, or genetic sexual attraction. When the false father isn't forthcoming, sexually, that is, her rejection turns to anger, and the fantasy remodels itself into something far more severe, such as rape."

"So, the psychosis manifests in stages?"

"Beginning with the original trauma."

"Have you met *Doctor* Anna Newsom?" Edwards says, with a tone that implies she's not deserving of the title.

"Not yet, but I skimmed through her book. I hear she met with Elizabeth Barrett for the first time, this week."

"Day before yesterday. An American you know."

"From the South. I thought the only things produced there were peanuts and bigots," Goddard quips.

"Full of new age tommyrot, as far I'm concerned. Not saying I wouldn't mind a roll in the oats with her, though."

"Then to what does she owe her success?"

"Juries love to be entertained, Fielding. My God, man, you of all people should know that! And the very idea of doing a show around her is madness."

"Frankly, I can't understand why Simon Mercer allowed it," Goddard says, reaching for his martini.

"Listen, Fielding, what I'm about to tell you must be held in strictest confidence."

Goddard takes another bite and continues working his plate.

"Hasn't it always been, John?"

Edwards pauses momentarily, glances from side to side and lowers his voice.

"Two days ago, Anna Newsom paid her first visit to the parsonage. I was able to get a glimpse at some of the footage."

Goddard looks up sharply.

"Elizabeth Barrett's bedroom to be exact," Edwards adds.

"How in the world did...?" Goddard responds, raising his voice.

"Shhhh," Edwards says, glancing to the table of patrons next to them. "Let's just say I have my ways."

"You could lose your show."

"Bollocks."

Goddard takes another sip of his drink and hesitates, and Edwards takes his silence as a cue to proceed.

"The day was dedicated to recording Newsom's description of Miss Barrett's bedroom. During one particular phase, she appears to be dramatically agitated, nearly to the point of fainting."

"Your martini, sir," the waiter says, setting the glass in front of Edwards.

"Go on," Goddard says.

"As she begins to describe the wallpaper in the bedroom..." Edward pauses with an uncharacteristic loss of words.

"Well...it just seems to..."

"Seems to what?"

"Peel! The bloody wallpaper begins to peel and curl up, away from the wall, without any apparent cause."

Goddard sets down his fork, reaches for his martini, and contemplates the possible meaning of what Edwards has just told him.

"You're sure it wasn't something one of your producers cooked up for the camera lens?"

Edwards takes another sip and smacks his lips.

"Cynthia Smythe may be a cunt... but she's not a liar."

"Then what the hell was going on?"

"I don't know. But my worry is that the defense is going to trot out this sort of bloody nonsense during the trial. Juries are seduced by this sort of vulgar spectacle, and I don't want to see the memory of a good man like David O'Rourke run into the ground by some new age, voodoo psychology. We've a time-honored discipline to protect, Fielding, remember that."

Goddard pauses for a moment and then goes back to working his plate.

"This is very noble of you, John."

"Nobility be damned, I want this girl unmasked for the bloody charlatan that she is," he says, then Edwards leans in over the table to make his final point.

"I want her undone."

Weighing his options, Goddard sets down his fork and wipes his mouth with his napkin.

"Well?" Edwards says.

Then, coming to a conclusion, Goddard reaches for his glass and raises it in a toast.

"To the undoing of Dr. Anna Newsom."

thirty-seven

"...Plus two bags 'o Aunt Sandy's famous cheddar chips!" the plump, affable female vendor says.

"Ooh, those look yummy," Lyla says, as she sneaks one of the French fries and pops it into her mouth. She scoops the two bags and the two beers off the counter and heads toward Anna, who is sitting on a bench overlooking the channel.

The organizers of the 'Chips on the Channel' festival had fretted about another storm, but much to their delight, the weekend dawned clear and bright and warm, and now the boardwalk and the pier were teeming with pedestrians on the prowl for their favorite fried potato.

"It's so peaceful here today," Anna says, pulling out her earbuds as Lyla approaches.

"One bag of cheddar chips and a bottle of Guinness. Just what the doctor ordered," Lyla says, as she passes them to Anna.

"There must be a hundred different vendors here this weekend."

"And our hotel, right across the street!" Lyla says, as she holds her bottle up for toast.

"Cheers!" Anna says.

As the two girls settle and dig into their chips, neither can help but think about the events in Elizabeth's bedroom three days earlier. Anna takes a sip of her beer and gazes out at the sailboats on the channel.

"We've seen a lot together, Lyla."

"Uh-huh."

"But nothing like this."

"I know," Lyla says, hesitating. "How's Elizabeth?"

"Recovering. Simon said she was calling for the guard,

screaming, I guess, when she blacked out."

"You and she passed information, didn't you?"

"It appears that way."

Anna takes another bite and another sip of beer. She wants to talk, and Lyla lets her go at her own pace.

"David O'Rourke wore a bag over his head. That's the image I was able to retrieve from her. And images of the farm are what she received from me."

"And the tearing and curling of the wallpaper?"

"Causal Tele-transmutation. Me to her. Her to me. And in this case, me to the wallpaper."

"But isn't it a crazy coincidence?" Lyla asks.

"That the man who is raping her owns a farm eerily similar to the one depicted on the wallpaper in the room where the crime is being committed?" Anna replies.

"Right. How?"

"Because there is no such thing as coincidence," Anna says, taking another sip of beer, "I prefer calling it synchronicity. We may be surprised by how the universe works, but God never is."

Just at that moment, Lyla glances up to see Mitchell crossing the street from The Sandringham.

"Truer words never spoken," Lyla says, with a wry smile.

"Hmmm?" Anna replies, not yet seeing Mitchell.

"Mornin, ladies!"

At the sound of his voice Anna turns and looks up at the familiar up-turned smile and the head of thick, curly black hair.

"The gentleman at the front desk said something had drawn you from your rooms. So, using scientific deduction I determined that chips and a cold beverage would be the most likely culprits!"

"Well done!" Lyla says.

"Good morning, Mitchell."

"Anna."

Locked onto Anna's eyes, Mitchell hesitates before speaking again.

"Anyway, I'm here to see how Anna was doing. Quite a thing you went through in the bedroom," he says, producing a small bouquet of flowers from behind his back. "I think there's something you're not telling me."

"I'll explain later," Anna says, reaching for the flowers. "How thoughtful."

"Why aren't you in London?" Lyla asks.

"Kept us over just in case. Almost forgot."

Mitchell hands Lyla the morning paper that he had been carrying under his arm.

"Hot off the press, as you Americans say. Have a gander under the fold."

Lyla slides over and Mitchell takes a seat on the opposite side. She opens the paper and flips it over to the bottom section of the front page.

"Public Defender Closer to Serial Rape," Lyla says, reading aloud.

"You're kidding? Suspiciously premature don't you think?" Anna says, taking a quick sniff of the flowers.

"Oh-oh, get a load of this," Lyla says, as she continues reading.

"Nineteenth century wallpaper may hold the key to proving a case of serial rape against well liked and now infamous dairy farmer."

"Now how in the hell did they get that?" Lyla says.

"No tellin'. Maybe Simon is close to someone in the press," Mitchell replies as Anna takes another sip of beer.

"Simon may be a nice guy, but he's nobody's fool," she says. "I don't think he would reveal his hand unless he was absolutely sure of what he was holding and we're not there yet. It must be coming from the BBC," Anna concludes, shooting Mitchell an accusatory look.

"No way. The tapes are kept in a locked vault. The only person with access is Hal and one of the tech geeks. It can't happen, I assure you."

"By the way, you look pretty good in this picture," Lyla says, with a smirk.

"Oh, Christ. How in the hell did they get *that?*" Anna says, reaching for the paper.

"Hey, you know. Just had a thought," Mitchell says, out of the blue. "Henry has the day off and since the weather is so agreeable, why don't I take you girls for a ride? 'Cross the channel. Grab a bite on the water somewhere. Cockles and faggots!"

"Sorry?" Anna and Lyla say, nearly simultaneously.

"Welsh. For mussels and meatballs!"

The girls look at one another for a moment, and then Anna responds.

"No, sorry. You two go, I've got some reading I'd like to catch up on and..."

"No, you don't," Lyla says, "you've got some relaxing to catch up on, and I think Mitchell, cockles and faggots notwithstanding, has a super idea. I'm taking my chips and my half bottle of Guinness and leaving."

Lyla stands and begins heading in the direction of the pier, leaving an obvious gap in the bench.

"Ciao, you two."

"No, really, I..." Anna says, trying to undo what's been done, but she knows it's too late.

"Brilliant! I'll get the car and pull up to the hotel while you jump across and do whatever it is you girls do when you're getting ready to go somewhere. Cheers," Mitchell says, and with an upturned grin and a glint in his eye, he takes off across the street.

"Dammit." Anna says, under her breath.

Although her gut is telling her otherwise, Anna relents and takes Mitchell up on his offer. She's seen so little of the English countryside, and, besides, *what could possibly happen?* she tells herself.

In her room, she slips into her black leggings, a lavender sweater and scarf, and a black, rainproof vest. She brushes her hair and pulls it into a low, scattered ponytail and perks herself up with some lipstick and mascara.

When she exits the hotel, Mitchell waves from the shiny, black Range Rover idling at the curb; and, as she rounds the front of the vehicle, she takes note of his vanity plate.

"HI ON TV?" Anna says, jumping into the passenger seat.

"Me vanity plate."

"I gathered that."

Mitchell smiles, throws the Range Rover into gear and pulls out of the hotel driveway, heading north on Knightstone Road.

"Brilliant lunch places in Cardiff. Right over there."

Mitchell points to their left, across the channel to the lush, low lying hills dappled by cumulus clouds.

"Look, hot air balloons," Anna remarks.

"Ever been up?" he asks.

"Not a chance."

"C'mon, where's your spirit of adventure?"

"Those things catch on fire! Haven't you seen the videos on You Tube?"

"That's what I'm saying, where's your spirit of adventure?" Mitchell quips.

"Parked between caution and common sense," Anna replies.

"Dear God, what bloody fun is that?"

"I don't have any fun, I thought you knew that by now," Anna says, glancing out the corner of her eye.

"Funny, I've heard you Southern girls like a good time."

The words are barely out of Mitchell's mouth, and he knows he's made a mistake. Anna goes stone silent and the temperature in the car hits zero.

"Sorry about that."

If he's going to salvage the afternoon, Mitchell knows he better get them back on track.

"Anyway, thought we'd take the coast up to Clevedon and then jump on the M5."

"Let's just go back," Anna says, coolly.

"Turn 'round, you mean?"

Anna thinks for a moment, debating whether or not to put a sword in the day.

"On second thought, would you mind if we swung by the O'Rourke place?"

"The dairy farm?"

"Just for a minute. It's just outside Clevedon. A place called Claverham."

"I don't know..." Mitchell says, suddenly growing pensive.

"What's wrong?"

"Never been to the scene of a murder."

Anna can't help some small satisfaction at the sudden discovery of Mitchell's Achilles heel.

"You were going to have to do it at some point, right?"

"For the show. That's different."

"You're squeamish!" she says.

"Am not!" he replies. "Being in the place where a man was skewered to death is not my idea of a pleasant afternoon. That's all."

"Now who's the one with no spirit of adventure?"

Mitchell makes the right on Lower Claverham road as the GPS calls out their location.

"...destination ahead...one half kilometer...on the right."

"There it is! See the barn and silo?" Anna says.

"In my sights."

"Slow down, please."

As they approach the farm, Anna's pulse quickens, and Mitchell stops the Range Rover at the far-right corner of the property line.

"What would you like me to do?"

"Pull up to the entrance of the driveway, please."

The Range Rover moves another two hundred yards down Lower Claverham and comes to a stop, giving Anna the exact same view as the images on the wallpaper in Elizabeth's bedroom.

"It's bloody uncanny," Mitchell says.

"It's not just similar. It's exactly the same!" Anna says, reaching for her phone.

She jumps out of the Range Rover and begins snapping pictures, describing what she sees and making sure to replicate the framing and focal length as she remembers it appearing on the wallpaper.

"Same house. Same maple tree, although much bigger now. Same fences, haystacks, and silo. Everything in its right place."

Anna is so mesmerized by what she sees that she fails to notice the large sign next to the road.

"Up for sale," Mitchell says.

"What's that?" Anna replies, as she snaps the last picture and lowers her phone.

"They're selling the place."

"Can't you feel it? There's so much sadness here," she says.

"I suppose there would be," Mitchell adds, as Anna gets back into the vehicle.

"Let's get closer."

"No, I don't think that…"

"Chicken?" Anna says, with a smirk.

"Really?" Mitchell says, taking the challenge, and he turns up the gravel driveway lined with fences and stops about halfway to the house.

"Look," Anna says, "even the cut-outs on the shutters are the same… roosters."

Devon hears the sound of tires on the gravel driveway and steps out of the equipment barn wiping his hands on a greasy rag. Thanks to the newspaper and television reports, the farm has seen countless morbid curiosity seekers, some brazen enough to attempt a selfie at the very spot where his father was murdered.

But, now that the farm is up for sale, his older brother, Samuel, has advised him that shooting a potential buyer wouldn't be good for anyone, so he stops and waits.

"What do you say, let's go in."

"No, Anna."

"We'll say we're interested in buying the place."

But before Mitchell can stop her, Anna jumps back out of the Range Rover and heads up the driveway toward the house.

Devon ducks back into the barn and retrieves a shotgun that had been leaning just inside the door.

"Hey!" Devon yells, as he moves towards her.

Anna turns at the sound of his voice.

"We, um, saw the for-sale sign," Anna yells, pointing in the direction of the sign near the road.

"Why didn't you see the number for the bloody realtor then?" Devon says, stopping about forty feet away.

"I, um…"

"By the way, where you fuckin' from anyway?"

"The, um… States."

Not liking the look of Devon or the shotgun, Mitchell steps out and joins Anna on the driveway.

"Afternoon," Mitchell says, in his friendliest voice.

"So it is. What the fuck do you want?"

Anna and Mitchell begin to answer simultaneously.

"We, um…well, we were…"

And then Anna lets Mitchell take over. He clears his throat and assumes his most trustworthy persona.

"I'm embarrassed to say, but me wife here has been, um…threatenin' divorce… if I don't get her out of the city."

"Bloody, hell! You're a bloody speculator!"

"No, no! He's a… a dentist. And a darn good one," Anna says, jumping in. "And it's true, my doctor says the city is bad for my nerves. Let us take a look. Please? We won't be long."

Devon thinks for a moment, but then it starts to drizzle, and Walker, the farm hand, calls out to him from inside the barn.

"Devon! Quick hand, son!"

Devon turns his head toward the barn and thinks for a

moment.

"Alright then. I'll meet you on the front porch, but you're not going any farther than the front room."

"Yes, of course. Thank you," Anna says, reassuringly.

As Devon heads back to the barn, Anna and Mitchell make their way up the front steps of the farmhouse.

"Anna, don't," Mitchell says, as Anna reaches for the doorknob, "didn't you hear what he bloody said?"

"Mitchell, can't you feel her?" Anna whispers, as she opens the door and steps inside.

"Who?"

"O'Rourke's wife. She's here. Upstairs."

"Shit, Anna," Mitchell says, as he follows her in and closes the door. "Must be why he doesn't want us here."

Finished in the barn, Devon makes his way across the field and notices that Anna and Mitchell are not on the porch.

Standing in the living room, Mitchell glances out the front window and sees Devon circling the Range Rover.

"Dammit."

"What's wrong?" Anna whispers.

"Look."

Devon stops at the front and bends down to see Mitchell's vanity plate.

"Dentist, me fuckin' ass," Devon says, under his breath.

Suddenly, there's a ringing from inside the vehicle. Devon stands, makes his way to Anna's open window, and glances inside.

Resting between the seat and the console is Anna's cellphone, and on the screen is Simon Mercer's caller ID. His jaw tightening, Devon reaches in and pulls it out of the window, then stares back at the house.

"Oh God, my cell phone!" Anna cries.

"You left it in the car?!"

"It must have slipped off my lap!"

Devon tosses the phone back through the window, reaches into his pocket for a handful of shotgun shells and opens the breach of the shotgun.

"We're fuckin' toast!" Mitchell says, "let's get the hell outta here!"

"Where, which way?" Anna says, spinning on her heels.

"Follow me, there must be a side entrance."

Anna and Mitchell bolt out of the living room and into the kitchen. Mitchell stops for a moment, his mind racing through several alternatives.

"Where is he???" Anna says.

Mitchell turns. Through the space between the kitchen door and the door frame, he can see Devon with the shotgun standing on the porch, facing the Range Rover.

"Waiting for us!" Mitchell says, in a loud whisper.

Suddenly, he has an idea.

"Give me your scarf!"

"What!!! This is the only Gucci I have!!!"

"Now, dammit!"

Not pleased, Anna takes the scarf from her neck and hands it to him.

"Stand outside the door and when I tell you, run like hell back to the Rover."

"Okay, okay," Anna says.

Mitchell takes the scarf, goes to the stove and turns one of the knobs. It makes a clicking sound but doesn't light.

"Dammit, c'mon, you mother f..."

He goes to another, and this time the burner erupts with an excess of gas, nearly singing his eyebrows.

He lights the scarf and then holds it up to the smoke alarm in the middle of the kitchen ceiling. Nothing.

"Mitchell!" Anna whispers as loud as she can, "what's happening?"

"C'mon, c'mon you bloody...."

Suddenly, the alarm screeches into life.

"NOW! NOW!" Mitchell yells, dropping the scarf, and like a shot, he's out the kitchen door and he and Anna break into a full sprint around the house and down through the front yard.

On the front porch Devon spins on his heels, first in one direction, then the other, and finally tears off in the direction of the kitchen where he finds the burning scarf in the middle of the kitchen floor.

"Fuckers!" he says, and realizing he's been had, breaks into a tear back through the house.

As they dive into the Range Rover, Mitchell fires up the engine, slams it into reverse and floors it down the gravel driveway.

Facing forward, Anna sees the screen door of the farmhouse fly open.

"THERE HE IS !!!" Anna screams, as Devon stomps out onto the porch and raises the shotgun.

"HANG ON!!!" Mitchell yells, and Anna covers her eyes.

Devon fires once, the shot misses, and he pumps and fires again. With gravel flying in all directions Mitchell stands on the brakes, throwing them back in their seats, and then whips the wheel to the right, hurling the 7500-pound Range Rover into a 180-degree spin toward the main road.

Then he crushes the accelerator until his Michelins dig in far enough to make purchase; placing Devon and the shotgun a safe distance in his rearview mirror.

Reaching the end of the driveway and with both of them swamped in adrenalin, Mitchell slows and drifts into a right turn onto the main road in the direction of Clevedon.

"Fuck!!!" he says, panting and turning to Anna, "any more bright ideas???"

Anna picks her cell phone up from the floor and looks at Mitchell. For a moment, they stare at each other in disbelief and then break into uncontrollable laughter.

Although it's not in Cardiff, the Moon and Sixpence, a cozy pub on the water in Clevedon, did the trick. After what they had just been through, the need for alcohol trumped sightseeing across the channel; and now, they were sitting side-by-side at a table by a window overlooking the pier and Mitchell is polishing off his second double Jack Daniels.

"My husband is a dentist, fuckin' priceless!" Mitchell says, running his hand through his thick, curly hair and laughing,

"I couldn't have been a bloody brain surgeon?"

"You don't look like a brain surgeon, okay," Anna says, and then fires a rejoinder of her own, attempting and nearly succeeding at a perfect imitation.

"...I'm embarrassed to say, but me wife has been threatenin' divorce if I don't get her out of the city," Anna says, incredulous. "Really?"

"What's wrong with that? I saw it in a movie once."

"You did not," Anna teases, as the waitress delivers their next round.

"'Ere we go. 'Nother double for the gentleman and a beautiful glass 'o Guinness for our guest from the States."

"'Nick 'o time, me dear nurse, and don't be a stranger," Mitchell says, reaching for his glass.

"So, tell me, what's the occasion?" the waitress asks.

Taking a gulp and then glancing at Anna, Mitchell feigns bravado.

"We stared death in the face and had the better of it!" he says, raising his glass in a toast.

"No! Now, don't you be playing with me...."

"No, seriously! He's right. We did..." Anna says, with a hiccup, "and we did!"

"Well, in that case, the next round is on the house!"

"Bloody brilliant!" Mitchell says, as they watch the waitress walk away.

"Do you mind? "Anna says, turning to him.

"What's that?"

"If I have a sip?"

"Of Mr. Jack Daniels? Of course not," Mitchell says, as she reaches for the glass.

For years to come, Mitchell would be able to recount, nearly

perfectly, what was about to take place. He and Anna were sitting in a booth at the table in front of the six-panel, mullioned window.

Of the two panes of glass on the bottom row, one was clear, yet rippled with age, with a view across Marine Parade Road to the channel beyond. The other was stained glass.

The sun, he recalls, was a finger's width from dropping behind the hills of Cardiff.

As Anna reached for his drink and brought it to her lips, she glanced up at him. For Mitchell, it was as if the rest of the room had ceased to exist. Now he saw only the delicate features of Anna's face, aglow with the last light of the sun, and the rose and lavender hues streaming from the stained glass dappled through her tousled, auburn hair.

And the whole effect was amplified by the grayish, green eyes the shade of moss and the lips that form a small heart at the philtrum just beneath the slightly upturned nose. Billions of photons that had labored millions of years to escape the pull of the sun were now conspiring to undo him.

After the sip, Anna let out an endearing little gasp at the burn of the whiskey and before she knew it, Mitchell leaned in and put his mouth on hers.

For a moment she held her ground, but in the next she softened, and the smoky singe of the whiskey mingled with the sweetness of her lipstick on his tongue.

It only lasted a few seconds, and when it was over, Anna pulled away ever so slightly, opened her eyes and whispered,

"Where did you learn to drive like that?"

But before Mitchell could answer, she thrust her fingers into the thick, black hair on the back of his head and dove into him with a kiss as hard as any he'd ever experienced.

thirty-eight

Lyla is just reaching for the lamp next to her bed when her phone rings.

"Are you just getting back?" she says.

"A few minutes ago," Anna replies.

"That was some ride in the country," Lyla says, checking the time on her phone. "It's ten-thirty, girl, you've got a big day tomorrow."

"We got a little sidetracked."

"With that curly black hair and those dark, brown eyes, I'm not surprised."

"Very funny. We went to the O'Rourke place."

"Without me?"

"Lyla, you won't believe it. The farm on the wallpaper is exactly...." Anna says, and then stops.

"Better yet, hang on...."

Anna opens her photos app, selects several pictures of the farm, and texts them to Lyla.

"Okay, I just sent them."

Lyla watches her notifications for the arrival of the photos and as soon as they come in, she opens and then scrolls through them.

"Omg," Lyla says, under her breath.

"I just felt a shiver go down your spine," Anna says.

"Come over. I'll get these up on the computer."

Lyla barely has time to jump out of bed and start her computer and she hears the soft rap on her door.

"It's open," she says.

Anna pads into Lyla's room in robe and slippers sipping a bottle of mineral water.

"You've got me freaked, girl. Glass of wine?"

"I think I'm done for the day."

Anna pulls a chair up to Lyla's desk and watches as Lyla opens the photos folder from the parsonage. She selects several close-ups of the farm wallpaper that Anna photographed in Elizabeth's bedroom, and then places them side by side with the photos of the actual farm that Anna took that morning.

"The fence, the road leading to the house, the maple tree..."

"Look, how about the clothesline and the haystack and the silo and the barn. All in exactly the same place," Anna adds.

"One could quibble about tiny details, like the maple tree, it's much bigger now, but for all intents..." Lyla says, and then Anna finishes her thought.

"They're identical. Which means that either the wallpaper was inspired by the farm, or the farm was inspired by the wallpaper."

Lyla stands and begins to pace the room.

"Okay, listen to this. Let's just say that David O'Rourke didn't always deliver to the parsonage. That the housekeeper or even the pastor made pick up trips to the farm. It's possible that Elizabeth went along for the ride. She's a bright girl, the similarities between the real farm and the image on her wallpaper would have been obvious, and when the rapes began..."

"...She connected the dots. Not only was she using the wallpaper image as her Psychic Lightning Rod, her escape from reality, she was tying it directly to the perpetrator," Anna says.

"And when the wallpaper began to peel during your first visit, it's just as you said, the Causal Tele-transmutation was moving from you to her, her to you, and you to the wallpaper."

"She may not have consciously known we were in the room, but her subconscious knew precisely where we were," Anna replies.

"Exactly," Lyla says.

"Now it's just a matter of getting her to say it. And when she does..." Anna says.

"You've got her defense."

thirty-nine

Simon Mercer had arranged with the prosecutor, Diana Lynch, and Chief Inspector Hayden to conduct Anna's interviews with Elizabeth Barrett away from the juvenile detention facility where Dr. Fielding Goddard had conducted his. Anna's thinking was that a neutral, non-threatening environment would likely be more conducive to success.

It was agreed that, although Elizabeth would be escorted by armed guards, none of them would be in her presence while the sessions were taking place. The area Anna had chosen for the psychological evaluations was a small meeting room on the third floor of The Sandringham Hotel.

She had a sofa and two chairs along with a coffee table and two side tables brought into the room and arranged to afford Elizabeth an unobstructed view of the Bristol Channel and the Grand Pier.

While some forensic psychologists rely on an environment devoid of stimulation, Anna's belief is that peaceful, visual stimulation works to trigger the areas of the brain where images of traumatic events are stored, thus making their retrieval more possible.

Per Mitchell's request, four small cameras had been placed in discreet locations within the room. Two would afford a wide shot taking in the entire scene. Each of the other two would be focused on Anna and Elizabeth respectively.

Mitchell also added a two-way microphone that would allow him to speak directly into the room if it were to become necessary and he placed a video monitor in the room adjacent to the interview room where Lyla will be stationed.

"Everything is ready here," Lyla says into her cellphone.

"Just finishing up, I'll be right down."

Just as Anna is about to put her phone in her pocket it dings with a text.

'Good luck today. M.'

Chief Inspector Hayden is just finishing his survey of the interview room when Anna appears through the door.

"Good afternoon, Chief Inspector," Anna says, reaching for his hand.

"Good day, Dr. Newsom. Mr. Mercer here has told me all about you."

"And you weren't bored to tears?" Anna says, glancing at Simon.

"On the contrary. You seem to have quite the knack with this sort of business. Frankly, it's the reason we agreed to your request. And in spite of what you may have read, we're as eager for the truth as you are. Wish we could do something about the bloody reporters, though. Free press and all that bloody rubbish. Price of democracy, I suppose."

"It's comforting to know we're on the same page, Chief Inspector. This is my associate, Lyla Patterson."

"Pleasure, Ms. Patterson," he says, as they shake hands.

"Ms. Lynch won't be joining us today. Other matters."

"Just us mice then," Simon says, as Lyla turns to Anna.

"I'll be in the next room."

In the production van, Mitchell is just finishing with his sound and video checks as Hal enters the van carrying two large, grease-stained bags and several bottles of soft drinks.

"We're eating like Welshmen!"

"Good heaven...what in the name of....?"

"Cockle and clam fritters and Spanish fried anchovies!"

"My God, man, smells to high heaven!"

"Because they're bloody delicious!"

"Just don't drop any of that down the seat cushions."

As Hal plops himself down on the sofa behind him, Mitchell keys his microphone.

"Good afternoon," he says, his voice coming through the speaker in the interview room and surprising Anna.

"Oh, um, hi," Anna replies, not knowing at first where the voice is coming from.

"Claire is outside the room if you need anything," Mitchell says, just as the armed security detail transporting Elizabeth Barrett rounds the corner from Royal Parade onto Victoria Square.

Sensing commotion on the street below, Anna moves to one of the windows and watches as the knot of reporters and cameramen across the road come alive.

Two vehicles, a van in the lead followed by a sedan, pull to a stop in front of the hotel. Within seconds, two armed guards exit the lead vehicle, with the smaller of the two carrying an assault rifle.

The larger of the two guards moves to the rear and opens the passenger door of the sedan. A few moments pass and then Elizabeth Barrett steps out, along with a third guard, triggering an avalanche of strobe lights and shouted questions hurled from the reporters.

The guard kneels and removes the chains from her ankles, but leaves the ones on her wrists.

As they climb the curb, Anna steps away from the window, takes one last look at herself in the mirror on the wall and takes her position. She's learned that making a good first impression goes a long way in securing the trust of her patients, and that body language plays a vital role.

Rather than sitting behind a desk, which would appear authoritative and remote, Anna stands in the middle of the room facing the open door. Sometimes she has her hands folded in front of her, but today she has them behind her back. And, rather than her usual black leggings and tops, she's dressed in soothing neutral tones with a sweater over a blouse that carry hints of pastels.

She listens carefully as the elevator at the end of the hall reaches the floor and groans to a stop. It opens with three short squeaks followed by the echo of male voices and the strangely satisfying jangle of metal on metal.

Anna has just enough time to take another deep breath as Elizabeth and the guard appear in the hallway, stopping just outside the open doorway of the room.

"That's her," Mitchell says, spotting Elizabeth.

Hal takes a bite of fried anchovy and looks up to the monitors, licking his fingers.

"Interesting child. Got that 'Village of the Damned' look, wouldn't you say?"

"Amazing what trauma can do to a person," Mitchell says.

Anna allows herself a moment to take the measure of the young woman in front of her. In spite of the prison apparel, Anna realizes she was not prepared for how striking Elizabeth would be.

"Hi, Elizabeth."

"Go on, say 'ello to the lady," the guard says, but Elizabeth doesn't say a word.

"That's quite alright, officer. I'll take it from here," Anna says, "can you remove her wrists bracelets, please?"

The guard, surprised at the request, looks toward Chief Inspector Hayden, who is standing off to his left and out of Anna's sight.

"Do as she asks," Anna hears Hayden say from the hallway.

"Yessir," the guard says, shrugging his shoulders and reaches for the key on a lanyard around his waist. He removes the wrist bracelets, and then steps off in Hayden's direction, leaving Elizabeth alone, framed in Anna's doorway.

In the brief seconds since Elizabeth's appearance, Anna has been able to take note of several things. First, is her long, raven colored hair. She has it parted in the middle and nearly perfectly straight, reaching the middle of her back.

Next, are the arctic blue eyes, which seemed to be focused on a point several feet beyond Anna. Most striking of all, however, is the contrast between her hair and her skin, which is white as chalk.

Also undeniable is her complete emotional detachment from reality.

"Elizabeth. My name is Anna."

Elizabeth hesitates, and then responds in a voice that displays further evidence of a flat aspect.

"Are me mum and dad here?"

Anna turns and walks slowly back toward the front of the room, hoping that it will provide a safe space for Elizabeth to enter, but when she turns around to face her, Elizabeth is still standing in the doorway.

"If you don't mind, I'm going to sit," Anna says.

Anna chooses the chair to the right, in front of the windows and facing into the room, allowing Elizabeth the chair with a view out the windows to the channel.

"Do you know why I asked the Chief Inspector to bring you here?"

Elizabeth doesn't answer.

"I asked you here because I need your help."

"To find me mum and dad?" Elizabeth says.

"Your mom and dad are dead, Elizabeth."

"That's not true. They're in India. On a mission for God, and now they're coming home."

"They're still in India, Elizabeth."

"Then how can they be dead?"

"They drowned. In a reservoir."

Anna looks down at her hands, then continues, playacting her story.

"I asked you here, because, well, there's a man..." Anna says.

"Everyone is lying to me."

"I've known this man for many years."

"And now you're lying to me."

"This man, he, um, says he likes me. He gives me things," Anna says.

"They're not dead," Elizabeth says, quietly, "how can they be dead when they were on a mission for God?"

"And he does things to me."

This last comment from Anna sparks something in Elizabeth, and she shifts her gaze, and focuses out the windows to the Grand Pier and the channel beyond.

"Those men. What are they doing?"

"Which men?"

"Out there. Looking at the sea. Is that where me mum and dad are? Are they looking for me mum and dad?"

Anna turns and glances out the window.

"No. They're fishing."

Elizabeth hesitates.

"Do they have penises?" Elizabeth says, reminding Anna of the conversation with Simon.

"I suppose they must."

"They should be arrested."

"For having penises?"

"For having penises, and for lying."

Elizabeth hesitates for a moment, putting a thought together.

"Is God a man?"

"Some say so."

"Then God has a penis."

"No, I don't think...."

"Why not? He's a man, isn't he?"

"Well, that's..."

"Then he's a liar also."

Elizabeth blinks once, then a second time; and then her eyes shift from the scene out the window to Anna and the interior of the room, and she blinks again as if she's seeing them for the first time.

"What things?"

"I'm sorry?" Anna says.

"The man. What things does he do to you?"

Anna stands and walk to one of the windows, looking out

toward the street so that her back is to Elizabeth.

"Vile.... Unspeakable things. So much so..."

"...that you're afraid to speak about them?"

Anna turns from the window, feigning surprise.

"Yes, how did you know?"

She watches as Elizabeth begins to move and then step slowly across the threshold into the room.

"You're pretty," Elizabeth says.

"I don't think so."

"It's awful to be pretty, don't you think?" Elizabeth asks.

"Why would you say that?"

"You know as well as I. Isn't that why you brought me here?"

In the adjacent room, Lyla looks at her watch and jots down a few notes.

"What is all this? Seems like they're going around in circles," Hayden says, "I'm stepping out for some air, get anyone anything?

"I'm good," Simon says, "Lyla?"

"Me too."

On the monitors in the production van, Mitchell watches as Elizabeth begins to move slowly through the doorway.

"Anna Newsom's quite the actress," Hal quips.

"All part of the job, I would imagine," Mitchell replies.

As Elizabeth reaches the center of the room, Anna suddenly becomes aware of a strange smell. Not fishy or mammalian, but oily and earthy and primordial, nonetheless.

And because she's not sensing it directly through her nose, Anna instinctively recognizes it as the second onset of ESS, or Empathic Shared Sensation, the first of which she experienced in Elizabeth's bedroom.

The smell must have something to do with David O'Rourke, she thinks, making a note to herself, and then turns and walks back to the chair in which she had been seated, but remains standing, her back to the window.

Elizabeth moves slowly to the chair opposite, stops next

to it, and continues speaking. The two women are facing one another again, but much closer now.

"The man…"

"Yes?" Anna says.

"Does he promise you things?" Elizabeth asks.

"Such as?"

"Sweets."

"Yes."

"Does he take your clothes?" Elizabeth asks, then looks down at the chair, embarrassed at the question.

"My clothes?"

"Yes. When he's through."

Elizabeth's questions are revelatory, so Anna proceeds to guide her along this path of discovery. Elizabeth takes Anna's answers as a sign of growing mutual trust and senses that she has nothing to lose by taking a seat in the chair. Anna follows Elizabeth's lead and sits as well.

"As a matter of fact, he does," Anna replies, he, um, takes my…"

"Your underwear," Elizabeth says.

Anna takes a deep breath and her heart quickens as the empathic sensations she's receiving from deep within Elizabeth's brain grow stronger and more pronounced.

She's learned from experience that the sensations can affect not just one, but many, if not all, of the senses; and that they could manifest one at a time or all at once, and that an onslaught of sensations could come at any time.

"Is she okay?" Hal asks, sensing a shift in Anna.

Mitchell turns to James.

"Camera two."

James hits a button and a close-up of Anna appears on the main monitor.

"We had some time together this weekend," Mitchell says.

"That must be it," Hal says, jokingly.

Mitchell throws a dismissive look in Hal's direction and

continues.

"Anyway, she told me some things. In addition to what she does as a forensic psychologist, she's, uh, also a kind of psychic."

"Don't say? Reads minds? That sorta thing?"

"Apparently, so." Mitchell says.

"I'm sorry, Elizabeth. What was that?" Anna asks, now struggling to manage multiple sensations:

The oily smell, the cold, coarse hands coming to rest on her calves, then traveling slowly, up the inside of her legs, and the fingers curling around the laced edges of her silk underwear...

"About your underwear..." Elizabeth says, her voice bringing Anna back to the present.

"Yes?"

"Did you always have to make excuses for having lost them?" Elizabeth asks.

"Yes. How do you know?" Anna replies.

"Because I did, too."

"My God, man. I feel like a bloody voyeur," Hal says.

"Know what you mean. Take a walk, get some air. I'll keep watch," Mitchell replies, then turns to James. "Kill the speakers but keep watch on the needles."

"Roger that," James says, cutting the audio into the production van.

In the adjacent room, Lyla looks at her watch, then back up to the monitor.

"She needs to take a break," Lyla says, to Simon.

"How soon?"

"Right now."

"How do you know?"

"The way she's resting her chin on her hand. It's a signal!"

As soon as Elizabeth is safely out of the room, Anna bolts

into the bathroom, falls on her knees, and begins heaving into the toilet bowl. Not only did the session make her incredibly nauseous, but she now had the additional worry that it had ended far too abruptly, possibly with the loss of Elizabeth's trust.

"Anna?" Lyla says, with her most comforting voice through the bathroom door.

"What?" Anna manages, through the spasms.

"Are you okay?"

"Do I sound okay?"

"I'm sorry, Simon, I don't think this is something I can go on with," Anna says, as she exits the bathroom, wiping her face with a towel.

"What?"

"This is such an…an invasion of privacy. And today was just the beginning. You can see what's coming."

"Are you saying you can't continue with the sessions?"

"Not this way."

"But doing the sessions here was your idea," he says.

"The location is fine. Perfectly actually."

"What is it, then?"

"It's just that, it's being seen and heard by people who have no real need for any of it, and somehow it's making a difference in how the sensations are affecting me."

"She actually feels as though she were the one…you know…being…" Lyla says.

"I'm aware of that. We've discussed her abilities at length."

"Remember, Simon. I wasn't comfortable with this from the beginning…" Anna says, and is about to continue when Mitchell rounds the corner into the room.

"Hey, I've been listening to what's…" he says, when he's stopped in his tracks by the heavy atmosphere in the room.

"See what I mean?" Anna says.

"What did I do?" Mitchell quips.

"Mitchell, give us a moment, please," Simon says.

"I was just going to say I have an idea. I know this is going to get bloody personal..."

"Mitchell, please, stay out of it, okay?" Anna snaps.

Stung by Anna's sharp dismissal, Mitchell raises his hands in mock surrender and walks backwards out of the room.

Simon looks to Lyla for some kind of life raft and runs his hand over the thinning hair on scalp, weighing his options.

"Anna's right, her sessions with Elizabeth are far more important than one more award on Cynthia Smythe's shelf."

Chief Inspector Hayden has stopped at the end of the hallway and is conversing with the smaller of the two officers when his cellphone rings.

"Hayden here. O'Rourke's widow? She what? You're sure? I'm leaving now, should be there in half an hour."

Hayden hangs up and heads to the stairwell.

"Call it a day! Get the girl back to detention!" he says, barking at the officer.

"Right away, sir!"

Hayden darts down the stairwell and out of the hotel to his waiting patrol car. He dives into the front seat, turns on his siren and flashing lights, then hits auto dial on his phone and whips out of Victoria Square onto Parade Avenue.

"Diana, Hayden."

"Over so soon?"

"For the day, anyway. Listen, I just got a call and David O'Rourke's widow is ready to be seen. Heading there now before she changes her mind."

"Call me after."

Hayden hangs up, tosses his phone onto the dashboard and hits the accelerator.

forty

Hayden's old Renault takes the right turn off the main road onto the gravel drive that leads up to David O'Rourke's farmhouse. Hayden parks, walks to the front door, but before he can knock the door, swings open and Samuel O'Rourke, 22, steps out onto the porch.

"You must be Hayden."

"And you must be Samuel," Hayden says, reaching for Samuel's hand but is denied a response.

"I should've been here that day. Bloody exams."

"Couldn't be helped, then. Where's your brother?"

"On an errand."

"And how's your mother?"

"Better the last few days. The meds are helpin' her sleep, and we're hopin' to get her back on solid food this week."

They stare at one another for a beat, and then Samuel clenches his jaw and looks up at the passing cars on the main highway.

"Me brother and I 'ave heard what they're fuckin' saying."

"Sorry, son. The public defender's office is like a bloody sieve."

"Bloody bastards are what they are," Samuel replies.

"What about your mother? Has she heard?"

Samuel looks back to Hayden and drills a look into him.

"We've managed to keep her from the telly and the bloody rags, and she hasn't seen a soul. You think I'm going 'fuckin' tell her?"

"I have to speak to her son."

"This is her doin'. We're against it, me brother and I. Why the fuck does she need to know? Told that to your man on the phone. Something happens to her now, I'm holdin' you

276

and your whole crew of bloody blighters responsible! You got that?"

Samuel hesitates, allowing his last words to hang in the air, and then opens the door. Hayden takes off his hat and enters the house.

He takes a few steps and stops, taking in the thick history of the place. The house was built sometime in the early 1800's and has been in the O'Rourke family for nearly the same amount of time.

"This way," Samuel says, leading Hayden into the living room, which is lined with family photos and assorted memorabilia.

"Mother?"

Hayden pulls up next to Samuel and takes off his hat. He had gotten a glimpse of May just after the murder when the paramedics were attempting to revive her. But today, had he seen her on the street, he probably wouldn't have recognized her.

"Someone here to see you," Samuel says.

Hayden estimates that she's lost close to thirty pounds, not that she was a large woman to begin with, and she had been easy to look at. Three weeks later, she's grown grey and hollowed out, giving the impression that she's been living on a planet with ten times the gravity of the one she's on.

"Mrs. O'Rourke. I'm Chief Inspector Hayden."

"Good. My son told me someone had gotten my message."

Hayden takes note of the weakness of her voice.

"May I sit?"

"Of course," she says, and Hayden settles into the old wooden chair facing the stuffed high-back in which May is seated.

"Before I fade entirely from this world, I want to know about the girl."

"She's under heavy guard," Hayden replies.

"Being fed, I hope."

"Why wouldn't she be?"

"Fattened for slaughter, then. Marvelous."

Hayden fiddles with hat, readying himself to break the news.

"Mrs. O'Rourke, there's something you should know."

"Nothing can touch me now, Chief Inspector."

Hayden looks up at Samuel, then back to May and continues.

"We think the girl is going to make a claim."

"She claimed him. Isn't that enough?"

"An accusation, to be more precise."

"An accusation? Of what? Against whom?"

"Against your husband."

Not understanding, May looks from Hayden to Samuel and back again.

"All indications are that the defense is going to say, that, uh, your husband, had been, um..."

"Been what, Inspector?"

"Well, there's no delicate way to put it, you see."

Growing impatient, Samuel begins pacing from one side of the room to the other.

"Hayden! Get on with it, man."

"I'm not a child, Inspector," May adds.

"The defense is going to say that your husband had been sexually molesting the girl."

Not quite believing what she's heard, May tilts her head to one side, and for several seconds Hayden's words hang in the air.

"Pardon me, Chief Inspector, but, what was that you said?" May says, her voice suddenly stronger.

"The girl is going to say that she was raped. Not once, but regularly... over several years."

Reliving the story, Hayden said that he thought May O'Rourke either didn't hear what he had said; couldn't comprehend it; or had retreated to an even deeper place inside herself. Whichever it was, she and the entire room had suddenly gone stone cold still.

Her breathing was diminished, and her eyes had become fixed in a death stare aimed directly at Hayden.

"Mother!!!" Samuel yells, shattering the eerie silence.

Then, without warning and like a demon shot straight out of hell, May explodes into a paroxysm of maniacal laughter. The outburst is so sudden, and so thoroughly odious that it forces Hayden to jerk back in his chair and Samuel to retreat several paces.

"Hayden, God damn you, look what you've done!!!" Samuel yells. Hayden, for his part, holds his ground.

"Shut up! Where's the brandy?"

"Are you bloody buggers?" Samuel says.

"Tell me, dammit!"

"Find it yourself!!!"

Hayden jumps out of the chair and rushes to the kitchen. He flings open several cupboards until he finds a bottle above the stove.

May is still hysterical when Hayden returns with the glass. He approaches her cautiously and she begins to quiet.

"Here, take some of this," Hayden says.

"It'll bloody kill her, she hasn't eaten in three weeks!"

"Quiet!" May says, her hands shaking as she takes the glass from Hayden's hand. "And what if it does?"

May manages to take a sip and grimaces, feeling the burn. She then takes a second sip and begins to speak, measuring each word.

"Twelve years ago, this past summer, David and I were preparing for the summer fair in Cardiff. We were loading the Guernsies onto the lorry and everything was fine until the last one which, that season, had always been the troublemaker.

David had the lead, but she wouldn't budge, so he handed it to me and walked around back to give her a shove. When he did…She went off."

"Went off? How so?" Hayden asks.

May hesitates to take another sip of the brandy.

"Hooved him right in the abdomen. Split him open from the navel down through, well, everything."

"Mother!!! What is all this?" Samuel says, incredulous.

May pauses for a few seconds and looks down into her glass.

"You boys were young. We never told you."

Hayden struggles to find the right words.

"Mrs. O'Rourke, I, um…,"

"There's nothing to say, Inspector. He survived, obviously, but was certainly not the man he was before the accident."

May looks up from her glass.

"Do you…understand the point I'm trying to make, Chief Inspector?"

"Well, I…"

"For twelve years my husband was incapable of thinking about, much less doin' what you say they will accuse him of."

May pauses, and then turns to look at Samuel, who stares back, dumbfounded.

"I'm sorry you had to hear it this way, son."

Hayden glances at Samuel, then turns, grabs his hat and is about to leave the room when May stops him.

"Promise me something, Chief Inspector? That you won't let them do that to my husband?"

Hayden hesitates and manages a look of encouragement. As he heads for the front door, Samuel chases after him.

"Chief Inspector! You heard her! Me brother and I had no idea!"

Hayden pauses and turns and lowers his voice so May won't hear.

"Last week a brick went through the livin' room window of a house in West Park. It was Mr. Mercer's choice not to press charges. I'm advising you to keep a tight rein on that brother of yours or you'll be visitin' him in Cookham Wood. That's a bloody promise."

Hayden puts on his hat, turns and exits, shutting the front

door behind him.

"Diana! Where are you?" Hayden barks into his phone, as he races down the gravel driveway of the O'Rourke farm.

"Looking down the barrel of a Beefeaters."

"Stay where you are."

"You spoke to her?"

"Seems that Mercer and everyone around him are headed down the primrose path. At The Crown, are you?"

"Jersey Lily."

"Daresay you'll be well ahead of me."

"It'll be fun watching you catch up."

Hayden stuffs his phone into his coat pocket and kicks up gravel as he spins the steering wheel of his old Renault onto the main road in front of the farm.

Traffic is surprisingly light, and Hayden makes The Jersey Lily from the O'Rourke farm in less than thirty minutes. He parks the Renault across the street, hangs his hat and coat on a rack near the front door, and turning toward the bar, spots Diana Lynch, seated at the far end.

"You barely left me time for another," Diana quips, as Hayden takes the chair next to her.

"What's your pleasure, mate?" asks the bartender who places a drink coaster in front of Hayden.

"Jameson. Double."

Diana drains the last of her current Beefeater and with her teeth slides the olive from the toothpick.

"So…" she says, chewing, "how did we fare out there?"

The bartender returns with the drinks and fresh napkins.

"Tab?"

"Please," Diana replies.

Hayden takes a long sip of his drink, then turns in his stool and lowers his voice.

"It appears to be Christmas in October. For you, anyway."

The comment gets Diana's attention and, as she sips from her freshened drink, she studies Hayden over the rim of the glass.

"Widow, poor thing. Nearly out of her mind. What you'd expect, really. But not so far gone as to be without need of setting the record straight," he says; and, as he takes another healthy sip, Diana happens to glance up at the television above the bar.

Hayden follows her gaze, and, although the sound is too low to hear, she and Hayden watch a news clip of Elizabeth Barrett and the two-armed guards entering The Sandringham Hotel earlier that afternoon.

"Tell me," she says.

"Seems that twelve years ago one of O'Rourke's disgruntled dairy cows put a hoof clean through his privates."

"WHAT?" Diana says, nearly choking on her drink, then lowers her voice. "You mean to say that…?"

"Lost it all. Twigs and Berries, Bells and Whistle, whatever you want to call 'em."

"And they were able to keep it secret?"

"For twelve years. Not even the two sons. Until she told me this afternoon, she and the doctors, who are, of course, legally bound to secrecy, were the only ones that knew."

Diana pauses a moment to think and then replies.

"And still are. Unless their testimony is to be used for the purpose of exonerating their client," Diana says.

"Poor bloke," Hayden says, shaking his head, "Goddard was right. David O'Rourke was innocent, and that makes Elizabeth Barrett a cold-blooded murderer."

"What about poor Mrs. O'Rourke? I doubt the Queen herself has gone twelve years without some sort of bit and bob."

Embarrassed at the thought, Hayden clears his throat.

"Yes, well, one wouldn't think so now, would one?"

Diana raises two fingers toward the bartender, signaling for two more drinks.

"So, um, where do we go from here?" Hayden says.

"We let Mercer and the girl from the States go down the primrose path toward the so-called cliff of yours. And when the time is right..."

"You'll pull the rug out from under 'em."

"Mixed metaphors, but a plan nonetheless, Chief Inspector," Diana says.

forty-one

"You haven't touched your dinner," Lyla says, looking across the table at Anna.

"Why did I let myself get talked into this mess? We could be back home in Macon right now."

"You were trying to do the right thing. It may still be the right thing. You've just got to…"

"What?"

"Chill a bit."

"Chill? Really?"

"Yes, really. Simon was right. The sessions would have been recorded at the detention center anyway and you've been on camera how many times before this? So, what's so different now?"

"I don't know."

"C'mon girl, you know exactly what the difference is, and it begins with an 'M'.

"Please, not this again."

"How can a world class psychologist be so self-deceiving? Hello! Can someone here answer that question?" Lyla says, pretending to offer the question to the room.

"Very funny."

"Feeling that you're being raped, especially in front of someone whom you have feelings for, is not only embarrassing but it's confusing and disgusting, and you're afraid that it's going to destroy any possibility of having any sexual attraction toward Mitchell, just as it has with Ethan.

"Nice try, but you're wrong. I have absolutely NO interest in that self-satisfied, egomaniac."

"And there it is. Somewhere in the back of that little pretty head, something is saying that, by denying yourself a relationship with him, it will actually preserve the possibility of having one."

"Nice theory, but it's laughable."

"Listen, Anna, you have a God given ability to feel the things other people have experienced. And that's good for the work you do, but it's also destroying your ability to have a normal relationship."

Anna settles for a moment, letting Lyla's words percolate. She takes a sip of her wine and tears beginning welling in her eyes.

"Everything goes back to that goddam houseboat," Anna says, the tears begin running down her cheeks.

"Everything. The good and the bad. What you have to do is keep the good and ditch the bad," Lyla says.

"I don't know how."

"And I don't have the answer."

"Thanks a lot."

"That's not to say that it can't or won't happen," Lyla says. "C'mon, let's get you home."

"Will you call Simon for me?"

"What should I say?"

Anna wipes the tears from her eyes and sucks in the sniffles.

"We'll stay the course."

"That's my girl.

forty-two

The Royal Thames Yacht Club, established in 1775, is John Edwards' favorite haunt, and for good reason. For one thing, membership is limited, which appeals to his elevated sense of self. In addition, a potential candidate must be sponsored by another member, which usually results in immediate access to the 'The Club's' inner circles.

It doesn't hurt, of course, if the sponsor is one of the royal family, such as Prince Andrew, whom Edwards attended school with at Heatherdown Prep.

"Good day, Mr. Edwards," the young, female receptionist says, with a pleasant smile.

"Afternoon, Rebecca."

"Sailing today, sir?"

"My dear girl. Haven't you seen the maritime reports?"

"No, sir. Been answerin' the phone all day," she says, as if the job required herculean effort.

"You see, Rebecca…"

Edwards leans in over the reception desk, assuming a dramatic air.

"…The Edwards family are descended from a long line of 'fair-weather' yachtsmen, as it were."

"Okay."

"And today's forecast is for dark and stormy seas…"

"Okay…"

"…followed by scattered sightings of icebergs…"

"Okay."

"…floating in copious amounts of bourbon."

The final comment leaves the clueless, young girl at a loss for words.

"Besides, I haven't been able to replace my sous chef," Edwards says, with a wink and begins to move off into the main lounge when she stops him.

"Oh, Mr. Edwards."

"Yes?" he says, turning on his heels.

"I did see your last show!" she says, smiling broadly.

"You don't say?"

"Me boyfriend is a psychology major and…"

"Bloody good for him. What did you think?"

Not expecting the question, the smile disappears and her brow furrows.

"Well, can't say, really."

"Sorry?"

"He turned downed the sound… as, um, he had other things on his mind, you see."

"Now there's a man who's going places in this world," Edwards says with a smile and a wink; and, as turns and heads toward the main lounge his cell phone rings.

Goddard, he says to himself looking at the caller ID and answers.

"Fielding! How are things in Bristol today?"

"Better than ever, John."

"You sound downright enthusiastic. Hard to do for men our age," Edwards says.

"Are you sitting down?" Goddard asks.

"Sounds like it's either very good or very bad."

"It's very good."

"Give me five minutes. I'll call you back."

At the bar Edwards orders a double bourbon on the rocks then takes his drink to a secluded corner of the lounge.

"Here I am," Edwards says, as Goddard answers.

"Sustenance in hand, I assume?"

"Yes. Thank heaven," Edwards says, taking a deep sip, "so, tell me."

"I met with Diana Lynch, this morning."

"Ah, the Prosecutor for the Crown with, dare I say, the

most perfectly rounded rear in the Commonwealth."

"Ahem, yes, well…"

"Wasted on that girlfriend of hers, wouldn't you say?"

"Well, I…"

"Oh, go on, man. Looking never hurt anyone, now did it?" Edwards says, as he winks to a passing waitress.

"Anyway, Diana met with Chief Inspector Hayden last evening," Goddard says.

"Intriguing opening."

"It gets better. Hayden was able to get a statement from O'Rourke's widow."

"You don't say?"

"The poor thing wanted to know how Elizabeth Barrett was doing and when she could expect the execution."

"Delusional, then."

"Exaggeration, of course, but not far from it, apparently. He told her the girl was doing fine and then felt compelled to advise her about the accusations that would be forthcoming against her husband."

"And?"

"Apparently, she went as still as a corpse, and then exploded into some kind of maniacal laughter."

"That's bloody odd."

"Not really, and here's why. She told Hayden that twelve years ago her husband was, well, run through by one of his dairy cows."

"Good heavens," Edwards replies, taking a sip of his drink.

"Not only did he lose his desire for love-making as it were, he lost the tools with which to do it."

"Fielding, you're pulling my leg."

"'Fraid not, John. Diana's already reached out to his doctors and they're willing to confirm the story, to save the man's reputation, of course."

"My lord…"

"One more thing."

"Go on…"

"The rape tests have come back. Negative."

"Aha!" Edwards says, loud enough to turn heads in the bar.

"Right. Looks like it's just as we've thought," Goddard says.

"O'Rourke was nothing but a fantasy."

"Promise you won't breathe a word of it. I was able to get it from an old friend in the lab who'll get the axe for sure if he's discovered," Goddard says.

"What about Simon and the American girl?" Edwards asks.

"Miss Newsom is scheduled to have her second session with the girl tomorrow," Goddard replies. They're headed toward the cliff in full belief that O'Rourke was a sex-crazed maniac."

"Just had a thought," Edwards says, coming off a deep pull on his drink.

"What if I go to Cynthia Smythe and tell her that I'd like to do a live segment with Anna Newsom, on the nightly news, as a follow up to her work?"

"And…?"

"We expose the testimony from O'Rourke's widow…"

"On live television?" Goddard asks.

"On live television."

"My God, John, you are the devil."

forty-three

Anna's worries about Elizabeth not wanting to continue were unfounded, and she agrees to meet with Anna for a second time. Lyla was able to reach Simon before he canceled the BBC, so the recordings are to go on as scheduled.

The session was scheduled for 10:00 a.m. It was Anna's thinking that if the morning didn't prove fruitful, they would be able to continue through the afternoon, allowing for a lunch break.

She also made the conscious decision to wear a similar outfit so as not to chance an unnecessary distraction. The armed security detail arrived precisely at 9:50, and they delivered Elizabeth to Anna's room at 9:58.

"Good morning, Elizabeth," Anna says, as Elizabeth appears in her doorway, but Anna is greeted with silence.

"How are you today?"

"Have you found me mum and dad? Is that why I'm here?"

Elizabeth's opening leaves Anna disappointed. She had hoped that the session would begin somewhat further down the road, closer to where they ended yesterday. She would have to start over.

"No, Elizabeth. I've asked you here because I need your help. Do you remember?"

"I, um..."

"You look very nice today. Do you mind if I sit?" Anna asks, but Elizabeth remains silent and Anna takes the same chair as before.

"I've left that chair for you. So, you can watch the boats on the channel. And there's water in the pitcher. If you'd prefer something else, please let me know. "

Although Anna isn't expecting it so soon, Elizabeth takes

a small step through the doorway and then another.

"I remember now. You need help. With the man," she says.

"Yes. Yes, I do."

Much to Anna's delight, Elizabeth continues walking toward the center of the room and comes to rest next to her chair.

Lyla and Simon are again positioned in front of the monitor in the adjoining room, and Lyla is busy taking notes of what's being said and at what time it appears on the recording.

"I also remember that we were talking about our... um..."

"Underwear?" Elizabeth says.

"Yes."

"The ones that me mum and dad bought for me. Some were white, like seagulls," she says, glancing out the channel.

"And the others?" Anna asks.

"All colors really, but pink and purple were my favorites. Especially ones with flowers."

"I bet they were pretty."

"They went missing," Elizabeth says, as she scans the Grand Pier and the channel. "What happened to all the water?

"The tide is out," Anna replies.

"Where does the water go when the tide is out?

"I don't know. I've never thought about it." Anna replies.

Elizabeth stops for a moment.

"What color was your underwear?" she asks.

"Blue and green. But they disappeared. Like the water."

"Did the man take them?"

"Yes."

Elizabeth shifts her gaze from the channel and re-focuses inside the room. She begins to move, then hesitates, then begins again and circles to the front of the chair and sits.

In the production van and at Simon's request, Mitchell has arranged for the audio to be muted to allow Anna and Elizabeth a modicum of privacy.

Claire is again posted outside the door to the room. Encouraged by the progress she's making, Anna decides to enter new territory.

"The man who likes me, who is doing things to me…"

"Yes?" Elizabeth says.

"He, um, works on a farm," Anna says.

"Here we go," Simon says.

"Four minutes, thirty-seven seconds," Lyla notes.

Immediately after saying the word 'farm', Anna notices a nearly imperceptible, involuntary twitch of Elizabeth's right leg and both her hands. Within herself, a feeling like a dull, electrical shock signals the onset of ESS.

Anna knows that from this point she'll feel everything that Elizabeth describes.

"What kind of farm?" Elizabeth asks.

"A dairy farm."

Anna watches Elizabeth closely, taking note of her breathing, which ratchets up a notch. Elizabeth cocks her head to one side and begins to speak again.

"He comes to you on Friday," Elizabeth says.

"Yes."

"With everyone gone to the fish market."

"That's right Elizabeth, Benjamin and Margret both. "

"But the house is locked."

"They lock it when they leave," Anna replies.

"And you don't know how he gets in."

"No."

Elizabeth hesitates, and Anna watches as Elizabeth's eye movements shift direction indicating an attempt at memory retrieval.

"It may be dark or sunny or warm or cold outside."

"That's right," Anna says.

"Yet you know he's coming, because it's Friday morning, and you're lying in bed waiting."

"Waiting?" Anna asks.

"For the shadow. The shadow that falls on the wall of the hallway that you can just see through the crack of your bedroom door."

"Yes. That's right, Elizabeth."

"And when you see it, your stomach jumps to your throat.

"And then?"

"You turn away, and as you turn away, you hear the squeak of the door hinges and the creak in the floorboards under his feet."

"Yes."

"And then the smell...like...like..."

"Oily rags?" Anna says.

"Yes! And the sound of his...breathing...wheezing, through the bag on his head."

"What kind of bag, Elizabeth?"

"I don't know. Except..."

"Yes?"

"It's thick, like canvas, and it scratches."

"Go on, Elizabeth."

"There's a cord around the neck, and there's a name. A man's name. Faded and difficult to read. It's begins with a B... Bar...Bar..."

"Barclay?" Anna says, receiving the message.

"Yes. No. Barclay's, with an 'S'".

"Like the bank, then."

"Four holes. He's cut four holes, and I can see his eyes and his nose and his fat, ugly mouth."

Elizabeth stops, her breathing shallow and accelerating, the trauma fighting its way to the surface, and Anna is swamped now by the thoughts and the sensations Elizabeth herself is experiencing.

"The man, Elizabeth," Anna says. "Are his hands... "

"Rough. Like a worker. I can feel his hands, on me ankles, pushing away me nightclothes."

"Why don't you scream or yell out for help?"

"I can't. It's as though I'm..."

"What?" Anna says.

"Being held down. As if someone is sitting upon me chest and..."

"Go on."

"...and me arms and legs. I can only turn...me head...and...look over at..." Elizabeth says.

"What?" Anna asks. "Look at what?"

"The wallpaper... and the...the...so many of them..."

"The what, Elizabeth? So many of what?" Anna asks.

"Farms. All in a row."

"In a row?"

"Mary, Mary, quite contrary, how does your garden grow? With silver bells and cockle shells..." Elizabeth says, beginning the childhood rhyme.

"And pretty maids all in a row." Anna replies, finishing it.

"Yes. And then, suddenly, I feel the cold, rough hands moving slowly from me ankles, up, under me nightclothes and inside me legs."

"Go on, Elizabeth, don't be afraid," Anna says, although her own body is shaking.

"It makes no sense."

"What doesn't, Elizabeth?"

"I imagine I'm...I'm walking up the road to the farm, and it's a hot day and I need a drink of water...and I feel his hand cupping me between me legs."

"And then, then you stop..."

Elizabeth shakes her head 'no' and then changes her mind.

"Yes! I stop to pet the dogs and to have a wave at the farmhand crossing the field. And when I get closer, I, I... see a..."

"A woman!" Anna says.

"And she asks if my name is Elizabeth."

"And you say..."

"Yes, it is, I tell her."

Elizabeth stops to collect herself.

"I feel his fingers now, cold and rough sliding up beneath me underwear. 'David has told me all about you', she says. 'There's lemonade and cookies in the kitchen. And then...'"

At the mention of the name *'David'* the tremors in Anna intensify.

"My underwear is **being pulled down me legs,** and the woman says, '*Help yourself. Have all you want. I made them just for you, and when David is finished with his chores, he'll take you home.*'"

"David? DAVID! TAKE ME HOME!, I yell and then, in my ear, *I feel the hot breath and the wet tongue and the roughness of the bag* and the voice of the man on top of me saying, "*quiet now... be a good girl...quiet now...be a good girl...* through the hole in the bag."

Anna lets Elizabeth settle for a few moments so she herself can catch her breath and slow her heartbeat.

Breathe...breathe...breathe... she says to herself, her heart thumping in her chest.

"Was it always like this, Elizabeth?"

Suddenly, it seems as though Elizabeth has turned a corner. Her eyes are brighter, and she seems to be more in touch with her surroundings, almost as if she's seeing the room for the first time.

Anna instinctively knows that this is a critical point, and she decides to pose the question.

"Is that why you killed him?" Anna says.

"I had to make him stop. He was doin' disgusting things to me. And ...and...

"And what, Elizabeth."

"He was cheatin' on his wife to boot."

Anna kneels in front of the toilet, and even though she's terribly nauseous and racked with spasms, she cannot get herself to vomit. All she can manage through the dry heaves is a mouthful of saliva which she spits into the toilet.

During the first session in the bedroom and the two sessions with Elizabeth personally, the two of them had been lashed together physically and mentally, more so than even the most famous cases of shared experiences between identical twins.

The hot water takes forever in this hotel, she says to herself, and when it's as hot as she can bear it, she steps into the shower and stands, motionless, as the stream of water hits the top of her head and cascades down around her body, which is still quivering from the shock.

After a few minutes, she steps out of the shower, towels off, and slips into her robe. She crosses the room to her bed, lays down and closes her eyes. Across Parade Avenue, the screeching of the seagulls that had been foraging in the mud signals the return of high tide.

Just as the thought crosses her mind that she owes her parents a call, a text comes through from her mother.

Aunt Trudy is in the hospital. You probably don't care, and I wouldn't blame you, but I just wanted you to know. When are you coming home?

Anna sighs, tosses her phone down on the bed next to her, and closes her eyes.

Why wouldn't I care? But being reminded of the rape and the houseboat and all the turmoil that followed wasn't something that she needed right now.

Never in her wildest dreams would Anna have thought that her own rape would send her down the road to Forensic Psychology or to Empathic Shared Sensations or to Psychic Lightning Rods or Causal Tele-transmutation or to writing a book or the BBC. Yet, it did. And here she was; her Vocation and her Cross.

The sounds of the traffic on Parade Avenue mixes with the laughter of the children on the miniature golf links next door and, just as she's about to fall into sleep, her phone dings with yet another text. This one is from her literary agent, Evelyn Hardwick.

'Word on the street is things are going swimmingly and sales of your book hit a weekly record. BTW John Edwards has requested a live interview the night after you return to London. I'd say 'yes' if I were you.' AFN. Evelyn.

A live interview with John Edwards? There was no way

Anna was going to get a nap in now.

"Hi Elizabeth, did you have lunch?"

"Yes."

Anna and Elizabeth are seated in the same chairs as they occupied during the morning's session.

"What did you have?" Anna asks.

"A turkey sandwich and a Coke. What did you have?"

"I didn't eat. I tried to sleep."

"You must be hungry," Elizabeth says.

"Not really."

"It's too loud to take a nap at the center," Elizabeth says, and then turns her head toward the windows facing Victoria Square across from the hotel.

"Don't the children keep you awake?"

"The children?"

"Playing miniature golf. I see them when I come to the hotel."

"Would you like to play sometime, Elizabeth?"

"I'm too old now."

"Maybe I can convince Chief Inspector Hayden to let us play a game when we're finished," Anna says. "Do you remember why we're here?"

"I think so."

"Before we stopped for lunch, we were talking about the farm, weren't we?"

"Yes."

"And the man."

"Yes."

"And what the man was doing to you."

Elizabeth grows silent at this point.

"Elizabeth, do you remember what the woman was saying?"

"The woman?"

Anna looks down at her notes.

"You said, 'My underwear is being pulled down me legs

and the woman says, '*Help yourself. Have all you want. I made them just for you and when David is finished with his chores, he'll take you home.*'"

"Yes, she said that."

"Who is David, Elizabeth?"

"The man who's going to take me home."

"But you are home, you're in your bed in your room at the parsonage."

"No, I'm, I'm at the farm."

Anna reads from her notes again.

"*David? DAVID! TAKE ME HOME!, I yell and then, in my ear,* **I feel the hot breath and the wet tongue and the roughness of the bag** *and the voice of the man on top of me saying,* "**quiet now…be a good girl…quiet now…be a good girl…** *through the hole in the bag.*"

"Did I say that?"

"Yes. Don't you remember?"

"Yes."

As happened in the previous session, Anna knows she's reached a critical juncture in her questioning and decides to take it to the next level.

"There is only one man, Elizabeth."

"I'm sorry?" Elizabeth replies.

"Only one man. Think about that."

Anna gives Elizabeth a few moments before she continues.

"David, the man who is to take you home, is also the one on top of you, doing the terrible things to you."

Elizabeth stops now, so deep in thought and without expression that Anna is fearful that she's lost her.

"How is that possible?" Elizabeth finally says.

"Think about it, Elizabeth. Think about what I'm saying."

"No, it's not poss…wait."

"What, Elizabeth? What?"

"When…when I yell for David to finish his chores and take me home, the man on top of me says…"

"Says, what, Elizabeth?"

"He says, '*be a good girl...quiet now...be a good girl. David is right here to take you home... David is right here to take you home...David is right here to take you home.*'"

Having just led Elizabeth over the finish line, Anna sits back with a sigh of relief.

When the news broke, it broke hard and fast, sending shockwaves through the community of Clevedon and the small hamlets surrounding it.

Whether you were a casual acquaintance, a good friend, or a long-time business associate of the man, one could scarcely believe the official announcement that had been forthcoming from the Public Defender's office.

That the defense of Elizabeth Barrett for the murder of dairy farmer David O'Rourke would be based on justifiable homicide due to serial rape.

As Chief Inspector Hayden and Prosecutor for the Queen, Diana Lynch, had discussed, the evidence for David O'Rourke's innocence would be withheld until the time when it would have the greatest effect.

forty-four

Mitchell, Hal and Claire bound into Nick's as soon as they're able to wrap production for the day. The place is jammed, but they're lucky enough to get a table which is on the other side of the room from Anna and Lyla who are seated at the bar.

Hal says, "What's your pleasure, kids?"

"Stout please," Claire replies, followed by Mitchell.

"Double Jack," he says.

"No surprise there," Hal quips, as he heads for the bar.

Claire announces that she's going to the loo, leaving Mitchell alone, which gives him a chance to study Anna from a distance. The sessions have been tough on her and, had he known in advance what to expect, he could have done more to insulate her from the things that he himself had control over.

Anyway, it's over now, she'll be heading home, he tells himself.

Hal collects the drinks from the bar and is heading back to their table as Claire exits the restroom and stops to say hello to Anna and Lyla.

"This rape business is all that anyone is talkin' about," Hal says, as he arrives with the drinks. "Cynthia Smythe had her finger in the wind on this one."

"She certainly did," Mitchell says, and as Hal takes his seat, Mitchell raises his glass.

"To Cynthia's finger!" he says, with no little sarcasm, followed by a large gulp from his glass.

"Cynthialis Digitalis!" Hal responds, eliciting from Mitchell a guffaw that nearly has him choking on his drink.

Mitchell recovers and glances up over the rim of his glass. Claire and Anna and Lyla are talking politely and seem to be getting on together.

"Got it bad, don't ya, mate?" Hal says, watching Mitchell watch Anna.

"Piss off."

Then Claire turns and points in Mitchell's direction. Anna looks over her shoulder, and Mitchell believes, or maybe imagines, he's not quite sure, that a small smile crossed Anna lips when she saw him.

He's learned his lesson, however, and isn't about to take the step of walking over and saying hello based on such a flimsy appraisal. Not with this girl anyway.

Suddenly, David O'Rourke's image pops up on the television behind the bar. The bartender, responding from a request in the crowd, turns up the volume.

'...this afternoon came the long-awaited announcement that Elizabeth Barrett, who some have dubbed the Lizzy Borden of Bristol Channel, will go to trial accusing her victim, David O'Rourke, of serial rape.'

"Oh, shit," Hal says, from inside his drink, "here it comes."

The response from the rowdy patrons is immediate and is a mix of boos, hisses, and hollers.

As Claire leaves the bar, Lyla turns to Anna.

"You sure you don't want to join us?"

The words are barely out of her mouth when the image on the television shifts to a photograph of Anna.

'Simon Mercer, the public defender assigned to Elizabeth's case, called upon the American, forensic psychologist, Dr. Anna Newsom to....'

"Oh, God," Anna says, seeing her image, and puts her hand to her head, trying not to be recognized, but it's too late.

"Seems like we've a celebrity in our midst," a drunken man seated two down from Anna bellows out.

"Where!? How so!?" another pipes up and then a drunken middle-aged woman stands and points directly at her.

"That's her! The bloody American! The one on the telly!"

"Come on, let's get out of here," Anna says, jumping up from the stool.

Lyla throws a couple of bills on the bar, and the two of them attempt to weave their way through the crowd, most of whom hurl epithets at her for helping destroy the reputation of one of their own.

Mitchell watches as Anna and Lyla exit through the front door.

"Is something wrong? I invited her to sit with us," Claire says as she reaches the table.

"It's alright. Better this way," Mitchell replies.

"Good, you're not cooking yet," Simon says, as he enters the kitchen.

"Not sure how to take that," Karen replies, offering him a cheek that he promptly takes advantage of.

"Let's give the pots and pans a night off. What do you say?"

"No argument here. I just remembered, we've got a gift certificate to the Curtiss Steakhouse."

"No argument here, either. How about a drink first?"

Karen smiles and takes off her apron, as Simon heads for the kitchen cabinet and his usual bottle of scotch.

"What in the...?" he says, pulling a bottle of unopened Glenlivet single malt from the shelf.

"Win the National Lottery, did we?"

"Had a feeling we'd be celebrating. You deserve it."

Simon peels the wrapper from the bottle and reaches for two tumblers.

"Anna Newsom came through. Just as we hoped," he says.

Going to the ice maker in the fridge, he tosses a couple of cubes into each glass, then pours two fingers for each of them.

"And you've got the case you've been wishing for."

They clink glasses and take a sip, and then Simon takes his usual position leaning against the counter.

"And just as we suspected. The girl had been raped. For years. By a man, no one, not even God, would have expected."

"Will Anna be present for the trial?" Karen asks.

"Don't know. Haven't broached that with her, yet. We've got a little time, and I'd like things to settle a bit. We've got a lot of folks very upset."

Simon drains the last of his drink, and sets the glass in the sink.

"Whaddya say? I'm starved."

"Give me a minute to change," she says, returning the kiss on his cheek and then adds, "so proud of you," as she exits the kitchen.

Entering the farmhouse, Devon slams the front door behind him.

"GODDAM IT!" he yells, loud enough for May and Samuel to hear from the upstairs bedroom.

"Go see what the matter is now," May says to Samuel, who picks up her empty soup bowl from the tray table in front of her.

Bounding down the stairs, Samuel confronts Devon who is pacing like a madman.

"What in the hell do you think you're…" Samuel begins to say when Devon fires back."

"YOU SEE THE FUCKIN' NEWS?" he shouts, pulling a folded tabloid from his back pocket.

"Shut up! Keep your fuckin' voice down. Come with me."

Samuel leads the way into the kitchen, and Devon follows.

"Lotta good it did, her talking to the police," Devon says.

Samuel tosses the soup bowl into the sink and turns.

"What are you saying? You're fuckin' hammered," Samuel yells, under his breath.

"Not fuckin' enough," Devon replies. "Here."

Samuel hesitates, then takes the tabloid from Devon and unfolds it.

"GO AHEAD! READ IT!" Devon yells.

For a brief moment it seems the two are going to get into

a brawl, but Samuel knows that he would probably be on the losing end of any physical confrontation.

"OUTLOUD!" Devon says.

Samuel shoots Devon a look and then starts reading:

> *"Murdered dairy farmer delivered more than milk and eggs. This afternoon, rumors that dairyman David O'Rourke had been implicated in a series of rapes against the underaged girl that skewered him with a knitting needle became more than rumors. They became the basis for Elizabeth Barrett's defense. Justifiable homicide."*

Samuel lowers the paper. It had been his and his mother's decision not to tell Devon of the Chief Inspector's visit the previous week, as Devon had no need of knowing the extent of the injuries their father had sustained. But now that the charges of serial rape would form the basis of Elizabeth's defense, Samuel was at a loss for what to do.

"SO? ARE WE JUST GOIN' TO SIT AND TAKE IT?" Devon yells, under his breath?

"For now, yes," Samuel says.

"WELL I'M NOT!!!"

Devon turns and is about to bound out of the house when Samuel stops in.

"DEVON! They know it was you who threw the brick."

Not wanting to hear any of it, Devon spins on his heels.

"DEVON! Samuel yells again, "one more stunt like that and you'll be in prison blowing gang bangers. Guaranteed."

Devon sobers for a moment, and Samuel thinks that perhaps he's seen the light, but, then, just as quickly, Devon turns and storms out of the house, slamming the door behind him.

"Blevins!" Benjamin calls out, as he stands in the doorway of the darkened church; the blue, evening light filtering in from behind him.

"Just wrapping up me weekly chores, sir," Blevins yells from the choir loft.

After his arrival at the Church of the Divinity, Blevins had insisted upon taking over the duties, not only of music director, but of maintenance foreman on Benjamin's pride and joy, the eighteenth-century Brindle pipe organ.

"Listen, Blevins, I've a bit of news. Thought we could share a sip down in me office," Benjamin calls out.

Blevins grabs one of his old rags and begins wiping his hands.

"An offer that brings a tear to me eye," he says, with good humor, toward the voice in the dark below.

Benjamin, physically and emotionally spent from all the trauma surrounding the O'Rourke murder, takes a seat in his chair on the altar as he waits for Blevins to make his way down from the loft.

"'Nigh time to order more lubricant and I'm afraid to say we may be destined for a new reservoir in the near future," Blevins says, as he steps from the darkness into the pool of light over the altar.

"Spare me the pounds and pence report for the evening won't you, Blevins?"

"Sorry, sir. Saved for another day, it is," he says. "Remarkable, though, how much like children those grand old machines are; always in need of nurture and sustenance and a loving touch."

Benjamin smiles, slowly stands, and moves to the basement door. He flips a switch and they both head down the stone staircase worn by centuries of footfall.

"Watch your step, Blevins." Benjamin says.

When they reach the bottom, they turn and wind their through the dank hallway and into Benjamin's office.

"Been an age since I was in this room," Blevins remarks as he takes the chair on the outside of the desk.

"The last was probably the day you arrived," Benjamin replies, "me own small sanctuary; for the time being, that is. So many of us come and gone; in better times and in worse, I'm afraid."

Blevins takes the chair on the outside of the desk as Benjamin moves to the wooden shelf on the far wall.

"Don't tell Margret," Benjamin says, and, with a mischievous glint raises the crucifix, turns it over, and carefully extracts the small key inserted into its base. He sets the crucifix back on the shelf, then settles into his chair and unlocks the lower drawer of his desk.

"Me lips are sealed," Blevins says.

Benjamin retrieves the bottle of whiskey and two glass tumblers, pushes away some papers, and sets them both on the desk, pouring a healthy amount of whiskey into each.

He hands one of the glasses to Blevins, they raise them in a toast, and without further ceremony, they consign the warm, satisfying liquid to the purpose for which is was created.

Blevins smacks his lips and wipes his mouth, as Benjamin graciously pours another round.

"Nasty business we're suffering through Blevins," Benjamin says, braced somewhat by the effects of the whiskey.

"Haven't let me self ponder it too heavily, sir. Hard on the spirit, it is."

"I wanted to tell you, in person, Blevins."

"What's that, sir?"

"The news. Made public just tonight."

"Go on, sir."

Benjamin takes another deep sip.

"Those in charge have determined that Elizabeth, my niece, had been..."

Benjamin looks down at his hands and they begin to shake.

"My God, I can't bring myself to say it."

"I've 'eard the rumors, sir. Been hard to avoid, really,"

"Yes, well, apparently they're true. She had been and was being compromised by that man, David O'Rourke, God help his soul, for nearly the amount of time she had been with us.

The man we had so warmly and willingly invited into our lives."

"Terrible news, this," Blevins says. "O'Rourke seemed like such a trusting soul. What's the world coming to?"

"I've no idea, Blevins. No idea."

"But you've got to be somewhat relieved, sir."

"What's that? How so?" Benjamin says, somewhat confused by the statement.

"Well, sir, you know how people are. Especially those given to excessive expressions of faith. They chirp and chatter at the smallest transgression. Suffice it to say that any shadow of suspicion, no matter how misplaced or trivial, that any person may have had against yourself, is now removed. Expunged, as they say."

"I uh, don't know what to say, Blevins; except, well, I suppose you're right. Thank you."

Benjamin drains the last of his whiskey and stands.

"God have mercy on me poor niece," he says, as he heads toward the wooden shelf.

"And may God have mercy on poor David O'Rourke," Blevins adds, as he watches Benjamin take the key to his desk drawer and re-insert into the base of the crucifix.

In the weeks that followed, people would tell the following story; that when Samuel and Devon O'Rourke walked into the Black Horse pub, every head turned, glasses quit clinking, darts stopped thumping into targets and pints of beer hovered in suspended animation above table and bar.

"Why are we here?" Devon says, through clenched jaws, eyes fixed forward as they walk.

"Cause I've something to tell you," Samuel replies, "now sit your ass down," he says, leading him to a corner table.

"Eve'nin' Samuel," the bartender says, with an obvious touch of sympathy in his voice.

"Two pints, Stewart."

As the bartender fills their glasses, Samuel sneaks a look

around the room. Not a single pair of eyes rise up to meet his.

"Here you go, then." the bartender says, and as Samuel reaches for his wallet he adds, "forget it."

"No, really..." Samuel says, responding to the offer.

"I insist."

"Thanks, Stewart," Samuel says, after a slight hesitation, then delivers the beer to their table and sits.

Devon grabs one of the glasses and immediately downs half of it.

"It better be fuckin' good," he says, wiping his mouth on his sleeve.

Samuel hesitates, debating how to start, then decides to be direct.

"He didn't do it."

"No shit, Sherlock. Tell them that!" Devon yells, loud enough for everyone in the room to hear and bringing the place to another standstill.

"Shut up and listen, dammit."

Samuel takes a pull on his beer, leans into Devon, and begins to tell him the real story of what happened to their father.

"There's no fuckin' way!" Devon says, in complete denial, "he would have told us!"

"He didn't want us knowin'! Could 'ya blame him?"

The two boys quiet for a moment as Samuel lets the news take hold. Devon is the first to speak.

"Fuck! So, here we sit, sons of a murdered rapist or sons of a bloody eunuch!"

Devon takes another pull on his beer, leans back in his chair, and runs his hand through his hair. Then he looks out into space, reliving the moment he came upon his dead father.

"You know...the look on his face was...something I..."

"I'm sorry I wasn't here," Samuel says, looking into his glass.

"Maybe this is just a fuckin' nightmare."

"But it's not."

"It's some kind of hell, then." Devon says, as his lower lip begins to quiver, and Samuel can see that he's using every bit of strength he has to keep from breaking.

"Why him? Why did… she… have to do that… to him?

Devon sucks the moisture back into his nose and runs his shirt sleeve across his eyes.

"Chrissake, he wouldn't even swat a goddam fly."

Then, suddenly, Devon's demeanor changes.

"I'm going to the fuckin' newspapers!"

"The hell you are! We're goin' to keep our fuckin' mouths shut until Elizabeth Barrett gets what she deserves. Understand that?"

Devon gulps down the rest of his beer and beats it to the door. Samuel, trying to salvage some kind of dignity, finishes his and stands, raising a hand in the bartender's direction, as if it were just another ordinary evening.

forty-five

Anna wakes early and is finished packing with time to spare, and decides to spend her last few minutes in Weston with a walk on the Grand Pier. The tide is out, and the seagulls are having a field day in the thick mud, as they squawk and fight over the cockles, mussels and clams.

The plan is to go back to London for a couple of days before leaving for the States.

She's been invited to do a live guest appearance with John Edwards on the BBC evening news to discuss as much as she's able to discuss of the O'Rourke case. And, as much as she dreads seeing the man again, she feels it's something she's obligated to do.

In addition, Simon would like her to be present for the trial, but it hasn't yet been scheduled, so she has time to return home and regroup before she even has to think about returning.

Heading back toward shore, she buys a cup of coffee and a toasted tea cake and can't help smiling at the memory of the young, acne-faced teen who had so perfunctorily revealed the mystery of this regional, culinary delight. And although only a week ago, it now seems miles away in her rearview mirror, framed by the events surrounding Elizabeth Barrett and the O'Rourke murder.

She sits on a bench adjacent to the merry go 'round, then takes a bite from the tea cake, followed by a sip of the hot, dark liquid.

It's getting cold here. Time to go home, she thinks to herself, even though it would have been fun to have stayed long enough for the big Octoberfest celebration coming up in a couple of weeks. She's gotten to like England and its customs and its people, and will miss it all, to be sure.

A young mother passes, wheeling her stroller and her two-year-old and, stops a moment to let the child ooh-and-ahh at the merry go 'round which this morning appears to be under repair.

And then she smells it. It's not the exact smell that had accompanied Elizabeth into the room during their first session, but close enough; not fishy or mammalian, but oily and earthy. And unlike when she first noticed it, this morning she's perceiving it directly through her olfactory.

What's going on here? she asks herself; and when she goes to deposit her coffee cup into the trash receptacle near the merry go 'round, it's obvious that the smell is coming from the ride.

That's when she notices that several of the brightly-colored, plastic horses have been removed and are laying about, and that a worker, standing on a ladder, has his head buried within the inner workings inside the ceiling.

"Excuse me," Anna says, reluctant to disturb him.

The worker pokes out his head and reaches for a rag slipped through a belt loop on his pants.

"Two thirty this afternoon," he says. "No earlier."

"No, sorry...I...."

"Well, what is it then?"

"I, um, couldn't help notice, if you don't mind me asking, that smell?"

The man wipes his hands on the rag, slips it through his belt loops, and then tosses it in Anna's direction.

"Never been around machinery before?"

Anna catches the rag on the fly, and she can see that it impresses him.

"No, I, um..." Anna says.

"Go ahead, have a sniff," the worker says, which Anna does, confirming her belief that it is indeed, the same smell.

"Grease. Stinks to high heaven, especially when it's lived out its purpose. But it runs the world, it does. "

"Grease? Really?" Anna says, more to herself than to the worker.

"My rag, please?"

"Oh. Right."

Anna tosses the rag back up to the worker and for a second time he's impressed that she's able to send it straight into his waiting hand.

"Should be on the pitch with an arm like that," he quips with a wink, then stuffs the rag back through his belt loop.

"Seems like forever, Miss Anna," Henry says, as he opens the door of his cab.

"Good morning, Henry," Anna replies, as she and Lyla climb into the backseat, "it does, doesn't it?"

"Hi, Henry, how have you been?" Lyla adds.

"Without me two favorite clients? A might lonely, I'd say."

"We missed you, too," Anna says.

"Well, from what me wife has told me, you've been pre-occupied with some rather nasty business."

"Anna's done a remarkable job, Henry," Lyla adds.

"That poor, young Barrett girl. Put upon that way. And, from all accounts, by an upstanding pillar of the community."

"Oh, darn it," Anna says, looking down at her white leggings.

"What's that, miss?"

"How did that happen?" Lyla asks.

"A man at the pier was working on a ride. I must've brushed up against something. I've got grease all over me."

"My, that does bring back a memory or two. Before I began drivin' lorries, I was what they called a grease monkey in Her Majesty's Navy. I didn't see the world, but me lovely new bride saw her share of soiled overalls, that's for sure."

"Darn it, these were my favorite leggings, too."

"Not to worry, miss. Hot water and dish soap does the trick."

"Or just give them to the hotel," Lyla adds, with a wink.

"Nobody thinks about grease until it's time to get something done. It runs the world, it does."

"That's funny," Anna says, turning to Lyla, "that's what the man working on the merry go 'round, said."

Whether by accident or intent, Anna has been given the same room as she had before, and Lyla is in the room next to her.

The only remaining items on the schedule is the live interview with John Edwards tomorrow at six, which she's dreading. The morning after, she gets to go home.

Looking out at the view of London and the Thames below, it's hard to believe that it's only been four weeks since she saw it for the first time.

She boots her computer and puts on her collection of her favorite bluegrass tunes, and then unpacks; not everything, but the few items she'll need for the rest of the trip.

She undresses and, taking Henry's advice, fills the bathroom sink with warm, soapy water and submerges the leggings. After a bath and a quick bite, they both went to bed.

The following morning, Lyla got an early start on the day. Since it was to be their last, she had made a list the night before of all the things she wanted to see and do and was intent on doing them all from the first to the last, starting with Harrod's.

Anna, on the other hand, decided she would sleep in. Sleep as much as she could, in fact, until the moment arrived when she had to face John Edwards again, this time on live television.

She had been experiencing waves of anxiety and feelings of impending doom ever since Evelyn Hardwick had brought up the interview in her text message, and Anna's conversation with Cynthia Smythe soon after did little to assuage the feelings.

Perhaps it was the residual effects of the sessions with Eliza-

beth, Anna tried telling herself, but she knew better. She dreaded it, but as long as she was doing it, of course, she wanted it to go well.

She wanted it to go well so she could get back to the hotel, have a nice dinner, and get a good night's sleep. So, the next morning she could get on a plane and fly back to her comfortable job and her many friends in the peaceful Southern town of Macon, Georgia, and consign John Edwards and Mitchell Walker and Weston Super Mud to a distant memory.

Anna pulls the covers up over her head, and eventually falls back to sleep. Her alarm wakes her at four-fifteen. She takes a long bath in the tub overlooking London and lingers as evening twilight descended over the city.

Lyla suggested that she dress in black, which she was going to do anyway. She decided on a small amount of make-up and mascara and went lightly on the lipstick, vowing to not let the young, BBC make-up girl get anywhere near her.

Even though Henry's remedy for her white leggings did the trick, Anna resorts to her black leggings with a white blouse and a black jacket. And she pulls her hair into a low ponytail, using a tufted purple hair tie.

forty-six

"'Ello ladies!" Henry says, with his usual punctilious, joie de vivre. "Miss Smythe wants you dispatched to the studio at 6:00 p.m, and 6:00 p.m. it shall be."

"Hi, Henry. I guess you'll be waiting to bring us back to the hotel?" Anna says, with a slightly nervous quiver.

"Of course, miss. Not about to let the likes of you two wander the streets, easy prey to the cunning advances of any Tom, Dick, or Harry," he says with a wink into his rearview mirror.

Anna and Lyla can't help shooting each other a quick glance and a small snicker.

"Hey, Henry. Can you tell us. What's a toasted tea cake?" Lyla says, intent on keeping up the banter.

"Don't tell me that you two girls, smart as you are, fell for that old chestnut?"

"Chestnut?" they both reply at the same time.

"Been around since World War Two. Locals put up signs in front of their shops saying, *'Toasted Tea Cakes',* just so the American soldiers would come in and make fools of themselves asking what a toasted tea cake was. Once they heard the answer, they felt like dunderheads."

"No, come on, really?" Lyla replies, skeptically.

"It was in some, small manner our way of demonstratin' against what most felt was an invasion of our country by the American cousins."

"So, they left the signs up for the rest of us?" Lyla quips.

As Lyla and Henry continue to talk, Anna notices the small camera that Mitchell had placed in Henry's cab.

How in the world did agree to this? she asks herself and is still pondering a way out of the interview, when they pull up

315

to the main entrance of the BBC's broadcast center.

"Auntie's doorstep with two minutes to spare," Henry declares, proudly.

"Auntie?" Lyla says, under her breath to Anna, who is reaching for her door handle.

"I'll get that, miss," Henry says, and as he jumps out of the cab, Anna turns to Lyla to answer.

"Auntie. It's what they call her. I mean this place. The BBC. It's weird, I know."

"But, sooooo British," Lyla adds.

"Right."

"Mitch?" Freddy calls out from the bathroom.

Freddy, short for Frederica, is Mitchell's on again, off again, love interest.

"What's up?" Mitchells replies, from the kitchen.

"All out of TP, love."

"Under the sink."

Where else would it be, Mitchell says to himself. He removes two steaks from the refrigerator and sets them on the counter next to the stove, checks his watch, and then goes into the living room and switches on his large, flat screen TV.

"Why do you men always run out?" Freddy says, making her appearance into the room.

"Must be in our DNA."

Live television is not part of Mitchell's job at the BBC, so he has the night off. Since returning from Weston, he's been busy tidying up the loose ends around the O'Rourke project, and Hal has delivered all the recordings to Cynthia Smythe.

The cameras, however, will not be removed until the beginning of the week when the strike crew is due to arrive from London.

"By the way, love…"

"What?" Mitchell says, turning from the television.

"You're out of chardonnay."

"In the freezer."

Mitchell turns up the sound and sets the remote back on the coffee table.

"One thing about this new place..." Freddy says, wine glass in hand, as she pads into the living room.

"What's that?"

"I certainly don't miss the horrid wallpaper."

"That was Carolyn's idea."

"I don't miss her, either," she says, sinking into Mitchell's contemporary mohair sofa. She takes a sip and then eyes Mitchell over the top of her glass.

"Why did you marry her, anyway?"

"Stability," Mitchell answers, without thinking.

Freddy chews her cheek for a moment and then stands. She wanders over to Mitchell, throws an arm around his neck and dives into his mouth.

"Doesn't get more stable than this, love," she says, and the words have barely left her lips when Mitchell's cell phone rings. He pulls away and accepts the call.

"Hal."

"You watching?"

"Yeah."

"Catch you tomorrow then," Hal says, signing off.

Mitchell picks up his remote and turns toward the television.

"Do we have to?" Freddy says.

"Yes. Why don't you season the steaks?"

Mitchell wanders over to his bar and pours himself another Jack Daniels. As he's heading back toward the television, the show begins.

"Something with that murder?" Freddy says, from the kitchen.

"Yes," Mitchell says, again, turning up the sound as Rebecca Portman, the BBC evening news anchor, begins to introduce the live segment with John Edwards.

"*...this evening, in response to the overwhelming interest in* the O'Rourke rape and murder case, our resident 'Maven-On-Any-thing-Mind', John Edwards, is here in the studio with us. John…"

"*Rebecca. Thank you for having me,*" Edwards says, forcing his voice to its deepest possible register.

Mitchell's phone dings with an incoming text from Hal.

'*Maven on anything mind? How do they come up with this shit?*'

Edwards turns from Rebecca Portman and looks directly into the camera.

"*Rebecca, as you know, the entire country has been riveted by the case of Elizabeth Barrett, the fifteen-year-old accused of murdering Clevedon dairy farmer, David O'Rourke, whom she now claims had been raping her for years prior. With me tonight is Dr. Anna Newsom…*"

Mitchell watches as the scene cuts from a close-up of Edwards to a two shot of the set, which includes Anna, who is sitting to his right. She smiled slightly at the mention of her name, turned politely to the camera and then back to Edwards; and, to Mitchell, she looks like she's getting the hang of it.

"Hey, something going on between you two?" Freddy says, picking up on the subtle change in Mitchell's demeanor upon seeing Anna.

"Hell no," Mitchell says.

"*If you've been following the case, you'll know that Miss Newsom was brought in all the way from the States to perform analysis on the accused. Good evening, Miss Newsom.*"

"***Good evening.***" Anna says, somewhat miffed at not being called "doctor."

"*Can you briefly explain to the audience what your work on this case entailed?*"

"***Of course. I was hired by the defense to examine, through*** *analysis, the accused, and to come to a conclusion about the motives for the murder and the nature and veracity of her claims, if there were any."*

"And we now know what those claims are, don't we?"

"Yes. I'm quite certain, and this is how I advised Simon Mercer, the public defender, that Miss Barrett had been raped, serially, over several years by the victim, David O'Rourke and that this is what led her to take the action that she did."

"You mean, running the man through with a stainless steel, knitting needle," Edwards says, with no little sarcasm.

Sitting at their kitchen table, Simon Mercer and his wife, Karen, watch the interview as Karen empties white paper bags of fish and chips onto plates.

"I don't trust him," Simon says, then he takes a deep breath and a long pull from his bottle of beer.

"Don't worry, she'll be fine. Although he does seem a bit ill-tempered tonight, doesn't he?" Karen says.

"Now, Miss Newsom. How can you be so sure of your conclusion?"

Mitchell's phone dings with another message from Hal.

'that bit, calling her miss instead of Dr. is intentional.'
'prick'. Mitchell responds, with a text of his own.

Cynthia Smythe, who is sitting at the console in the control room, leans into the director, who is sitting next to her.

"Does Edwards have an earpiece?"

"Of course."

"Then tell him not to pull that shit again."

"I'm not at liberty, Mr. Edwards, to discuss all the details about the case. Suffice it to say, that all of the facts and all of the evidence to support my conclusion will be brought forth during the trial of Miss Barrett."

"Miss…ahem, I'm sorry, Doctor, is it safe to say that you've become quite a celebrity around this work of yours?"

"I wouldn't say, celebrity, no."

"Well, you have a book on the New York Times Bestsellers List, that certainly says celebrity to me."

"It's a response to my work. Not me personally. Celebrity is a cult of personality."

"Speaking of your work, remind our viewers how you arrive at your conclusions when involved in something like this."

"I have my own, scientific process. A process which I discovered and developed and thoroughly vetted. We discussed this thoroughly on the series which you yourself presented."

"Have you ever been wrong, Dr. Newsom?"

"You've asked me that before. No. Not that I know of."

"Well, I'm not sure that even Sigmund Freud could have made that claim," Edwards says, with a chuckle.

Before Anna knows what's happening Edwards reaches to one side and retrieves a file folder.

"In my hands, I have a statement from David O'Rourke's doctors."

Anna pales, unsure now of where this is headed.

"Doctors? Autopsy doctors?"

"No. Medical doctors. Would you like to read it?"

"Why wasn't this provided to the defense?"

"It would have been. In due time. But now it's been given to me."

Sensing the trap, Anna doesn't respond.

"Then allow me."

"What the fuck is going on here?" Cynthia Smythe says to the director seated next to her.

"No fucking clue," the director replies.

Edwards opens the folder and, with great relish, removes

the pages, puts on his glasses, and begins reading.

    "'We, the undersigned, set forth the following; That on the twenty third of July, in the year 2008, one David O'Rourke incurred a life-threatening injury to his abdomen and pelvis inflicted by one of his dairy animals, a Guernsey cow. After the victim was stabilized, Dr. Higgins and myself were brought in to save, whatever we could, of Mr. O'Rourke's sexual organs. I am saddened to say that we were not successful in our endeavors. Mr. O'Rourke, on the day of the accident, was for all intents, neutered; rendered incapable of sexual desire and incapable of any means by which to express it.'"

"Oh! My! God!" Lyla says, out loud, to herself, watching from the greenroom of the studio.

"That goddam, bloody prick!" Mitchell says, gulping Jack Daniels from his glass.

"What's just happened!" Karen says, turning to Simon, who is already up from the table and heading toward the front door.

"I'm going to London!" he yells, grabbing his coat and hat from the rack.

"It's 6:15 Simon!" Karen cries, but Simon is already out the door.

Cynthia Smythe, hyper aware of the humiliation Anna has just suffered at the hands of John Edwards, stands and bolts toward the door leading to the studio, yelling at the director.

"Go to a fucking break!"

"Give Edwards a thirty second...." the director begins to say, when Cynthia fires back.

"Now, goddam it!" she commands, exploding through the door. "Edwards, is fucking toast."

At her parent's home in Macon, Frank and Vivian had just sat down to a lunch of tuna sandwiches and potato chips.

Anna had told them of the live show, and they were able to

tune in on their cable provider. Against Anna's wishes, Vivian had announced it to several of her friends, as well, so the audience in Macon had swelled to well over twenty viewers, which were now front-row witnesses to Anna's humiliation.

"Mitchell!" Freddy yells, but it's the interview that has sent him sprinting into the kitchen. He downs his drink and tosses his glass in the sink.

"What! he says, glancing at her.

"I burned the steaks," Freddy says, oven mitts grasping a wine glass in one hand and a large fork in the other.

Without acknowledging her, Mitchell yells,

"Fuck! Fuck. Fuck. Fuck," then grabs his coat and storms out of the apartment, the slamming door sounding much like a sonic boom.

Clueless as to what has just transpired, Freddy takes a sip from her wineglass and shrugs.

"It's just steak," she says, under her breath.

Anna wasn't surprised that Edwards had sought to make a fool of her, as her intuition had not failed her. What blindsided her was the severity of the attack, and his unadulterated hatred of her that he so gleefully displayed on British television.

At the same moment the floor manager told John Edwards to go to a break, Anna shot straight up off the chair, ripped the microphone from her collar, and bolted from the studio.

Assuming that Anna would be in the chair when they returned from the break, Lyla took the opportunity to go to the loo.

Henry was in his cab and had his head in the sports page of the paper, so didn't see Anna storm out of the broadcast center; and by the time anyone realized she had left, Anna was halfway down Woods Lane.

First came a text from Simon,

'Don't know what all this is about. I'm driving in now. See you

at the hotel.'

The next text was from her father.

'What just happened there, Sparky? I thought
     they were supposed to be on your side.'

The next was a phone call from Cynthia Smythe that Anna sent directly to voicemail.

Then came a text from Lyla.

'OMG! Where are you? I was in the bathroom for like a nano-second and you were gone!'

Anna ignores them all and opens her contacts, retrieves Mitchell's address, and enters it into her GPS.

Asshole, she says to herself, and, dodging traffic, stomps across Wood Lane heading toward Kensington Place, angrier than she's ever been.

By the time Lyla jumps into Henry's cab, Anna has a three-minute head start. Lyla is assuming that Anna would be heading back toward the hotel, presumably taking the full length of the seven mile walk to clear her head and hopefully, cool off.

"I still don't see her!" Henry says, glancing from left to right through his windshield. "What, may I ask, happened to the poor child?"

"John Edwards. That's what happened," Lyla replies, her hands cupped around her eyes, searching the sidewalks outside her window.

"I see." Henry says, in a somber tone.

"What's that big building there, on the right?" Lyla says, suddenly.

"Oh, my. That's the Romanian embassy, miss. Pray to the Lord that she isn't in there," he says.

The closer Anna gets to Mitchell's flat, the more determined she is to have it out with him; as she's sure that there was no way for him not to have known what John Edwards was cooking up.

As luck would have it, just as Anna gets to Campden Hill Square, the skies open with a downpour so fierce that, by the time she rounds the corner to Kensington Place, she's drenched, making her angrier still. To make matters worse, the street numbers are worn and barely discernible, so it takes another minute or two before she finds Mitchell's address.

Now, mad as hell, chilled to the bone, hair plastered against her head, and eye-liner and mascara dripping down her face, Anna climbs the stairs to the flat, steels herself and rings the doorbell. Once. Twice. No answer.

He lied. He said he was going to watch the interview from home, and he lied. Double asshole.

Anna quickly turns to see if Mitchell's Range Rover is parked out on the street, and, while she's squinting through the rain, she hears the door open behind her.

She whips around, ready to pounce, but instead of Mitchell standing in the door, it's Freddy, with a glass of wine in her hand. Anna's heart sinks.

"Um. Can…I…help you?" Freddy says, giving Anna the once-over. "Whoever you are."

"Where's Mitchell?"

"That's none of your business," Freddy says, unsure of who Anna is or what possible intentions she may have. But as she studies Anna a little more closely, her demeanor changes.

"Well, knock me over with a feather," Freddy says, "aren't you the pretty little thing that was on the telly this eve'nin?"

"And that's none of *YOUR* business," Anna snaps, spinning on her heels.

Heading back down the steps, Anna retrieves her phone and calls Simon.

"Anna! Where are you?" he says, nearly breathless.

"It doesn't matter. Don't come."

"But…" Simon says.

"I'm way over this, Simon. The whole damn thing. You. Mitchell. John Edwards, the BBC.

"But…"

"Don't! I'm going home."

"But we're not done."

"Oh yes, we are. Good-bye, Simon."

Anna switches to her GPS and searches for The Shard which she's saved, and then calls Lyla.

"Thank God!" Lyla says, relieved. "We thought you jumped off London Bridge."

"It's not too late."

"I wouldn't blame you. That was pretty rough."

"I'm walking back to the hotel."

"But it's pouring!"

"Really, I don't care. When you have a chance, please arrange the trip home. The sooner the better."

"Of course," Lyla says, "sorry it ended this way."

"Me, too."

The rain has eased by the time Anna gets to The Shard, but, just as she's heading up the drive to the entrance, Mitchell bolts out the front doors, forcing Anna to spin and head in the opposite direction.

"Anna! Stop!" Mitchell cries, but she keeps walking, and Mitchell runs after her. He grabs her arm, Anna pulls it away, speeds up, and turns toward the walkway that leads to the Thames.

Mitchell hesitates for a moment, and then continues after her.

"Anna, please, it's not what you think. I had no fucking clue that Edwards would pull a stunt like that."

"Like hell you didn't!" Anna says, turning over her shoulder.

"Anna, I swear. On everything that is right and holy," Mitchell says.

Suddenly, Anna stops and turns.

"Right and holy? Now, that's a laugh. That, that, whoever, that's in your apartment didn't seem so right and holy!" Anna yells, then spins back and continues walking.

"Oh, now I get it. So that's what this is about?" he yells.

Anna gets to the walkway overlooking the Thames and stops at the railing. Mitchell stops as well, but a few paces away.

"It's about everything," she says, softer now.

"Listen, whether you believe me or not, I think what fucking Edwards did tonight was wrong and despicable, which is why I came after you..."

"...Which is why you left a cozy little evening at home is what you mean."

"What's with you, anyway?"

Anna hesitates and walks a few paces down the railing before stopping again.

"I'm screwed up, okay?"

"Don't say that."

"Why, not? It's true."

Mitchell pauses and runs his hand through his wet hair, debating with himself about going on with the conversation.

"Look, Anna, Lyla and I had a few moments alone last week."

"Congratulations, another notch in your bedpost."

"That's fucking insulting."

Anna slows for a bit, giving Mitchell an opening.

"Sorry."

"She, uh, well...she told me some things that..."

"That what?"

"Some things that she thought I should know."

"She had no business, Mitchell..."

"Of course, she did. Yes, she's your employee, but she's also a friend. And I'm glad she did. It explains things."

"Oh, I see. It explains why I didn't jump into bed with the wonderful Mitchell Walker the first chance I had! Is that it?"

"No. And you know it. She told me how you're...um... affected by things and that you're a...clairvoy...."

"No, not clairvoyant. I'm a clair-cognizant. An empath in other words."

"That's it," he says, "and that you actually experience what your victims experience."

"Unfortunately. Yes."

"Why is it unfortunate?"

"Why do you think?"

Mitchell pauses for a moment, letting the ramifications of it all sink in.

"It's starting to pour again. You're going to catch pneumonia," he says.

"What difference would it make?"

"It would make a difference to me," Mitchell says, "let's get you upstairs and into a warm bath."

forty-seven

Still shivering, Anna climbs out of her robe and into the warmth of the bath and reaches for her glass of red wine. In the living room, Mitchell pours himself a glass and steps to the floor-to-ceiling windows to take in the view and can't help thinking how much hatred he has for John Edwards. As he takes a sip, his phone dings.

'Got tired of waiting. BTW, Blondie was here. F.U.'

He pockets his phone, then wanders toward the partition separating the main living area from the bathroom and notices that, because of a one-foot gap between it and the windows, he can see Anna's reflection.

"Hey, you okay in there?" he says, as he watches her.

"I'm sorry," Anna says, from the opposite side of the wall.

"Sorry for what?"

"Everything."

"You talkin' to me?" he says.

Mitchell takes another sip and then leans against the wall, watching her.

"For one hundred pounds, who said it and in what movie?"

Anna thinks for a moment and then Mitchell hears her answer.

"De Niro. Taxi Driver," Anna replies, sinking a little farther into the warm water. "One of my favorites."

"You know, you're like no one I've ever met," Mitchell says, leaving the reflection and heading back toward the bottle of wine.

"Frigid. Afraid of sex. I don't doubt it."

"How do you know it's not a temporary condition?" he says, pouring himself another glass.

"Because I've been this way my entire life," Anna says, gazing out at the lights of London.

She'd been having fun with the conversation, but this last statement has driven home the sad reality of her condition.

Mitchell goes back to the windows and takes another look at Anna's reflection.

"You're low on wine," he says.

"How do you know that?"

"I'm a mind reader, too." Mitchell says, studying her. "Just joking, of course, but how is it possible?"

"What?"

"Your ability to feel what other people feel? I mean, it's not scientifically proven, is it? Extrasensory perception and all that?"

Anna takes another sip, thinking about how to answer the question.

"Modern science...and it's embrace of the material world as the total of reality has done humanity a great disservice, Mitchell. What we need is an interpretation of the world that unifies all aspects of reality; mind and matter, and not just what can be measured with a ruler."

"Never thought about it quite like that. You should write a book about it," he replies.

"I've been working on it."

Anna sips the last of her wine and sets the glass back on the table next to the tub. She reaches for her towel and, as she begins to stand and as much as he doesn't want to, Mitchell turns away.

Anna climbs out of the tub, dries herself off, and throws on a robe. She towel-dries her hair, lets it stay tousled, then grabs her wine glass and heads into the living room.

Mitchell pours her another glass, and Anna walks over to the windows.

"When I first got here, I tried to imagine what the sky must have looked like during the bombing raids," she says.

"German pilots, those that survived, said the flak was so thick you could walk across it," Mitchell replies.

"Flak?"

"Anti-aircraft fire. It's an abbreviation of, let's see if I can remember… *Fliegerabwehrkanone.*"

"You know German."

"Only a few words from the war that we learned in school."

Mitchell turns toward Anna.

"See the London Eye. The big Ferris wheel?"

"It's hard to miss."

"In 1942, there was a Woolworth's just a few blocks from there. One morning, after a night of fighting fires ignited by German bombers, my great grandfather stopped to have something cool to drink. Moments later, a German rocket, the V-1, fell right on top of it. Blew the store and half the neighborhood to smithereens."

"How awful," Anna says.

Mitchell looks down into his wine glass and for a moment he's lost in the past.

"Hey," Anna says, bringing Mitchell back to the moment.

When he looks up, Anna raises her hand and, using her index finger, gently raises each corner of Mitchell's mouth, putting a smile on his face.

"That's more like it," she says; and as the now familiar glint returns to his deep brown eyes, he gazes into each of hers, sending a shudder down the length of her body.

What has this girl… this American girl, done to me? Mitchell asks himself.

It's only been a week since their visit to the O'Rourke farm, but since their kiss in the Moon and Sixpence, Mitchell has been consumed with the thought of being with Anna again, of being undone again; by the grayish, green eyes the shade of moss and the delicate lips that form a small heart just beneath the slightly upturned nose.

And although he would never admit it to anyone, he was frantic with the possibility that it would never happen. And wasn't that part of the fascination? That this willowy, almost waifish, Southerner could get the better of the great Mitchell Walker. England's Valentino! Lover of Women! Envy of Men!

As he leans into her, with their lips no more than an inch apart, he feels her breath mingling with his, and he lingers, savoring the exotic alloy of cabernet and Beer Nuts and freshly powdered female skin. Anna glances at his lips and back into his eyes, and then her phone rings.

"I should see who it is," she whispers, but, as she's about to pull away, he closes the gap and kisses her. Once. Twice. Then kisses her check. He puts her hair behind her ear and, as he moves around to her neck, he hears Anna quickly inhale.

"What are you feeling?" Mitchell whispers.

"I...don't know."

"Are you afraid?"

"Yes."

"Then let's take it slow."

"Mitchell, it won't work."

"Shhh..." he says and as feels her muscles slacken, he guides his lips down into her collar bone, then gently pulls back her robe and moves down and around her shoulder.

Somewhere in the distance Anna can hear Cynthia Smythe leaving a message.

'Anna. Cynthia. I'm so sorry. I tried catching you before you left, but you're a might faster than me. I have no idea where you are or how any of this happened. John Edwards may think this is over but it's not. Call me when you can.'

"Should I call her?" Anna whispers.

"Come with me," Mitchell says, softly, as he guides them over to the sofa. He takes the wine glass from Anna's hand and has her sit. Then he places both glasses on the small end table and kneels in front of her.

He takes both her hands in his, studies them for a moment, and looks up. He can see that she is breathing harder now. He kisses each hand, one at a time, and then leans in to her mouth, lightly at first, waiting for a response.

After a moment's hesitation, she reciprocates. He releases her hands and she wraps her arms around his neck, her fingers clutching the thick hair on the back of his head.

"Oh God, Mitchell…" Anna says, pulling back.

"Tell me what you're feeling."

"It's dark and enormous and hovering over me."

Mitchell kisses her again, and this time Anna thrusts her tongue into his mouth, then just as quickly retreats. She starts to tremble, her breathing heavy and erratic.

"Oh God," she cries.

"What? WHAT IS IT? Anna, tell me!!!"

"I…I…."

Suddenly, Mitchell pulls back from her.

"Let's stop. We've got to stop."

"NO!" Anna cries out, "LET ME TRY. PLEASE!"

Anna pulls him toward her and kisses him just as she did in the Moon and Sixpence, hard and deep; and then, without warning, she pulls one of her hands from his head and opens her robe.

"Kiss me there! Please," she gasps.

"Are you sure?" Mitchell whispers.

"Yes, yes, let me try!"

Mitchell gives her a peck on the lips, and then begins kissing her down her neck.

"NO, PLEASE, DON'T!" Anna blurts out, pushing away at him as the memories of her client's rapes tear through her brain and body.

"But you just…" Mitchell begins to say.

"I KNOW, I KNOW, I KNOW…"

"I'm sorry, Anna, I don't know what…."

"Don't stop. Please, don't stop!!!" she cries, as she reaches for Mitchell and pulls him closer. Mitchell hesitates, then moves lower. He kisses her perfect, pale breasts and runs his tongue around each areola.

He moves farther down the center of her stomach and to each side of her pelvis, then centers himself and descends further until his tongue detects the downy edge of her pubic hair.

He feels Anna shudder, not once or twice or even subtle, but hard and repetitive.

Thinking she is pleased, he continues.

"NOOOOO!!!!" Anna screams, forcing Mitchell to bolt up-right and now he sees that her shudders were not paroxysms of passion but fierce, unrelenting sobs.

"MITCHELL! I'M SORRY! she cries, reaching for him, but in the next moment she is pushing him away.

"PLEASE GET AWAY FROM ME. GO, PLEASE, GO!" Anna cries again, but now it's directed at someone or something in her head, and, as her voice fades, Mitchell falls back onto the floor, shaken.

He stands and plucks his wine glass off the end table, then pours himself a full glass, which he immediately drains.

He goes to Anna's bed and pulls back the blankets, then walks to the sofa and picks her up in his arms.

After he lays her down and pulls the covers up around her neck, he draws the curtains and switches off the lamp next to the sofa. As he opens the door to leave, a single shaft of light il-luminates Anna's bed.

"I'd say it was a bloody good start, wouldn't you?"

"Good night, Mitchell," she says, through her tears, "I'm sorry, but it's just not going to work."

Mitchell hesitates for a moment, considering a reply, but then changes his mind and turns and exits, closing the door behind him.

forty-eight

The following morning, Celwin Blevins is swirling a hunk of brown bread through the egg yolk of his proper English breakfast when a local fisherman strides into the Tides Cafe with a morning paper, the floorboards creaking under his waders.

"Couldn't have fuckin' done it!" the fisherman says, holding the paper above his head, "that's what they're saying! Didn't have the bloody tools, poor bastard!"

Blevins head shoots up at the sound of the fisherman's voice.

"What's that you say?" Blevins asks, wiping his mouth and beard of egg.

"See fer yourself!" the fisherman says, shoving the paper into Blevins' face. "O'Rourke is bloody innocent!"

"I told you so!" another man yells from across the room, "David O'Rourke was as good as they come!"

"They've crucified the poor soul!" yells another.

Blevins grabs the paper and furrows his brow as he studies the headline.

"Bloody nonsense," he says, shoving the paper back, but he knows better.

He stands, throws down his napkin, and drops a few coins onto the table. He grabs his coat and hat off of one of the wooden pegs on the wall next to the door and exits the ramshackle, working class cafe.

Outside, he buttons his coat against the howling wind, turns up his collar and hesitates, taking in the view of the Clevedon Pier reaching out toward his Welsh homeland across the channel. The sky is low and dark, and fog wraps the coastline like cotton, reminding him of the view he had of Ireland from the village of Porthgain, when he was a child.

Before the fisherman stormed in with the morning paper, Blevins was actually light-hearted and looking forward to spending the day with his beloved Brindle organ.

He turns to his left, walks down to the corner, and fishes a coin out of his pants pocket as he steps into one of Britain's iconic red phone booths.

He drops the coin into the slot, then reaches for his wallet. He flips it open, reaches under his driver's permit and extracts the business card of Hugh Archer, the reporter for the tabloid, The Evening Tattler.

Had one been an observer watching from across the street, you would have sworn that the call lasted no more than a few seconds, because it was all the time Blevins needed to reveal the real identity of the rapist.

"Never mind the recompense, Mr. Archer," Blevins says, with a tone of somber resignation of what was now to come. "It's for the good of the church. I'll be rewarded in the next life."

"Sure wish I had your optimism. Mr. Blevins," Archer says. "'Bout the afterlife that is. I'll make sure this gets to the right people."

"Right. Of course. I'm certain you will." Blevins says, then hangs up with the look of a man who has sentenced his best friend to death.

Devon is spraying down the milking parlor as Samuel strides into the barn with the newspaper.

"Here!" he yells, over the sound of the high-pressure water hose.

Devon rips the paper from Samuel's hand and glances at the headline.

"I fuckin' told you it would be okay," Samuel says, as Devon shoves the paper back at him.

"Okay? You think this is okay? Now the whole bloody world knows!"

"So, fuckin' what? At least we can hold our heads up and say for certain that our father wasn't a bloody rapist!"

Devon shuts the taps from the boiler, then grabs a rag and wipes his hands. He shakes a cigarette from a package in his shirt pocket and lights it.

"When the fuck did you start smokin' again?" Samuel asks.

"None of your bloody business," he says, and he stomps toward the barn door.

"You headed somewhere?" Samuel yells.

"Yeah. I'm thirsty."

Anna doesn't wake until noon. Still in her robe, it seems she didn't move a muscle the entire night. She climbs out of bed, wanders over to the windows and raises the curtains on a brooding sky, then notices the empty bottle of wine.

Mitchell, she says to herself, and then the memories of the whole, bloody day come rushing back.

She showers and dresses in dark leggings and a black turtleneck, then sends a text to Lyla, asking about their return trip home.

'*Working on it. Are you just getting up?*' Lyla replies.

'*Yep.*'

'Glad you got some rest. What are you doing today?'

'*Going out for awhile.*'

'*Have you seen the paper?*' Lyla asks.

'*No. Should I?*'

'*Yes. Sorry, Caleb's calling. CULater.*'

Anna throws a scarf around her neck, grabs her heaviest coat from the closet, and heads toward the elevator. In the lobby she pours herself a cup of coffee from the complimentary service cart and buys a newspaper, which she rolls and stuffs into her coat pocket, then heads out onto the cold.

As she rounds the corner of the hotel toward the Thames, the bitter wind hits her square in the face, making her eyes water. She pulls her scarf up over her nose and makes it to Horniman's Pub a second before the skies open.

Anna hangs her coat on a hook next to a small booth by the windows, then slips the paper out of the pocket and takes a seat.

"Afternoon, ma'am, here's our lunch menu," the friendly young waitress says, "something to drink?"

"House chardonnay?" Anna says.

"Perfect, back in a jiff."

Watching the boat traffic on the river and the pedestrians scrambling to get out of the rain, Anna pauses a moment to steel herself, then takes a deep breath and opens the paper.

It's worse than she imagined. The paper has dedicated its entire front page to the revelation of David O'Rourke's innocence and she and Simon's role in promoting him as a serial rapist.

'O'Rourke Absolved of Heinous Crimes.' The headline reads.

'Murdered Dairyman Was Castrated in Freak Accident Twelve Years Before Being Accused of Rape.' Says the bi-line.

Below the headlines are photographs of David O'Rourke, Simon Mercer, Diana Lynch, and herself, with captions identifying each of them and their roles in the case.

Anna feels as though she's about to be sick. Then her phone rings.

"Simon."

"Hi Anna. I'm assuming you've seen the papers?"

"Uh, huh."

"Not to pile it on, but I felt you should know. The rape test came back. Negative."

For several seconds Anna doesn't say a word.

"Ma'am? Is something wrong?" The young waitress says, as she arrives with Anna's glass of wine.

"Ma'am?"

"Anna? You there?" Simon says.

forty-nine

"Good afternoon, Miss Strawsby," Chief Inspector Hayden says, tipping his hat as Margret opens the front door of the parsonage.

"Oh, it's you," Margret says, with an obvious tone of disappointment sprinkled with apprehension.

"You sound like me wife."

"And like her, I'd like to say it's a pleasure, but somehow your appearance at our front door is more like the presage of an impending swarm of locust rather than a friendly visit."

Margret looks out past Hayden, toward the street and sees, once again, several patrol vehicles and uniformed officers.

"And I wish today were different, but I'm afraid it's not," Hayden says, as he reaches into his coat pocket and retrieves an envelope, which he hands to Margret.

"This is a search warrant."

Margret's eyes widen.

"A search warrant? My heavens, whatever for?"

"Is Pastor Wetherford at home?"

"In his study, but he's busy working on…"

"Call him down, please."

"Chief Inspector, I'm afraid you don't understand, you see…"

"Call him down, please. I won't ask again. I'd like the two of you to wait outside, in one of our patrol cars. Officer Langdon here will accompany you."

"Wait? In the patrol car? Well, I never…"

"What is this, Chief Inspector?" Benjamin says, as he and Margret come down the stairs, "I will not, nor will I allow Ms. Strawsby to be subjected to this outrage, or exposed to the ridicule of the press, or made a laughingstock in front of our good neighbors."

Hayden thinks for a moment and then relents, partially.

"Alright. In the kitchen, then," he says, nodding to the officer.

"And you're not to interact or impede in any fashion with the searching of the home. Is that understood?"

"Well, of course! Why would ...?" Benjamin begins to say, as he and Margret are escorted down the hallway and into the kitchen.

The search of the parsonage takes well over an hour, and Hayden is standing in the hall when one of his men comes up through the stairway leading to the basement.

"Nothing in the house, Chief Inspector."

"Start on the church, then."

Hayden and four officers cross the lawn toward the church and enter through the large doors.

"You there!" Hayden says, calling up to the choir loft.

"Sorry?" Blevins says, over the railing.

"Come down here."

Blevins stops his maintenance work on the Brindle organ, grabs a rag, and comes down the stairs from the loft.

"What's your name?"

"Blevins, sir. Celwin Blevins. I'm the organist."

"Well, this afternoon you're the tour guide."

"Sorry, sir?"

"Take me downstairs."

Blevins leads Hayden and the officers around the rear of the altar and to the steps leading to the basement.

"Where are the lights?" Hayden barks.

"Sorry, sir, there on the wall," Blevins says, as the officers remove the flashlights from the straps on their belts. One flips the switch on the wall and the group, headed by Blevins, descends the worn stone steps. Upon reaching the lower level Hayden turns to his men.

"You two, that way," he says, and then he and Blevins and the two remaining officers head in the opposite direction. Getting to the end of hallway they stop at the last door on the left.

"What's in here?" Hayden asks.

"Pastor's office, sir."

"Open it," he says, to Blevins.

Blevins hesitates.

"But...."

"I said, open it."

Reluctantly, he does as Hayden asks. As the door swings open, Hayden and the two officers pour inside. Hayden flips the switch, bathing the small, dank room in a yellowish cast.

"What's he do in here?" Hayden asks, as he begins a cursory examination of the room.

"Pastor's work, sir."

"And what would that be?"

"Writing the homilies. Paying the bills. Communicatin' with members of the congregation."

"Uh-huh."

"What about on Fridays?" Hayden asks, out of the blue.

"Sorry, sir?"

"Fridays. Did he work in here on Friday's?"

"Fridays were days set aside for the fish market, sir."

"But he wasn't always at the fish market, was he?"

As Blevins watches the officer's move about the room, one of them sits behind Benjamin's desk and begins opening drawers.

The officer begins with the first, topmost drawer, shuffling items, and then works his way through the middle drawer and down to the larger, bottom drawer.

"This one's locked," the officer says to Hayden, who turns to Blevins.

"Open it."

"'Ave no idea, how sir," Blevins replies. "That's off limits to anyone other than the pastor, sir."

340

"Where's the key?" Hayden says, glancing toward Blevins, then waits and watches. A seasoned officer with years of investigative experience, Hayden immediately picks up on Blevins' involuntary eye movement in the direction of the shelf with the crucifix.

"Check everything on that shelf," Hayden says, barking to the officers who then begin a detailed inspection of the two candlesticks, an enormous bible and several assorted items which appear to be vestiges of the Roman Catholics.

Hayden studies Blevins' face for a reaction. And like a gambler sitting at the roulette wheel when the ball drops onto his chosen number, Blevins' eyes widen when one of the officers puts his hands on the crucifix.

"It's there. In the crucifix!" Hayden says, to the officer.

"NO!" Blevins shouts out.

"One more word and I'll run you in for obstruction."

"In the base, man," Hayden says, to the officer.

"Sorry, sir?"

"Turn it over, dammit!"

The officer does as Hayden asks.

"Just a label of some kind, sir."

"Peel it off!" Hayden barks.

As the officer peels away the label, he exposes the slit into which the desk drawer key had been inserted.

"Found it sir."

"You know about this?" Hayden says, to Blevins.

"No! And I would be derelict in my…" Blevins starts to say when Hayden stops him.

"Shut up. Give it to me," Hayden snaps.

The officer hands him the key and Hayden sits into the chair behind the desk. He inserts the key into the lock and turns it, then he opens the drawer and begins removing the contents.

First, is the whisky bottle. Next are the two tumblers. Following that are several books, none of which appears to be a diary, and lastly, under several manila folders, he finds what he's been looking for.

Hayden takes his handkerchief from his pocket, places it between his thumb and forefinger and reaching into the desk drawer removes the item.

He lays it on the desk and opens the handkerchief, revealing a brown, canvas sack with crudely cut holes for two eyes, a nose and a mouth.

Running down the length of the bag, from between the eyes and past the mouth, is the word *'Barclays'.*

As Hayden and the four officers bound down the hallway and into the kitchen, Benjamin and Margret are seated at the table, each with a cup of tea.

"Ah, Chief Inspector, finished so…" Benjamin begins to say, but he's immediately interrupted. Hayden nods to two of the officers who take positions behind his chair.

"Benjamin Wetherford, you are under arrest for the serial rape and the abuse of a minor, your niece, Miss Elizabeth Barrett."

The statement is so sharp and so sudden and so entirely devastating that both Benjamin and Margret are dumbstruck, rocked to their cores, and left speechless.

"Mr. Wetherford, please stand."

Margret's hand, clasping a napkin, rushes to her mouth and she lets out a loud gasp. Sitting across the table is the man she had thought she had known, the man for whom she had worked, admired and trusted; who, in an instant, has been reduced, to a quaking, quivering mass.

"Margret, I…" Benjamin tries to speak, but cannot.

He stands and lets out a moan. His knees buckle and he begins to move toward the floor when he's caught by the arms of the officers standing behind him.

Immediately, the officer standing to his right rear produces a pair of handcuffs and snaps them, one after the other, around Benjamin's wrists as Hayden reads him his rights.

In the choir loft, Blevins is just reaching the tops of the stairs when he glances out the small window that looks out across the large lawn toward the parsonage and the road beyond.

First Hayden appears and then the officers escorting Benjamin. As they arrive at the patrol car, Blevins watches as one officer pushes Benjamin's head down and into the vehicle, an authoritative gesture meant to subdue and humiliate. As Benjamin sinks into the rear seat, the door closes and he disappears behind the reflection of clouds and sky in the rear window.

Blevins makes a sign of the cross; a throwback to his Catholic youth, then he turns and makes his way to the bench in front of the organ. He rests his head in his hands, says a silent prayer and then begins playing Hyfrodol, in Benjamin's honor.

fifty

Using an old, embroidered potholder, Celwin Blevins removes the boiling water from the stove and dispenses it into his ceramic Welsh teapot.

He's lived in this two-room flat above a small, exotic bird shop since moving from Wales seven years ago; and while cramped and susceptible to the piercing winds coming off the channel, Blevins, nevertheless, declares that it suits him just fine.

'Neither a showoff, nor a braggart be,' he's fond of saying, and when he's had a few sherries or whiskeys, may even venture into the realm of Shakespeare.

'Who knows himself a braggart, let him fear this, for it will come to pass that every braggart shall be found an ass.'

And so, like his father before him and his father before that, Celwin Blevins has led a life of quiet solitude, fearing and loving God, in that order, and doing his best to utilize his God-given talent for music, even if his short, chubby fingers prevented him from realizing his dream of becoming a world-renowned pianist.

Another of God's little jokes, he would tell himself.

The Sunday after Benjamin's arrest dawned clear and unseasonably warm, giving Blevins the impression that The Almighty was rewarding him for the deed he had done. Even though he had no idea how many, or if any, of the congregation would be in attendance, he had been working on the sermon ever since Benjamin was taken into custody, as it wasn't unusual for a deacon, an organ player, or a congregant for that matter, to assume the role of pastor in the event of his absence.

After drinking his tea and eating a breakfast of toast and

344

eggs fried in bacon grease, Blevins showers and then dresses.

Today is an occasion for my best suit, he tells himself. He reaches into the small, eighteenth century pine armoire next to his twin sized, metal framed bed with frayed cotton sheets topped with a heavy wool blanket, and extracts his trusty, blue pin-stripe. His funeral suit. He does his best to put a shine on his shoes and brushes his beard and his thick gray hair before donning his overcoat.

"Good day, Mr. Blevins," one of his neighbors calls out in passing as Blevins walks to a side street where he parks his car, a 1986 Opel Rekord. A modest vehicle, to be sure.

"That it 'tis, madam, that it 'tis," he says, tipping an imaginary hat.

Blevins bought the car in Wales, from a man who had purchased it new, in Germany, for his wife, who soon after discovered she had little desire for the car or for him, but had great need of their house and nearly all of what remained in their joint bank accounts.

Blevins paid a sum well under the value of the car and believed, for a time after at least, that the good fortune was an auspicious sign of things to come.

Driving through the farmland from Clevedon, Blevins debated with himself on how to approach the morning's service.

Should I stand at the large doors, welcoming the congregation? Or would it be a presumption to assume the place of Pastor Benjamin so soon after his fall from grace? Perhaps some music. Yes! that's it! That's surely the way to begin! I'll sit at the old Brindle and play Hyfrodol in Benjamin's honor until the church is full and the congregation wanting.

The music will end and for many minutes I will do nothing, letting them stir. And when the moment has ripened, I'll stand and walk slowly down the old wooden staircase. I'll cross over to the main aisle and make me way to the pulpit, then ascend the twelve steps cut from the single block of Jurassic limestone quarried in Cardigan, Wales.

Upon reaching the top I'll settle and fix my gaze on the eight-

eenth-century Bible and wait for the coughs and murmurs and the clearing of throats to echo their last. And then, with the decorum demanded by the moment, I'll begin.

And so, he did.

"Good morning," Blevins says, looking out at the sea of expectant faces as variations of the salutation echo in return.

A full house. Good, he says to himself.

Fire and brimstone was not Benjamin's style, nor did he think it was a message that played well in the twenty-first century. Blevins, on the other hand, felt that the church's modern-day retreat from clearly stated principles of right and wrong bore most of the responsibility for the last gasps of Christianity.

'Without boundaries,' Blevins always said, *'people are free to roam too close to the cliffs,'* and this morning he senses that the faithful, gathered in front of him, are ready for something more.

Men sit with hats in hand, displaying stoic faces in the shape of question marks as women bury their sniffles into lace handkerchiefs; all wondering how such evil could have taken place right in their own church.

Like Benjamin and the countless pastors and priests before him, Blevins glances above the heads of the congregants and out through the large front doors carved from English walnut.

Today, because of the fine weather, there are hundreds of sails on the channel, and several species of sea birds swirl and frolic in the blue sky which folds itself around the crisp outline of Wales in the distance.

He comes back to the moment, looks from one side of the church to the other, and begins.

"What is sin?" he says, letting the question hang in the air for several seconds, the congregants stirring and murmuring in their seats.

"The age-old-question isn't it? he adds, looking up, waiting for a response. "Well, is it not?"

And then, out of the corner of his eye, Blevins spots a man stand up in the left rear of the church.

"Yes. It 'tis!" the man says.

"Thank you. And no one thought and wrote more about sin than did St. Augustine. And no one knew about sin, the nature of sin, more than he. Do any of you, from those long-lost days in Sunday school, remember at least one of his observations regarding sin?"

This question, too, hangs in the air.

"No one? Come now, dear people, someone must remember some utterance from the great saint."

Now, an older woman, on the right, raises her hand.

"Please, madam," Blevins says.

"Do I have to stand?" the woman asks, shyly, as some around her titter.

"No, no, my dear woman. Please, stay seated," Blevins responds.

"It's been so long, but I'll try," she begins. "It was something like...'The evil in me...was...foul. But I loved it. I loved my own perdition and my own faults and...and...'"

The woman begins to blush and seeing her embarrassment, Blevins finishes the quote for her.

"'...and not the things for which I committed wrong, but the wrong itself.' Very good, madam.

You see, dear friends, St. Augustine knew sin and he knew it well. He saw that sin was a trap. But a trap set by whom? By God? By the devil? Or by our very nature?"

"The devil!" a man shouts out.

"But the devil is a fallen angel, created by God!" yells another.

"And so is our human nature. And as you can see, we are all, right. The Church of the Divinity has suffered a tremendous blow. Benjamin Wetherford was a man whom you knew and loved and trusted. And I, right along with you. But he was a man, nonetheless. And what awaits him now, we cannot know..."

'The flesh lusteth against the spirit, and the spirit against the flesh,' said the Apostle Paul. *'The thorns of lust rose above my head and there was no hand to root them out!'* Augustine cried!"

"Amen!" Comes the enthusiastic response.

"Remember now what I'm about to tell you. The devil will drag you down... ONLY, AS FAR AS YOU YOURSELF ARE WILLING TO DESCEND!!! REMEMBER THAT!"

We humans ARE CO-AUTHORS OF OUR OWN FATE!!! AND THE DEVIL IS THE ONE HANDING US THE PEN WITH WHICH TO WRITE IT!!!"

Blevins waits for the reverberation of his voice to fade and then softens his voice.

"I am but a simple man of music, and I find myself, much to my consternation, because of circumstances I wish I could have avoided, addressing you as the temporary pastor of your church, until a new one can be found."

Blevins closes the Bible and begins to descend the stone staircase. Although he can't be sure, it seems that he has made an impression with at least some of the congregants, who now whisper excitedly. As was the usual practice, several of the men stood and went to the altar where they retrieved baskets for the offering, which they then proceeded to pass out to the front rows of the pews.

Blevins had decided that he would climb back up the narrow wooden stairs to the choir loft, which he now did, and wait to see if the response to his sermon would be a positive one. The swiftness with which the men reached into their wallets did not disappoint him and so he began playing *'GRACE GREATER THAN OUR SIN'* on the magnificent old Brindle.

"An amazing sermon, Blevins. Didn't know you had it in you, old boy!" an elderly gentleman says, "terrible news about Pastor Benjamin, however."

"Yes, indeed," Blevins replies, and as the man and his wife

begin to walk away, he suddenly turns back.

"Almost forgot," the man says, "the key to the collection box is hanging within the fabric on the rear of Benjamin's…I mean the, um, altar chair. There should be bank bags there as well."

"Yes, thank you. Benjamin trusted me with such information years ago."

"Very well, then," the man says, as he and his wife head off to the parking lot, the last to leave.

Blevins smiles after them for as long as he thinks a pastor should, then heads back inside the now empty church. He makes his way to the altar and to Benjamin's altar chair.

He retrieves the key and one of the canvas cash bags and goes to the large, bronze collection box, which features two winged angels facing one another over a locked door.

Blevins inserts the key, opens the door and empties the box, then takes the bag full of cash and coin around the altar and descends the steps to the basement.

In the office, he places the money bag onto Benjamin's desk and sits, taking a moment to imagine himself in the role of pastor.

He reaches for the bottom drawer and pulls out the bottle of whisky and a tumbler. He pours himself three quarters of a glass, then takes a sip, licking his lips and wiping his mouth on his sleeve as he studies the money bag with the word Barclay's printed down the center.

Then, out loud, he begins to recite portions of his morning's sermon.

"*'The flesh lusteth against the spirit, and the spirit against the flesh, said the Apostle Paul! The thorns of lust rose above my head and there was no hand to root them out!* Augustine cried!"

Blevins pours himself another drink and downs it in one gulp, and then stands and begins delivering the last part of his sermon.

"WE HUMANS ARE CO-AUTHORS OF OUR OWN FATE!!! AND THE DEVIL IS THE ONE HANDING US THE PEN WITH

WHICH TO WRITE IT!!!"

He pauses, then weaving from the effect of the whiskey, he collapses back into Benjamin's chair and lowers his voice.

"Augustine was right. There are no hands to root them out..." he says, to himself, under his breath.

The Cock and Whistle was busy for a Sunday night, but Blevins' early arrival meant that he was able to stake out a place at the bar, which soon after filled to capacity.

"Another round for me and me mates!" Blevins says, waving his empty glass at the bartender, sending up a round of cheers from those sitting nearby.

"Sure about that, friend?" the bartender says.

"Never more certain of anything in me life," Blevins says, weaving and slurring his speech.

The bartender counts out seven shot glasses, pours whiskey into each of them and passes them out along the bar.

"On me tab," Blevins says.

"Sorry, friend. Let's take care of what's been drunk."

"And who made you king?"

The bartender, who's had about enough of the evening, raises a clenched fist.

"This is who made me king. Any questions?"

Blevins thinks better about answering.

"Forty pounds, twenty," the bartender says.

Blevins sways as he gets up from his stool, then reaching into his pocket produces a wad of bills that prompts a double-take from the bartender.

"Win The National, did we?"

"My good man," Blevins says, slurring his speech, "isn't it obvious that I... am a man of means?"

Blevins peels several bills and places them neatly on the bar in front of the bartender, then reaches for his glass and downs it, motioning for the bartender to come closer.

"Yeah, what is it?"

"Who's the owner of the jobblies down the way?" Blevins

says, glancing down to the end of the bar.

The bartender follows Blevins' gaze to an attractive woman who appears to be the life of the party.

"Sight young for an old man like you, ain't she, friend?"

Blevins reaches into his pocket, peels another bill from the wad, and sets it on the bar. The bartender looks down, hesitates for a moment, then palms it and slides it off the bar and into his pocket.

"Mabel. Mabel Prine."

Blevins downs his drink, wipes his mouth on his sleeve, and gets up from his stool. Seated at a table some distance away are two men, one of whom recognizes him.

"Blimey. Isn't that Ben Wetherford's organ man?"

"Was. Wetherford's holy days have come to an end, me friend."

"And it looks like his is just beginin'. On the pull, he is."

"Drunk as a monkey, too, if you ask me."

The men shake their heads and watch as Blevins reaches Mabel Prine, who is sitting at the far end of the bar surrounded by a group of boisterous friends.

"May I ask what the young lady is enjoyin' this fine eve'nin'? Blevins says, over Mabel Prine's left shoulder.

Not hearing him, Mabel continues giggling and chatting with the younger men and women huddled around her.

"Excuse me," Blevins says, but it comes right at the punch line of a joke, so his words are lost under a second, cacophonous burst of laughter.

Undeterred, yet growing agitated, he waits, letting the laughter fade, then taps her on the shoulder. Surprised, Mabel whips her head in his direction, her long, kinky red hair practically hitting Blevins in the face.

Instead of what she expected, she comes face to face with a person who, in her mind, is a doddering old fool. Her laughter morphs into disgust.

"Yeah. What do you want?" she says.

"I was asking' what the young lady is enjoyin' this

eve'nin'?"

Mabel's friends, taking notice of Blevins, begin to snigger and make disparaging remarks.

"First, I ain't that young, and secondly, I certainly ain't no lady."

The rejoinder spikes the level of frivolity in Mabel's group.

"C'mon, 'ole man, shove off," says one of Mabel's male friends.

"See here, there's no need for…" Blevins says.

"And secondly, no thirdly…I ain't so certain you could afford me."

At this remark her friends explode into a merciless cacophony of hoots and howls and, as she swings back toward her friends, Mabel accidentally sweeps her car keys off of the bar and onto to the floor at Blevins' feet.

Blevins takes notice and reaches down to pick them up but before setting them back on the bar, he takes note of the medallion on her keychain, identifying her car as a Fiat Abarth.

He glances over his shoulder to see how much of the bar has been witness to his humiliation at the hands of Mabel Prine. Satisfied that it went basically unnoticed, he turns back toward his stool, but sees that it's now occupied. With nowhere to go, he opts for the quickest way out and heads toward the front door.

Out on the street he stops for a moment, swaying. He turns the collar up on his coat, puts on his gloves, and looks up and down Alexandra Road, the west end of which leads to the Clevedon Pier.

He turns in the direction of the channel and, as he begins to cross Copse Road, spots the orange-colored Fiat parked slapdash in front of a row of trees.

To match the color of her hair no doubt, he thinks to himself.

Blevins stumbles and nearly falls stepping off the curb, but makes his way to the Abarth and tests the driver's door.

It's locked. He glances around and decides that her choice of parking spot, so close to the copse of trees, must certainly be a gift. And not necessarily from God.

fifty-one

Anna is just stepping out of the shower when her phone rings. She grabs a towel and wraps it around herself and then pads into the bedroom.

The number is one that she recognizes. It's shown up several times in the past few days, and it appears the caller is phoning from somewhere in England, but fearing a prank or a threat, Anna hasn't answered. Today, she feels like there's nothing left to lose.

"Hello, it's Anna," she says, apprehensively.

"My goodness! Is it actually you?" the elderly woman caller says.

"This morning, I'm not so sure."

"This is the number I was given. Is this Miss Anna Newsom?"

"I'm afraid so."

"How thrilling! This is Isabel Quivers."

"Isabel...Quiv..."

For a moment Anna can't place the name, and then it dawns on her.

"Isabel Quivers! Of course! Your granddaughter, Sarah, is the flight attendant!"

"Yes!"

"I've been trying to reach you for days."

"I'm sorry, I..."

"No apologies, please. Lord knows, you've had a full plate, my dear girl. I'm calling, first, to say thank you for the autographed copy of your wonderful book."

"Well, you're very welcome."

"Secondly, I, along with everyone else in England, have been following your case with utmost interest, and when I saw the news about the farmhouse and the wallpaper in the room where the terrible things are said to have taken place, well, I knew that I must reach out to you."

"Go on," Anna says, slowly sitting on the bed.

"Well, for years, I've painted pictures of English scenes. Countrysides, seasides, cottages, gardens. You know, everything typically quaint and cozy and British."

"Now I remember!" Anna says. "I saw a coffee table edition of your work in Pritchards, when I was there for my book signing!"

"Yes. Not a big seller, I'm afraid. The younger generation has no interest in an old woman's scratchings, and the older generation, God Bless their souls, have all the books they'll ever need.

In any case, I wanted to let you know that the farm, on the wallpaper in the bedroom of the parsonage, is one of mine."

"One of yours? Your work?"

"Precisely! Page thirty-two of the book in Pritchards, if memory serves."

"But, how did…?"

"As a child, my family spent summers in Weston, on the ocean. Art was always my first love and when, as an adult I took it as a vocation, I gravitated to the quaint, seaside tableaus and lovely, rolling farmland so typical of the area."

"Miss Quivers, I..."

"Please, call me, Isabel."

"Okay, then. Isabel. I can't thank you enough for..."

Anna wants to thank her, but can't bring herself to tell Isabel that her memory, even if accurate is moot at this point.

"It's my pleasure, my dear. I'll tell Sarah we spoke. She's somewhere in Africa at the moment, but when she...." Isabel says, but then suddenly remembers something.

"Why, I haven't thought about this in years, but..."

"Sorry?"

"In those early years, I became close friends with a girl, about my age, her name was...was... Agatha. Yes, that's it."

"Yes..."

"And Agatha lived in the parsonage. Her father was the pastor at the time."

"Go on."

"How strange, I haven't thought about her in years, decades actually. Yes, now, I remember...wait, there's something else..."

For a moment, Isabel grows quiet, and Anna thinks that perhaps her call was dropped.

"Isabel? Are you there?"

"Yes, dear, sorry."

"It's been decades since I've thought of her and that big, strange house. We had the best time, playing hide and seek and running around like the devil.

And then one day...by chance, you see...well, we came upon a, well, a passageway."

"A passageway?"

"Dark as night. Eldritch it was. It ran from the basement of the parsonage to the church. Right under the lawn. It was long forgotten and damp as the dickins but we discovered it and kept it as our little secret. Our hiding place. Our playhouse."

Isabel trails off in a reverie of her youthful years.

"Isabel? Are you still there?" Anna says, and then she returns to the present.

"Oh, sorry, yes. Anyway, I've kept you long enough, my dear. You have my number now, if there's anything I can do, please call. Cheerio!"

"Goodbye, Isabel. And thank you!" Anna says, ending the call.

"It says here, that, '*when the Reformation began the church of England began converting churches that had once been Roman Catholic and that many priests and nuns were threatened with their lives. Therefore, it wasn't uncommon for them to build safe rooms or other means of escape.*'"

Lyla takes another sip of coffee and continues reading

from her phone.

"'If one got on the King's bad side, he would declare them a traitor. His first victim was a twenty-eight-year-old nun who claimed to have visions, and she eventually confessed to having faked trances, to heresy and to treason. On April 20, 1534, she was hanged and beheaded along with five of her supporters, two monks, two friars and a priest. Her head was then spiked on London Bridge.'"

"You can see London Bridge from here," Anna says, looking down at the Thames from Lyla's room.

"Can you say zero tolerance? Anyway, do you really think that's what the passageway was for?" Lyla says, but Anna doesn't respond.

"Anna?"

"It's all a moot point now. The farm, the wallpaper. How could I have gotten it so wrong?" Anna says, then she comes back to the present, "going to my room to pack."

"Me, too. Henry will be here at one o'clock tomorrow," Lyla adds.

"It'll be nice getting home, won't it?"

"Yes."

Walking from Lyla's room to hers, Anna's phone rings and she sees that it's Cynthia Smythe.

I've dodged her long enough, she says to herself and answers it.

"Cynthia," Anna says, with a chill in her voice.

"I know you've been avoiding me."

"I was just going upstairs to pack. Lyla has arranged a flight for tomorrow."

"I can't say I blame you, but I think you're making a mistake, Anna."

"How dare you?"

"I know you feel betrayed, but believe me, it was all John Edwards' doing. He's a bloody asshole of the first order and a chauvinist and a misogynist to boot."

"Then why did you put me on his show?"

"Honestly? Because in you I though he had met his match."

"Oh, please, don't patronize me," Anna replies, "I'm a psychologist, remember?"

"Well, why wouldn't I have? Your work is brilliant and you've a tremendously successful book. I put you on his show so you could tear him to pieces. Trust me, it would have been good for ratings."

"Fine job I did of that."

"Anna, listen. I can feel it in my bones, this thing is not over. I'd like you to do one more session with Elizabeth Barrett."

Anna goes silent as she considers what Cynthia has said.

"Anna? Are You there?"

"Um, yeah, I'm here."

"And if it makes you feel any better, Edwards been put on indefinite suspension."

"It doesn't, but it serves him right. I'll think about it."

"Your flight's tomorrow, remember. You'll have to cancel."

"I'll let you know," Anna says and she and Cynthia are both about to hang up when Anna stops her.

"Listen, Cynthia, if we do another session, I'd like it to be in her bedroom at the parsonage."

"If Simon can arrange it, you've got it."

"And could you please have Henry here at two this afternoon?"

"Of course."

"If anything changes, I'll text you," Anna says.

"Dr. Newsom to see you."

"Thank you, Justin. Show her in."

After her call with Cynthia Smythe, Anna felt like she needed to speak with someone she knew she could trust, and

Adrienne Owens, the Director who had invited her to speak at the Institute of Psychiatry, Psychology and Neuroscience, seemed the perfect choice.

"Anna, so good to see you again!" Adrienne says, reaching for Anna's hand with both of hers.

"Hello, Adrienne. Thanks for having me on such short notice."

"Not at all, dear. I've been thinking of you since that appalling display put on by John Edwards. I've been chock-a-block ever since but finally had a free moment and was about to give you a call when, lo and behold, my phone rings!"

"Funny how that happens," Anna says with a smile and Adrienne leans in and gives Anna a little wink.

"We know better, don't we, dear? Come on, let's have a seat."

Adrienne leads Anna to the two high-backed chairs inside her office just as Justin arrives with two cups of coffee.

"Coffee with milk, if memory serves," he says, handing Anna her cup.

"Yes, thank you." Anna says, wrapping her hands around the warmth. She takes a sip, then begins.

"Well, let me start by saying that regardless of what John Edwards' motives were, he clearly showed that I was wrong... and..."

"My God, I imagine it was much like a Christian being thrown to the lions, wasn't it?" Adrienne says.

"You're not far off."

"Look, dear, if you don't mind me saying, you're not seeing things clearly."

"How so?"

"The point is that you were wrong insofar as you were denied all of the relevant facts."

"Okay."

"Surely, if you knew ahead of time that David O'Rourke had been, well, castrated, you wouldn't have come up with the conclusion you did, now would you?"

"Of course not."

"Facts matter, my dear. *Especially* to psychologists," Adrienne says, and just as she had done in their last meeting, she leans forward, totally focused on Anna's presence.

"Justin, myself, and a few of my students watched the interview in this very room. And at the end it became apparent to all of us that Edwards was using your incorrect conclusion regarding the guilt of David O'Rourke as an argument to shatter the sum total of your theories and methodologies. That was his true motive."

"Well, maybe he was right."

"Wrong. Don't fall into that trap a second time. The revelation that David O'Rourke was incapable of the crimes, shocking as it may have been to learn of it in that manner, does not mitigate against the fact that Elizabeth Barrett used the farmhouse image on the wallpaper in her bedroom as a psychological escape from obvious trauma. Your theory is the correct one, because your interviews and analysis of her says so. It was simply incomplete."

"But they've arrested Benjamin Wetherford, the pastor."

"In your heart of hearts, do you really believe he's guilty?"

"They found hard evidence in his office, the mask that Elizabeth described in our sessions as being worn by the rapist. But, to answer your question, no."

"Don't you see what's happening?"

"Sorry?"

"You're working for three people now."

"I don't understand."

"The pastor, to prove his innocence. Elizabeth, to save her life. And yourself, to prove beyond a doubt the veracity of your theories. If you don't believe he's guilty, then you must follow those instincts."

Adrienne lets Anna consider all that's she said.

"Cynthia Smythe, the producer at the BBC, would like me to do one more interview with Elizabeth Barrett.

"And why wouldn't you do it?" Adrienne says.

Anna doesn't answer but looks deeply into Adrienne's eyes.

"Do it, Anna. You're most of the way there. You've nothing to lose and everything to gain. Do it."

fifty-two

Blevins is in his bath when the news comes over the old radio sitting on a table in his kitchen. Since moving to the flat above the exotic bird, store he has made it a practice, during the day, to keep the radio at a volume that drowns out the shrieks and squawks filtering through his floorboards.

'...just in to Radio BBC Bristol. A woman's partially nude body was found early this morning amidst the pylons under the Clevedon pier.'

A small, satisfied smile creeps over Blevins faces as he pulls the plug out of the drain.

'...the identity of the woman has not been forthcoming, but unconfirmed reports have it that this may be yet another victim in the series of rapes that have plagued the area in the last month...'

He grabs a towel and steps out of the stained clawfoot tub, catching his image in the cheap, full length mirror on the wall. What he sees is a pudgy old man with unkempt gray hair and a scraggly silver beard. Had he been a musical virtuoso or a renowned physicist, his eccentric appearance would have been celebrated. But he is neither of those, and it infuriates him.

Wrapping himself in the towel, Blevins steps to the sink and runs the water, then soaps his face in the small mirror above and runs a razor in the sparse areas around his beard.

He rinses and pats himself dry, hesitates for a moment, and then reaches for the red and black pair of lady's underwear hanging from the faux brass light fixture next to the mirror.

Studying the delicate intricacies of the lace, he runs his fingers over the letters, 'MP' embroidered into the crotch, then closes his eyes and pulls them up to his face, luxuriating in Mabel Prime's scent.

'*...on another note, the controversy raging around the murder of local dairy farmer David O'Rourke takes yet another turn...*'

Disturbed by what he hears, Blevins lowers the panties and walks into the kitchen.

'*...with the announcement that Dr. Anna Newsom, forensic psychologist from the US, will stage yet another exploratory interview with the murder suspect, Elizabeth Barrett.*'

At the mention of Elizabeth Barrett's name, Blevins recoils.

The bitch! he says, to himself. *The arrest of Benjamin should have been the end of it!*

'*...the difference being the session will take place in the bedroom where fifteen-year-old Elizabeth claims she was raped.*'

Jolted on hearing the news, Blevins grabs one of two overstuffed pillows off of his tattered sofa, draws the zipper, and quickly stuffs Mabel's underwear inside. He then punches a preset on his radio, cranks the volume to maximum, and rushes into his room to dress.

Downstairs in the exotic bird shop, the shopkeeper is waiting on a customer who is just purchasing a blue and white budgie when the ceiling suddenly starts reverberating with The Ride of the Valkyries. They both look up at the ceiling and then back to one another.

"Strange one, he," the shopkeeper says.

Hayden parks and makes his way to the underside of Clevedon Pier where he's met by Officer Poole.

"Chief Inspector."

"G'day, Poole."

"Looks like the same handiwork, sir."

Hayden glances out at the knot of onlookers that have gathered about a hundred yards from shore.

"Reporters?"

"Yes."

"Get them out."

"Straight away, sir, and watch your step, sir. Might slippery."

Hayden makes his way over the slimy rocks and joins the group, then glances down at Mabel's half nude body. Another officer steps in alongside him.

"Fields."

"Chief Inspector. She was found by that clammer over there," he says, pointing to an elderly woman in waders being interviewed by yet another policeman.

"Her sister phoned a couple of hours ago saying she never come home last night. Mabel Prine's the name."

"Missing her undergarments, was she?

"Correct, sir."

"Make sure we get a proper DNA sample and expedite the rape

"Third one this month, Chief Inspector."

"I can count, Fields, thank you very much."

"That was rather perfunctory, miss, everything alright?" Henry says, as Anna jumps into the cab.

"Yes, Henry, everything's alright," Anna says, pulling her phone from her pocket.

"Well, I'd be less than honest with me self, If I didn't say that I was just a little concerned about you these last few days."

"I'm fine, really, Henry," Anna says, raising her phone to her ear.

Lyla is just placing the last item in her large suitcase when her phone rings.

"Hey, how did it go?" she says.

"You haven't packed yet, have you?"

"Um, yeah. The last thing I heard you say was, 'I'm going to pack.' What's going on?"

"I'll tell you over dinner. In the meantime, cancel the flight."

"Oh, no, Anna, really?"

"Yes. Lives are at stake."

"Mine is one of them if I don't get home soon." Lyla says.

"I'm sorry, Lyla, just a few more days."

"Fine, but you'll have to be the one to tell Caleb."

"I'll promise him a steak dinner when we get home. Bye."

Anna hangs up and then redials Simon Mercer, but he doesn't pick up, so she leaves a voicemail.

"Simon, Anna. Let's do one more session... in Elizabeth's bedroom."

fifty-three

As Blevins pulls his rusting Opel Rekord into the gravel parking lot of the church, he takes note that the throng of reporters has begun to re-materialize across the street from the parsonage. With no activity for the last few days, they had migrated to more fertile grounds, or lacking such, had simply resorted to harassing members of the royal family.

But after hearing the reports about the return of the infamous Elizabeth Barrett, they smelled blood and were now reassembling with the fervor of hormonal schoolgirls at a Justin Bieber concert.

One enterprising young journalist spots Blevins and breaks from the pack, yelling for his cameraman to join him as he dashes across the lawn. Blevins is just climbing out of the Opel as they reach him.

"Your name, sir?"

"Blevins."

"What do you do here?"

"I'm the Director of Music."

It's only a moment before the other reporters notice the activity and they too begin darting across the lawn in Blevins' direction.

"Do you know Elizabeth Barrett?"

"No. Not very well."

"Is it true that the pastor had been raping her?"

"I'm not in a position to know."

"Perhaps you yourself had a go at the girl?"

Blevins shoots the reporter a dirty look.

"But it was right under your very nose!"

"I'm sorry, but you're in my way..." Blevins says, as he forces his way between the young reporter and the cameraman.

"And you're claiming ignorance?"

"I told you, I was in no position to know."

"Then what do you know of the American girl, Newsom?"

Blevins lets the question float past him, but the next one he answers, anxious to keep up the appearance of business as usual.

"Is there anything you'd like your parishioners to know?"

"They are, uh... they're not my parishioners, per se. But as long as they'll have me, we will go on, doing God's work and praying for the soul of Benjamin Wetherford. Good day."

As Blevins pushes his way through, the reporters mumble and reluctantly begin to disperse, and, as he passes the first reporter, he overhears him speaking to his cameraman.

"Let's find the American," the reporter says, under his breath.

"I've a friend at BBC. They're at the Sandringham," the cameraman replies.

Blevins takes note of '*the American and Sandringham*', then quickly covers the twenty or so paces to the side door of the church and slams it behind him. He rushes to the massive, main entrance doors and tests the lock, making sure that they too are secure, then climbs the creaky wooden staircase that leads to the choir loft and his beloved Brindle.

Blevins takes a moment to collect his thoughts, then takes off his jacket and tosses it on the organ bench. Leaning against the back wall of the loft is a decades-old ladder used to light candles during major church services such as Christmas and Easter.

He takes hold of the ladder and moves it into the darkest corner, which is to the left and rear of the loft. Next, he rushes to the Brindle organ, grabs a small jar containing a mixture of nuts and bolts, dumps them onto the floor, and jams the jar it into his pants pocket.

With the light from a candle leading the way, Blevins

climbs the ladder until he's nearly at the uppermost rung, then raises it and squints into the darkness.

For a few seconds, most of the details in the rafters are nearly indiscernible from the dark wood of the walls and ceiling.

But as his eyes adjust, he starts to see the faint smudge of a thick tangle of webbing, and then, a shadow. As he moves the candle the shadow shifts and then, for a split second, the creature flinches, giving itself away.

Indigenous to Great Britain, the False Widow is a cousin to the American Black Widow but far larger and many times more lethal. This particular specimen is nearly two inches in length with the customary shiny black legs and the bulging mid-section that displays a whitish, yellowish pattern in the shape of a human skull.

The False Widow flinches again as Blevins sets the candle on a nearby rafter, casting decades, if not centuries worth of dust and debris onto the web and the floor, fourteen feet below.

Reaching into his pocket, Blevins removes the small glass jar and unscrews the lid.

FAST AS LIGHTNING IS HOW I MUST BE, he says to himself, then realizes that a False Widow up his sleeve would spell the end of him. He sets the jar and lid on the rafter, then rolls up his sleeves and primes himself for the assault.

NO! AS CUNNING AS A FOX AND FAST AS LIGHTNING! That's more like it, and with lid in one hand and jar in the other, he moves in for the assault.

When he was a child in Wales, he and his friends would play the game of 'statue' on the green hillsides overlooking the Celtic Sea and he recalls it now.

LIKE A STATUE. LIKE A STATUE BE! he commands, allowing himself to move toward the False Widow no more than a few centimeters at a time.

A quick calculation tells him that covering the twenty inches between he and it will take him at least a minute, and he begins to sweat under the strain of controlling his arm and leg muscles, which are beginning to tremble.

WHEN TO STRIKE? That is the question isn't it? But isn't that the question for most things in life? *WHEN TO STRIKE?*

*TOO FAR AWAY AND YOU RISK LOSING YOUR PREY; TOO CLOSE AND YOU RISK LOSING YOUR LIFE. A FINELY TUNED AP-PROACH IS WHAT ONE NEEDS IN ALL SITUATIONS. PERHAPS I'LL PEN A BOOK ABOUT IT ONE DAY...*he daydreams.

And then, without warning, his right arm jerks involuntary and, for the merest fraction of a second, the bottom of the jar touches the spider's webbing causing the False Widow to lurch ever so slightly toward Blevins and the center of the web. Blevins flinches and nearly loses his footing. Fourteen feet, he reminds himself glancing down at the floor.

PREY IS WHAT SHE'S THINKING. A FAT, FEISTY FLY OR A SAVORY MOTH! PREY AND PRAYER. PRAYER AND PREY. PREY AND... HOW IRONIC PRAY AND PREY!!!...IS SHE CONJURING A MENTAL IMAGE OF SUCH? WELL, IT'S NOT TO BE. NOT TODAY, ANYWAY...

And then, in a blinding flash, without thinking and every instinct commanding him to do so, Blevins simultaneously fires both the jar and lid forward around the False Widow, sealing it inside.

Blevins gasps with relief and nearly loses his balance again but recovers. Taking a deep breath, he quickly tightens the lid. In his fingers, he can feel the vibrations of the creature clawing against the walls of its glass prison.

Blevins parks in a spot on a side street behind The San-dringham and walks past the miniature golf course to Parade Avenue. Next to the small coffee shop is a kiosk that features an assortment of flowers and potted plants.

He purchases a small bouquet of pansies, then walks to the newsstand and buys a paper. With pansies in hand and newspaper under his arm, Blevins enters the hotel and walks up to the front desk.

"Sir?" Williams, the clerk says.

"May I have these delivered to Miss Anna Newsom, please?"

"Of course," Williams says, and goes back to what he was doing but Blevins remains at the desk.

"I'm sorry, was there something else?"

"Well, you see, pansies are incredibly delicate little things and I'd hate for them to be…"

"I'll see that they're taken right up, sir," Williams says, somewhat peeved and then hits the bell on the counter.

Satisfied, Blevins finds a seat in the corner of the lobby that's of out view of the front desk, but at the same time affords him a view of the elevator.

With barely time to open his paper, he spots a bellman, pansies in hand, headed to the lift. Blevins stands and makes his way across the lobby, but instead of getting into the elevator with the bellman, Blevins takes the stairs adjacent to the lift shaft.

As he climbs the first flight, Blevins hears it stop with a rumble and a whine on the second floor. He hears three squeaks as the doors open and, as he reaches the top of the second flight, he spots the bellman headed down the hallway.

As luck would have it, the maid is servicing Anna's room, so the door is swung wide open. Blevins hides himself behind a pillar and then watches as the bellman enters with the pansies and exits without them.

He comes out from behind the pillar, and as he and the bellman pass in the hallway, Blevins nods in his direction, the bellman responding with a smile.

Reaching Anna's room, he stops and peers in. The maid has the radio tuned to a pop music station and is nowhere to be seen; in the loo, Blevins presumes. And then, yet another stroke of luck. The bed has been made.

With no time to waste, he rushes to the near corner at the foot of the bed and throws back the blanket and top sheet. He reaches for the glass jar in his pocket, takes one last look at the

False Widow, and unscrews the lid. He turns the bottle over and watches until the creature falls out, and then stuffs the bottle back into his pocket, returns the bedding to its proper place, and exits the room.

Not thirty seconds later the maid enters the bedroom from the bathroom and taking one last glance around the room she notices the corner of the bed.

"Blimey. How did that happen?"

She quickly straightens her tidy hospital corner, pats it once for effect and then heads out into the hallway, closing Anna's door behind her.

fifty-four

"I don't have much of an appetite, wanna walk to Nick's for a drink?" Lyla asks.

"It's too cold. Besides, it'll get too late."

"Okay, how about room service?"

"Perfect. Come over here and we can go over tomorrow."

Anna hangs up and goes to her closet looking for something warm to wear. Traffic had been heavy on the way back from her meeting with Adrienne Owens, and between answering emails and speaking with her parents, Anna hadn't had a moment to settle in and relax.

"Hey," Lyla says, as she comes through the door.

"How did Caleb take the news?"

"He was in a sports bar and couldn't make out a word I said. So, I texted him an, typical Caleb, no response."

"I'm sure you'll hear from him."

"Yeah, but will it be this year? That's the question."

Lyla grabs the room service menu from off the coffee table and sits on the edge of Anna's bed, just next to where Blevins planted the False Widow.

"How about a large order of fries and two bottles of chardonnay, no make it a Merlot."

"Oh God, no. One and done. Then to bed."

"We'll save the celebration for tomorrow night, then," Lyla says, with a hopeful smile, placing the menu back on Anna's dresser.

"What's with the pansies? Fan mail?"

"No idea. They were just sitting there when I got back to the room."

An hour later, with the fries nearly gone and the bottle of

Merlot a distant memory, Anna and Lyla sit quietly, Lyla allowing Anna the space to prepare herself for the day to come.

"Is there anything I can do?" Lyla asks, after a long silence.

"Just be there."

"I won't let you out of my sight," Lyla says, taking her last sip of wine. "Promise."

"I don't know, Lyla, I just feel that tomorrow is going to be different, somehow."

"Well, why shouldn't it be? The whole case is completely inside out, unlike anything you've ever dealt with."

Anna turns toward Lyla, somewhat surprised that she herself hadn't considered that.

"It is, isn't it?"

"Yes. You have a girl that's been serially raped. And the murder of a man, at her hands, that we now know was absolutely incapable of the crime. On one hand, she's either a fantasy-driven, cold blooded murderer. Or, as the prosecution would now have us believe, poor Benjamin Wetherford was the rapist, and the murder of David O'Rourke was simply a terrible, tragic mistake."

Anna sets down her empty wine glass and proceeds to hold up one finger for each of the points she's making.

"Option one. Elizabeth. Cold-blooded murderer."

"Right."

"Option two. The pastor is the rapist and Elizabeth killed O'Rourke in a case of mistaken identity."

"Uh-huh."

"Option three? Elizabeth is not a cold-blooded killer and Benjamin Wetherford is not the rapist."

"You just sent a chill up my spine," Lyla says, her tone thick with foreboding.

"We better get some sleep," Anna replies, signaling an end to the evening.

Anna has slipped into her white boxers and white tank top and switches off all the lights in the room, except for the one next to her bed. She peels back her covers and slips in between the crisp linen sheets, then switches off the light, plunging the room into darkness, save for the sharp slivers of amber streetlight that manage to squeeze between the slats of the Venetian blinds. Just as she's about to drop, off her phone dings with a text.

'Think I'm falling in love with you. M.'

Anna doesn't respond and is about to put the phone down when it dings again.

'This just in. I'm sure I'm falling in love with you.'

Anna sleeps soundly until 2:00 a.m. and is awakened by the hoots and hollers of horny young men, presumably having just ejected themselves from one of the local bars. Anna reaches for her glass of water, takes a sip, and then lays back down.

Lodged in the corner and trapped between the sheets, the False Widow is aroused by Anna's movements. It's also her time to hunt.

As Anna drifts back to sleep, the False Widow makes her way out of the corner of the bed sheets and, as it reaches Anna's left foot, Anna begins to dream that it's summer and she and Chloe have just spent the day in the sun on top of the houseboat and each have gotten a sunburn.

The False Widow climbs across Anna's toes and back down to the sheet. She's looking for a way out, a place where she can spin her web and wait for prey. And as she searches, Anna's dream jumps to her bedroom in Macon, and the sunburn, covering nearly all of her body, is turning into a tormenting itch.

What most people don't know is that each leg of a spider has seven segments and they all end in two or three claws. And it's these claws that Anna feels so distinctly now. Like tiny needles they pinch and puncture with an intensity and an itch made all the more maddening within the context of the dream.

It begins at Anna's ankles, then moves up her calves,

crosses one knee and travels up her left thigh until it reaches her stomach.

In the dream, Anna scratches and cries out; but here in bed, in REM sleep, an evolutionary safeguard has 'turned off' Anna's muscles, preventing her from moving.

The False Widow crawls over Anna's breasts, up her neck, then continues moving up to Anna's face.

Now, in her dream, the tormenting itch morphs into the bony fingers of a rapist and in horror, Anna screams in her sleep and swipes at the imaginary hand, flicking the False Widow from her cheek.

Startled and gasping, Anna opens her eyes just as a lightning bolt from somewhere over the channel sends a momentary flash through the Venetian blinds and onto her pillow; illuminating the False Widow, which is now just inches away and crawling back in Anna's direction.

Anna screams again and flings the pillow and the False Widow onto the floor. She jumps out of bed, switches on her light, and spots the ghastly thing scampering toward the corner near the windows.

Scrambling to the coffee table, she grabs the heavy telephone directory, then rushes back to the corner of the room, but the False Widow has disappeared. She fears it might have made it behind the radiator, but then spots the grotesque thing climbing the wall just outside the edge of the draperies.

With all her might, she heaves the four-hundred-page book against the wall, killing the spider instantly, then screams again, gasping for air and running her hands up and down her body as if the thing was still somewhere on her.

For a few seconds, Anna stands in the middle of the room trying to calm herself. She takes another sip of water and is about to sit down on the bed, but jumps up, thinking better of it. Instead, she goes to her closet, retrieves her heaviest coat, then curls up in the chair she had been occupying earlier in the evening.

Shaken by the presence of the giant arthropod, and having no idea of whether there were others and where they could be, Anna never really got back to sleep.

Not a way to start the day, she says to herself as the gray light of dawn begins to filter into the room.

Especially like the day I'm about to have.

She gets herself up from the chair and wanders over to the corner of the room. The telephone directory hasn't moved.

That's a good thing.

Anna showers and dresses and, knowing that it's going to be cold and damp in the parsonage, opts for her heavy, cream colored sweater and a black headband to bookend her black leggings. She throws a scarf around her neck and grabs her coat and her Tumi backpack and heads out the door.

"Good morning, Miss Newsom," the clerk says, as Anna exits the elevator to the lobby.

"Morning, Williams," Anna replies, tossing the heavy phone on the desk in front of him.

Williams glances at the book and then up at Anna, unsure of what it's all about.

"Something the matter, miss?"

Anna doesn't say a word, but simply reaches for the page she has bookmarked with the room service menu. She flips it open to reveal the dead False Widow, smashed flat and looking even larger than it did in life.

Williams struggles with a response.

"Oh, my Lord."

Anna exits and goes to the small cafe next door for a coffee, foregoing anything solid. A young Arab family, a mother and father and two small children, all in traditional clothing, are playing miniature golf around the moats and castles and windmills laid out next to the hotel.

Anna wonders what they were expecting from a trip to the beach this time of year, when it's so typically cold and rainy, but much to the delight of their parents, the children don't seem to mind, giving Anna the hope that it may end up a successful vacation after all.

Funny how sometimes we humans have more compassion for strangers than we do for family or friends, she thinks to herself as she crosses Parade Street to the Grand Pier.

She takes a bench facing the channel and notices that the merry go 'round has been healed, the amusing mechanic nowhere in sight.

Anna sips her coffee and looks out toward the water, trying to shake herself of the False Widow, and at the same time brace herself for the day to come.

The sky is slate gray and the sea, now at high tide, is the same pallor, adding to the illusion that Wales has detached itself from Earth and is now floating in space.

fifty-five

The BBC crew that had been assigned to wrap the equipment out of the parsonage and church had been delayed a week, so all the cameras and support equipment are still in place when Mitchell arrives.

He pulls his Range Rover to within walking distance of the BBC production van and notices that the encampment of reporters, pop-up tents, cameras, and lighting gear has nearly doubled since he was last here, but are still, for the time being at least, safely corralled behind police barricades.

As Mitchell exits the vehicle, he's instantly assaulted by a barrage of questions and curses, fired one atop the other.

"Hey Range Rover! Fuckin' one percenter!"
"Why is the bloody BBC involved?"
"Why are they doing another session?"
"Did you have a go at her?"
"How about the American?"
"Have you met Elizabeth Barrett?"
"Was the pastor having his way with the little thing?"
"Should the church be shuttered?'
"If David O'Rourke was innocent why was he murdered?"

If that wasn't enough, the reporters have now been joined by a group of women associated with the *'Me Too'* movement who are demanding Elizabeth's immediate release.

Hal pulls up behind Mitchell and climbs out of his van, carrying 'thank you' snacks for the crew; a large pink box loaded with tea cakes, donuts and assorted pastries.

"Obnoxious buggers," Hal says, reacting to the crowd of

reporters.

"How in the hell did they know we'd be here?"

Mitchell and Hal give one another a look, and then it dawns on them both at the same time.

"Edwards," Mitchell says.

A sly look crosses Hal's face. He reaches into the box, pulls out a large, iced pastry, and heaves it across the road and into the throng of reporters, a few of whom proceed to swarm and grapple for the sweet treat like female wedding guests clawing over a thrown garter.

Mitchell chuckles and turns to Hal.

"They're just so bloody easy," Mitchell says.

"Right," Hal replies, chuckling, as he takes a bite from his donut.

Mitchell walks through the front door of the parsonage and meets Clare, who is just reaching the bottom of the stairs.

"Morning, sir."

"Good morning, Clare. Steven here?"

"Was, first thing. All cameras are a go and audio is fine, from our end at least."

"If I need a mobile unit, who's in charge?"

"Bennett on camera. Lizzy on boom."

"Fine. I'd like you here when Anna arrives. Get her something to eat and drink if she'd like, and then jump upstairs. Elizabeth Barrett is due to arrive thirty minutes after Anna."

"Who'll take care of her?"

"One of the officers. No need for us to hold her hand."

Mitchell turns and as he exits the front door, he meets Anna and Lyla climbing the steps. Seeing one another, he and Anna freeze and for a few seconds nothing is said. Lyla can't help but notice.

"Good morning, Mitchell. Sorry we're late," she says.

"No problem," Mitchell replies. "I um… anyway, Clare is waiting for you two inside."

Anna doesn't say a word, but as she and Lyla pass him on the porch, Mitchell takes Anna's arm and she pauses.

"I meant what I said last night," he says, his eyes fixed on hers.

Anna gives him a small, sweet smile and Mitchell reciprocates, but as Anna starts to walk away Mitchell turns serious and holds her back.

"They found another girl. Under the Clevedon pier."

"I know," Anna replies.

"But the pastor's in jail...so..."

"So, who did it then?" Anna says, finishing his thought. "That's why we're here today, Mitchell."

"Right. Of course. Just...be careful, okay?"

He releases her arm and as Anna disappears behind the large front door, Lyla lags behind.

"She had a terrible night."

"What happened?"

"I'm no expert in arthropods, but I'd say someone may have it in for our girl," Lyla says, turning to go inside.

"Wait? What!!!? Arthropods?" Mitchell says. "You can't just throw out a statement like that and let it lay!"

"She doesn't want me to say anything."

"Tell me."

Lyla turns from the front door and steps back toward Mitchell, lowering her voice.

"Yesterday a pot of pansies materialized from out of nowhere and ended up in Anna's room."

"Okay."

"Then in the middle of the night, a spider the size of Manhattan crawled out from under her sheets."

"Good heavens."

"She killed the damn thing."

"Where is it now?"

"Somewhere in Scotland Yard. Anna brought it down to the front desk and the clerk, poor soul, was scared stiff and had no idea what to do with it so, I called the police."

Mitchell goes silent for a moment, trying to put two and two together.

"Remember what Anna says, there are no coincidences. I think someone used the pansies as an excuse to get into the room and then planted the spider. Someone may be trying to kill her, Mitchell," Lyla says, before turning and entering the parsonage.

From the window in the choir loft, Blevins watched as Henry's cab pulled up to the front of the parsonage.

As the reporters began to scurry about, he saw when they began flailing their arms and hurling questions; and he paid particular attention as Henry got out and went to the rear door of the cab.

If Anna was dead, then Blevins could consider himself home free. He could go on with his double-life, even become acting pastor, a position that would provide him an endless stream of cash and an array of potential quarry, albeit older.

But if Anna were still alive, he would either have to flee or find another way to finish her off.

His heart pounding in his chest, Blevins waits as Lyla exits the cab and Henry closes her door. *WALK TO THE FRONT AND GET IN THE CAB! NOW!* Blevins screams to himself, firing telepathic commands across the open yard.

For a second, maybe less, Henry turns and is about to walk to the driver's door; but then, as if he had absentmindedly forgotten, he turns and walks around the back of the vehicle.

NO! NO! YOU IDIOT! BUT WAIT! IT COULD BE SOMEONE ELSE!!! Blevins prays, but it's not to be.

As Henry opens the second rear door, Anna steps out, reaches for her Tumi backpack and begins making her way up the front sidewalk.

"DAMMIT TO HELL! he yells out, the False Widow having failed him. He jerks away from the window, frantic for a solution.

I've got to think, he tells himself. *I've got to think.*

Anna hangs her heavy coat on the rack next to the door and heads down the hallway to the kitchen.

"Good morning, Simon."

"Anna! Good morning," Simon says, as he turns from the coffee urn.

"How was the drive?"

"Bloody awful. Thought I'd beat it by getting an early start. Lot of good it did." he says, stirring the liquid in his cup.

"Hi, Dr. Newsom." Clare says, as she enters and begins freshening the breakfast items on the table. "If there's anything you'd like that you don't see, please let me know."

As she's about to leave the room, Clare puts her hand to her earpiece.

"Roger that," she says and turns to Anna.

"Mitchell says Elizabeth should be here in twenty minutes."

Simon waits until Clare has left the room and then continues.

"Listen, Anna, I don't know how all this got so off the rails. O'Rourke's innocence; I shudder at what we were going to do to the man, and now Benjamin Wetherford arrested. I was so certain in the beginning, but now, I've no idea of what to make of this case anymore."

"Simon?"

"Not to mention this whole, bloody television mess. It had nothing whatsoever to do with what I asked of you, and it's become a bloody sideshow, a distraction.

It may be a feather in the cap for Cynthia Smythe, but it's one huge pain in the arse for me and for you."

"Simon?" Anna says, again.

"Yes?"

Simon can be so endearing at times, Anna says to herself, and she can't help but break into a small smile. She walks over and gives him a small kiss on the cheek

"You brought me here to do a job, and I intend to finish it."

As Anna gets to the upper floor, she takes a peak into Elizabeth's bedroom and is pleased to note that it appears as though nothing has been altered since she was last here; the knitting needles, the quaint English antiques, the torn and curled wallpaper; just as they left it.

Claire shows them to the room across the hall and Lyla begins to prepare for the session, setting her computer on a small table in front of one of the high-backed, Victorian chairs.

"Any idea on how you're going to start?" Lyla says, trying to make conversation and put Anna at ease, but immediately regrets asking the question. She has been through enough of these to know that Anna can't begin until she's made an assessment of Elizabeth's state of mind.

"Sorry, stupid question."

"No, it's not. I was asking myself the same thing."

Anna moves to the windows and looks out across the gloomy patchwork of fields and hedgerows that slope toward the channel, and then, intuitively, she glances to her right and across the street.

"Elizabeth's here," Anna says, taking a deep breath.

In the BBC production van, Mitchell has taken his place at the console and studies the several monitors displaying the four cameras positioned within Elizabeth's bedroom.

"Recording?" Mitchell says, turning to James, his technician.

"Rolling," James replies.

Mitchell watches as Anna enters Elizabeth's bedroom. She walks to the middle of the room, turns toward the door and folds her hands in front of her. Mitchell takes note of the time and waits.

At six minutes and twelve seconds, Mitchell sees Elizabeth Barrett appear in the doorway to the bedroom.

"She just walked in," Mitchell says, to Hal who is just taking a seat behind him.

"Good morning, Elizabeth," Anna says, but for several more seconds nothing else happens.

What Mitchell can't see, or anyone else, for that matter, is the dull, electrical shock that shoots through Anna marking the onset of ESS, and the sudden wave of empathic sensations that are now beginning to flow from Elizabeth.

"Slight vertigo," Anna says.

In the opposite room Lyla checks her watch and makes a note of the time.

"What does that mean again?" Simon says, watching over Lyla's shoulder.

"She's beginning to have ESS with Elizabeth."

"Oh, right. Of course."

Suddenly, Mitchell catches movement in one of the monitors that display video coming from the cameras placed in the church.

"Who's that?" he says, to James, but then sees that it's Blevins. "Never mind. It's just the organist."

"Elizabeth, do you remember me?" Anna says, beginning to access Elizabeth's state of mind.

"Why am I here?"

"Because I need your help."

"I helped before and nothing changed."

"That's because we're not finished yet. Why don't you come into the room?" Anna says, taking a step back.

"No."

"Why not?"

"Because."

"Because...?"

"I hate this room. And he'll come, I know he will," Elizabeth says.

To Anna, Elizabeth still projects a flat aspect, despite their progress.

"Who? Who'll come?"

"David."

"David is dead, Elizabeth," Anna reminds her.

"Dead? How?"

"He was killed. Don't you remember? At the farm."

"The farm?"

At the mention of the word, 'farm', Anna notices that Elizabeth brightens slightly, and Anna senses in herself a momentary rise of positive emotion.

"Yes. You told me. Don't you remember telling me? He was killed at the farm."

Once again, at the mention of the word 'farm', Anna picks up a positive reaction from Elizabeth.

"There we go. Tell me about the farm," Anna says.

"There's a woman and she tells me that there is lemonade and cookies in the kitchen."

"Why did she tell you that, Elizabeth? Were there lemonade and cookies?"

"Yes, but... I don't know...maybe."

Now, to Anna's delight, Elizabeth begins to move. She steps over the threshold and into the room, allowing herself to look at the wallpaper and the rows of farm images, the multitude of which appears to momentarily confuse her.

"Why am I here?"

Anna reaches for her notebook and continues, intentionally moving further ahead in Elizabeth's story.

"Elizabeth, when I saw you last, you said,

My underwear is being pulled down me legs and the woman says, Help yourself. Have all you want. I made them just for you and when David is finished with his chores he'll take you home.'

"Do you remember saying that?"

"I think so."

"I want to help you, Elizabeth. Please believe that."

"What would you like me to do?"

"Why don't you lay down?"

"OH, NO, PLEASE...DO I HAVE TO?"

"You'll be more comfortable..."

"NO, PLEASE..."

"You don't want to live the rest of your life in prison, do you?"

The proposition makes Elizabeth freeze.

"But why should I? I didn't do anything wrong, it was him!"

Anna turns and sits on the padded stool in front of the antique vanity and decides to take a chance and move into an area of questioning they haven't yet explored.

"Elizabeth, let me ask you this. What if it wasn't David, at all?"

"Beg your pardon. What? What are you saying?"

"What if it was someone else and you just thought it was David. Perhaps you simply made a mistake."

"A MISTAKE?" Elizabeth says, her brows furrowing and immediately Anna could kick herself for making such a blunder.

In the church, Blevins stands immobilized in the loft, desperately weighing his options.

He can stay the course, hoping that Anna's gambit with Elizabeth fails; scrape together the cash and valuables from the church and escape to France or Germany or Switzerland in his Opel Rekord; or he can hold out for total victory while at the same time preparing to destroy himself and everything around him should Anna prevail.

And then he remembers the old Welsh proverb that his father used to quote;

The Wise Man Hopes For The Best,
And Prepares For The Worst.

THAT'S IT THEN! He says to himself. *AM I NOT A WISE MAN? PERHAPS THE WISEST! I'LL RISE VICTORIOUS OR GO DOWN IN A BLAZING INFERNO! FAMOUS I'LL BE, IF PUSH COMES TO SHOVE! AND WHAT IF IS SHOULD COME TO THAT?* Blevins muses.

A perfect end to an imperfect life. His right brain conspired to sabotage him in mathematics, and his sausage fingers made a mockery of his aptitude for music.

BUT WAIT! NOT IMPERFECT! NO! WHATEVER YOU DO, BE THE BEST YOU CAN BE AT IT! his father used to say, and who, now, could deny that once he had found his calling, Blevins had done just that.

How many women, defiled? How many young girls, ravished? Celwin Blevins, the Mighty Marauder of the Inner Sanctum, the Holy of Holies! The Divine Honey Pot! And only three dead. The last being Mabel Prine. Not a bad accounting!

He carefully makes his way down the creaky staircase and crosses the vast floor of the church in record time. He descends the stone steps to the basement and bursts into Benjamin's office.

PLANTING THE CASH BAG FASHIONED INTO A MASK IN HIS DESK DRAWER; A STROKE OF GENIUS! he thinks to himself and crosses to the opposite wall. He pulls back the faded print of Martin Luther nailing his 95 Theses to the door of the Castle Church in Wittenburg, revealing the safe in the wall behind it.

Poor, stupid Benjamin thought it was his secret and his alone, that no one else knew! But Blevins knew, having hid in the room one night not long after arriving at the parsonage.

Blevins knew all of it. The safe. The whiskey. And the outlawed Catholic bible hidden inside the floorboards.

Blevins had partaken of the first two, but only in moderation, so as to not attract attention, and he had ignored the third. But the young girl who came to live at the parsonage shortly after the death of her parents? That was a different story.

Elizabeth lays back, her head coming to rest on a pillowcase embroidered by Adelaide Wetherford.

"What happened on Fridays, Elizabeth?"

"Uncle Benjamin and Margret would be on to the fish market."

"What time would they leave?"

"It was early. In the winter, it would be dark," Elizabeth replies.

"When did David, or shall we say, 'the man', begin coming to you? Do you mind if we just call him 'the man'?

"No. That's...fine. I, um, just after I arrived."

"How did he know to come on Fridays?"

"Because they were gone, and that's when his schedule had him at the parsonage."

"Whose schedule?"

"David's."

"Did he come the day you killed him?" Anna asks.

"I killed him?"

"Didn't you say you did?"

"Yes. But he didn't visit me."

"And why not?"

"Because Uncle Benjamin and Margret were back much too soon, and they surprised him. I saw his truck on the street beneath my window."

Anna carefully proceeds to the next level of questioning.

"Elizabeth...did you ever see his face?"

"It was always covered."

"By the bag?"

"Yes."

"I would hear the kitchen door close and soon after there would come the sound of Uncle Benjamin starting the car."

"Go on."

"And I would wait. Paralyzed. During the winter, when it was dark out, I would see his shadow, through the crack in my door. His shadow would always proceed him."

"And in the summer?"

"If there weren't clouds, the sunlight would filter in from the eastern windows. I would hear his steps on the stairwell and wait. I prayed and prayed that he wouldn't come, but it never did any good, he always would; and then, there it would be, lit by the sunlight, that God awful…, THE BAG OVER HIS HEAD!….Oh…NO…NO…WHY ME???" Elizabeth cries out and, as she does, it sends shockwaves through Anna's body.

In the production van, James turns to Mitchell.

"Poor kid. Rough going."

"Rough indeed," Mitchell replies, imagining what Anna must be going through as well.

"Anna?"

"Yes, Elizabeth?"

"Are you okay?"

"Thank you for asking. Yes, I'm fine. Go on."

"I, um, turn to face the wall and to the farms, so many of them but all the same. The road up to the house and the white fences and the dogs and the man waving. It all seemed so merry. And then… and then…"

"I'm here, Elizabeth."

"I, I feel, the hot breath and the wet tongue lapping at me through the roughness of the bag…and then he, and then he…"

"He what?"

"He would start at me ankles…licking…kissing and go up the inside of me legs…until he, OH GOD, until he…would curl his rough, fat fingers through me undies and, and pull them slowly down, so slowly, and I WOULD BE PRAYING TO GOD TO MAKE HIM GO FASTER, TO GET IT OVER WITH!!!"

Blevins empties the cash from the wall safe into one of the Barclay Bank bags, then retrieves the whiskey bottle from the bottle drawer of Benjamin's desk. In the next room, next to the antiquated furnace, sit several jugs of kerosene. He grabs as many as he can, balancing the armload under his chin, and makes his way up and out of the basement.

In Elizabeth's bedroom, Anna continues with her questioning.

"But he didn't go faster, did he, Elizabeth?"

"No. He went as slow as he liked."

"Was it always the same?"

"I don't remember," Elizabeth responds.

"And the woman?"

"The one with the lemonade and cookies? She was always there. *'David has told me all about you'*, she says. *'There's lemonade and cookies in the kitchen. And then...'*"

"Then...?"

"Then she says, *'Help yourself. Have all you want. I made them just for you and when David is finished with his chores, he'll take you home.'*"

Wheezing and coughing, Blevins reaches the top of the wooden stairway in the choir loft and stops to catch his breath. Glancing again to the lawn below, he remembers the times when his mother would call across the yard from the living room window.

'CELWIN! CELWIN! TIME FOR PRACTICE!' she would bellow.

And where was young Celwin? In the basement of the house next door, with young Annabelle, the neighbor's daughter; his fat fingers being put to better use.

Blevins sets everything down near his beloved Brindle organ and unscrews the top of the whiskey bottle.

Three gulps should do nicely, he thinks, then wipes his mouth on his sleeve.

fifty-six

"Pardon me, Sir…" Officer Poole says, as he raps on the open door of Hayden's office.

"What it is, Poole?"

"DNA report on the young lady found under the pier. She was raped alright."

"And…?"

"Curious thing. Seems that several years ago, there was a series of similar attacks on young women in the town of Stoke-on-Trent."

"How so?"

"Whoever done it put the pinch on their undergarments, as well."

"What's so curious about that? If they're deranged enough to rape, they'll do about anything, wouldn't you say?"

"That's not it. There was a church, you see. A small, non-denominational sort, new age kind of affair. No official association with any mainstream religion, as it were. You know, the oddball sort."

"I do know," Hayden says, clearing his throat. "Me sister attends one. Regularly."

"Oh. So sorry, sir. Anyway, this so-called church, The Sunrise Church of the New Dawn, burned down one night. Rumor was the self-ordained pastor absconded with the collection box. Never rebuilt, of course, lack of funds and all that."

"Poole?"

"Yessir?"

"The point?"

"Yessir, well, to come around it from the long way sir, the rapes stopped just after the fire."

"Mere coincidence, wouldn't you say?"

"You tell me, sir. The name of the choir master, and the owner of our newly found DNA, was one Celwin Connor Blevins."

Hayden thinks for a moment, putting two and two together, and then in the next instant, it dawns on him.

"MY, GOD, MAN!!!" he says, jumping up and grabbing his hat and coat off the rack next to his door. "GET UP A PATROL SQUAD! ELIZABETH BARRETT IS AT THE PARSONAGE, TODAY!"

fifty-seven

"Elizabeth, you said that the woman told you that David would take you home after he was finished with his chores."

"Yes."

"What chores, Elizabeth?"

"His tongue, I can feel his tongue, and then his fingers between me legs...and then going up and, and..."

"It's okay. Go on."

"It would stop and all of a sudden I would feel him inside me...or sometimes he would sit on me and...and..." Elizabeth begins to gag, and she snaps her head to the side.

"Put himself in me mouth."

THIS POOR CHILD, Anna thinks, but she, along with Elizabeth is also tormented.

"I didn't dare open my eyes."

"No...no...of course not," Anna gasps.

"And then, finally, he would lay on top of me and put himself inside me and begin rocking back and forth, back and forth."

Elizabeth is heaving, struggling for air and Anna is nauseous to the point of vomiting.

"Go...on...Eliz... ab...eth...please..."

Now, as suddenly as it did during Anna's first session in the room, the wallpaper begins to tear and curl, climbing up the walls; this time, however, it's preceded by the amplified sounds of tearing and ripping.

"OH, GOD! WHAT'S HAPPENING!" Elizabeth screams.

"James!" Mitchell yells. "Close up on the wall over Elizabeth!"

"My God, man," Hal says, watching the monitors.

"I...I...would yell out, begging for help...screaming,

DAVID! DAVID! DAVID! TAKE ME HOME!"

"And…and…then?"

"And then, in my ear, I feel the hot breath and the wet tongue and the roughness of the bag and the voice of the man on top of me saying, *'quiet now…be a good girl…quiet now…be a good girl'…* through the hole in the bag."

"THERE!" Anna yells out, "YOU HEARD A VOICE!"

"YES! YES! I DID, I TOLD YOU THAT I DID!" Elizabeth screams.

Now, without warning, the sound of tearing and ripping fuses with the roar of a rushing wind.

"HELP ME, PLEASE!!!" Elizabeth cries, and then, in horror, Anna watches as the stainless-steel knitting needles begin to slowly rise up and out of the wicker basket.

"OH, MY GOD! HELP ME!!!"

"I'M HERE, ELIZABETH, I'M HERE!" Anna screams, knowing now that they're both caught up in an extreme form of Causal Tele-transmutation; and as the steel knitting needles begin dropping to the floor, Adelaide's needlepoints shake and rattle against the wall, and the antique Hollywood dolls start flinging themselves across the room, landing slapdash at odd angles.

Suddenly, as quickly as it started, everything slows to a dead stop, and the roar rushes from the room and fades to a deafening silence.

In the BBC production van, all that can be heard is the sound of Elizabeth's whimpering and Anna's struggles to catch her breath.

"Jesus Christ," Hal says, "Are they okay?"

"Mitchell?" James says.

"Just stay wide on all the cameras and wait. Lyla, are you there?"

"I'm here, Mitchell."

"What should we do?"

"I don't know, Mitchell, I don't know."

"Wait, she sees something," Hal says.

Turning toward the video monitors they watch as Anna raises her head and gazes in the direction of the shelves where the Hollywood dolls had been.

"What's that sound?" Simon says.

"I don't know," Lyla replies.

But in the room, Anna knows exactly what it is. The miniature MAGNUS organ sitting on the shelf above the dolls has begun playing, BY ITSELF, as if mocking all of them.

"WHAT IS THAT, WHERE'S IT COMING FROM!?" Mitchell asks.

"IT'S IN THE ROOM!" James replies.

And not just any composition. It's playing Bach's Toccata and Fugue in D Minor. Blevins' favorite composition.

"THE ORGAN, ELIZABETH!" Anna cries.

"JESUS CHRIST!" Mitchell yells out. "James, camera two! Tilt down and zoom in on that bloody thing!!!"

Simon, in the room with Lyla, can hardly believe what he's seeing and hearing.

"I SAY! WHAT IN HEAVEN'S NAME...THE INFERNAL THING IS PLAYING ITSELF! WE SHOULD STOP! NOW!"

"No! Simon, she's so close now!" Lyla says.

"ELIZABETH!?" Anna cries, taking hold of Elizabeth's shoulders.

"WHAT IS IT? PLEASE MAKE IT STOP!" Elizabeth screams, her hands over her ears.

"YOU'VE...YOU'VE HEARD DAVID O'ROURKE'S VOICE, HAVEN'T YOU?" WHEN HE WOULD SAY HELLO...WHEN HE GAVE YOU THE TOY TRUCK..."

"YES! I HAVE! I HAVE..." Elizabeth says, beginning to sob, "PLEASE MAKE IT STOP!"

"ELIZABETH...WE'RE ALMOST DONE. IT'S ALMOST OVER," Anna says.

"PLEASE..."

"AND WAS HIS VOICE, THE VOICE YOU HEARD THROUGH THE BAG?"

On hearing the question, Elizabeth thinks for a moment bursts into shrieks of grief and remorse.

"NO! NO! NO! OH MY GOD, IT WASN'T THE SAME! IT WASN'T THE SAME VOICE!!! IT WAS A DIFFERENT VOICE!!! OH MY GOD, WHAT HAVE I DONE!!!

In an instant, like a flash of light ripping from one hemisphere of her brain to the other, Anna visualizes a long, dark hole boring itself through the center of the earth.

ISABEL'S PASSAGEWAY!!! her own voice screams in her head. *ISABEL'S PASSAGEWAY!!!*

With Elizabeth's sobbing screams and the Bach fugue echoing in her ears, Anna bolts out of the bedroom and heads for the middle stairwell of the parsonage.

"LYLA! TAKE CARE OF ELIZABETH!"

"ANNA! DON'T!" Lyla screams, but it's too late. "Mitchell? Can you hear me!"

"WHAT IN THE HELL IS SHE DOING?" Mitchell yells, into his mic.

"I think she's headed down to the basement!" Lyla says.

"The basement? What the…"

"There's an underground passageway that runs from the house to the church!" Lyla says.

"WHAT? WHERE IS IT!" Mitchell yells in response.

"I've no idea! Just somewhere in the basement!" Lyla replies.

"Fuck! And no one bloody told me?" Mitchell says, whipping his head around to Hal.

"Had no idea, either," Hal says. "We're losin' control here, Mitch."

"Bloody, fuckin' right we are," Mitchell says, then keys his microphone so all his assistants can hear what he has to say.

"Listen up! I want Bennett and Lizzy to grab their equipment and head across the lawn to the church. Now!"

"NO!" Hal says.

"Oh, shit. Right. The boys across the street," Mitchell says and keys his microphone again. "Bennett and Lizzy meet me in the hallway."

"Roger that, Mitchell!" Claire says, into her microphone, followed by Bennett and Lizzy and several others.

Anna runs to the first floor, crosses a small hallway, and heads down the much narrower stairs to the basement door.

"DAMMIT," she says, fumbling in the dark, then finds the switch. A single bare bulb, casting a dingy, yellowish light, illuminates a dust covered maze of rotting supports and used furniture. In the corner is the black, hulking shape of a furnace, its metal arms stretching out like an oversized sea monster.

Anna quickly hits the flashlight on her phone and begins searching the perimeter. Most of the walls are made of up large cobbles cemented together and she sees nothing like a door or passageway.

IT'S GOT TO BE HERE! Anna thinks to herself and is about to give up when she spots a small table pushed up against the wall under the stairwell. An embroidered tablecloth draped over its edge reaches to the floor.

Anna crawls under the stairwell, throws the tablecloth aside and peers in.

There, in front of her, is a roughhewn hole in the basement wall. It's roughly three feet square, framing total blackness beyond.

Oh, God, am I actually going to do this?

Not giving herself the chance to talk herself out of it, Anna sucks in several gulps of air and disappears inside.

Isabel Quivers had been right, and the years had not diminished her memories of the place. It was dark and dank, '*Eldritch*', was ultimately how Isabel had described it, and Anna promises herself that if she makes it out alive, she's going to look up the word.

Anna inches forward, her hands and knees scraping on the rutted surface left by the hasty removal of stone several centuries before.

It occurs to her that the tunnel is more hiding place than passageway, but today, for Anna, it's more like a portal to hell.

The path is strewn with dead rats and animal bones, and bats hang from the ceiling just inches above her head. As she approaches, they stir and flap and flutter toward the far end.

NOT IN MY HAIR, PLEASE! JUST DON'T GET STUCK IN MY HAIR!

Moisture oozes from the walls and collects in moldy pools with a stench that is making her gag, and now she's wondering if it's she herself and not Elizabeth that is driving her on.

Mitchell bursts through the front doors of the parsonage just as Claire is getting to the front door.

"WHERE'S THE BLOODY BASEMENT!" he yells.

"Down the middle stairwell, sir! follow me!" Claire fires back.

"GET THE OTHERS AND HAVE THEM FOLLOW!"

After ten minutes that seem like an eternity, Anna detects a smudge of light filtering down from the roof and, as she gets closer, she realizes that the tunnel doesn't end in the basement but under the church floor; and to her horror, a thick iron grate is set in cement along the top.

BREATHE, Anna. BREATHE! she says to herself, but she begins to panic; her breathing quickens, and her heart begins to race. She grabs hold of the grate and tries to steady herself.

BREATHE IN... COUNT TO FOUR. BREATH OUT... COUNT TO SIX.

Anna says a quick prayer and, as she begins to feel herself settle, pushes against the grate. It doesn't budge.

"DAMMIT!" she yells out.

If she can't get it open, her only option is to go back the way she came, which she's dreading.

"SHIT!"

Terrified and exhausted, she does the only thing she can do. She rolls over and lays on her back, her hair dragging in filth, and using her legs, pushes as hard as she can.

ONCE. NOTHING. TWICE. NOTHING.

Then she remembers something she learned in martial arts. She anchors each arm against the rough walls of the tunnel and, using them as leverage, kicks the iron gate with both feet as hard as she possibly can;

ONCE, TWICE, THREE TIMES, and slowly she feels it begin to tear free.

JUST A FEW MORE! she yells, grunting, and then, all at once, the iron grate rips through the rotted cement.

Anna scrambles up and out of the hole, stops to get her bearings, and sees that she's behind the altar. She runs around to the front and then spots Blevins in the filtered light coming through the window in the choir loft.

As quietly as she can, Anna pads across the large stones in the church floor and begins climbing the old wooden staircase, but just as she's nearing the top, it creaks beneath her feet.

Blevins looks up sharply, sensing her presence behind the shiplap partition.

"You've come for me, haven't you?" he says, into space. "You didn't think I heard you, coming up through the floor?"

Anna doesn't respond.

"It's no good. I know you're there. I can hear you breathe."

Anna gasps and glances quickly out the window, which is now at her back. She looks down at the floor, some twenty feet below; but in the next instant, turns back and continues up the last few steps, her heart in her throat.

And then she smells it. The same oily, earthy smell of grease that she encountered during her first visit with Elizabeth at The Sandringham and again at the merry go 'round at the Grand Pier.

As she rounds the corner of the shiplap partition, Anna stops, baffled by what she sees, but finally understanding the origin of the smell. And she recognizes Blevins from the newspaper reports.

The graying man, unkempt and corpulent, has torn the old Brindle apart and has detached several of the brass pipes responsible for creating the organ's sound.

His hands are covered in grease, and in his fingers are draped an assortment of brightly colored girl's underwear.

"Seems you've caught me red handed," Blevins says, and Anna can see immediately that Blevins is totally and utterly mad.

"CLAIRE, GIVE ME YOUR FLASHLIGHT!" Mitchell says, crouching at the hole in the basement wall.

Claire, squatting behind him, switches on the flashlight and hands it to Mitchell, who then shoots the beam down the length of the tunnel.

"ANNA!" he yells, hearing his echo through the shaft. "ANNA!!!"

But there's no response.

"DAMMIT! CAN'T EVEN SEE THE END OF THE BLOODY THING!" Mitchell says, but then, in the BBC production van, James spots Anna on the video monitors and keys his microphone.

"Mitchell! She's not in the tunnel! She's in the church!"

"SHIT!" Mitchell says, scrambling out and up from the hole.

Blevins sets the underwear on his bench, reaches for one of the brass pipes from the organ, and picks up one of the stainless-steel knitting needles from Elizabeth's bedroom. For a moment, the shiny metal glints in the light from the window, the reflection hitting Anna in the eye.

He inserts it into the brass pipe, fishes around, and then carefully extracts yet one more pair, this one with tiny blue flowers set against a bright yellow background.

"Forget-Me-Nots. Suitably named, don't you think?" he says, setting the pair alongside the others. "What exactly do you expect to do here, Miss Newsom?"

"I needed to be sure it was you."

"And now you know. Are you satisfied? Are you going to arrest me?'

"I'm…I'm going to try to help you."

"Don't be ridiculous."

Blevins reaches for the whiskey bottle and takes a long pull, sucking in air at the burn of the liquid, then wipes his mouth with the back of his hand.

"You…you… couldn't have always been this way." Anna says.

"Oh, my dear. That's where you're mistaken. I burst from my mother's loins depraved and unprincipled, and I fully intend to go on this way. I've got it quite good here, now, you see."

Blevins weaves for a moment as the whiskey takes its full effect.

"It's unfortunate, really, that we should have met this way," he says, fiddling with the stainless-steel knitting needle. "I rather would have liked to know you better."

"I can run. You'll never catch me."

"You're not the type, my dear. I've known them all, and you're not the type."

Then, from out of nowhere, there are voices, yelling and pounding on the large wooden doors at the front of the church.

Blevins stops, takes another pull on the bottle of whiskey, and reconsiders.

AM I NOT A WISE MAN? PERHAPS THE WISEST! I'LL RISE VICTORIOUS OR GO DOWN IN A BLAZING INFERNO!

Knowing now that escape is improbable, Blevins reaches for the lit candle sitting on top of the wooden railing.

"YOU BLOODY BITCH," he says, raising his voice over the yelling and pounding from below.

He walks to the last of the kerosene cans and kicks it

over. Anna glances at the flame of the candle and watches as the flammable liquid pools in the cracks and crevices of the ancient wooden floor, and suddenly comes the terrible realization that she's torn between her native instinct to save another human being and her desire to destroy him.

HOW EASY IT WOULD BE TO PUSH HIM OVER THE RAILING...

The thought has barely formed itself when she glances up and catches the demonic expression rippling across Blevins' face as he consigns the candle to gravity.

The size of the ignition causes Blevins to lurch backward and Anna to throw her arms in front of her face. As he does, he steps onto one of the brass organ pipes laying on the floor.

He pivots on it for a moment and, as the pipe slides out from under his foot, it sends Blevins backwards against the railing.

"Oh God!!!" Anna cries, catching sight of him through the flames, *NO, NO, NO, I DIDN'T MEAN IT, I DIDN'T MEAN IT!!!* and she tries to move in his direction, but the flames are holding her back.

For a second or two, Blevins is balanced between heaven and earth, but in the next instant his weight begins to shift rearward and his eyes open wide in horror.

"NO!!!" Anna screams.

But it's too late. As he falls backwards over the railing, Blevins has just enough time to remembers the words...

'The thorns of lust rose above my head and there was no hand to root them out.'

...before tumbling head over heels and crashing face down onto the stone floor of the church, forty feet below.

Anna screams again, coughing on the smoke from the flames that are now climbing the legs of the Brindle; feasting on its greasy lubricant and the magnificent bird's-eye maple taken so long ago from the ancient forests of northern Wales.

Anna spins and charges down the wooden stairs to the

church, reaching the bottom just as Chief Inspector Hayden and his men burst through the side entrance next to the altar.

Mitchell and the camera crew follows, Mitchell shouting orders to capture as much video as they can.

"My God, Anna, you had us worried!" Lyla says, as Simon runs up to join her.

"What in heaven's name...?" he says, seeing Blevins on the stone floor.

Embers and chunks of burning beams have begun dropping and it's becoming apparent the whole choir loft is in danger of collapsing.

"I WANT EVERYONE OUT OF HERE, NOW!" Hayden yells.

Simon grabs Anna and rushes her toward the large front doors which have been flung open by the police.

"HIM AS WELL!!!" Hayden yells again, this time at two officers who grab hold of Blevins' body and move toward to the doors.

Reaching the open air, Anna stops and leans on her knees trying to cough out the smoke and get her breath back. Glancing up, she catches sight of several police officers working to keep the crowd of reporters at bay.

In the production van, Mitchell's assistant watches the video monitors as the Brindle organ, its larger brass pipes reaching through the flames like arms begging for forgiveness, begins to sink through the collapsing floor of the choir loft.

Anna straightens and moves toward the police officers who are setting Blevins' body down on the lawn between the two buildings.

Coming to rest between the two officers, she sees that Blevins' eyes are wide open and staring at a point somewhere outside of Earth's orbit, the stainless-steel knitting needle still clutched in his hand.

As the discordant whine of fire engine sirens grow in the distance, something happens inside of Anna.

Months later, when writing about it for her next book she says,

'…it was as if the monster that had clutched at my insides for so many years simply let go and drifted up and out of my body and I was thirteen again, laying in the sun on top of the houseboat in Branson, Missouri.'

On the lawn, she feels Mitchell come up behind her and stop just over her shoulder.

"I wanted to save him, I really did," Anna says, her eyes starting to well up.

"Don't doubt that at all," Mitchell says. "Let's get you home."

Anna looks up, sniffles, and wipes the tears from her cheeks.

"Yeah."

fifty-eight

Henry waited outside The Sandringham as Anna and Lyla packed. Anna was able to wash the dirt and bat dung out of her hair, then Henry drove the two of them back to London and The Shangri-La.

They had promised themselves one last bath in their amazing tubs before leaving, and now, with a glass of wine in her hand and bluegrass playing on her phone, Anna leans back and takes in the lights of London spreading out below her.

I can see it in their paintings
And I can hear it in the wind,
hear it rise and descend
Through the many-colored trees,
Forms a many-colored breeze
Made of many-colored leaves,
departing ever so gracefully...

The final session with Elizabeth has left Anna spent, completely emptied. And, as she's experienced in the past, her body continues to ring - vibrate is more like it; long after the shared sensations have ended. The feelings will go on for hours and, in this case, perhaps days; and the sensation is so intense that, when Anna closes her eyes, she has the feeling that, if she concentrated hard enough, she could make herself levitate.

After Blevins was killed and they were leaving the church, everyone was caught up in the pandemonium created by the reporters who ended up breaching the police barricades.

Mitchell had to fight his way back into the BBC production van while barking orders to his crew, and Anna and Lyla were whisked away by Hayden into Henry's waiting cab, so she didn't have the opportunity to give Mitchell a proper goodbye.

Anna reaches for her towel and is about to climb out of the tub when her phone dings.

'Hate to see you leave. Safe trip. M.
BTW it all ended way too soon'.

She considers a response then types.

'Yes, it did. Thank you for everything.
I'll never forget you.'

The next day Anna sleeps until noon, which is as late as she dares, and Henry gets them to the airport in plenty of time for their 4:00pm flight.

"There you are, ladies! With time to spare for a cup of tea!" Henry declares, as he deposits their luggage on the curb.

Lyla grabs her suitcase and heads toward the terminal, and Anna lags behind to say a proper goodbye.

"Miss, before I forget!" Henry says.

Reaching into the front seat of his cab he produces a copy of The Spider on the Ceiling.

"Would you mind, miss?" he asks, pulling a pen from his shirt pocket.

"I'd be delighted!" Anna replies.

She opens the book and writes: *'to Henry, the best driver in London, with love, Dr. Anna Newsom.'* and as she hands it back, her eyes begin to tear.

"Now, now, miss. There'll be none of those," Henry says, and, with that, Anna leans in and gives him a big hug.

Anna sniffles a bit, wipes a tear from her cheek, and then turns and grabs her suitcase. Henry watches until she disappears safely into the crowd heading into the terminal, then gets into his cab and pulls slowly out into traffic.

"Two toasted tea cakes. Two diet Cokes," Lyla says, as she plops down next to Anna in the waiting area.

"Toasted tea cakes? Really?"

"It's our last chance!" Lyla says.

Anna smiles and shakes her head, and then her attention

is drawn to the voice of a young, female reporter coming from the large, flat screen TV.

"It was late afternoon yesterday when the Elizabeth Barrett murder mystery came to a dramatic end..."

The scene shifts to a wide shot of the parsonage and the church when her voice is drowned out by the boarding announcement coming over the PA system.

"Saved by the bell," Anna says, as she stands and grabs her carry ons.

"Sure you don't wanna wait a minute and watch this?" Lyla asks.

"Absolutely positive," Anna says, without the slightest hesitation, and begins to move toward the door of the jetway.

"Ladies and gentlemen, welcome to British Airways, Flight 1011 to Atlanta, Georgia. At this time, please turn off all cellphones..."

The words are no sooner out of the flight attendant's mouth when Lyla's phone rings.

"It's probably Caleb," Anna says, as she pulls her blanket up around her.

Lyla looks at her phone and doesn't recognize the number, but sees that it's from somewhere in England. She decides to give it a quick answer and lowers her voice to a whisper.

"Hi, it's Lyla."

"Why are you whispering?" Chief Inspector Hayden says.

"On the plane, we're about to take off."

"Okay, I'll make this quick. Our little friend, the one that paid a visit to Miss Newsom the other night, was a False Widow. Deadly as they come. Thought you'd like to know. Cheerio, miss. And have a safe flight home."

"Bye, thanks," Lyla says, ending the call.

"What was all that about?" Anna says.

"Wrong number."

The flight home was long, but Anna was able to sleep most of the way and woke only for a few minutes as the Airbus was crossing the coast of Newfoundland.

She raised her window shade to get a peek and watched as the lights of St. John slid past and disappeared behind the dark, hulking shape of the engine.

Caleb was at the airport to greet Lyla and gave her a kiss that lasted well beyond what was appropriate for public places, and of course, someone yelled out, 'Get a room!'

Anna's father, Frank, was there as well.

"It's good to have you home, Sparky," he says, grabbing her luggage. "Your mother's been worried sick."

When they arrived, Anna said hello to her mother and went right to bed.

"What's gotten into her?" Vivian says, to Frank after Anna's longer than usual hug in the kitchen.

"Seems different, doesn't she?" he replies.

fifty-nine

For a week, Anna slept-in, ate home cooked meals, and played with Louis, and eventually decided it was time to pack up and go to her own place and to her regular job.

She had clients to catch up on, and she promised Adrienne Owens at the Institute of Psychology an update on Elizabeth Barrett and the tragic murder of David O'Rourke.

Benjamin Wetherford had been released and he returned to the church, and Margret, his housekeeper, agreed to stay on as long as she could take a month's-long vacation somewhere, anywhere, as long as it wasn't in Clevedon.

Elizabeth's trial was scheduled to take place sometime in December and it was yet to be decided whether Anna would need to be in attendance.

Anna and Lyla got back into their routines in the office, with Anna seeing clients and Lyla keeping track of appointments and billing; and about a month after getting home, Anna decided it was time to make good on her promise to buy Caleb a steak dinner.

"Hey, sorry I'm late," Anna says, as she gets to the table, prompting Caleb to look up from his menu.

"Good. I could eat a cow. Hey, Anna."

"Hi, Caleb."

"Actually, you are going to eat a cow," Lyla quips.

"Oh. Right," Caleb replies, flipping the menu around to read the name of the restaurant, Sammy's Original Steakhouse.

"Something to drink?" the waitress says, as she gets to their table.

"How about a....um...gin and tonic. For old time's sake," Anna says, with a smile in Lyla's direction.

"Make it two," Lyla adds.

"Three," Caleb says.

As the waitress walks away with their drink orders, Caleb glances up over his menu.

"Speaking of gin and tonics, did Lyla tell you the news about that director?" he says, but before Anna has a chance to react, Lyla kicks Caleb under the table.

"Owww! What???"

Anna glances sharply at Caleb and then at Lyla and then back at Caleb again.

"What news? What director?" Anna says.

"That's what I get for sharing with Mr. Big Mouth."

"Sharing what!? What's going on!? Is this about Mitchell?"

"Yeah, that's his name! I couldn't remember," Caleb says.

"Would you please shut up? Here, eat something!" Lyla says, tossing the breadbasket in front of him.

"I...was...going to tell you. When the time was right," Lyla adds.

"Time was right? For what?"

"Okay, three gin and tonics," the waitress says, as she arrives and begins setting them down.

"I, um... I got a call from Simon a couple of days ago."

"Yeah..." Anna says, taking a sip of her drink.

"It seems that Mitchell is going to, um...get married again."

"Married? Really?" Anna says, peering out over the rim of her glass. "And Simon called you? Instead of me?"

"He wasn't sure how you'd take it."

"Wasn't sure how I'd take it? And to whom, may I ask? Or didn't he tell you that?"

Lyla looks to Caleb and then back to Anna.

"Some woman with a guy's name. Billy...Danny..."

"Freddy!?" Anna says.

"That's it," Lyla says, sipping from her drink.

This was the last straw. Anna jumps up from the table, throws a few bills on the table, grabs her purse and her phone and stomps out of the restaurant.

"Just as I thought," Lyla says, as she and Caleb watch Anna charge out of the restaurant.

"She really has it for that guy, doesn't she?" he says, and then points at Anna's gin and tonic.

"Wanna split that?"

Anna storms through the front door, throws her purse on the table, goes to the cupboard and pours herself a glass of wine, then stomps over to Louis who's sitting in her favorite chair.

"Off!" she says, and Louis reluctantly agrees.

Anna sits, takes a sip, and then two seconds later bounces up, grabs her phone off the kitchen table and pounds out a text to Mitchell who is just getting out of the shower.

'Just heard the good news. Freddy? Really?'

Mitchell considers responding with a text, but then decides to call her instead, and Anna is pouring a third glass of wine when her phone rings.

"Listen. I'm sorry," he says.

"Why couldn't you have just picked up the phone?"

"Didn't think it mattered that much."

"And when did you and Simon become such confidants?

"I don't know...we..."

"You know, Mitchell, it's your life. You can marry whomever you want, whenever you want."

"Oh, really. I've been granted to live my life as I see fit from the great Dr. Newsom. I wanted you, remember? But that wasn't about to happen, was it?"

"No. It wasn't."

"That's it, then," Mitchell says.

"But Freddy?"

"Didn't you just say that..."

"I don't care what I just said."

"You don't know her, Anna. She's bright and fun and we get

411

along together. More than I can say for a lot of women I've met, and, in the end, that's all that matters, isn't it?"

Anna slows for a moment and takes another gulp of wine.

"That's all that matters. You're right. I hope you know what you're doing," Anna says, then hangs up and throws her phone at the sofa.

To say that being in the office with Anna for the next week was a living hell would be an understatement, and Lyla is seriously on the verge of quitting when Anna storms in one day.

"Do me a favor?"

"Kill myself?"

"Don't be silly. Get online and book the next available flight to London for me."

"Anna, what? No..."

"I'm serious. I don't care if it's in steerage."

"You can't break up an engagement. You know it's wrong, and you don't have it in you."

"Bullshit, If I don't. Mitchell is going to be miserable. Or broke. Or both!" Anna yells, and then storms into her office and slams the door.

Lyle shrugs her shoulders and goes to her computer and manages to get Anna a middle seat in coach on a flight later that evening.

Anna drops Louis off at her parents' and doesn't tell them where she's going or why, but just that she's going to be away for a few days.

As usual, Frank takes her to the airport, but he barely has time to pull to the curb before Anna jumps out, grabs her bags and heads inside the terminal.

"Love you too, honey," he says, to himself, watching as she disappears inside.

The flight was pure torture, and Anna had no one to blame but herself. She was stuck in a middle seat between a teenage boy who constantly farted and an enormous woman who ate chocolates all the way.

To make matters worse, when they arrived that afternoon, Anna discovered that the woman had let one of her chocolates fall onto Anna's side of the armrest and, as luck would have it, Anna ground it into the seat of her white jeans.

"Uh, lady?" the farting teenager said as Anna stood after landing.

"Yes?" Anna replied.

But all the kid could do was point to her rear end, now covered in Russell Stovers.

"Freddy?" Mitchell says, laying on the mohair sofa in his living room.

"Darling?" she replies.

"What are we having, again?" he asks, sipping from a tumbler of Jack Daniels.

"You wanted a typically British dinner, and that's what you're having," Freddy says, from the kitchen; then she grabs her glass of wine, heads to the sofa and plops herself next to Mitchell.

"Roast beef. Potato. Yorkshire pudding; peas, carrots, and cauliflower. You know, it's not just any girl that would do this," she says.

"Don't I ever. Can you cancel the cauliflower?

"Too late, it's on its way."

Freddy has no sooner said the words when there's a knock at the door and she goes to answer it.

"Delivery, ma'am."

Mitchell jumps up from the sofa and heads to the dining table which is set for an elegant meal.

Rather than bothering Henry, Anna stood in the queue and got a cab. As it turns out, the traffic is light, and they make great time into the city.

"You seem in a hurry, miss," the driver says.

"Yes. I am."

"First time in London?" he asks, looking into his rearview mirror.

"No."

"You know, you look mighty familiar, miss."

"I'm sorry, are we almost there?"

"Right around the corner, miss."

Mitchell takes another gulp from his whiskey glass and looks at his watch.

"She'll be here any minute," he says, and within seconds the doorbell rings.

"Not nervous, are you?" Freddy asks.

"Hell, no. Why should I be?" Mitchell says.

He heads to the door, takes a deep breath, and swings it open.

First, there's no doubt that Anna's had a rough trip and it's all Mitchell can do to keep from bursting out laughing. Secondly, the look on her face tells him she's loaded for bear.

"Anna, my God!" Mitchell says, pretending her presence at his door is a complete surprise. "How in the hell, why in the world…. what are you doing here…?"

"Never mind all that. I'd like a word with you," Anna says, stomping through the door and running her hand through her hair trying to look more presentable.

Without warning, Freddy steps in next to Mitchell, something Anna hadn't counted on.

"Good heavens, this one is across the pond more often than Elton John," Freddy says, then gives Mitchell a kiss on the cheek.

Anna's jaw tightens and she glances from Mitchell to Freddy, and then back to Mitchell again.

"I, um, Mitchell? Can we have a word in private please?"

Freddy drains the last of her wine, sets down the glass, and grabs her purse and coat from the rack near the door.

"Don't mind me. You two have a bloody fine dinner. I've got a date."

The statement from Freddy leaves Anna stunned.

"What? I'm sorry...What!? A DATE? I thought that you and Mitchell...?"

"Nice seeing you again, miss. No wonder he's head over arse in love with you," Freddy says, then she slips by Anna and heads out the door, leaving the two of them alone.

Mitchell doesn't say a word as Freddy shuts the door behind her. The plane flight has left Anna exhausted and it takes her a few seconds to put two and two together.

"Do you mean to tell me that...?"

"What?"

"That you and Freddy aren't...."

"Getting married? No."

"But then...?" Anna says.

"Made up. The whole bloody thing."

"Simon and Lyla, and Caleb...?"

"Like I said. A complete and utter fabrication."

Now Anna's realization turns to anger.

"Why, you...you...conceited, manipulative, ego-maniacal..." Anna says, nearly apoplectic that he would stoop to such a stunt.

"What? Go on..." Mitchell replies, egging her on.

"...LITTLE SHIT! THAT'S WHAT!"

Anna spins on her heels and bolts for the door and Mitchell reaches for her arm, but she pulls free.

"Reverse psychology. Isn't that what it's called? Mitchell says, as Anna swings opens the door and heads out onto the porch.

"Believe me, I wasn't all that sure it would work," he says, calling out to her.

Anna's about to head down the steps, but instead she slows and settles and for a few seconds she watches the traffic on Kensington Place and says nothing.

"That night... in my hotel room...what was it you said... when you were leaving?"

"I said, I thought it was a bloody good start."

Anna takes a breath and as she turns and walks back

through the door Mitchell can see that she's softened.

"We can take it slow?" she asks.

"As slow as you like," he says.

And with that Mitchell's eyes begin to glint and his mouth takes on the familiar upturned smile, and Anna realizes she has no choice now but to kiss him as deeply and for as long as she possibly can.

THE SPIDER ON THE CEILING

ABOUT THE AUTHOR

Michael Joseph Grasso

 Michael Grasso has always been a story-teller. In his first career, he wrote, produced, and directed television commercials in nearly every category of the industry. His directorial work garnered major awards and worldwide recognition including the prestigious Gold Lion from the Cannes Film Festival. He was twice nominated by the Director's Guild of America for Director of the Year award. More recently, he wrote and directed his first feature film, The Umbrella Man, which is currently available on Amazon and iTunes. The Spider on the Ceiling is his first novel and is based on an original story by the author. Michael and his wife Maureen reside in Carlsbad, California, with their dog Bayley.

Made in the USA
Columbia, SC
02 May 2020